# PACK RUIN

# PACK RUIN
## THE SPLINTERED BOND

MERRI BRIGHT

Editing by Aubergine Editing

Cover by Get Covers

*For Iris*

# CONTENTS

# AUTHOR'S NOTE AND CONTENT ADVISORIES

Thank you so much for reading Pack Ruin. This book contains on-page, graphic violence/death, profanity, intimate activities involving more than one partner, physical assault, mention of past sexual assault, gore and off-page dismemberment, gun violence, and mentions of past domestic abuse. There is a scene involving one of the MMCs being coerced/forced to be intimate with a woman outside the harem.

Please be kind to yourself when choosing to read.

# I

## CROSSING OVER
### FLOR

*Colorado, at the Mountain pack border*

My mama once told me a true mate can cut you deeper, hurt you worse, than any other creature on earth. She said there's no way to heal from that pain. She made me promise never to take a mate, and if I met my true mate, to run.

As I stood on the border of the Mountain packlands, ankle-deep in a shallow river that wound through a pine forest with not a road nor telephone line in sight, I thought for the first time that she'd been completely wrong. Two strong, honorable males stood at my sides, and I knew, deep down, neither one of them would hurt me intentionally.

Unless you counted how bad it hurt to look at them, standing naked as jaybirds under the midday sun. Though it was more of a pleasant ache than a hurt, since they were doing their very best to drive me crazy with want.

My fingers itched to touch their exposed skin. My private parts were threatening to form a river of their own. I clenched my thighs together, annoyed and slightly humiliated.

"Stop that," I demanded as Brand, my massive, heavily muscled mate flexed his biceps slightly and broadened his stance, like he was trying to make it easier for me to see just how ripped he was.

His abs stood out like a ladder I wanted to climb, the dark hair down his chest and torso doing nothing to hide how toned he was. Another significant part of him stood out as well, bobbing at me like it was trying to say hello, or call me over.

Brand even reached down and picked up a handful of water, dripping it down his chest and making me the world's thirstiest shifter as my eyes ached to track the droplets on their journey south of his belly button.

But I was supposed to focus, and breathe, and connect with my inner self, not my inner hussy. I needed to shift, to find a way to bring out my wolf.

So I refused to let my gaze dip below his waist, which meant I had to keep my head tilted up. *Way* up. Brand was over seven feet of grade-A wolf shifter, after all, and I was just over five feet on a tall day.

"Stop what, my lovely wildflower?" he teased. "All I'm doing is standing here, looking at my perfect mate. Bathing in the rivers of my packlands, as we all must do before crossing the border." His heated gaze raked me from head to toe, lingering on the silver mate mark he'd placed at the juncture of my neck and shoulder, then moving over my small breasts, his slight smile growing contemplative as he took in the old five-armed scar that radiated from my heart.

When he licked his lips slightly as he peeked lower, I groaned. "Stop looking so sexy." I shivered, though I wasn't sure if it was with the cold or from the growl he was making as he stalked toward me.

Eyes glinting, he waded through the water to my side, lifting me up and devouring me in a long kiss, a battle of lips and tongues, his beard rasping against my face and reminding me what it felt like to have his mouth farther down—

A shower of cold water drenched me from my hair all the way to my ass.

"*Ahhh!* Fucking Glenda, I will end you!" I threatened, scrambling away from Brand and facing the other male.

Glen grinned at me like an idiot, hands on his hips, the sun painting the curls around his face a brighter gold. He wasn't as massive as Brand, and it was hard not to stare at his honed body and his perfectly curved... I slammed my eyes shut.

"I'm freezing, you rat's ass!"

"I know. Makes your nips tight like little cherr—*oof!*" I opened my eyes to see Brand looming over Glen, who was now on his bare ass in the shallow water.

"Respect my little queen, brother."

"I do respect her," Glen replied softly. "Sorry, Flor. I was just playing." I shivered, but nodded.

"You won't be cold when you shift," Brand told me. "Let's try again. Focus. Breathe."

I sighed. "I've been trying for a half hour. My eyes are crossing, and I'm halfway to hypothermia. Nothing's gonna happen."

He tsked. "Your teeth and claws emerged last time. I know you can do it."

I knew no such thing. But apparently, modern technology was all but forbidden on the Mountain packlands. We'd left the car in a clearing with a few old pickup trucks a mile back. Brand had promised that some pack members would go back for our luggage, explaining that his pack had rituals for entering and leaving their lands. "The old ways," he'd murmured as we'd all stripped and left our clothing in the car we'd been in for thirty-six hours.

Brand and Glen had taken turns driving all the way from Ontario, going as fast as they dared, unwilling to stop for more than a few minutes at a time to stretch, eat, and change drivers. I'd never even been in a car until a few months ago, so I had slept and stared out the window, taking in the countryside and cities bigger than I'd dreamed could exist, wondering what the reception would be at Mountain.

I was sure they would welcome me as Brand's mate. But once they discovered I also had a bond to Finnick, the Eastern pack's Alpha Heir, would I still be welcome?

Or would they shout that I was a witch, and try to kill me? Would they allow Glen, who was technically a rogue since he'd abjured his pack to stay near me, onto their packlands?

I'd loved Brand's father, Samuel, when I met him before. I hoped he would at least listen to what we had to say before making any decisions. But Samuel was waiting in the Alpha's Den, Brand's childhood home, and all visiting shifters had to cleanse themselves in the water of the pack, take fur, and run on four feet to be welcomed by the Alpha.

"If I can't shift, you should go on without me."

Brand and Glen were both silent for a long moment, then burst into laughter. I scooped up a handful of water and threw it at them. Glen rose, shaking himself. "You're getting closer, Flor. Don't stress. Want to watch me shift again?" Without waiting for an answer, he began his own shift, his limbs growing more slender, his neck longer, hair unfurling all over his flesh.

His shift was quick and shockingly beautiful, as his blond curls seemed to ripple and lengthen, covering his entire body until he wore a gorgeous gray pelt. In less than a minute, he was completely transformed, but his playful nature was every bit the same. He jumped through the shallow water, licking my face, then chasing after a brown trout that darted past.

"He makes it look easy," I grumbled.

"It should be," Brand said softly. "If you can't shift, we can walk to the Den together in human form. I think Dad would use his Alpha command to help you shift, if you asked him."

"But he's not my Al—" I began, then stopped, blinking. "He is, though. I'm your mate, and he's my Alpha." I almost smiled. For once, I had an Alpha who might be worth the title.

Brand's mouth twitched under his beard. "Try once more. Let me use our connection?" I nodded. "Ground yourself in our bond, reach for me, and I'll help you envision the shift."

My heart lighter, I agreed, taking his hands. I closed my eyes, picturing the bond between us—a glowing, golden cord that connected to my heart and pumped energy and love into my center. I took it in my hand, then noted a few hazy shimmers in the corner of my mind's eye.

Next to Brand's bond, there was a smudged place that felt like the opposite of Brand's connection to me. It was siphoning energy away from my core, but the connection was tenuous. The steady, leaking stream of energy from my spirit to that one was obvious.

And obviously weakening my wolf. I let myself taste the flavor of the silver smudge, and my mouth filled with rot.

Decay, death. Blood clotting and meat going bad.

Panic had me struggling to find my wolf, to connect somehow. I smelled my own blood as my nail beds sliced open and my teeth emerged too fast.

"She's doing it!" Glen shouted.

"No. Something's wrong," Brand growled.

Something was very wrong. I knew at once who was taking from me. It was like a string had been plucked, and was humming with the last few notes of a song that was ending.

Luke. Luke was dying.

My wolf howled inside. *Not dying*, she mourned silently. *Not dying.*

*Dead.*

# 2

## LIVE
### BRAND

My blood turned to ice, colder than the water around my feet, as my little mate—caught in the earliest stage of her shift—shuddered, foam collecting at her mouth and blood seeping from her eyes.

She stopped breathing, and I shouted, "*No!*"

Glen was beside me as I laid her on the bank inside the Mountain border, weakness filling my own limbs, my own soul, as she began to pull energy from me down our bond.

"Take it," I whispered, though it felt like knives slicing away my soul. "Take all of me, but live, my love. Live."

Glen had pressed his hand to the center of her scarred chest, and was doing compressions, chanting the same word I was sending down the bond. "Live. Live. Live."

Her blood flowed, thanks to him. But she was growing colder, more still.

Forcing myself to adjust my position so that her head was in my lap, I closed my eyes, praying for insight. I breathed deeply, focusing on what had happened. Whatever it was, the attack had not come from the physical world. She was dying from a spiritual wound.

I knew more about those than most. I'd watched my father slipping away from the world when my mother died. I understood now how he'd felt then. If she wasn't alive, he didn't want to be. He'd admitted once that it had felt like his soul was bleeding to death. That he'd cauterized it, and stayed, but only for me.

"Our souls weren't just connected, son," he'd admitted, the only time he'd allowed himself to speak of it. "Our souls were one. I could feel everything she felt. I could see through her wolf's eyes. And when she was taken... it was as if my eyes had been gouged out. I sent every scrap of energy I had to her wolf, until I knew I would die. I prayed for death. I begged the moon to take me."

I'd cried like a baby when he said that, though I hadn't been a child for a long time by then. He held me until I could listen again. "And then you laid your small hand on me and called me back. You needed me, you cried. You needed your father. The moon spoke into my soul, and commanded me to live for you."

Shaking away the memory, I focused on the golden cord that held me to Flor's dimming light. *Our souls were one,* Dad had said. My soul and Flor's had only just begun to connect. Still, I threw my consciousness down the golden line and poured everything I had into widening my connection to Flor's soul, and making us one.

Her wolf was there, and I had an impression of a snarl, and then a whimper, and bright topaz eyes warning me away. Wanting to protect me.

But her wolf was too weak to stop me, and once I pictured what I was attempting—that I was fighting to save them both—her wolf subsided.

In that moment, I saw into the light of her being, as if every thread that made up her spirit lay spread out before me. I hadn't even known such a thing could happen. That the innermost fabric of a shifter could be visible to her mate's inner sight. But Flor's wolf soul opened before me, and I rushed inside.

Her inner being was as scarred as her chest, jagged lines of energy tracing patterns on the roof of her spirit. What should have been filled with her fierce power was emptying, silently draining her as quickly as a burst dam.

When I dove deeper into her, I saw the problem immediately. A sucking vortex was taking her light down, swallowing it, and pulling my golden glow with it.

But the lines were glowing, too. Were they her other bonds?

I concentrated on a green, glowing one that was far narrower than mine. As if the one at the end of it was far away.

*Finnick.* I grasped the green cord and called out his name in my mind. Begged for his help.

He answered without words. In an instant, I felt his energy swarm up the bond and pour into Flor's soul. It rushed in like a steady, cool stream, bright and harsh.

It wasn't enough. She needed more power.

More connections.

Glen was next to me, keeping her heart beating. The incomplete bond between them was so tenuous, when I grasped for it in that spirit state, he fell to the ground, snarling.

"Brand! What the fuck? She's not breathing. I have to keep her blood moving!"

He was right. I let loose, and he cursed, picking himself up and starting the chest compressions on our mate again.

Was she already dead? I hesitated, and my wolf surged, taking control.

My wolf nature had always been closer to the surface. Sometimes, it was hard to keep my human form, and being this near to my home had made it even more difficult. My wolf was stronger than my human side, so I shifted quickly, keeping Flor's head on my paws. He ran on spirit paws into her soul, filling it with his own energy, demanding her to fight.

Her wolf whimpered in reply. *Dead. Dead.*

*NO. LIVE!*

No sooner had my wolf barked the command than another presence was there. A dark, feral energy that raced toward the silvery-gray vortex and began to fill it with red and blue light. My wolf recognized it as magic. It was forbidden. Wrong.

But if it saved her, I didn't care if it was the darkest, most evil sorcery ever to exist. I didn't care if it would taint my own soul.

An odd, metallic laughter filled my mind. *It is, brother mate. And it may.*

My wolf laid its ears back, but relaxed as I felt Flor's heart begin to beat steadily. I held my breath as the vortex of energy started to swirl more slowly. The slice and pull of my energy as it filled her, and the vortex, grew less painful.

*Well done. Hold her. I will try to save him.* The voice grew fainter before it vanished into dark laughter. *So many courting gifts, my sweet one. Such an expensive little mate.*

My wolf passed out from the effort of keeping my mate alive, and I shifted back while unconscious.

When I opened my eyes, Glen was holding Flor on his lap. I sat up, my own limbs weak and shaking, as if I'd been ill for months. "Is she..."

Glen nodded, but his gaze remained fixed on the forest. "Your mate is fine, Alpha Heir Becker," he stated clearly. "She is unconscious and will need to be carried to the Den to recover."

I swiveled my head when I heard cursing. A group of my father's wolves stood under the canopy of the forest, milling around in confusion. I wasn't sure how long they'd been there, but they glared at Glen like he was the enemy.

One of them was in human form, and he stepped forward. It was Josiah, one of the males who I'd trained with for years. "Alpha Heir?" His expression was stunned when he met my gaze. He dropped his immediately, but peered back up from the corner of his eye. Suspicious. Nervous. As if he didn't recognize me. "Is it really you?"

"What do you mean?" I snarled. "You don't recognize me, Josiah?"

He tilted his head to the side, exposing his neck in a sign of submission. "My apologies. I do know you. But you've... you've changed."

I blinked, looking to Glen for an explanation. He shook his head. "You'll have to see it to believe it, brother."

# 3

## FLOWERS AND WEATHER
### GRIGOR

I had lived for centuries with a raging fire inside that wanted nothing more than to be let out to burn the world. The magical abilities my mother had passed on to me, combined with the cruel power and madness of my father's line, had made me unstoppable once I killed him. I'd been uncontrollable in those early years, murdering indiscriminately.

I'd felt no remorse. Killing had felt good, like snapping a candle flame out with my fingers. It was almost amusing to watch the light fade in the eyes of those who were less than me.

In my childhood, against the wishes of my mother, I'd found a way to shape my magic. I'd assumed a wolf form the same color as my father's, but hid my skill from him. Hid the threat of my growing power. I had only just grown strong enough to punish him for all he'd done to my mother and to me, when he struck out.

And lit the match of my rage. My madness.

He'd been the Grand Alpha of the Eastern Hemisphere, unassailable, an enormous wolf and a powerful Alpha. But

12

he'd died like all the others, unaware of how strong magic could be when wielded by one with both witchcraft and wolfcraft in his veins.

To my surprise, over the years, I'd found my wolf spirit wasn't an extension of my own spirit, as it was for most shifters. He was a complete, disparate entity inside me. A malevolent one, to be sure, but clever, with his own desires and needs.

His own madness.

He was with me now, fully present as we tortured a male we'd found in a rogue encampment, the only living shifter close enough to sense. He'd been gnawing on a human femur, utterly feral, unaware of my approach. But luckily for me, he could still speak.

"Please," the rogue begged, his own eyes half white with insanity, the trickles of blood seeping from them a nice contrast against the creamy color. "Lemme go, I don't know nothin' more." His teeth were long, almost curving out the sides of his mouth, distorting his speech.

This happened to rogues, when they'd been without a leader for too long. Their wolves became feral, desperate for structure. Eventually, they clawed their own throats to shreds, after they'd taken out their rage on as many others as they could find in their search for the safety and peace of a pack.

"You don't know why the Sergeant at Arms from Northern stopped at your squalid little camp?" I squeezed his neck, allowing my nails to lengthen and pierce his flesh a bit deeper. "You have no idea what he wanted?"

I'd been following the Sergeant after his defection from Northern. My wolf had fought me at first, needing to be close to his mate-to-be. But I reminded him that we had courting gifts to arrange, and suggested that our perfect little blade would be far more likely to accept us as we were, if we sweetened the mating pot a bit.

I wasn't the tallest, or the youngest, or the most handsome of her suitors. But I would prove to her that I was the most devoted and protective. My little *behrserk* loved blood, and I could show her my love in ways her other, more traditional males might overlook.

"You didn't hear a single word? Maybe you don't need those ears." I moved one hand to the side of his head, cleaving away one of the useless appendages with a whip of magic.

The acrid stench of urine filled the air, along with the rich copper of his blood. "Flowers," he gasped, his eyes bulging out. "Weather."

I released the pressure, surprised. That was the truth. But it made no sense, unless... "Did they speak in some sort of code?"

"I dunno, I really d—" He let out a satisfying gurgle as his head sailed away from his neck, and I dropped his body, done here. Sergeant was probably at Southern's borders by now, if that was his true goal. I had a feeling he wasn't going to follow protocol and announce his arrival to the pack leaders, who were mostly Council Enforcers at this point.

The Mountain guards who had stayed when my mate left had been relieved of their duties after two dozen of the Southern Enforcers had been mysteriously slaughtered in the night, their remains arranged in a startling pattern. I smiled, remembering how hard it had been to balance all the skulls just so.

She would love it.

I looked around the deserted rogue camp, listening for any other heartbeats, or panicked breathing. Unfortunately, the Sergeant had already killed or chased away all the others in this group.

I broke into a jog and then a run, seeking out his trail, which was faint, almost indiscernible. I admired his skills.

I'd almost hate to kill him.

SOUTHERN HAD a stench all its own. Some of it was the kind of stink that offended the nostrils. Septic tanks that needed to be pumped competed with the natural bogs that dotted the length of the border between the inhabited areas and the forest.

Some of it was a stench that ate at the soul. Despair and poverty, terror and pain.

Ignoring it all, I perched near the top of a loblolly pine, an odd lethargy creeping over me as I waited for my quarry to pass below me.

I'd scented but not seen a group of rogues I found here months before, the ones led by the feral woman. I had caught glimpses of her from a distance. She had what I assumed was white hair, though it was hard to tell through the grease and dirt. Back then, she'd worn rags and scraps of animal hides stitched together with burlap twine and silver tape. Gaunt and rangy, her muscles had appeared almost atrophied, like she'd been starved her entire life. She'd also kept her face turned to the ground, as if she'd been trained to do that at some point, or forced to. I needed to get a closer look at her.

The scraps of conversation and rumor I'd put together made me wonder who she was to my Flor, and I decided I would search for her and her ragged group of a dozen males if I had time. But that woman was not my prey on this hunt. The Sergeant at Arms was.

He'd been almost utterly silent as he approached the packlands, forcing me to expend magic to cover my own scent and the sounds of my breathing and heart. Once I'd done that, I'd moved into place, though it had been far harder than I liked to climb the tree. The distance from my little mate was wearing on me. I needed to kill this man, and go to her. She would be at Mountain now.

I extended my claws and readied myself for the leap, only stopping when he spoke a single word. A name.

"Lily," Sergeant called out quietly as he moved through the dense Southern forest near the very farthest western border. "Lily," he called louder. Then, "Lily Rain!"

Flowers and weather indeed. *Lily Rain.*

"Lily, come out. I smell you. I know you're here."

To my surprise, a cackle of laughter came from the ground itself. I watched, stunned, as the white-haired woman stepped out of a tunnel of some kind. The opening had been well covered with pine needles and leaf mulch, the opening at the base of a boulder. I smelled silver on the air, and a hint of magic.

"Lily," Sergeant rasped, moving quickly toward her. But the rogue leader held up a blade. It was far cleaner than the woman herself. Her head swiveled upward as she turned at Sergeant's approach, and I almost flinched when I saw her face more clearly.

What I had assumed were wrinkles were scars. The woman had been marked somehow, tortured by magic or by her mate. The marks were old, so they'd weathered into her skin. They began at her eyes, continuing down her face and neck where the ragged furs she'd fashioned into clothing began. Her arms had the same peculiar texture, the scars fine and numerous, like wrinkled skin on an elderly human.

Her voice wasn't that of an old woman, though, and she spoke clearly. "No one here has a name, shifter. We've all had them stripped away, stolen and broken and torn out of us."

"Your name is Lily Rain, though." His voice cracked. "You don't look like... but you're her. What happened, Lily? What happened to you?"

Her eyes flashed a familiar gold before she turned her gaze back to the ground, muttering something. I leaned forward to hear the answer, but almost fell as something wrenched at me, like a bolt plunging into my heart.

I knew who was hurting: the only one I had allowed a connection to my soul.

Well, I'd more or less forced a connection when she wasn't looking, but still. My perfect, bright blade was in pain, far away. I closed my eyes and sent my awareness down the secret thread of magic I'd hooked into her soul.

She was being drawn deep into an abyss of pain. Into a death that reeked of old and new curses, and more quickly than should have been possible. I scrambled to find a way to hold onto her, but the connection I had forged was too tenuous. I kept reaching, heard a chanting, "Live, live, live," from somewhere, and at last, felt the shocked touch of another soul on mine.

The Mountain mate. He'd built a bridge between their wolves, a broad, solid connection that might save her. Or kill him as well.

He was channeling his entire soul into hers. "*NO. LIVE!*" he spirit-shouted as my queen, our queen, began to lose herself to the vortex.

Only he was keeping her tethered to this world.

Jealousy cut me deeper than silver. I needed my little *behrserk* to see me as the most devoted, not him. I almost grunted aloud as I sent as much magic as I could spare toward him and her, singeing my own bond to her in the process. I ignored the pain.

The Mountain mate worried that I was tainting them with darkness. I laughed, beginning to pull myself away. If he knew just how true that was, he would have already killed me. Or attempted to.

Below me, Lily was leading Sergeant into the earth, into the tunnel. I would follow them later. For now, I had unpleasant, necessary work to do.

*Well done,* I sent to the Mountain mate as he sent even more of his wolf's energy into our mate's drained spirit, not sure if he could understand me. *Hold her. I will try to save him.*

To do that, though, I had to untangle us all. I examined the magical knots, growing angrier by the heartbeat. I could see the real trouble was here in Southern. There was no help for it.

I would have to stay and protect the worthless one. She was connected to him, and he was vulnerable.

I almost pitied him.

I threaded my own magic down into the tangle of bright and dark cords that stretched out in three different directions. The Southern mate's silver-gray cord had become a suction. A curse had all but killed him, and would soon devour my mate-to-be.

*Nyet.* I would never let that happen. But there was only one way to save her. A distasteful solution, and one I had a feeling I would regret for the rest of my life.

I hesitated for an instant, but her pain tore at me.

Quickly, I did what I had to do to save her and the rest of her mates.

Someone would die for this. Some witch had done this to the worthless mate, and endangered my little one, my bright shadow. I had to stay, and be the tool for her vengeance.

Incensed, my long-rabid inner wolf foamed at the mouth, snapping invisible teeth at the delay.

I slipped down the tree in silence, moving without leaving a single footprint or hint of my scent, and headed straight for the festering heart of the Southern pack.

Maybe I would save the witch's teeth and make them into beads for my little blade to wear. She would like that, I was certain.

*So many courting gifts, my sweet one. Such an expensive little mate.*

*Just as you should be.*

# 4

## ASSUMPTIONS

### FLOR

I woke with a gasp that turned into a sob.

Luke was dead. I'd felt him slip away, heard his wolf's howl cut off and somehow, even without a completed mate bond, knew a part of my own soul had gone dead. I'd thought I would die, too. Then I'd sensed... Someone had stopped me from following him into the darkness.

*Who?* In my next breath, I had my answer.

"Flor?" Brand's voice opened my eyes, though light from somewhere had me slamming them shut again.

"Too bright," I rasped, the feeling of nails being driven into my skull easing when the light dimmed. I struggled to sit up, Brand's warm hand somehow snuffing out the pain a bit more. Warmth and comfort radiated from the spot, and I braved the agony to turn my head toward him. He had a blue pottery mug in one hand, steam rising from it. It smelled of licorice and mint and something floral.

"An old family recipe for healing," he said quietly. "My grandma made it for you." He held the mug to my mouth, and I took a cautious sip.

"Your grandma?" I whispered.

"She's been checking on you for the past two days. She was worried about you. We all were."

"Two days?" He didn't answer, just gave me another sip.

Brand had mentioned his family on the ride from Ontario. He had no siblings, but had always wanted some, although Glen and Finnick had filled that void once they were old enough to travel to each other's packs. Still, he had four cousins, an aunt and uncle, one grandfather, and two grandmothers, all living at Mountain, though not all of them lived in or even near the Alpha's Den.

I would meet more of Brand's family today. My family. The thought warmed me almost as much as the tea. I rubbed my eyes, took another sip, and turned back toward Brand to ask about his grandma.

But he turned to one side, hiding his face. Like he was ashamed, or angry.

Confused, I automatically reached for the bond between us, and flinched. It felt burned, like a fire had cauterized our connection somehow, the emotions numbed. I swallowed hard, wondering what had gone wrong.

Then I remembered. The river, the pain, the way my own life was draining out as Luke pulled on it. Pulled away.

"Luke is dead," I whispered. But something about that seemed wrong. "Isn't he?"

Brand let out a breath before he answered, his head still turned away. "I'm not sure. It felt like he died, or at least a part of him. I... connected with him through your bond. Even though neither of you claimed each other. It didn't seem to matter. But Dad called Southern yesterday. He's alive."

"Your dad spoke to him?"

"No. He spoke to the guy in charge there, an Enforcer from Finnick's pack. They have him breathing on human machines, staying in a room in the Pack House with a doctor from Eastern checking in on him, but he's not responding. At least, that's what the Council told Dad when they called here yesterday."

A chill ran through me. "The Council called?"

"Aidan McDonnell himself." An image of Finnick's douchecanoe of a father popped into mind. I'd disliked him at first sight, after he made it clear he thought I was trash. "They had someone watching our border, maybe even tracking us as we drove here, and they saw us at the river. Dad would have kept it secret, but he had to admit that Glen was on our land."

"Why is it even their business? He's not hurting anyone."

"He's an Alpha's child who went rogue. Alpha McDonnell said he needs to be taught a lesson, made an example of, so none of the others like him 'get ideas.' They're insisting on having him put to death. Margarette and Bradley have asked for an emergency meeting of the four pack Alphas. They're on their way to New York now to meet with the asshole and beg for a stay of execution. But they'd have to rewrite pack law to get him out of it entirely, and that requires a majority vote, at least three of the four Alphas voting for the change. With Luke out of the picture, and Dad here..."

My heart ached for Glen's parents. "Where is Glen now?"

Brand sighed heavily. "He's in our cell."

My blood went cold at his words. Instantly, I was back in the cell at Southern, silver bars all around me, the hard concrete of the floor icy and cold on my bruised legs. The barren room wasn't the worst thing about that cell. The silver in the bars was what made even sitting inside a torture of its own. My spit had tasted of the metal for weeks after I got out.

Brand's pack wouldn't have a cell like that, though. His father wasn't like Alpha Callaway. They knew Glen, liked him. They wouldn't... I stopped myself. Assumptions like that were what had landed me in a hunt at Northern on my first day.

For all I knew, Brand's dad cared more for pack law than doing what was right.

"Will he do it? Will your dad execute Glen?"

A deep voice I'd heard before came from the doorway. "I've never disobeyed a Council directive. Never broken pack law. But I cannot say what I will decide. Not after what's happened to you, son."

"Alpha Becker." I sat up a bit straighter as the massive Alpha entered the room.

"Call me Samuel, or Dad," he corrected, stopping at the foot of the bed, with a nod to Brand.

Who still hadn't looked at me. What was going on?

"I was... overjoyed... to hear of your mating with my son," Samuel said, his expression grave. "Although the circumstances were not ideal."

"I would do it all over again, but without the stabbing," I joked weakly.

No one laughed. Brand stood abruptly and walked to the fireplace, stoking the embers there.

Okay, something was really wrong.

I took a second to peer around in the dim light and get my bearings. The furniture here was all enormous, made to fit people much bigger than normal. I probably looked like a

23

child on top of the rough-hewn log bed that was piled high with downy comforters and quilts. The chocolate-brown leather chairs against the opposite wall beside a tall, curtained window were just as outsized, as was the gray river rock fireplace, where a small fire now burned, thanks to Brand. I was dressed in a fancy nightgown, long and made of gorgeous white satin, with embroidered running wolves stitched in gold at the neckline and hem.

Samuel had on normal clothes, jeans and a blue flannel shirt. Brand wore dark gray sweatpants but no shirt, like he'd been training, or wanted to be ready to shift. They both waited in silence while I breathed, and took everything in.

The room was filled with scents: smoke, pine, and the tea I was drinking. But there was my own jasmine and cinnamon, along with a few others that I couldn't make out. My wolf probably could, if I ever shifted.

I thought back to the river. "Did I shift, when... when I blacked out?" I couldn't let myself think of why I'd blacked out, couldn't think of Luke. Even if I tried to tell myself I didn't care about him, no matter how many times I reminded myself that he'd failed me over and over when I was growing up at Southern, my heart still pounded when I thought of him.

My lips still hummed with the memory of our one kiss.

I wouldn't say anything about him in front of Brand's dad, not yet. Anyway, I wasn't certain if Samuel knew about my weird-as-hell mating bonds, or what he might do when he found out. Better to keep my neck covered and my unusual mating shit to myself.

"No," Brand said, without turning his head. "You began to, and then... you passed out. At first, we were worried you were dying. Your pulse was almost indiscernible."

"What happened then?" I took another sip of tea as Samuel explained what had happened since the river crossing. He didn't mention what had caused my "seizure," and I didn't volunteer anything.

"You and Brand both passed out on the bank, just inside our packlands. Glen spoke to the shifters I sent to meet you. He explained everything." He directed a look of concern at his son, who had picked up a small wooden carving from the table, and was turning it over in his hands. "Well, all that *could* be explained."

When Samuel looked out the window, still obviously unsettled, I scooted over on the bed toward Brand. He still wouldn't look at me.

Something was wrong. Very wrong.

Samuel cleared his throat. "Dinner's in an hour. Brand can show you the way."

"Look at me," I said quietly to my mate as Samuel slipped out the door more silently than anything that big should be able to move. "Brand, what's wrong? Why won't you look at me?"

"I... Something changed, Flor. Something happened to me when you were slipping away."

*Oh shit.* Had my wolf scratched him while I was blacked out, and scarred him? Ruined his face? I was the only creature in the world who could cause lasting damage to this male, without using silver. If I had, I would never forgive myself.

"Bearman?" I whispered.

He didn't answer. I held my breath as he crossed to the window and opened the curtain the smallest bit, his hands trembling visibly. My head wasn't hurting now, but the light made it hard to focus on his face when he turned.

Steeling myself, I reached into the bond again and sent

a wave of what I hoped was reassurance to him. I blinked, waiting for my eyes to adjust. I was ready for scars, or something like that. I assumed my wolf had scratched him while I was out.

But his face hadn't changed. Or so I thought.

His eyes were closed at first, but when he opened them, I gasped aloud. It took me a second to remember how to speak, and only one word came out. "*How?*"

He wasn't disfigured. He was... transformed.

Before I knew what I was doing, I'd crawled out of bed on weak legs and crossed to him, my hands on his arms, then his shoulders. He was so tall, there was no way to look directly into his face unless he kneeled. He'd closed his eyes again, and his brow was furrowed in what looked like—*felt* like—fear.

I had a horrible thought. "Can you see?"

"Yes. That hasn't changed."

*Thank goodness.* I pulled him down gently until he was kneeling in front of me, then used my fingers to trace gentle circles on his face. "Why won't you look at me?"

His eyelids fluttered open again, and for a long moment, I stared, keeping my own expression soft and accepting. His eyes had been chocolate brown before, gorgeous deep pools a richer shade than his hair, and I'd loved them. Now, they were pure white.

No, not quite pure. I moved his face up to the light. "They're the same color as the moon."

The irises were whiter than the sclera, almost glowing like the moon when it was full. There was a narrow darker line between the sclera and iris, and the pupil was still present, though it had faded to a pale silver-gray. He swallowed hard, trembling even more now that I could really see them.

"Brand, they're beautiful." It was true. They were magical, almost hypnotic.

For a moment, he slumped and buried his face in my stomach, his broad shoulders heaving as he breathed deeply.

"How, Bearman?" I asked again. He stood and lifted me into his arms, not answering. Instead, he carried me back to the bed, curling up behind me, his chest to my back.

"I don't know. My grandmother says she read about a shifter who had eyes like this in one of our histories. She's been in the library since we arrived, trying to find the reference." He nuzzled my shoulder, nipping at the ends of my hair.

I pulled away and turned to face him again, taking in the changes in his expression. His eyes were odd, almost eerie, now. But looking into them... settled something deep inside me. I'd only ever felt this way when I stared at the moon, on nights when I'd found a safe hiding place, knowing I'd make it until dawn without being found by the Hunt.

"Do you hate them?" Brand asked roughly.

"I love them," I replied instantly. "They're part of you, and I told you before—I love you, Brand. Maybe more now." I felt disbelief in the bond, and swallowed hard. I wasn't good at talking about my feelings, but for my Bearman, I'd find the words to make him understand. "I know you said love wasn't words. But you're the only one I've ever said those words to, other than my mother and Del. I loved my mother, even though she wasn't sane. She was broken before I was even born. I loved Del, and he was missing a leg. Why would you think I would love you less, just because your eyes have changed?"

I scooted up and kissed both eyelids, gently, then pulled

back. "I waited my whole life for someone who would prove to me that not all males who wanted me were the same. That not all of you would hurt me, given the chance. I'm grateful every day that you claimed me, even though I was unranked. Maybe those eyes are the moon's way of saying 'you're welcome.'"

"Ah, my love." He brought me up to his face, kissing me tenderly. "You teach me every day how to be strong. Thank you for the reminder."

Suddenly, his eyes were the least important thing about him. I felt his length hard against my leg, and reached down, lifting the nightgown out of the way.

"Flor, what are you—" he began as I rolled over until I was sitting on top of him. He only had on sweatpants, easy enough to push down. He helped me, his bright, magical gaze on my face filled with wonder as I ran my fingers through the hairs on his chest, soaking in his warmth.

The white gown mirrored the shade of his eyes as it pooled between us, concealing the places where my bare thighs surrounded his hips. One of his hands moved up from my knee to my thigh, and then over one hip, finding my core. Those strong, thick fingers moved from my opening to the place that already ached for his touch. He circled there for a moment, until my breathing grew choppy and my vision hazy.

I pushed myself down on top of him, closing my eyes as I slipped over him in small movements, taking him inside me.

Accepting him.

The stretch of him was every bit as intense as it had been before, but this time, it echoed the gentle, persistent ache in my heart. "You are mine, Brand Becker. Mine to love, and comfort, and hold, no matter what. I will never let you go." The ache grew lighter, even as the spirals of plea-sure grew more intense.

"My love," Brand managed to say, before his voice broke.

"Yes. Yours." I leaned forward so that the top of his length pressed against the center of my pleasure. I wasn't close—or at least I didn't think so—but it didn't matter. What mattered was this moment. Our connection.

I moved slowly, staring down at his eyes, which grew brighter as he approached his peak. To my surprise, my own climax rolled over me at the same moment that he cried out, in a slow, luxurious wave of pleasure. Like a blessing.

"If I need to remind you how I feel about you every day," I whispered when we were done, and I was lying on his broad chest, "then I will make that sacrifice. I will suffer through as many orgasms as it takes."

His chest bobbed up and down in silent laughter, and I let myself smile. Even if the rest of my life was a shit heap, this part—where I could make my mate laugh and forget his worries for a moment—was golden.

# 5

## STARVING

### FLOR

We might have stayed in bed for another full day, but my stomach insisted on getting up. "You're hungry," Brand grumbled when it let out a loud gurgle that sounded a little like a cat yowling. "What kind of mate am I, letting you go hungry?" He launched himself from the bed, holding me like a baby, or possibly a football, as he carried me to the doorway.

"Brand, I only have on a nightgown," I squealed as we moved down a hallway decorated with what appeared to be family photos and paintings of shifters in wolf and human form. Some looked really old, but I couldn't focus on them at the speed Brand was walking.

"It covers everything," he replied, hauling me down a winding staircase made of enormous logs. Everything in the whole house was oversized, like the pictures of fancy ski lodges I'd seen in magazines.

Northern's Lodge had been big on the outside, but the rooms had seemed normally proportioned. This room was vast, the ceilings vaulted high, with rough-cut pine beams stretching from one side to the other and enormous leather sofas and armchairs, as well as gorgeous carved wooden tables and cabinets.

I heard voices down one hall, but Brand tacked away, toward a room that smelled like dozens of kinds of food, and something else... I sniffed.

*Oh no.*

"Brand, put me down," I hissed in his ear, struggling. "I reek of sex."

"Good. You smell like your mate," he growled, and his eyes glinted bright. "Smell like a claimed female." He ran his nose along my throat, scenting my skin above the neck-line of the gown, before he pushed open a door.

The room behind it was noisy, filled with the lush scents and sounds of a meal being prepared, and a plump, older woman with gray hair, who was humming and moving pots and pans around as we walked in.

"Grandma Ida, my mate is starving. Help."

She spun to face us, a wooden spoon in her hand. She had on a pair of denim overalls, a red checkered shirt, and an apron that said *Team Jacob* in block letters. She was one of the roundest shifters I'd ever seen, from her apple cheeks all the way down to her short legs. I grinned. She was almost as short as me.

Her face was immediately wreathed in a matching smile when she saw us, and she rushed across the kitchen with her arms outstretched. At the last second, she stopped mere inches away, her nostrils twitching. I blushed, knowing what she'd scented.

But she mock-scowled at him, not me. "Brand, really? You didn't even let your new mate take a shower?"

"She was hungry, Grandma Ida. Her stomach was growling."

Ida's dark eyebrows lowered, like he'd shared something awful. "Understandable then," she agreed, pointing to an empty chair with her spoon. "Put her there, and start feeding her. Biscuits for now, but we'll have a proper meal in no time."

*Feeding me?* Brand took her at her word, setting me on his lap and not allowing me to touch the warm biscuits in the basket Ida set in front of us, along with butter and honey. Instead, he smeared chunks with the soft butter, drizzled honey over the pieces, and lifted them with his hand to my mouth. It felt ridiculous, and decadent, but I allowed it.

While Brand fed me, Ida chattered at us from the stove, mentioning dozens of names of pack members. "Oh, I can't wait for you to make some friends here, Flor. You're newly shifted, yes? I'll invite some of our newer wolves around. Tomas, Layla, Grace, Raymond, Brianna, and Rebin all shifted this year for the first time.

"Rebin got caught mid-shift, but Annalise—she's a dear friend, a female who's been living wild for two decades—well, she'd come in for provisions and saw the shift. She went up to him and laid her hand on his back, and wouldn't you know? He was her true mate. After all this time! We'd worried she'd gone feral, by the look of her. Of course, she's a few years older than him, but you wouldn't have known it from the way those two started honoring the moon right there in front of the whole pack—ah, Samuel! I wondered when Verona would let you out of the library. Take a seat."

"Thanks, Mom." The Alpha pressed a kiss to the older woman's forehead before sitting on the other side of the rough-hewn oak table, and I took the opportunity to wriggle into my own chair, though Brand grumbled.

Ida gestured for her grandson to help her with the food, and I peered around, ignoring Samuel's piercing gaze as he sipped some coffee. The room was a kitchen, not a formal room like the Hillier family ate in at Northern. I preferred it, though, and it was still nicer than Southern's fanciest dining room.

The rustic table was long enough for a dozen shifters, with copper pots and pans hung high overhead down its length, and plenty of space behind our chairs for the ovens and countertops. It looked like Ida had been preparing a feast for days.

She and Brand covered the tabletop with platters and baskets of every kind of food I could imagine. There was warm cornbread dripping with butter, more biscuits with a bowl of sausage gravy nearby, a venison roast, crackling duck, quail, beef meatballs, quiche stuffed with bacon and cheese, and mounds of crispy, buttery roasted potatoes.

And one bowl of salad, about the size of two of my fists.

"That's in case you're one of those skinny-on-purpose females," Ida said, pointing at it. She tilted her head back and looked down her button nose at me. "I've read about them in magazines. You look thin."

"I'll eat anything and everything you put in front of me," I replied, already piling food onto my plate as she pulled up her chair. I wasn't offended by her bluntness; she wasn't wrong. "I've been starved by others my whole life. I'm not stupid enough to starve myself." I moaned slightly as I nibbled at a potato, and Brand let out a rumbling purr.

"Starved?" Her moss-green eyes flared wide as I turned my head, pushing a lock of hair that had fallen over my eyes behind one ear. My hair had grown back ridiculously fast, so it covered the ear tag a lot of the time. When she noticed the round metal disk, she let out a hiss like an angry lynx.

I grabbed some butter and a small pot of honey for the

cornbread. "I was unranked at Southern. We didn't get food most days."

Ida rounded on Brand's father. "And this is the one your damned Council wants you to hand over? Why, so they can starve her more? My baby Brand's true mate. I'll tear the hide off any wolf who thinks to keep her from my kitchen." She picked up a platter full of steaks and piled two more on my plate.

Had she just said hand me over? She had.

I didn't stop eating at the revelation. I did lift an eyebrow at Samuel, who only sighed as she harangued him for a bit longer.

When Ida finally ran out of steam, she stood, grabbing the pitiful salad and putting a platter of fried chicken in its place. "Eat! I'm making more. Unranked... As if our Mother Moon would abide even the weakest of Her children going hungry."

I stuffed some chicken in my mouth as she set a whole bowl of macaroni and cheese beside my plate. The smell alone had my eyes rolling back in my head.

I spoke through a mouthful of cheesy pasta. "Brand, I hate to tell you now but... I'm not sure you're really my true mate." Samuel choked on something, but I ignored him and went on. "I'm pretty sure it's your Grandma Ida."

Ida cackled, but when she returned to the table, she had an empty plate. She whacked Samuel's head with her wooden spoon before she started spooning up healthy piles of food on the empty dish. Well, maybe not healthy. The portions were enormous, and she only stopped when the food was practically falling off the sides.

"Mom, what was that for?" The Alpha rubbed his head.

"For not doing what you know is right. You've got that sweet little Glennie down in the cell, starving to death—"

I sucked in a breath to demand he be let out, but Samuel's reply had me letting it out again. "Mom, he's not starving. You took him an entire side of beef this morning—"

"—and if you even think about sending him to those criminals in the big shitty—"

*The big shitty?* I mouthed at Brand.

His lips twisted, and he whispered, "The big city."

Ida was still talking as she rounded the table. "—you'll be the one starving, make no mistake. I've always known this Council experiment would fail, because it's not natural! Packs are meant to keep to their own borders, protect their own—"

Samuel cut her off. "I'm not giving him over if I can help it. And you *know* why we needed the Council."

Ida shook her head. "A War Council was what was formed, when it was needed. It should have been dissolved. You and I and every shifter who's read the books in that library upstairs know what happens when shifters concentrate power in one place for too long. We get shifters like that Grand Alpha of Alphas—curse his soul forever—and then that Dimitrivich, and the only ones who win are the packs without honor, and sneaky rats like that McDonnell fellow." Samuel's expression grew even more grim at the mention of Finnick's dad. "Brand, come get the doors for me. I'm going to feed our guest." Ida stomped off to the door, carrying the plate.

Brand pressed a kiss to my head and followed. "Yes, Grandma."

Once they'd left, I drank some water, since my mouth had gone suddenly dry. When I could speak again, I tried to sound casual. "Dimitrivich? What did she mean?"

Samuel sighed heavily. "Grigor Dimitrivich. The most evil shifter who ever lived."

"Lived?" I asked, looking around for something stronger than water to drink. If he was talking about my Grigor, I had a feeling it wasn't a tale I wanted to hear sober. "He's dead?"

"Every wolf alive should hope so," Samuel replied. I was afraid he might not say more; Samuel's mom might be a talker, but according to Brand, Samuel had always been quiet. But after he finished his food, he sat back, assessing me. "Your education was cut short."

"At Southern? If you mean I wasn't allowed to finish high school, yeah." I shrugged. "I guess Grigor Dimitrivich was the subject of some senior history class?"

"Yes. Part of the curriculum covering the Great Shifter War." His voice took on a teaching cadence, like he was echoing a lesson he'd learned from someone before. "He was born centuries before that, of course. Grigor Dimitrivich was said to be a black wolf, with glowing red eyes, smaller than most, due to his mother being starved when she was pregnant with him. There was a famine in Russia back then. His father was the last Alpha of Alphas, ruling over all of Eurasia.

"Grigor killed him, but instead of taking the throne, he torched his father's palace and fled, leaving even his own mate. Dimitrivich's great-great-grandson, many times over, of course, was famous even among humans, known as Raspu— What's wrong?" His jaw snapped shut.

I'd stood up without realizing it, and my teeth and nails had emerged slightly. "He had a mate?" I had no reason to be as pissed as I was, but my wolf was insisting I leave Mountain *now*, go and find Grigor, and beat the shit out of him. "He had a child?"

Samuel's face went still as he stared at me. Listening. "Your heart's racing. Why?"

"Ah, I'm not... No reason to be..." I knew Samuel would hear any lie I tried to tell, and for the first time in my life, I was at a loss for how to dance around the truth.

"What are you hiding?"

I'd been given Alpha commands before at Southern, horrible ones. I'd been forced to hold still while I was beaten and whipped. I'd watched other shifters be commanded to do despicable things, and to submit to even worse acts.

But I'd never known an Alpha could force a truth out of one of his own pack without even a hint of compulsion.

Not answering Samuel was impossible.

"Grigor Dimitrivich is the wolf who saved me at Northern, when I was abducted and given to the General. General Ivan."

To his credit, Samuel didn't react, though his power leaked into the room, making the air feel thick in my lungs. "He... saved you?"

"Yes."

"Did he tell you why? Do you have any idea what his connection with you might be?"

"Yes." I didn't even hesitate, and that was what made me understand something I'd never realized about Alpha power. I'd only ever seen it wielded like an ax or a hammer, splintering a shifter's will into fragments. But Samuel's power was like moss on stone, soft but unyielding.

"He said he was one of my... suitors. And I'm pretty sure he's the same one from your story." I swayed on my feet, slightly dizzy.

"One of your suitors?" Samuel's power leaked even

more, and my lungs hurt with each inhalation. "Where is he now?"

"I don't know. But he said... that he'd meet me... at—" I slapped a hand over my mouth, the scent of Samuel's rage in my nostrils.

He blinked, waiting. Keeping my hand over my mouth, I raised my other hand and slowly lifted a finger.

Just the middle one.

When he inhaled sharply, I dropped both my hands. "That was an asshole move, Alpha." I met his gaze, then deliberately lowered mine and turned my neck to the side, showing him I was choosing to submit. I glanced back up. "I want you to teach me how to do it, though."

For a long moment, he was still. Then his beard shook slightly. I had a strong suspicion he was laughing underneath it. "You'll be Alpha Mate of this pack someday, little Flor. I'll teach you everything you need to know to keep our pack safe. To protect them, and yourself, starting now." He circled the table and took my arm in his, leading me from the room and back up the sweeping staircase. "The wolf who is courting you is evil in its purest form, daughter. Please, do not believe what he has told you."

Evil in its purest form? Grigor, the one who'd saved me from the Russian general? Who'd healed Glen, and promised me a courting gift? I thought about the way his touch had blown through me like a cold wind. How he'd been enraged for me. How he'd so sweetly offered to tear off my attacker's hands and give them to me to burn.

Okay, so maybe he was a little unhinged. Or maybe a tiny bit evil. But what did it say about me that I found it deeply romantic? I wasn't the sort of woman to get silly over gifts like jewelry and flowers. Maybe I was the same kind of evil as Grigor.

"Promise me you'll be on your guard, Flor," Samuel urged.

I couldn't agree, so I stayed silent. Samuel clearly understood what that meant, and a look of disappointment and fear flickered over his stern features. "I'll let you read the histories and make your own decisions, then. Let me show you the heart of the Alpha's Den." He opened another door in the center of the hall, one elaborately carved with animals and trees, an enormous round moon at the top of the frame.

"The library."

# 6

## FLOWER ARRANGEMENTS
### GLEN

I heard footsteps coming down the concrete stairs into the cell, and adopted a pitiful expression, fully prepared to milk Ida's pity once more. Maybe she'd bring me ice cream if I looked forlorn enough.

My back to the wall, I reclined on the narrow bed with my head on the stack of pillows. This was actually far more comfortable than any prison cell had a right to be. It didn't hurt that Ida had brought me a half-dozen blankets and two pillows, as well as a small cooler to keep snacks in. She'd even brought extra sweatpants and shirts, so I had clean clothes.

"Here you go, sweet Glennie," a voice growled. "Heard you were starving."

The key was still in the lock when I jumped up. Brand stood there, a plate piled high with food in one hand. He met my gaze for an instant, and I tried not to react at the change in his eyes. They almost glowed in the low light of the cell, though the room had a small, barred window that let in fresh air.

I nodded and took the plate through the bars, spying

40

Ida at the top of the stairs. She waved at me before closing the upper door there and scooting off, probably back to the kitchen. She'd told me Brand wouldn't leave Flor's side, which was as it should be.

"Brand, is she up? Is she okay?"

He nodded curtly. "She's having dinner with Dad. She was hungry." He said the word like it implicated him in a crime.

"I bet she was. She slept for most of two days." Inside, my wolf paced, needing to be closer to her. I sat and distracted myself with the food Brand had brought. "Have we heard anything more about Luke?" Ida had whispered what she knew the last time she'd brought food down. Luke was alive, if only barely, at least according to Samuel's sources.

"You know the Council sent all the Mountain Enforcers home weeks ago, and replaced them with McDonnell's favorites. I heard Torran was there."

"Better than Niall."

We both sighed. Niall was an Enforcer about our age. He was everything an up-and-coming shifter should be: strong, a phenomenal fighter, clever, and resourceful. But he was lacking any sort of morality. The stories of what he'd done when he was "learning the ropes" under the Eastern pack's Head Enforcer, Torran, were the stuff of nightmares. I had a feeling we hadn't heard the worst of it; Finn had obviously been under Alpha command not to share details of his pack. But we knew enough.

At the last Conclave that had been held in Eastern, just over four years earlier, almost no females from the Mountain pack had stayed to the end. The women of Brand's pack had been mocked openly at many of the events, where they were outnumbered by the host pack.

But the poor treatment by the Eastern partygoers hadn't been why Samuel had forbidden any of his women to go to future Conclaves there.

It was how many had come home with haunted eyes and whispered tales of waking up in strange rooms in the Mansion, with markings and lacerations on their bodies that couldn't be explained. Some made with silver, that would never heal.

Far too many of those women said the last male they'd spoken to, or danced with, or brushed past, had been Niall.

Torran hadn't been implicated, but he'd been given the duty of discovering what had happened to the women. After months of searching, he'd pinned it all on a human visitor, who was conveniently too dead to question further when Samuel asked to do so.

If Torran was at Southern, acting as interim Alpha while Luke was in a coma, there was no telling what was happening to the rest of the Southern pack. And if Torran thought there was any chance he could take the Alpha position himself, Luke wouldn't be alive long enough for any protests to be heard.

"Has anyone located Callaway?" I wondered aloud.

"No." Brand took my empty plate back. "Supposedly, Torran has every male left alive looking for him."

"Every male left *alive*?"

Brand shrugged. "The Council liaison's words, not mine. Apparently, there have been even more deaths since the battle. All males." He hesitated. "Josiah told me yesterday that the bodies started piling up even before they left. That reporting it was what had the Council swooping in and putting Torran in charge. Josiah said the old Enforcers were being killed, a few each night, beginning as soon as we left Southern. Their bodies had no defensive wounds, but their hands and heads had been removed. They located the heads—the skulls—but a few other parts weren't found."

*Fuck.* My stomach churned. "Killed in human form?"

"Yes. Smothered, maybe."

For some reason, the rapist at Northern who had choked to death came to mind. He'd died with no obvious wounds.

Brand went on. "Josiah said the entrails of the murdered Enforcers were... arranged."

"Arranged?" I was curious, but found myself unable to care about the worthless shifters who'd participated in the Hunts, forcing Flor to hide every night of her life for four years.

"Mmhm. Pulled out and placed in shapes. Like flowers, they said."

I shuddered. That might have been the creepiest shit I'd heard in a while. "Only males, huh? Maybe the unranked there found their way into the kitchen like they did at my pa—at Northern." I had to remember, it wasn't my pack anymore.

I had no pack. *Fuck.* I really was a rogue.

"No. They put everyone on lockdown, forced the unranked into the dorms every night. They've been hunting the killer, or killers. They never found a trace, not one clue. But night after night, more headless bodies showed up. More flowers."

Our eyes met, and I knew we were both thinking the same thing. *Flowers. Flor.*

"Who could it—" Brand began.

"Doesn't matter." I cut him off, not wanting to mention the black wolf I'd seen running at the side of our car when we left Northern's borders. Flor had shared what had happened after she was abducted, and that the mysterious Russian who called himself Grigor had been the one we'd known as Joaquin Villalobos at Southern.

He'd followed her to Northern, obviously obsessed. I understood the feeling, though if he was the real Grigor Dimitrivich, I didn't want him anywhere near. Since he hadn't followed us all the way here, I hadn't been all that concerned. As long as he stayed away from Flor from now on, I wasn't going to try and find the sneaky fucker.

I had wondered where he'd gone before, and what he'd been up to, but as far as I was concerned, he could pick off every one of the assholes who'd hunted Flor.

I shrugged at Brand. "The only reason I'd need to know who killed them is if I planned to send some flowers of my own to whoever took care of those bastards. But we need to get back to Southern."

He nodded once. "To save Luke."

"To save Luke, which means saving Flor."

Brand shook his head, those odd, white eyes filled with wisdom and pain. "First, we need to convince my dad to go to war with the Council."

"You mean, to let me out of this room. Let me live."

"Exactly."

# 7

## ANCIENT HISTORY
### FLOR

S till in the long nightgown, I sat with a book on the table in front of me, one so old it was handbound and handwritten, staring at a picture of a wolf I knew. Brand's *other* grandmother—his mother's mother—stood behind me, her baleful glare burning a hole in the back of my head.

Samuel had escorted me into the library, introduced me to his mother-in-law, asked her to allow me free run of the space, and fled like a coward. She'd introduced herself as Verona Prestwick, warned me that she would tear off my hands if I so much as wrinkled a page of any book in the room, and then gone utterly silent.

Watching. Lurking, more like a dragon guarding its hoard than a wolf.

To be fair, she looked like a tall, skinny, older female version of my Mountain mate, her eyes the exact shade of brown his had been. She had a few wrinkles on her neck, but none around her eyes, like she'd stopped smiling a good long while back.

She'd sniffed at my gown and peered at the dangling

tag on my ear, but said nothing about the still-present odors of Brand's and my morning activities. I would have excused myself to change and shower, but for some reason, this felt similar to the time I'd come upon a mountain lion in the woods of Southern. Like it was smarter not to attract attention to myself for the moment.

After a few minutes of reading the book she'd given me, one that was all about my mysterious black wolf, I figured how I looked or even smelled was the last thing that mattered. My Grigor was famous. Well, infamous. He'd killed more shifters and humans than I was comfortable thinking about, especially since the phrase "wiped out whole villages" popped up a few times in reference to what they called his Reign of Terror.

In the 1500s.

*Fuck a damned duck.*

If it was my Grigor, he really was too old for me, by a few hundred years at least. I peered at the illustration of the original Grigor in human form, which was identical to the man I'd seen naked in the woods in Ontario, wondering why the eyes on the page seemed to follow me. The words beneath him were simple, but I read them again, my gut twisting.

*After killing his father in retribution for the death of his mate Anya, Grigor Dimitrivich rained down terror on both shifter and humankind, often slaughtering entire villages in a berserker rage. Born of a sorceress and an Alpha, he was as powerful as he was corrupt. The first War Council was established to defeat him, but when the European shifter army assembled, Grigor rendered ten thousand shifters unconscious in a burst of power, then vanished.*

I knew the important part was about the War Council,

and the whole sorceress mother thing, but my eyes kept returning to the name: Anya.

He had a mate. Had she been a true mate? Had he loved her? It had been over five hundred years since she'd died. Shit, could he still love her?

Ugh, I was pathetic. I glared at his picture, wondering how the hell I'd ended up mooning over the world's most evil witch wolf.

"Do you even know how to read?" Brand's grandmother snapped at last from behind me, each word icy.

That terrible flush of shame rushed through me, like it always had whenever I was teased about not knowing as much as others. Back at Southern, I would have stayed quiet, or maybe apologized. But I was Brand's mate—which might have been the problem, come to think of it. She didn't think I was worthy of him.

I wasn't. But he'd claimed me anyway.

I looked up from the illustration of Grigor. "I do know how to read, Granny Verona," I said, liking her flinch at the word Granny. "Not very well, to be honest. They kicked me out of school after ninth grade."

"What?" Her eyes narrowed, and I knew I was flushing red, but I held her gaze.

"After I turned fifteen, I had to work if I wanted to eat. I didn't get to go to school, or have books of my own. Well, I had a few. Old paperbacks, moldy ones that the other shifters had finished." I gently closed the cover of the book, stood, and carried it back to the shelf. "I would have given an arm for the chance to read all these. A chance to learn the history of our kind, to be able to learn firsthand what the pack law really said, and not just the parts Alpha Callaway read out loud." I thought about the library back at

Glen's pack, the sheer number of books there. "If I was ever rich, I'd probably spend as much money on books as food."

"You weren't allowed to have books? You didn't have a library at your pack?" She sounded as shocked as Margarette had been when she learned about the unranked not having food privileges.

"Of course not. Can you imagine what would have happened if we'd had this?" I waved at the rows of books, all neatly shelved, filling the room from floor to ceiling, then rested a hand on the stack that Verona had been reading when I came in. She'd told me she was hunting for information about shifters with white eyes, and the topmost book was titled *Legends of the Moonblessed*. I itched to read it, and all the rest. I needed the knowledge that was collected in this place. "These aren't just books, Verona. They're power."

She scowled, then sighed. "Damnit, I didn't want to like you. Every shifter within a hundred miles knows you've let more than one male claim you, which has not happened in" —she stood, sliding a book out of the stack and opening it to a page marked with a silk ribbon—"one hundred and forty-three years, to be precise. And those shifters were identical twins, which kept the packs from executing them. Some excuse about twin souls. Though they did cast them out."

My throat tightened. "Is this pack planning to cast me out? Cast us out?"

"Over my dead body, and as many of theirs as I would take out if they tried," she muttered. "No, whatever happened to my grandson's eyes has set the rumor mill going, but kept anyone from thinking there's a sinister connection."

I frowned. "Because they're the color of the moon?"

Her stern expression softened as she pulled up a chair next to mine. "Not only that. This pack knows him and his family. We've followed the old ways for a very long time, or tried to. They trust us to explain how all of this—your bonds, his eyes—is the moon's will."

I wasn't sure it was, but she snapped her fingers, instructing me to read over her shoulder as she found a page in the Legends tome, and I obeyed. "The Legend of the Moonblessed Alphas." I read aloud, and she listened with her eyes half closed.

*"Once upon a wolf moon, in the coldest winter the world has known, a pup was found outside the borders of a pack, alone and freezing. The Alpha Mate brought him into the pack, and nursed him alongside her own pup. The pups were inseparable.*

*When the two brothers grew old enough to shift, they went into the wilderness with the Alpha, who taught them to take fur and run with joy beneath the moon. Smaller than his brother, the adopted pup fell behind as they ran for the first time in wolf form.*

*That is what saved him.*

*Far ahead, the Alpha and his child were set upon by traitors to the pack, and though he fought with all his strength, the Alpha was murdered. The traitors also left the Alpha's pup for dead.*

*No one but the moon saw the wolf that found his dying brother. No one but the moon witnessed his pain.*

*And when the adopted brother prayed to the moon for help, no one knew how that help arrived.*

*But when the two brothers returned to the pack, one was a wolf with midnight fur, the other a bright white, with moon-blessed eyes, and both shared a bond as Alpha.*

*They ruled until the mountains crumbled, and the seas rose and washed away the forest, and the moon cast its shadow over the sun."*

I stopped reading. "It's a fairy tale."

"Yes. This one is the only reference to moonblessed eyes I've found in two days of searching."

"Is it enough to keep the pack from wanting to burn me at the stake? I already got that reaction from Northern." I tried not to let how much that had hurt show on my face, but I wasn't sure I succeeded. Verona's eyes flashed dark, and her lips tightened.

"I would imagine you did. That pack is all muscle and no memory of what we were given in the first place. And what is required of us in return."

"What is required, Verona?" I asked bluntly. "I don't know much about who we are. Shifters, I mean. I don't know enough, and I want to learn. I need to, for Brand."

The woman's face remained every bit as stern, but her gaze was filled with something like acceptance. "I'll teach you." Then she actually smiled. "But perhaps you could put on some clothing first."

# 8

## WHAT IS MAGIC?
### BRAND

I went from the cell straight to my father's office, not checking on Flor. I didn't have to anymore. More than just my eyes had been altered. I hadn't told her, though I knew I would need to, but the nature of our mate bond had changed entirely.

Instead of having a vague sense of her emotions, I now had a direct line to her thoughts. I could hear her speaking, though perhaps I only heard her thinking of what she might say. I knew she was with my grandmother in the library, which pleased me. After my mother's death, Grandmother had closed herself up with her books and stopped interacting with most of the pack.

I could feel that Flor truly liked her, and was... reading stories aloud to her? Yes. I could also sense that my little mate was feeling strong, fully healed. It was the perfect time to plead my case—and Glen's—with Dad.

He was on the sat phone when I stepped into his office, really a sitting room with a large desk for the paperwork that came with being an Alpha of one of the largest packs in the world. While he spoke, I took a seat on the firm leather sofa and waited.

It was beyond rare for him to take calls. Dad hated technology, and only allowed a few vehicles on our land, as well as one satellite phone for the Alpha's Den and one for the medical outpost. Most of our six thousand shifters lived in smaller sub-packs in the forests that stretched from Southern Wyoming, across Colorado, and down to Northern New Mexico. I had a feeling some of the ones closer to the border had scavenged some televisions and other tech, but for the most part, our pack lived like shifters had for centuries before: hunting, fishing, growing crops and herbs, making art, and running together under the moon.

Dad's voice on the phone was a snarl. "Aidan, you can't be serious. You're calling for the execution of one of our sons. An Alpha Heir. With no hearing, no special meetings —" He went silent, but his face grew flushed. "Of course I know you're the interim Head. Listen, Margarette and Bradley are on their way to you. I'm not making any decisions until you hear them out." A long pause. "Yes, he's in a silver-barred cell. I know the law better than you do."

He slammed the phone down on the desk after he hung up and stood, pacing. I waited for him to speak, knowing there was no need to plead my case. We both knew what was at stake.

"Brand, don't ask me to let him out," Dad grumbled. "You know I can't."

"Can't or won't?"

"Can't." His nostrils flared, and his ears grew tufts of hair at the edges. I gaped at his unusual loss of control. He paced for another moment before he faced me, regret etching his features. "To take my place on the Council, I had to submit to an Alpha command from Bradley. You know that. You know why."

I nodded. I had been a small child during the war, but had overheard more conversations about strategy and battle plans than a child should. Flor hadn't known anything about the causes of the war that had ended before she was born, but the other packs had better schooling. Even if the lessons weren't complete.

Everyone knew that Russian shifters had decided to invade North America twenty-four years before. It was common knowledge that rogues in our own country had joined them. But no one talked about where those "rogues" had come from.

They had been the Western pack, or what remained of it after they were disbanded, their Alpha executed at a Conclave around forty years ago. I rubbed my temples, my head aching even thinking about that pack. They had been punished for crimes against the moon, for using magic against the other packs at that Conclave, or at least that's what my grandmother had taught me. And it may have been the truth.

They had been cut off from the other packs forty years ago. But they were eradicated after the war, because they had enlisted the Russians to help them with their true goal: to regain the power that had been stripped away. They'd shown they would use any means to do so. Theft, betrayal. Even magic.

Their crimes during the war had been severe, but my father had confided once that he believed the response of the other packs had been equally heinous. His elders' roles in the extermination of an entire pack was only one of the reasons that after he came to power, Dad had tried to have as little to do with the outside world as possible. With any of the other packs.

When the war ended, all the mature shifters left alive gathered under the War Council's authority, and every mature wolf made a vow not to speak of the eradication. It was the strongest Alpha command that had ever been given, carefully constructed, and then repeated by all the gathered Alphas simultaneously. With none of the older shifters able to speak of that pack, none of the younger ones learned of it. In another two generations, it would be as if the Western pack had never existed. That communally accepted command had worked to make our kind nearly forget what had happened.

Forbidding the sharing of books that contained knowledge of magic, and the Western pack, had done the rest. Grandmother had found a way around that rule, of course, deciding on her own that locking those books away counted as "not sharing" them.

*Maybe Grandmother will loan those books to Flor. She needs to know the truth, and there's no place else to learn it.*

But Dad was speaking of another Alpha command, one that each member of the Council had to agree to, in order to take their place. "Is the command that strong?" I asked quietly.

His brow lowered. "I promised to follow pack law. Even though I can interpret that to suit our pack in many things, I cannot subvert a direct order from the Council Head."

"The Council Head was Bradley when you took that oath. You had no way of knowing, no way of thinking the position would shift to Aidan McDonnell," I murmured as he paced. Finn's father was more snake than wolf, slick and polished and deadly, and to my wolf, he stank of dishonor and deception at the best of times.

Dad stopped, hanging his head. "I know that now, and knew it then. I should have taken the position, instead of letting him have it, even for a day. The old ways are clear; only the strongest Alpha holds the right to lead."

I nodded grimly. Our family had always taken the old ways of shifters to heart. Physically weak challengers to an Alpha's position were easily defeated in combat.

Morally weak ones were more difficult to remove from power. That was why our pack held so closely to the law. If an Alpha were to break or bend pack law, it was far more dangerous than a lesser wolf's transgression. It led to Alphas drunk on power, ruling as tyrants. This was how many of our worst wars had been started over the centuries. How whole packs had been lost, and not only on this side of the globe.

Dad went on. "I'm far stronger than Aidan has ever been. I should have known better than to allow him to grab the reins of power." He scowled at the floor. "At least Bradley had honor. Aidan..."

I hadn't questioned him before, but I had to know. "What happened, Dad? After the battle at Southern two months back, when he was given the role."

"I wanted to invite you to listen in, son. But it was an emergency Council meeting." That meant only the ruling four Alphas and their Head Enforcers had a vote. I nodded my understanding, and he continued. "Calvin had fled. Only a few of us were there to vote: Aidan and Torran from Eastern, Margarette from Northern, Dean and me from Mountain. I wanted to go home. Even though Margarette had reservations, the rest of us agreed. Aidan would hold all the rights Bradley had as Council Head, until Bradley was well enough to return."

"Bradley *is* well, though."

"But outside of a called Council meeting, Aidan is the one who gets to make that decision. Bradley and Margarette are on their way there now, but I don't expect Aidan to hand over power easily." He dropped his head. "My guess is that Aidan will find some way to deny Bradley's fitness. I'll need to go to the city, too. I was an idiot, turning down the spot as interim Council leader. I knew Aidan would be a shit leader, but I wanted to get back to our pack." His voice was filled with shame. "I didn't think he could do much damage. I couldn't imagine he would go this far."

The hairs on the back of my neck stood up. "How far has he gone?"

Dad's bloodshot eyes met mine. "He's calling for Glen's immediate execution. He tried to give me an Alpha command over the phone." We both chuckled darkly at that. "I can ignore that. But the law regarding rogues was put in place long before him, as were the regulations on Alpha Heirs moving outside their packs without permission. At the least, according to Aidan, Glen is a rogue who needs to be punished for his crime."

"Aidan's worried we'll come to his packlands and get Finn out from under his thumb." I'd already shared my concerns about Finn's coerced return to the fold. Dad had not been all that surprised.

"Or that you'll go to Southern and rescue Luke," he replied. "The reports from our Enforcers who stayed behind —until they were evicted by Aidan's Council troops—were grim. They've done something to Luke."

"He almost died, Dad. He *was* dying, and Flor as well. And me..." I took a deep breath. "And Finn would have gone, too. Glen might still be safe, but I'm not sure."

"All of you?"

"All of us, Dad."

Startled, he met my eyes, and for the first time in forever, dropped his gaze first, though I didn't think he realized what he'd done. "They can never know. If they find out, they'll have you all executed."

"For what?"

"For witchcraft. Or worse."

"We're not witches." I hesitated. "At least, none of the Heirs are."

His eyes grew wide. "Are you saying—"

"No," I interrupted. "I'm not. But Dimitrivich was there in Northern, using magic. Saving her with it. I think... I think he was there, his spirit was there, when Luke was dying. I recognized his energy, when I went into her soul and—"

Dad was across the room, with a hand over my mouth in a heartbeat, stopping me. His eyes blazed fire, and he infused his voice with Alpha power. "You will *never* tell anyone how you saved her. Not a word of going into her soul. Only the moon has the power to do such things. Not you. Not your mate. You will never speak of what happened to another living creature—never, do you hear me?"

I waited for the Alpha compulsion to take hold, but it didn't. It felt like his command slid off me, albeit slowly, like sap dripping down a trunk. But I nodded, and he pulled his hand away. I managed to find my voice again, but only asked one question. "Why?"

His eyes were filled with fear when he replied in a whisper, "What do you think magic is, son?"

"How would I know?" I stood, anger making my limbs tremble. One of the only times Dad had ever shouted at me in true anger had been when I was young, asking about magic. I hadn't understood how the Russians could have killed so many of our strongest shifters. I'd shifted the week before that, and had scented something peculiar on a run. Following my nose, I'd found a gentle woman living in the center of our packlands, who never spoke, except to plants. She'd looked young, but her eyes had been ancient. She'd made me tea, given me my first carving knife, and then I'd watched her use magic to heal a sparrow's wing.

When I'd asked Dad about her, he'd warned me not to speak of it again. So I'd snuck into our pack's library and looked for books on magic. When Dad caught me there, trying to get into Grandmother's locked bookcase, he'd ranted about dark magic and how many friends had died because wolves had allied with witches.

He hadn't needed to teach me about that. I had grand-parents left alive, but many of my friends did not. At Northern, that generation had been killed almost entirely, the loss of their wisdom almost as painful as the dwindling numbers of children.

What did I know of precisely why they died, though? Of magic? Close to nothing. I'd been sheltered, I realized, in a way that weakened me. Perhaps all of us had.

"Nothing," I admitted at last. "No one speaks of it. I saw it used at Northern, by the Russian Ivan, but if there is more than one kind... How would I recognize it? How would I know what it looks like?"

Dad bared his teeth, a fierce smile this time. "I can't answer that. But I know where you can find out."

I said it for him. "The library."

GRANDMOTHER WAS CHIDING Flor as we pushed open the thick, hard-carved door of the room that had always been one of my favorites. "Listen, girlie, you need to put your whole name here in the book. It's our family tree, and you're in it."

I bristled at Grandmother's tone, but when the door was wide enough, I relaxed. She was standing in front of Flor, who was seated at one of the library tables with her back to the door. As Grandmother placed a pen on the table, she graced my mate's lowered head with a smile.

A *smile*. Dad and I both stopped in our tracks and exchanged glances. Grandmother almost never smiled, not after my mother's death.

I could tell that in our bond that Flor knew I was there, but neither woman so much as turned to acknowledge us. "I hate my middle name," she grumbled, ignoring the pen. "No one ever knew it besides my mom and my... my old piece-of-shit Alpha. This can be a fresh start, right? If I don't write it here, it doesn't exist."

Grandmother spoke softly, glancing up at me. "Names have power, Flor. Those who follow the old ways know more about that than you young, restless shifter packs."

"The old ways? I keep hearing vague things about those, whatever they are." My little mate sounded suspicious.

"The old ways are how the pack was meant to be structured. When shifters follow the old ways, the pack as a whole thrives. It's why our pack still has children being born every year, why we haven't lost the moon's favor like the others."

Flor sniffed. "Beggin' your pardon, but I'll withhold judgment. The last time a pack bragged about its amazing structure, it turned out to be Northern. The unranked there were treated like trash."

"Until you arrived," I agreed, crossing the room and greeting Grandmother with a kiss on her cool cheek. "Where's Grandfather?"

"Out teaching the young ones how to track," she replied, then turned, giving a slight bow of the head to Dad. "Why have you come to the library, Alpha?"

Grandmother hadn't always been formal around Dad, but since Mom died, she'd changed. I was almost certain it was her way of keeping her grief from showing. Grandfather coped with his by vanishing into the woods.

"Brand needs to read everything our library holds on the... forbidden topic." He had to work his mouth to get the last two words out.

Grandmother hmphed and stalked across the room, opening the locked case I'd tried to open all those years before, and pointing imperiously at the books and objects behind the doors. A faint scent of silver drifted out of the cabinet.

Dad obediently went to gather the books Grandmother indicated, then carried a small stack back to the table. He set them down as if they were venomous snakes instead of three dusty books.

"What are those?" Flor asked as I wrapped an arm around her. Not touching her felt wrong. In fact, as soon as I felt her skin under my hand, a surge of strength raced through me, as if I'd just shifted into my wolf form.

*Hmm.*

Flor shivered, but moved closer into my embrace. "The titles of them, I mean."

Dad's mouth slammed shut, and he shook his head silently, furious.

Flor hissed. "*He's* under a command? An Alpha?" Our eyes met; she'd seen this before at Northern, with Alpha Hillier. I wasn't sure if she understood this was the same command, affecting another Alpha. Dad grumbled under his breath.

Grandmother sneered. "Flor, they all are. Every Alpha in North America, and every mature member of all the packs. Nearly the only ones who aren't bound are the rogues, and most of them are too feral to speak."

Flor reached over to the stack of books and picked one up, her mouth moving to form a word. She let out the breath on a disgusted curse instead, and set it back down.

Grandmother went on. "It's obscene. The old ways never provided for the sort of monolithic pack structure that strips our Alpha of his rights." She spoke to Flor, but it was obvious she was dressing my father down. "My son-in-law chose to divert from the teachings of our pack when he took the oath in front of the *Council.*" I flinched at how hard she spat the last word. "But the command you're seeing was the most egregious abuse of Alpha power ever fashioned. Of course, it was done to 'protect' all the packs."

"Good intentions?" Flor murmured. "I know about those."

"Just so," Grandmother said, opening one of the books. "None of us can read these aloud. You may find them difficult even when reading silently. Your head might start to ache, and your nose may bleed. Please read them with a handkerchief close by. We don't want blood on the pages."

Dad motioned to me to gather chairs around the table, and I did, making sure to pull a narrow loveseat over for me and Flor.

Grandmother had gone back to haranguing her about completing her entry in our pack's lineage. "I'd let you read as well, but the only pack members allowed access to those books are immediate members of the Alpha's family. Ones who have been recorded in this book. Take the pen, and write your full name."

To my surprise, Flor acquiesced, accepting the feathered pen and scratching her name carefully on the page. Grandmother's eyes went wide as she watched, but when Flor went to set down the pen, she added, "Now your parents' names, of course."

Flor's shoulders slumped. "Do I have to?"

"You do," Grandmother and Dad said at the same time.

Flor's amber eyes met mine. Indecision and fear warred in her gaze, until I said, "My sweet mate. I already know. No one here will share the truth. I won't let anyone hurt you, no matter who your parents are." I hoped that was a promise I could keep.

Flor dropped her head, but then scratched a few more words on the page, a mulish expression on her face. "Fuck it. You'll all know before long anyway."

# 9

## MIDDLE NAMES
### FLOR

My hand shook slightly as I scratched my name on the slightly yellowed page. It felt like I was desecrating the ancient book that Verona had been so proud to show me. Every Alpha since the Mountain pack had been established, dozens of them, had their names there, as well as their mates and children. The line for Brand's mate was on the right side of the page, and I almost laughed out loud, thinking about how it would look to scribble in the other Alpha Heirs' names around his. Would I line them up underneath his? Put them in parentheses?

I was long past denying that there was some weird shit going on with my mate bonds. And something even more weird with my wolf. I still hadn't been able to shift, not that I would ask that of my wolf. She felt off, somehow. Like she was lying still, panting heavily, recovering.

But she was alive, and so were all my... well, all the guys.

I felt three sets of eyes on me as I finished my name and wrote in my mother's—Lily Rain Wills—but then got stuck. "Samuel," I said quietly. "Do you happen to know Alpha Callaway's middle name?"

He went silent, then cursed under his breath. Verona, who had been standing beside her chair, sat with an audible thump.

Brand was the one who answered. "Lee. Alpha Calvin Lee Callaway."

"Thanks." I met his bright gaze, the light in his eyes as beautiful and odd as it had been since I'd woken up. I glanced at the window. It was late evening now, and the moon was shining through a gap in the curtains.

"You know what this means, Brand," Samuel whispered. "She can't be here. She's an Alpha's *child*."

"She's my mate," Brand replied without blinking. "And no one will take her from me."

"I'm sworn to do so," Samuel growled. He was grabbing the armrests of his chair, the wood creaking in his tight grip. "Who else knows this?"

I shrugged. "Callaway." That was the only person still alive who knew.

"Luke," Brand said softly.

I shuffled my feet. "I think Margarette suspects, but she didn't press the issue."

"Finnick?" Samuel's voice was tight, but Brand shook his head. Samuel didn't seem comforted. "If anyone discovers this, if Aidan finds out... At the very least, I'll have to throw her into the cell with Glen. The Council must be notified—"

Brand began to growl, a low, threatening rumble.

"Mate bonds, mate bond preeminence," Verona began muttering and stood, rushing to a shelf. "We have almost everything ever recorded about pack law, the ancient laws, in this room. True mate bonds should always trump any other law. We just need to find the right way to frame it... There must be a way. There's always a way." She dropped another stack of books on the table. "You boys, read for a way out. Flor? Pass that over."

She held a hand out imperiously, and I closed the dusty book where I'd signed my name. I'd hoped she wouldn't look, but I saw her face change as she opened it back up and read it. She staggered for a moment before regaining her balance. Then, carefully, she placed the book back on the stand, and closed the glass doors around it as if she was trying to put a pin back in a grenade. She didn't say a word about what I'd written, and neither of the men asked, though I was almost certain Brand knew.

Brand knew everything, just like he knew when I'd had enough. "We need to sleep," he announced and held out a hand, nodding to his relatives, who were both reading furiously. Desperately. "Join me, little flower?" He led me to a side door, not toward the bedrooms.

"Where are we going?"

His smile was as bright as his gaze. "It's time for me to show you my lake."

"IS IT EVERYTHING YOU HOPED?" Brand asked the next morning as we sat side by side, staring out at the calm water.

"It's exactly as you described it," I whispered. "The most beautiful place I've ever been."

Brand had run beside me for three miles or so the night before, from the Alpha's Den to a cabin hidden in a grove of aspen trees. He'd insisted on carrying me over the threshold, muttering something about old ways.

Someone had obviously freshened up the small one-room bungalow, and left a picnic basket filled with food for breakfast. We'd slept, woken up and made slow, sweet love to each other, Brand's eyes gleaming like twin moons in the darkness. Then we'd gotten dressed in sets of generic forest-green sweats that had been stored in a cedar chest, and he'd led me to the water.

At first, the lake had been dark, reflecting stars. But as the sun rose, it had turned a lighter blue and gold, then pink, orange, and bright turquoise. Mountains on the far side of the valley reflected in the water, until it was a perfect mirror of the opposite shore and sky.

It truly was the most peaceful, gorgeous place I'd ever seen. Ducks called across the water, swallows dipped to drink as a soft breeze blew, and for the first time in my life, I felt utterly safe. And completely incomplete.

I tried not to show Brand what I was feeling, but he lifted me onto his lap, feeding me purple grapes and squares of cheese, and didn't mention the tears on my cheeks. "We'll all live together," he said at last. "Here, or somewhere like this. We'll build a home, with enough rooms for as many mates as you call to your side, my queen."

I pressed a kiss to his lips, his beard tickling my face, and sighed. "What did I do to deserve you, Brand Becker?"

He shrugged. "Must have been something pretty amazing. If I say so myself, I'm a catch." At the same moment he said that, a giant trout leaped out of the water. I snorted at Brand's teasing, then laughed at his pinkened cheeks.

"He's almost as much of a catch as me," a voice chimed in from the trees behind us.

"Glen?" I gasped and jumped up. "Did you escape?"

Blue eyes sparkled like the water, and white teeth flashed as he stepped out from under the trees, wearing dark gray sweatpants and a red flannel shirt.

"There's no cage that could keep me away from you, Flor." Glen struck a pose like a bodybuilder as I ran to him, except one of his hands was filled with flowers. "*Oof!* Woman, has Grandma Ida been feeding you?" he teased, pretending to stagger under my weight as I hugged him.

"How did you get out?" I ignored his teasing and pushed back to stare at his face. He seemed fine. Uninjured, but a little tired. There was a tension in his eyes, though. Fear.

Of course there was. He had an order of execution from the Council hanging over his head.

Before he could answer, Brand joined us. "Has Grandma Ida been feeding *you*, is the question? Say, baking you cakes with files in them?"

"Not a file." Glen grinned and pushed his curls away from his forehead, looking like a toothpaste commercial I'd seen once. "She slipped a key right underneath a tray of freshly baked chocolate chip cookies, though." He held the slightly bedraggled bouquet of wildflowers out to me. "I brought you a courting gift."

"A what now?" I sputtered.

"Damnit," Brand muttered for some reason.

Glen winked at him. "Better catch up, Bearman."

I smacked Glen's arm. "A courting gift? What are you thinking? You're a wanted criminal! You stupid ass, what in the hell are you doing out here in the open?" I grabbed the flowers in one hand and his forearm in the other, dragging him toward the cabin. Brand jogged ahead of us. "If anyone sees you—"

Brand snorted, holding the door for me to enter. "No one will. This lake is off limits."

"Whatever," I scoffed. "Packs are nosy. They don't stay out of somewhere just because you say so."

"They do if you beat the living shit out of any pack member who comes within a quarter mile of a place," Glen chipped in.

"No one should approach. Lock the door anyway, Glenda," Brand said calmly, then took the flowers and arranged them in a glass Mason jar, adding water and placing them on the small table.

After Glen shut and locked the door with a broad wooden bar, he looked around. "Reminds me of another lake cabin. I wonder if the bed is as comfy." He opened his arms and fell back onto it like a starfish.

I gawked. "How can you be so relaxed? Brand's dad is under some ultra-powerful Council command to do what they tell him and execu—" My voice cracked on the word, and Glen hopped back up, folding his arms around me.

"Shush now, princess. You know that won't happen. We're working on a plan."

I let myself go boneless in his arms as he lifted me up to hold me tighter, for a moment pretending that the world worked that way. That a strong, handsome man could just waltz in, declare that everything would be fine, rub his erection on your leg, and... rub it again, a little harder. I groaned in exasperation. "Glen, are you humping my leg?"

He gave a soft, "Woof."

Brand snorted softly. "I'm going to find a good branch." I had no idea what he meant by that, but Glen murmured a thank you, and the door closed behind my mate.

"Now that our chaperone is gone..." Glen yanked off his shirt, throwing it on the floor. Then he used his strong arms to maneuver me up and down so his erection was grinding into my thigh, and made what I thought might be his attempt at an O face.

"You're ridiculous," I muttered, allowing myself to appreciate the feeling of his warm skin under my hands as he nuzzled my neck. Glen had just enough chest hair to give my fingers something to tug on. I was doing just that when his mouth came close to Finnick's bite, and I shuddered at the tiny burst of cold pleasure that blossomed there. Could Finnick feel that?

It felt odd, having a mate so far away. Painful, and a tiny inner voice whispered that Finnick could have done what Glen did. He could have left his entire family and pack for me.

What a selfish thought. When had I turned into such a greedy bitch? It wasn't like I could fuck more than one at a ti... *Huh. That might be possible.*

My inner wolf roused at that thought, sending a few images.

"Ridiculous," I said again, but this time to myself.

Glen chuckled. "I don't know. This could be my last time to commit frottage on your person, sweet wolf." I didn't ask him what frottage meant; I could kind of put it together from context, and Glen's hands were doing something else now.

"What are you doing?" I moaned as he held me closer, using one hand to work the muscles of my neck.

"Shhh. Relax." He tugged at my sweatshirt, and I let him slip it off, over my head. Then, he pressed me down on the bed, rolled me over onto my stomach, and began to rub rhythmically, working from my neck down to my shoulders, then to my lower back, pressing deep into the tense muscles. "Have you ever had a massage?"

"No. I used to give Del massages, though," I said quietly, my heart aching as it always did when I thought of him. "His stump would hurt, especially at the end of a long day, or when it rained. I got pretty good at it."

"I'm so glad he had you."

"He was my... everything. My father figure."

"But not your father."

"No." I took a deep breath. Glen deserved to know that he wasn't the only one here against pack law. And I trusted him to keep my secret. I let that thought float through my head.

He was kind, funny, thoughtful and romantic. He'd raced to save me, and followed me without question. Once he'd realized how he'd been blinded to the injustices at Northern, and learned his own parents' place in it, he'd taken a stand.

He'd fought for me. If the Council got their way, he'd die for me, too. He deserved my trust.

"My biological father is Calvin Callaway." Glen hummed slightly, but didn't react. "You already knew?"

"I'd put a few things together. You know that the kind of power you have, so much that you could meet almost any other shifter's eyes and hold their gaze, is beyond rare? It only exists in the ruling Alpha families, pretty much. I knew whoever your dad was, he had to be someone powerful. And powerfully stupid, not to take care of you."

I almost laughed. Callaway was that. "Del was the best father I could have ever had. My real father in every way but one." Of course, that had to be the one way the Council cared about.

"I'm sorry you lost him. I'm sorry you had to live for so long in a pack run by your own father, who should have loved you..." He cursed, then let out a long breath, focusing on the massage again. "I wish I'd been there to take care of you. But I can do it now."

"You don't need to—ooh, that's the spot. Harder, right *there*." How was he finding every little knot of tension without me saying a word?

*Glen's incredible at this*, I thought, as my brain started to fizz. Wherever his bare hands met my skin, the whirlpool feeling I'd always gotten from him started up in my center, but somehow calmer this time.

His murmur felt like velvet on my skin as he leaned over me, slowly working the muscles down my spine in small, rolling movements. "If you accept me, princess, I'll do this every day. Any time you feel stress, any time you're sore, I'll rub you until you feel nothing but pleasure. Let you set the pace, spend every bit of my energy taking care of you. You deserve this. You deserve love."

My heart raced a little as I thought about all the times Glen had blurted out that he loved me. Had he meant that?

There was no other explanation. He'd left his pack, his family, his home, to follow me. When I thought about it, I wasn't certain I could say I loved him. But I could someday. I might already, a little.

I rolled until I was facing him. His blue eyes were wide, the pupils enormous as he took in my naked breasts. "Flor?"

My mouth had gone dry. There was no way I could ask for what I wanted, so I decided to let my body do the talking. With my hands on his wrists as he hovered over me, I arched my back up slightly, tilted my head so the unmarked side of my neck was exposed to him, and waited.

# IO

## AT LAST, ENOUGH

### GLEN

For my entire life, I'd known I wasn't enough.

My father and mother were so strong, so capable, and I'd accepted that I would never measure up, not really. I had plenty of power, but none of the relentless ambition my parents possessed.

I had inner strength, but it wasn't something to boast of. Especially when the closest friends I had were far stronger. Brand's burgeoning Alpha power had made my knees tremble a little the first time I met him, though we'd still been children. These days, with his eyes shining like twin moons, he seemed even more obviously one of the Moon Goddess's most blessed.

Finn had always been suave and sophisticated, far more politically astute than I could hope to be, with an array of dark talents that I wished he'd never had to learn. But I was thankful he called me a friend, as his loyalty knew no bounds. He would kill to protect me... and those he loved.

I'd known from the first day I met Flor that I was not worthy of her. She was fierce and wild, strong in ways I'd never imagined someone so young could be. And all I wanted to do was make her smile.

Well, maybe not all. I also wanted to make her cry out in pleasure, fall apart on my tongue, and look at me with even half the love that shone in her amber eyes as she gazed at Brand.

Of all the Heirs, I was the joker, the comedian. But right now, I couldn't even muster a smile. Flor was baring her throat, offering herself to me. I had to be certain she knew what her posture meant. And then I had to be absolutely certain that she knew I in no way deserved to claim her, or to wear her claim in return.

"Love, what are you doing? What are *we* doing?"

Her eyes snapped to mine, and a small smile played around the corners of those mysterious pink lips. "Glenda, for a wolf with your reputation, you're awfully slow on the uptake. I'm asking you to fuck me. Fuck me, and bite me. Claim me."

"I... I can't," I rasped, my throat suddenly dry.

She went still. "What do you mean? You don't want me?" I could see her closing up, almost feel her shrinking inside.

"No, Flor! I want you more than I want to breathe. But I don't deserve you." A droplet of water landed on her cheek. No, a tear. I let them fall, unashamed. I wouldn't hide anything from her. "You need mates who are stronger than you, or as strong. Ones who can protect you, who'll never dishonor you."

"Mates like Luke?" she mocked.

I shook my head. "Like Brand is. Like Finn will be. They have so much to offer y—"

One of her hands moved from my wrist to my lips, shushing me. "Glen. You said you loved me. Was that true?"

I nodded immediately. "Do you love me enough to stay with me, no matter what's coming? To..." She blushed, but forged ahead. "Enough to share me with Brand, and Finnick, and maybe even Luke and Grig—"

I shook my head. "Not him, Flor. You don't know what he is. What he's done."

I could tell she wasn't impressed. She shrugged. "Okay, then. With the other Heirs. Do you love me enough to put up with all my shit, and still smile at me at the end of the day?"

"For the rest of my life, no matter how long that is," I vowed.

Her smile crept back. "Then that's all you need to say to deserve me. I want you. I want you to claim me, and I want to claim you back. Because I'll do the same. I'll stay with you and fight for you, even if every stupid fuckhole of a pack on the continent chases you out for being a rogue. Even if we have to go somewhere, all of us, and form a pack of our own. I want to do it all with you."

We both went silent for a long moment, my heart pounding loud enough to hear, hers shining in her eyes.

Then she growled, "Now fuck me."

"No." I pressed a finger to her lips now. "I'll never fuck you, princess." She blinked, flushing again, until I went on. "I will always make love to you. Worship and honor and cherish you, from this day until the moon falls."

"Such a poet," she teased, as I leaned down and began my worship at her pert nipples, then along her neck. Her skin was warm and smooth as I finished removing her clothing, followed by mine. I took a long moment just to feel her, to memorize the way her skin changed as I stroked her. To listen as her breath came in shorter pants as I traced every gentle curve and slope of her honed body, ignoring the way her legs parted as she writhed.

"More," she begged. "Make love faster."

I almost laughed. "Hush now. 'You must allow me to tell you how ardently I admire and love you.'" I quoted her favorite line from *Pride and Prejudice*, then set my mouth to her breast again. She squirmed as I lavished attention on her nipples one at a time, quoting my favorite lines from Austen between kisses and gentle bites, then moving on to the Romantic poets.

Once she was lost in the sensations, I let one hand trail lazily down her torso until I reached the center of her pleasure, tracing slow circles around that spot, learning her desires. I was in no hurry at all. If time stopped right now, and I was caught in this moment for eternity, I would never complain.

She began to tremble as her first climax overtook her, and I watched her face transform, wishing I could capture that expression forever. I'd have to settle for making her come every day, so I could see it.

"So beautiful," I murmured, then moved down her body, reaching behind her to lift her hips up and taste her. Cinnamon and salt, jasmine and her own sweet nectar was the best meal I'd ever imagined. I lapped up her sweetness with my tongue, devouring her.

I'd made her come twice by the time I moved back up her body. As I stared down into her damp, flushed face, and whispered, "'And all that's best of dark and bright, meet in her aspect and her eyes,'" she snapped.

Her wolf rose, her eyes glowing with impatient fire as she growled a demand, "Claim me now, mate!"

"Yes, my love." I lowered myself until my mouth hovered over her inner thigh. My teeth had elongated, and I tasted the evidence of her pleasure as well as the tang of her blood as I claimed her.

Power flooded my veins. A maelstrom of power and energy, a hurricane of it. I felt it leaking from me, blazing in my eyes and down my throat as I swallowed. She rolled us over until she sat astride me, sliding down to encase my cock in her heat. Rising and falling, taking her pleasure.

Driving me to mine.

"I'm coming," I warned her as she shuddered on me, then leaned forward, her dainty, sharp teeth piercing the flesh at the juncture of my neck and shoulder, and driving in more deeply as I filled her.

A long moment passed where we stared into each other's eyes, connected. Complete.

Then her expression changed, filling with pain and shock, as if someone had stabbed her. She slapped a hand over the mating mark on her neck from Finn, and her eyes filled for just a moment with strange red sparks.

She blinked, and they were replaced by tears. Tears of... rage?

"That chickenshit!"

# II

## THE LONG HUNT
### FINNICK

The formal reception room in the Eastern pack's Mansion was always cold. It was even colder when you'd been held in a prison cell in the sublevels for a week with no clothing, almost no food, and no one for company other than the pack torturer, Niall.

*Fucking Niall.* I would kill him someday, and I'd make it as slow as he'd made this punishment over the past seven days.

The bastard tightened his grip on my arm, trying to force me to my knees on the marble floor. I resisted, keeping my eyes on the Louboutin spiked heels that graced the feet of the leader of the Eastern pack, even though I was dressed in a pair of threadbare shorts and nothing else, and dizzy with hunger and blood loss. I knew better than to show any signs of weakness.

"You made us wait, Finnick," my mother remarked from her antique ebony throne.

It wasn't really a throne, though it had cost as much as one at the Sotheby's auction where my father had purchased it for her, at her request. As if Mother ever made a request. Even the smallest of whims from her was a command, and not giving her exactly what she wanted, when she wanted it, resulted in consequences.

"I've been here for a week, Mother. If you were waiting, I was just below."

She scoffed. "You know I can't abide disrespect. And yet, you made me wait." She managed to sound as if she cared. "How many weeks were you at Northern, playing with your little friends? You're lucky I'm not sending you below for the same number of days."

I shivered, and Niall chuckled behind me. Father had sent me to one of the cells beneath the Mansion the moment I arrived home, and I hadn't even seen Mother. For all I knew, she had been at a spa while I was tortured.

I kept my voice calm. "I came as soon as I could. The Northern pack was attacked by rogues. They had an almost simultaneous attack from within, by Enforcers who rose up against Alpha Hillier."

"Of course, you didn't take the opportunity to remove him from the board," my father groused from the smaller chair a few feet away from his mate. He had a tumbler of whiskey in his hand, as usual, and drained it in one long gulp.

"Quiet," Mother snapped. My father flinched, but obeyed.

I held my gaze on her chin, refusing to drop it, though I felt blood seeping from my nostrils. Mother's power was far greater than my father's had ever been, though she was usually careful not to reveal the truth to anyone not in our inner circle.

Niall's hand trembled on my bicep as her waves of power beat down on us, and in seconds, he was slumped against me, using me as a support under the barrage. Normally, I would've crumbled under the force of her dominance, but this time, even after I'd been punished for a week, I was able to keep from collapsing.

*That's new,* I thought. *New and dangerous.*

Mother's eyes narrowed. She would hate that I wasn't kneeling yet. I hoped she would also respect it. She hated my father, mostly because he was weaker than her. Strength, power, and ruthlessness were all she valued, and for once, I had enough for her to notice.

It was my connection to Flor that had given me that power, though I'd rather spend seven more weeks in Niall's tender care than admit that.

I felt a deep surge of gratitude that her wolf had left the mating claim on my tongue. Our bond was hidden. Flor was safe, or as safe as she could be. I knew Brand would keep her as far from my packlands as he could. If she ever came here, there was no hope.

A short whimper came from the other side of the throne. My eyes flew to my little sister, Tana, who had fallen to her knees under the onslaught of Mother's power. Unlike me, Tana was dressed as if she were attending a cocktail party, though she was too young to drink. Or wear clothes that slipped off her shoulder inadvertently, revealing one of her breasts.

*Damnit.* Who had put her in that dress?

As if in answer, Niall made a grunting sound beside me, then noisily licked his lips, and it was all I could do not to elbow him in the gut. He'd had far too much fun over the past week, and it was only knowing that every hour he was beating or cutting me was an hour Tana was safe from him that had kept me from despair.

Her green eyes met mine, and I saw the embarrassment,

the shame, in them. I shook my head slightly. She loved to wear jeans and baggy sweaters she hand-knit for herself, and hated revealing clothing. Unless she was appearing in the reception room, she didn't even wear jewelry.

She had nothing to be ashamed of. I was the one who had left her here.

She shivered, unable to move the strap of her dress back into place, as Niall leered at her, his grip growing even tighter on my arm. The short, raw silk slip dress didn't have enough fabric to ward off the chill in the room either, and was the color of blood, clashing with Tana's bright auburn hair.

"Well, I'm so glad you were able to return home now." Mother's words were like an oily snake slithering through the room, but the sound broke the oppressive pressure as she pulled back most of her power. "We've had so much going on. Deals with PetroCorp and Imregin that needed your particular... skills to finalize."

"I'm sure Father could have filled in," I said. His eyes blazed as he finally paid attention. He and Mother had an arrangement of sorts that I wouldn't have believed could exist between two true mates, if I hadn't witnessed it once, when as a child I inadvertently opened a guest bedroom door to see them entangled with two other shifters, Mother wielding a knife on the rest.

The three days I'd then spent in the lower levels had only been half as horrific as witnessing their bloody sexual perversions.

"Maybe he needs another week to remember his place, Elina," he muttered.

The corners of Mother's mouth dipped, then firmed. "No. He wouldn't have time to heal. The Baranoff woman has to fly home tomorrow. He needs to take care of her tonight." She stared at me, waiting for something. I didn't even blink, and eventually, she went on. "I'm shocked it took word of your sister's mating ceremony to bring you back to your pack, Finnick. It's almost as if you've forgotten who you are. Who you... belong to."

She stood and glided toward me. She was wearing her usual custom-made, perfectly fitted black vicuña pantsuit. I tried not to inhale, but she came closer, pinching my chin between her thumb and two fingers, making me gasp slightly as she yanked my head to each side, looking for...

*Of course.* She was looking for a mate mark. She knew my power had increased, and she knew how that must have happened.

Before I could blink, she'd jerked me to my feet and torn my ragged shorts off with one shifted hand. She circled me, searching for what she suspected.

"Aidan, have your contact in the Northern pack taken care of," she said smoothly as she inspected me. "He fed you misinformation."

"Ah, about that contact..." Father hesitated. "He was put to death last week. Executed."

"The Hilliers discovered him?"

"No," Father snapped. "He was one of dozens. They restructured the pack, from what I heard. They executed some of their best Enforcers for petty crimes."

Mother tsked. "Stupid Bradley. Not the sort of shifter who should lead the Council, I'd say. When do they arrive again? I want to make sure we have everything ready."

"In an hour," Father replied, crossing to the door. "I've commanded forty additional Enforcers to be ready when they bring their request."

"How many Enforcers are they bringing?"

"Four. They left their new Heir at Northern."

"Patrick, yes. He's young. He won't pose much of a problem." Mother stepped back, her eyes skating over my skin once more. "An hour, hm? Barely time for Finnick to dress for his... date."

"Our agreement still stands," I said coldly. "If you want me to use my skills, that is." I didn't give specifics aloud, unsure how much Niall knew.

After the first few "assignments" I'd been given to help coax the wives of the corporate giants—and sometimes even the CEOs, on the occasions when they were female—Mother had hinted that Tana could also be used as an enticement for the men.

She'd been twelve.

My wolf had, for the first time in my life, gone nearly feral. I'd killed four of Mother's favorite Enforcers, as well as the human Chinese textiles dealer who had been the one to suggest the atrocity.

Once she understood she would lose my "skills" as well as the lives of any businessmen who dared touch Tana, we'd negotiated a deal.

Tana was safe until she turned eighteen. That day had not yet arrived, though it was only a few months away. I'd been working on a plan to get her out of our pack, but Flor's appearance had changed a lot of things.

"We shall see," Mother said in reply. "Tana has a fiancé now. Young love and all that."

I bared my teeth, feeling my wolf rise. I was still nowhere near as powerful as her, but I would die to protect my little sister. "If she is even touched before the age of maturity..." My wolf rose inside me, and I felt the unmistakable prickle of fur sprouting on my neck.

Mother hummed. "Our arrangement will stand, as long as you kneel." She meant it figuratively, but I dropped instantly, the hard stone bruising my knees. "Good. Remember to kneel for—what was her name? Ah, yes—Stella Baranoff, as well. She'll be in your room within the hour. Keep her occupied until dinner at nine." She snapped her fingers. "Niall? Make sure the cell Finnick was in is ready for new occupants, please."

"Yes, Alpha... Mate." He bowed and left, my parents following afterward without another word or look at their children. As I staggered back to my wing of the Mansion, Tana helping me to stay upright, I wondered if our situation could get worse.

When I heard the shouts of Bradley and Margarette Hillier ringing in the vaulted ceilings of the foyer, too distant to make out the words, but close enough to hear the anger and mocking tone of my father's yelling, I realized it already had.

My parents had been waiting for a long time to bring down the Hilliers and take over the North American Council. I hadn't been certain how far they would be willing to go, but I should have remembered what my father had said, the first time he'd placed a silver blade in my hand and forced me to slowly execute one of our own pack members. "The strength of the shifter isn't what matters. The number of wolves in a pack is nothing. It's how far one is willing to go to accomplish a plan... and how patient one is during a long hunt."

The Long Hunt. That was what I'd overheard my parents calling their secret bid for power. They'd maneuvered the other packs into this untenable place, playing the other members of the Council, while making certain no one suspected our pack was the root of so many of the problems. Southern had made a fantastic scapegoat, but our pack had far greater abuses taking place, and it wasn't only the unranked who suffered here.

"I tried to get you food, Finny," Tana whispered as we turned the corner. "But Mother has me on another diet. She's watching too closely."

I sighed. Mother was obsessed with appearances, and Tana's bone structure and build were more like the pictures I'd seen of our father's parents than Mother's.

A maid wearing a plain black dress with an apron, her head bowed, opened the heavy door to my wing. Neither one of us thanked her; we'd learned early that to draw any attention to the staff meant punishments for them and us.

And we never knew where or when our parents were watching. I glanced up to the corner of the hall. A small red eye gleamed there. "New addition?" I breathed.

Tana huffed. "They're in the bathrooms now, too. And our bedrooms."

"Shit." Tana was trembling, so I forced myself to smile. "Father selling rights to a reality show or something? Wolves Gone Wild? Shifters After Dark?"

It worked. Tana giggled, the same soft, innocent sound that had driven me to protect her at any cost to myself since I was ten. And I'd protect her now.

I leaned down, pretending to fall, and breathed in her ear, far too quietly for any microphone to pick up. "Your birthday is only a few months away. I have to get you out. I have a plan." I did. I'd used my time hanging from my wrists in the basement to come up with a desperate one.

"It's impossible." She didn't elaborate. They used locked doors, alarms, and trackers as well as their shifter senses to keep us in place.

"I have liquid cash and more stashed in banks outside

the country. I have allies in Europe, and their Alphas have made no pledges to keep you out."

*It would be an act of war,* she mouthed. *No one will take me.*

"If I give them the keys to Mother's kingdom, they will. You forget, I know where all the bodies are buried."

She gasped, her green eyes wider than I'd ever seen them. She knew I meant literal bodies. Some of them were shifters, some human. Most of the ones in the well-hidden mass graves behind the Mansion were people who would never be missed.

But Niall, Torran, and Mother had miscalculated after a ball four years before. They'd invited a young male to an after-party that got out of hand, and ended in his death.

He'd been the Heir of a small Italian pack, and Mother had done everything she could to conceal the crime. In the end, she'd ordered me to burn his corpse. I'd buried him instead. I'd dig him up with my claws and teeth if I needed, if it meant Tana would get free.

I kissed Tana's head and gently shooed her into her room, then went to my own. I ordered some food to be brought up, then ate, showered, and shaved. I'd just pulled on a robe when a knock came at the door, and a brassy, sultry voice called out, "Finnick? Are you decent?"

The door opened before I could draw a breath to answer, and I forced a smile at the bottle-blonde, fifty-two-year-old society matron who glided in wearing jewelry that cost as much as my little mate's Pack House would, and a blunt-toothed, greedy smile.

"No, I'm not decent, Stella. But then, neither are you." I crossed to the wet bar. I knocked back three fingers of the Macallan Lalique, then poured two more. "I hear you've

85

been kept waiting. I'm terribly sorry. How can I make it up to you?"

"Oh, I'm sure you'll think of something," she purred, her gaze taking me in, assessing me like I was a purchase she'd made, and she wasn't yet certain I'd been worth the cost.

I was exactly that: a purchase, part of a business deal. Flor had said again and again that she was nothing, that she was a reject. If she'd known who I really was, under the thin veneer of manners and expensive clothing, she would never have claimed me. She was worth a thousand of me, ten thousand. She was honor, strength, determination, and fierce will wrapped in a perfect, small, fiery package.

I was a whore.

My mother's whore, to be exact. My father's greatest disappointment.

My sister's only hope at escaping a living hell.

I lowered the lights so the healing wounds on my torso wouldn't be visible to her weak human gaze. The camera in the corner of my bedroom stared with a baleful red eye, though, as I let my robe fall, and I knew at least one of my parents would be watching. Making sure I did what I was told.

*Flor, forgive me,* I thought, as the woman pulled up her skirts, revealing her bare sex. My cock didn't even twitch, but that didn't mean anything. *I* didn't mean anything, not to these women.

"I think you should ask forgiveness from down there," she half-teased, half-ordered.

My wolf howled with rage and desperation as the stranger grasped my hair and pulled my face forward, between her legs. I swallowed bile, then opened my mouth, salty tears coursing from my eyes so quickly, it was almost all I could taste.

The mate mark on my tongue burned like acid as it touched the other woman. I swallowed bile and tears, and did what I had to, to save my sister. Even though it damned me.

*Forgive me, Flor.*

*Please forgive me.*

# 12
## A TERRIBLE SOLUTION
### FLOR

I'd never gone from bliss to pissed faster in my life.

Glen's blue eyes crackled with intensity as he held me while I trembled. "What happened?"

"Cityboy decided to cheat on his true mate," I gritted out, feeling blood where I'd bitten my tongue a few seconds before. I rolled to one side, pulling away from his hold and curling up into a ball as my wolf thrashed inside me.

"Are you sure?" Glen asked, and I directed a little of my rage at my newest mate.

"You think I'm lyin'?"

He shook his head, helping me sit up as we disentangled our limbs. The sweat and other fluids drying on my body were suddenly uncomfortable. I headed for the door, the feeling of an invisible knife stabbing into the mate mark Finnick had given me making me stumble. I stomped the rest of the way out of the cabin, picturing Finnick's face under my feet.

Behind me, Glen scooped up a blanket and followed. When Brand appeared from beneath the shade of the nearest trees, I shifted directions toward where he'd been waiting. Waiting for Glen to have a moment alone with me.

*Thoughtful mate. Unlike—* The mating mark flared again, sharper than ever. "Shitfire, that turtlefucking asshat! I will stew his damned balls for this!" I stopped at the edge of the water, panting from the barrage of pain. There was no escaping this feeling. I couldn't run from it. The cold water might numb it, but if I tried to swim now, I'd probably drown.

In seconds, Glen was on one side of me, Brand on the other. I let them hold me up as I cried into the lake.

When I could speak again, my voice was hoarse. "I never thought... I watched my mama go crazy from this. Watched her scream and cry every time my fucker of a father screwed one of the pack's other females. This is exactly why she made me promise not to let a true mate near me. This *exact* damned scenario."

"Little flower, don't say that you regret our mating," Brand murmured. "That would be a worse pain than I could bear." Our bond pulsed with a quiet sadness.

"Oh, Bearman, no!" I turned to him and held on, letting my tears wet his chest. I felt Glen come up behind me, his warmth comforting me, and I reached back to pull him closer. Their closeness helped, the pain in my narrow bond to Finnick fading to a manageable, yet sharp flicker.

"How could he?" Glen whispered. "I know how he feels about you, Flor. That man wanted nothing more than to be yours. For you to be his." His eyebrows flew up. "He's got a mating mark, too, doesn't he? This has to be agony for him, too. There's something you don't know."

Brand rumbled in agreement. "Before he went home, he told me that he had no choice. His little sister Tana was being forced into a mating. He had to go back to stop it."

"What?" I gasped.

"She's only seventeen," Glen added. "Super shy. Innocent. Who the hell are they asking her to—"

"Niall," Brand spat.

Glen went still. "Tell me you're joking."

I pulled back from both my mates. "Who's Niall?"

By the time Brand finished explaining, I felt sick, almost dizzy with an amorphous fear. Was I feeling *Finnick's* fear? I closed my eyes for a moment, trying to focus on the bond that had felt aching and distant.

My mate mark was still burning, but the emotional pain that had begun in the cabin was worse... and it wasn't coming from me. I knew Finnick was with another woman, was still with her, touching her. I felt rolling waves of possessiveness, an itchiness under my skin that mimicked my own mother's fits when I was little.

*Could it be...* I closed my eyes and focused on the bond, that narrow band of energy that led from my chest to somewhere far to the east. But the connection wasn't rich and full, like Brand's, and Glen's now.

It wasn't like what I had with either of them. Their bonds felt almost as if part of them had parked itself inside my heart. Finnick and I hadn't done whatever metaphysical thing it was—or more likely, a physical thing—to cement our claims.

Would I be in even more pain if we had? I remembered my mother's agony, so much that it had driven her insane, and had my answer.

When I opened my eyes with a sigh, Glen took my hand and guided me into the shallow water of the lake's edge. "Let's get clean, while we hash this out. There's something we're not seeing."

Brand jogged to the cabin to get us towels to dry

ourselves, then returned and waited on the rocks by the shore. He told us everything that had passed between him and Finnick back at Northern, while Glen and I washed ourselves clean in the cold water. "I didn't put it together before, but Finnick must have had an Alpha command placed on him. When he told me about Tana's mating, I asked for more information. He wanted to, but he wasn't able to talk about what was happening at his home. He tried to make me promise to keep you away."

"You told me on the trip here that Finnick said he couldn't be the mate I deserved," I mused aloud. "*Couldn't.* Not wouldn't."

"Are you feeling better?" Glen asked as he pulled me back to shore, dried us both off, and wrapped a towel around himself and a blanket around me.

I sat, shaking my head. "Not great. If he does *this* often, I'll get worse. That's what happened with Mama." I tried not to let myself think about what "this" was, what exactly he was doing with someone else, far away.

"Your mom? Tell me about her." Glen held me as we looked out at the lake, and I tried to remember everything I could about my mama.

"What do you want to hear?"

"Describe her, little flower." Brand had a lump of wood in one hand, the size of my fist, and was shaving at it with a pocketknife.

I smiled, picturing her from one of my favorite memories, one of my earliest ones. "She was a little taller than I am now, I think. She was thin like me, but her face was rounder. She had a dimple in one cheek, right here, when she smiled. Though she didn't smile a lot. Del was sweet on her. He used to make her caramels in the kitchen for her birthday." I closed my eyes and pictured her face, cheeks stuffed with sticky candy, laughter in her eyes, looking down at me.

The Alpha had been out on a long hunt that year, trying for white-tailed deer. There hadn't been any females in the group that went out, and Mama had felt better and better as the days went on. She'd been clear-eyed that day, the one when Del had made her birthday sweets.

I sniffed and leaned against Glen. "I think Mama wanted to be a good mother, but she couldn't. She was stuck in a trap." I blinked, then turned to Brand. "Finnick is, too, isn't he? He's being forced somehow. Made to…" My mark burned even more fiercely, and I whimpered until Glen and Brand both snuggled in close again.

Brand had carved a face in the wood, and he held it out to me.

"Is this the art you promised to tell me about?"

"It is," he said. "I make small things. Sculptures out of stone, and carvings out of wood. This isn't as small as the ones I usually do, though."

Glen laughed. "He made an entire chess set for my pack one year carved out of limestone, with the Queen as Mom, the King as Dad. Mom keeps it in with the pack's treasures, and won't let anyone touch it."

I held the chunk of carved wood up and gasped. My mother stared back at me, her dimple captured in the pine, curls tumbling down the sides of her face, her cheeks round and her lips full. The carving looked like it had been plucked straight from my memories.

"How, Brand? How did you…"

He wore a somber expression, and his moon-bright eyes were shuttered. "I've been carving a long time," was all he said.

That wasn't an answer. There was no way, unless…

"You can read my thoughts, can't you?" I asked, suddenly shy. Glen sucked in a breath.

"I can't help it, love," Brand replied quietly, with a furtive glance at my expression. I hoped he saw my wonder, and not anything else. "It's not just a mate bond now, the connection between us. Something happened, something that feels permanent. When I had to save you from being pulled down with Luke, it altered our bond." He swallowed. "Forgive me."

For some reason, those words echoed inside me. As if it wasn't just Brand saying them, but one of my other mates. Like a whisper, from far away: *Please forgive me.*

And when I murmured, "I do forgive you," it might have been a coincidence, but the burning in Finnick's mate mark stopped almost completely. *Huh.* I didn't have long to appreciate the lack of pain, as a howl came from the direction of the Alpha's Den.

Glen sighed. "Sounds like they realized I left. I'd better go back; I don't want to get Ida in trouble."

Brand snorted. "Don't worry about Grandma. Dad may be Alpha, but she rules the Den. But he's calling..." He went still as another howl went up, and then another, until there were dozens of wolves howling. Running toward the Den, it sounded like.

"Who's he calling, the whole pack?" I asked as we returned to the cabin and dressed, gathering our things.

Glen and Brand exchanged glances, but didn't answer. As we ran back to the house, wolf after wolf—some with two feet, but most with four—ran past us. More than one curled a lip at Glen, but most of them yipped a greeting.

When we reached the Den, Ida and Verona were there at the front door, arguing. Ida was clearly incensed, shaking a wooden spoon in the taller woman's face. "Just because you can't find a better solution doesn't mean you tell my son that. You know how he is about honor and duty. Black and white, day and night. He's a good Alpha, but at the end of the day, he's still a male and can't see the smaller paths through the forest!"

Verona bristled. "I didn't tell him I'd given up looking—in fact, I told him to wait! I'm not done with my research; I told him I had four more books to examine, but that stubborn son of yours has made up his mind, and you know—" Her narrow face turned toward us. "Ah, Flor! Maybe you can talk some sense into my idiot son-in-law."

"Samuel? Why would he want to talk with me?" I glanced at Brand, who shrugged and escorted me through the front doorway, prompting the women to follow. "Shouldn't Brand be the one—"

"No!" the women both shouted.

Verona's narrow shoulders bowed in. "That's the last thing we need. I'm afraid Ida's right. Samuel thinks he knows the right way forward. It is a way—it's just not the one anyone would want. Especially our dear boy Brand."

"It's what's best for the pack, Verona," Samuel said from the doorway to his office. "It's the only way I won't have to send Glen and Flor to the Council. And my son to his death from losing his mate, when they get their tainted hands on her."

"Brand, help him!" I gasped, but Brand didn't move from my side. His moon-bright eyes were fixed on his father, and an expression I'd never seen shone on his face. Horror and understanding. Anguish and resignation. Brand knew what was happening.

Samuel was shaking, his hands grasping the doorframe on both sides so hard, small splinters of wood were coming off in his clawed grip. His nose was bleeding, and his eyes shadowed. He almost looked like he'd gotten sick. Was he losing control of his wolf?

"What's wrong, Samuel?" Glen took a step toward the Alpha, who shook his head.

"Stay back. I'm fighting this damned leash as hard as I can, but..." He broke off, panting, his head hanging.

Ida huffed, folding her arms around herself. "That awful Aidan called again. He put the full force of the Council's command on my boy. He's been ordered to execute Glen immediately. He can't disobey... Well, he *can*. But it's killing him."

"I'll go," Glen offered, though he was still holding my hand. "Flor can stay here with Brand. I'll go to Southern and help Luke."

"Won't be... enough," Samuel groaned. "Flor. Once I knew her lineage, saw her name on that page..." Glen's eyebrows flew high, but no one else reacted. I'd need to tell Glen everything soon.

"Shit," I muttered. "I should've guessed. I suppose we'll all need to go."

But Brand was already shaking his head. "Pack law means he's honor-bound to make Flor leave, given her parentage. But the Council command is another thing. Even if Glen left now, Dad would be driven to hunt him down and obey their rule. Obey or die. Isn't that right, Dad?"

Samuel's head rose slowly, and I saw the mirror of Brand's expression on his older, lined face. "Years ago, I made a mistake that no Alpha of this pack will ever make again. I was so mired in my suffering, I gave my power to the Council. But you won't do that, son. You'll know who the enemy is now. You'll know how not to fall into that trap."

I didn't follow what he was saying, but the others all

reacted with shock. "I can't challenge you," Brand said softly, taking my free hand. "I won't. The pack needs you."

I blinked as I understood. "Challenge? You think if Brand takes your place as Alpha, then... Wait. Would that work?" My pulse quickened, a flare of hope exciting me. "Brand can be Alpha and not swear to the Council, right? Not get put under that command to obey Finnick's dad?"

Glen answered. "Right. None of our packs are required to belong to the Council. It means there would be no trading between Mountain and the others, no alliances against rogues, or sharing of information. It would be close to a declaration of war." When I took a breath to ask, he shook his head. "Of course, my parents wouldn't go along with it, and Mountain is the largest pack by far, with almost as many shifters as the other main packs combined. No one would come all the way across the country to attack a fortified, massive pack. But..."

I remembered something from back at Southern. When I'd asked if the Heirs had to kill their own parents to become Alpha, they'd assured me that wasn't the case. "But don't you have to go to the Council to transfer the Alpha power?"

Brand didn't speak, and neither did Samuel. They were staring at each other, dark brown eyes meeting moon-white ones, both filled with pain and resolve.

Verona answered me, her voice shaking. "Those are the new ways. Moving that power from Alpha to Heir takes more energy, more of the moon's blessings than any one wolf can hold."

"I challenged my grandfather," Samuel said after a long moment. "My father was dead, and Grandfather could no longer lead."

"No longer wanted to," Verona corrected. "His mate had gone on."

"It's not the same," Brand whispered. "You are not sick. Not dying. *No.*"

The tension in the room was palpable. Verona broke it, turning back to me. "The new way of sharing power has only been adopted in the past hundred years, and not by all packs. Only the North American and European ones, in fact. It takes a group of extremely powerful shifters—like the Council working together, with the combined strength of their individual packs behind them—to reassign the role of Alpha." Her nose wrinkled, like she'd smelled something bad. "Thousands of shifters, all lending their power to the task. The old ways are..."

"I already said I won't do it," Brand said softly, his grip on my hand almost too tight.

Watching Samuel crushing the solid wood of the door-frame in an effort not to lunge forward and attack Glen made me think that whatever the old ways were, they were worth a shot. "What are the old ways?"

Ida spoke quietly. "All it takes is the power of the moon and of blood. If Brand challenges his father and defeats him in combat, when Samuel dies, his power will pass to Brand." I had guessed this was coming, but hearing it made me feel sick. The old ways sucked.

"It's an easier transition under a full moon. That's not for well over a week," Verona muttered. "But I need more time. I can find some other way. There are texts in some of the cabinets I haven't read for decades—"

Samuel waved her to silence. "We don't *have* time. Bradley and Margarette arrived at Eastern to meet with Aidan. But someone has lodged an official complaint about Bradley's decision-making. He and Margarette are under investigation for executing their own Enforcers, and Aidan's refusing to give Bradley his seat back until the judgment." Blood was now running from his nose. "I won't make it there to contest the findings, and even if I did, I'd be under investigation as well. If I don't obey pack law and the Council Head's command, I'll die anyway, but slowly, and for nothing. You must challenge me, son."

Tears were pouring down my face. Of course Finnick's dad would do anything to hold onto his power. Of course Samuel would give up everything, even his life, to fight against that.

Samuel rasped, "There's no other way. Challenge me and defeat me tomorrow night. Swear to me you will never let the Council leash our pack again, and I will go to your mother's arms with joy. And pride, knowing you will be a far more worthy Alpha than any of your ancestors."

The pain from Finnick's mating mark was almost gone now, though not entirely. But the agony that flared from my heart was every bit as bad.

No, worse, because it wasn't all mine. My massive, strong, warmhearted mate was silently weeping next to me, tears running down his cheeks and into his dark beard as he stared with those beautiful moonblessed eyes at his dad. He opened his mouth, and I knew he would refuse. There was no way he would kill Samuel. His love for his father was so strong, I could sense it in every breath Brand took.

Of course, I'd been wrong before. And I was wrong now.

Brand's voice broke audibly as he addressed his father. His heart broke at the same moment, but I was the only one who felt it. "Alpha, I challenge you."

# 13

## IN THE EYES OF THE MOON
### FLOR

T'd had more than my fair share of bad days in my life. I'd been hurt in more ways than I cared to remember: beaten, starved, mocked, and whipped publicly. But the pain I felt as I sat in the basement of the Alpha's Den with the man I'd thought I would have years to get to know, who I'd imagined as a father figure now that Del was gone... it hurt worse than all of the beatings I'd taken at Southern put together.

Samuel lay where Glen had been just the day before, his massive frame dwarfing the small bed, and his face turned to the high, narrow window. He'd insisted on being locked down here, afraid he would be driven to harm Glen or me. Brand had only let me come to keep him company when I'd promised to stay on my side of the bars. Then he'd sent some of his friends, a few I'd met at the Enforcer Games at Southern, to call as many of the pack members as they could round up to stand as witnesses to the challenge.

When I'd asked how many that was, and learned there were over six thousand shifters in the pack, I'd been astounded. Southern only had a few hundred at the most, all living inside a razor-wire fenced compound. The humans nearby just thought we were some kind of odd religious cult.

The Mountain pack, Ida explained, had always had borders marked by the natural world—rivers, mountains, and valleys—and those were protected by patrols of wolves. The whole pack, males and females, took part in protecting an area of around fifty thousand square miles.

"Not just the ranked shifters?" I'd asked, wondering what I was missing.

"There is no rank in the eyes of the moon but that of Alpha, granddaughter," she'd replied as she'd given me a plate piled with food to take down to her son. "Enforcer and Head Enforcer are only job descriptions here that we use when interacting with outside shifters, no more or less important than teacher or pack herbalist, or mother. We are all children of the moon."

Brand had locked himself in the library with his grandmothers, and I kept feeling odd sensations in the bond. Tiny sparks of what might have been hope or curiosity, followed by waves of anger and despair. On my end, I'm sure he only felt how pissed I was. How could he have challenged his father? It was like he'd given up hope of finding a way out that didn't end in battle.

Glen had asked me to believe in Brand. But I still felt the burning pain of one mate I was trying not to give up on completely, since Finnick's mate mark still hurt like a hornet sting. Now? I was halfway to Ragetown, Population: 1, since Brand had hopped on the crazy train.

"You should go, Flor," Samuel said, not looking at me. "Let me rest before the fight."

"Maybe I'm trying to wear you down. It is my mate you're fighting." I got up and drank a sip of water from the bottle I'd brought down. My throat hurt from trying to convince Samuel not to go through with the challenge.

"You're too honorable for that kind of thing," he replied after a long moment. "You know, you remind me of my mate, Lore."

I'd seen her name in the family tree when I'd added mine. "Lorelei?"

Samuel smiled up at the ceiling. "She was tall, like her mother, with nice broad shoulders and hips. Good thing. When Brand was born, he weighed fourteen pounds." He laughed as I shuddered. "We wanted more children, but it never happened. So she poured all her affection into Brand. It's why he's so spoiled." We both chuckled at that. "Her love was like sunlight, soft and warm. But when she got riled up? She was a thunderstorm, raining hell down on anyone who hurt the ones she protected."

My heart ached. Usually, Samuel was reserved and quiet. But he'd obviously passed down a deeply romantic streak to Brand. And now, on what might be my last day to get to know him, he was opening up, sharing all the stories I should have had years to learn.

"I wish I'd known her." I wondered if she'd looked like Verona. If she'd loved books, or fighting, or something else. I made myself a promise to walk down the hall of portraits slower when I had a chance, and see if she was there.

"She would have loved everything about you."

"Even though I have more mates than a dog has ticks?" I grumbled.

He sighed. "She'd have crocheted matching wedding tuxedos for all your males."

"Crochet?" I couldn't even picture it.

Samuel laughed quietly. "She wasn't very good at it, but she loved to crochet. She made me a pair of shorts one year.

Yellow wool, in some sort of pattern she called granny squares. Itchy as hell. She asked me to wear them to the Conclave the first year after we mated. With a matching short-sleeve shirt thing."

"How did you get out of it?"

He huffed. "I didn't. I wore them, and fought every shifter who laughed." His lips twitched under his beard. "All seventy-three." I couldn't laugh; Brand would probably do the same thing for me. "Do you crochet?"

"Not a stitch. So don't worry, Brand's safe." I sighed when I realized what I'd said. He was anything but safe. He could die tonight, and it would be his own father who did it. Though even if Samuel was the one to fall, a part of Brand would disappear with him. I went on, as if I could talk away the sadness. "I did like to sketch, back at Southern. I could usually get hold of some old pencils and paper. I wasn't great—I'm not an artist like Brand—but it was fun. It was about the only fun I had, growing up."

Samuel sat up. "Brand needs fun." The light had diminished, so it was hard now to make out his features. "Promise me you'll enjoy every minute you have together. Even the hard ones. I'd pay any price for even one day more with my Lore. Even one kiss. Don't take my boy for granted."

"I never could. His love is more than I ever dreamed."

He reached through the bars, and I grasped his hand gently. "Don't take any of your mates for granted. You're going to change this world, Florida Wi..." We both held our breath for a moment before he finished, "Florida *Wills*." His smile widened as I stared into his eyes. Maybe he was weaker, or maybe I had grown stronger, but it wasn't hard to meet his gaze now.

"I'd settle for changing this fight," I admitted.

He opened his mouth to say something, but the door at the top of the stairs swung wide. Ida came down, her face blotchy and swollen from crying. She pulled a key from her pocket and opened the cell door while I slipped away, my lungs tight.

I looked for Brand in the library, but only Verona was there, furiously reading and taking notes. "Did you find a way out?" I asked quietly.

"Not yet." Her voice sounded as rough as mine. She had two books open in front of her, one antique and one brand new. "The old ways were recorded in our modern books, but they've been simplified over the years. The oldest recorded pack laws are where I've been trying to find another solution. A loophole, a precedent. Something." She pulled the older one of the books toward her and read aloud with increasing frustration. "*The passage of power from Alpha to Alpha shall take place under the eyes of the Moon Goddess and before Her gathered children. The decision of who receives the power is not made by tooth or claw, but by Her favor, which She makes known through blood and light.*"

*Blood and light?* "That doesn't make sense."

"They simplified the description of the old ritual in the most current pack law books." She pulled the freshly printed book closer.

I peeked at the page she tapped with one bony finger, scanning a few lines. This one was straightforward, even though the author had made it clear that these "old ways" were only included in this text as a historical footnote. The challenge had to be offered with witnesses, with a fight to the death that took place under a full moon. The winner was the shifter who survived. That was it.

"And then the power just... goes to the winner? Like... woo-woo magic shit?"

"You know magic is outlawed," she replied, but something in her tone made me curious.

"It is? I never learned about magic at all back at Southern. Why is it outlawed? The Russian, General Ivan, had a wand with magic. Where did it come from? Did we shifters have magic? And gave it up or something?"

Verona moved her mouth, like she was trying to chew gum, but couldn't speak. Finally, she took a breath and let it out. "You wrote your mother's name: Lily Rain Wills. I looked into all the Southern pack registries we have here. There is no recording of a Rain at Southern. Were there others with your name?"

"Ah, no," I answered. "Just me and my mother."

She hummed. "As I suspected. Mountain also has no Rain family. So I looked into the smaller packs that are allied with Southern, then Eastern, and Northern. There are no Rains. And then I remembered, I'd seen that name once before."

I blinked, wondering what she was getting at. Did I have some family she knew about? "Where?"

After a long moment, she walked to the back of the library, using a brass key to open a locked bookcase. She reached behind the shelved books to something hidden there. When she returned to the table, I saw what she'd retrieved. It was an antique-looking book that smelled like old blood and mildew, small enough to fit into my pocket and bound with faded red leather, with a brass hinge closure.

Verona placed it gently on the table. "You asked about magic. You should know, you should have been taught, that any use of magic is forbidden since the war with the Russians. Any hint that a wolf has magic can lead to banishment or death. Anyone possessing an item that has magical properties is to be executed."

I nodded. "Like Ivan's wand. Wait, what about Brand's eyes—"

"*Moonblessed*," she stated severely. "Mother Moon blessed him, just as the old stories mention. There was no magic involved, do you understand? Magic and the moon's blessings are not the same."

Something was off in her tone. Was she lying? Not exactly, but she was hiding something. Her mouth worked again, and I let it go. "Gotcha." I reached to pick up the book, my thumb landing on the catch. "Ow!" Something, a sharp tooth or splinter of metal in the design, had cut my thumb. A droplet of my blood welled up and landed on the hinge.

The metal closure released with a tiny click, and the book flipped open to the front page, as if an invisible hand had moved it. I stared down at the beautiful pictures, wolves and moons, that decorated the edges. They were lovely, but the title on the front page was the last thing I'd ever expected to see. Verona leaned over, peering at the page along with me. I read the words silently, but when I tried to read them aloud, she tapped my lips with one finger.

*What the hell?* I raised an eyebrow at Verona.

She just reached over and closed the book. "No one knows this exists, not even my son. It was left here by a shifter who shouldn't have been allowed to cross our borders. He was defecting from..." She swallowed hard. "In any case, he left us and went to Northern, and stayed."

"Have you read it?"

"I couldn't even open it."

I stuck my already-healed finger in my mouth, disturbed at that thought. "Why are you giving it to me?"

Her voice trembled as she replied, "Because I believe it belongs to you. To your line. But Flor, no one can ever know you have it."

I nodded dumbly and tucked the book into my pocket, the words I'd read humming in my mind, over and over, like a spell. The words and the oddly familiar name that had been printed on the first page, and the spine.

*Western Witchcraft, Eastern Wolfcraft: The Journal of Sergeant J. Rain of the Western Pack.*

# 14

## A WASTE OF A LIFE
### BRAND

My little mate didn't understand why I'd challenged my father. I wasn't sure I did either. But when my grandmother had explained to Flor the movement of power, and how it was once driven by the moon, something had hummed inside me, like a tuning fork, perfectly on pitch.

This was right. This moment, how it was unfolding, was precisely what was needed to... to what? I wasn't sure, but it didn't matter. I was committed now. The fight would begin in only a few minutes.

"Brand! What's happening?" Voices I'd known my whole life called out to me, concerned. Shifters had run all night, traveling across mountains and crossing rivers to arrive in time. It was obvious some of them didn't eschew all the modern conveniences like Dad, since I'd heard motors and even a small helicopter that landed only miles away from the Den. The pack was coming, thousands of them, the air humming with anticipation and fear.

I knew why. My father was an exceptional Alpha. He'd shown how to lead a pack with wisdom and care... and how to keep leading, even in the face of devastating loss. I feared our pack would need those lessons even more, if what I'd heard from Glen was true. He'd called his brother Patrick on Dad's sat phone, who had shared that Northern was preparing for war.

Both Bradley and Margarette were being held in an unknown part of the Mansion at Eastern, and no one—not even Patrick—had been allowed to speak with them. As Dad had told us, they were being formally investigated by the Council. When Patrick had asked which Council members had voted to incarcerate his parents, he'd just been told a majority of the remaining Council members had agreed.

"Dad would never have done that, and neither would Dean," I'd assured him. Dean, who wore the title of Mountain's Head Enforcer when necessary, would never go along with the McDonnells, or Torran. "It's a lie."

"I know that," Patrick had snarled. "But McDonnell is a snake. He claimed Eastern and Southern both voted to lock them up. It was two against two, and Aidan as Council Head had final authority."

Snakes indeed. After Luke had been incapacitated, McDonnell had appointed Torran, his Head Enforcer, to the interim Alpha position at Southern. Though Torran didn't have the Alpha's authority, he held the vote for Council purposes.

Even if I won the challenge tonight, I would not have a vote on the Council until I joined it. And to do that meant pledging allegiance to Aidan, putting myself under his power. So the only option to free Bradley and Margarette, and get a fair hearing for Glen and Flor, was war.

War... or perhaps, if we could somehow bring Luke back from the brink of death, he could cast his vote and stop the investigation. Without Southern's support, Aidan would have to allow a trial. Even though there was no way of knowing if he would follow the law, as a sworn member of the Council, he had to, or he would end up like my father. Dying.

"Brand?" I heard my mate calling out over the massive crowd of pack members who were gathering in the field behind the Den. Of course, she was one of the shortest shifters in the throng, and I couldn't see her.

My wolf snarled inside, hating that. We should always be able to lay eyes on our wildflower. It helped us to keep her safe.

"Mate?" I roared back. A hush fell over the noisy crowd as she made her way toward me, her bright red hair shining like a beacon. Like a field of grass being blown by wind, the shifters she passed dropped to one knee in a rippling wave, acknowledging her.

Flor's face was bright red by the time she reached me. "What are they doing?" she hissed, obviously uncomfortable.

"Honoring my mate," I replied before I picked her up and kissed her thoroughly. "You're the future Alpha Mate of this pack, my love."

"I don't want to be Alpha Mate," she whispered into my neck as the crowd around us whispered and hummed. "I want your dad to stay alive and in charge. Please don't do this."

"He's in a trap, Flor," I answered quietly. "The Council is a cage. Maybe it kept our packs safe after the war, but Eastern has grabbed the reins of power now. I have to save him."

"Save him?" Her amber eyes glinted as she stared into mine. "You have a plan?"

"I have a *hope*," I corrected.

"Fuck. I hate hope," she grumbled, threading her fingers through the hair on my chest.

I kissed her silky hair and set her down. "How about trust, then? Trust me when I say that if there's any way out of this, any way to save him, I'll do it. But I cannot lose this fight. I will not endanger you, my flower." I stepped back, and Glen joined her, taking her hand. The noise from the crowd grew louder again, with a hard edge.

"Quiet!" My father's voice thundered over the gathering, and he stepped into the clearing. The moonlight shone down on his dark hair and beard, painting them with silver. Instantly, everyone moved back, creating an open space for the fight. "Mountain, your Alpha has been challenged. I welcome the challenge. I will fight my best, but if I fall... I believe our pack will rise stronger."

"Is he going to throw the fight?" Flor muttered.

Hearing her, Dad shook his head. "I would never dishonor my son, or my pack, in such a way." He smiled. "I also would never lie to myself. Brand is the best fighter in any pack. The strongest, with the most to live for. You, my daughter." Flor muffled a sob. "Tonight, we honor the old ways."

The pack roared in protest. They knew what that meant.

Dad's eyes blazed as he stripped off his clothing and stood naked beneath the moon. "Mountain! You are called by your Alpha to witness this challenge, and to honor the moon's judgment. Do you accept this responsibility?" The gathering darkness was filled with howls of acceptance and grief. "Who challenges for the position of Alpha of the Mountain pack?"

"I do." I stripped off my own clothing and walked

toward my father, looking around at the members of my pack who still kneeled. At Flor, who was clutching Glen's arm. At my grandparents who had gathered, all of them shifted into wolf form, at the edge of the circle.

Then I met my father's gaze. He was strong and a viciously capable fighter. But he had taught me everything he knew. As I gazed at him, the corners of his mouth turned up, and all of his love poured out of his dark gaze into my bright one.

He knew.

There was no way out of this fight now. At the end, I would be Alpha.

And an orphan.

The pack quieted, the sounds of breathing, shuffling paws and feet, and the evening wind all that broke the stillness until my father spoke. "Brand Becker, you have challenged for the position of Alpha, so I choose the form. *Shift.*"

His command, filled with Alpha power, rolled over me. I shook it off without a thought. "You first."

The crowd gasped. He'd done that on purpose, I knew. To show our pack that I was worthy. That I had enough power to lead. He'd done it so no one would question me when I led them into war.

Dad began his shift into his enormous, dark sable wolf form, and I dropped to all fours, shifting as well. In one breath, I was a man. In the next, I was howling my challenge to the night sky. Another gasp went up from the crowd, and I knew why. I'd shifted faster than my father, faster than any wolf they'd ever seen. I waited for Dad to finish his change. As soon as he had, he struck, snarling.

I'd fought against him in human and wolf form thousands of times, and we both knew each other's strengths and weaknesses. Dad was still strong, still used his teeth and claws with equal terrifying efficiency, and I bled within the first few seconds of the fight. He was every bit as fast as he had ever been. He fought hard, making sure the pack saw that he wasn't handing me his position. I was earning it.

But I had changed, and not just my eyes. Bonding with Flor had given me more strength than I'd had on my own. When the bond between us had deepened, that power had increased even more. Now, I had access to a level of strength I'd never imagined. There was a reserve that I could sense alongside my own power, like a river of energy.

A river that flowed to me though my little mate. *Glen*, I thought. I had access to Glen's power, too. I felt him, some-how, in the wide bond that stretched from me to Flor, and was now tethered in his soul as well. *Holy shit*. He was stronger than I'd realized, and he was offering me his strength freely, pushing it to me, through her. All I needed to do was accept it.

As if that realization had opened the channel wider, I found myself moving faster, avoiding my father's lunges and attacks without a thought, my teeth finding their way into his fur faster than he could move to protect himself. I bit and held on, dragging sharp teeth through soft flesh, claws through thick fur into the muscles beneath. The scent of blood filled the air, and painted the packed earth where we fought.

I didn't want to hurt my father, but my wolf knew this was needed, and fought with startling efficiency, aiming sharp teeth at the most vulnerable places, slicing through tendons and muscle with ease. Each movement was precise, each attack measured to bring this fight to an end as soon as possible.

Finally, my father collapsed, his back legs unable to support his weight. I hesitated. He could heal, given time. I hadn't bitten so deeply that he would bleed out.

My own wounds were superficial, except for one nasty bite in my flank, and a set of claw marks that ran across my muzzle. I snarled low, stepping forward, angrier than I should be. This moment was a travesty. Even my wolf saw it as what it was: a waste of a life, of a strong wolf who had many years left.

A cloud had moved in front of the moon, and at that moment, it cleared, sending a beam of light down to his blood-soaked fur. My father groaned, extending his neck, waiting for the strike. I could feel the moon's power now, bathing me in possibility. Preparing me for my new place.

*Possibility.* Grandmother's words echoed in my mind. *Moving that power takes more energy, more of the moon's blessings than any one wolf can hold.*

*Possibility.* Was it possible that I could change the outcome that had seemed so inevitable? With the strength I had now... perhaps. As I listened to my little mate's thoughts, the silent mourning that echoed in her mind, even as she stood proud and tall, her expression stoic, I knew I had to try.

Setting my teeth to his throat, I bit down as gently as a mother wolf carrying a pup. I called to her in our bond. *Mate.*

She answered, stepping into the circle, leaving Glen at the edge. Her feet were bare and human, but her eyes glowed with gold fire as she knelt at my side. With my teeth still holding my father's neck, I went still, diving into that place where I had widened the bond. Flor met me there. Her wolf, her red-black fur gleaming, pressed its muzzle to my side.

*Can we?* I wasn't sure what I was asking.

It didn't matter. Her reply was instant. *Yes.*

Glen's voice echoed her. *Yes.*

*More than any one wolf can hold,* I thought to them both. The moon, and blood, and our intention.

I let go of my father's neck and turned my bloodstained muzzle to the sky, loosing a deep, long howl. *I am Alpha,* I called to the moon. *I am Alpha!*

The pack joined me, though the closest wolves seemed confused. The ones who could see that my father still breathed. Still lived.

*I am Alpha!* I howled.

*Alpha! Alpha! Alpha!* the pack repeated.

The moon's light shimmered, painting us all silver, and I felt a surge of power falling as if from the sky itself, onto me. Crushing me. I was driven to my belly, my head bursting with light, with energy. Too much.

I felt Glen reach for some of the power, some of the weight. Then Flor rested her hand on my neck. She cursed and fell to her knees. "Shitfucking son of a bitch! *Ah!*"

Someone gasped. Someone laughed. I shivered with apprehension. I could smell her blood on the night air and knew she was being crushed alongside me.

My father growled, snapping at my muzzle. Demanding. I knew, if I killed him, the power would flow smoothly into me. He'd told me how it felt, when he became Alpha. "The power will flow to you naturally, once I'm gone," he'd whispered that morning. "The moon will guide it to you."

But that wasn't happening. With my father still alive, there were two branches the shining river of the pack's power could follow. Two pulls, two competing tides. Perhaps if I was trying to encompass a smaller pack, one with weaker members—Southern, for instance—it would have worked. Or if the other Alpha was far weaker than my dad, or had held the pack for less time.

I'd been a fool, to think that I could stretch wide enough to fit my pack's bonds inside my own spirit. I was born to be Alpha someday, but reckless to think I could do it on my own, pull the bonds of six thousand souls to mine, with only a new mate bond giving me added strength. Even if that mate was a wonder. Even if she brought the power of the Northern Heir along with her.

Flor was still being drained by Luke. It was a slow dripping of power away from her, but present. Finn's betrayal had wounded her even deeper, and her wolf's heart had been weakened. Glen was strong, but cut off from his own pack.

It wasn't working. We were all dying, would all die together: Flor and Glen, Luke and Finn. I tried to hold the pack, to wrap the power that flooded me in bands made of my willpower alone. They burned away like cobwebs.

I felt something hemorrhage in my brain. Heard Flor cry out. Dad growled again and stretched his neck long, his expression panicked. I could almost read his thoughts: *There is no other way. Don't make me lose my son.* A tear fell from his bloody eye.

I set my teeth back to his neck, praying for the Moon Goddess to help. But it wasn't the moon that saved us. Another invisible presence, a dark, sly energy slid through the bond.

My father's head slumped as he fell to the ground. And the pack fell into my soul.

# 15

## A RUINED PACK
### GRIGOR

The wing of the Southern Pack House where Luke Callaway's sickroom resided was dark and deserted. Almost too quiet, except for the sound of the machine that pumped air into his lungs and the buzz of electricity that ran the device.

I stood in a shaft of moonlight, unconcerned that I would be seen. No one in the pack cared enough about this male to check on him. I wasn't even certain the pack knew he was alive. If this could be called living.

I stared at his gaunt, wasted face, half-obscured by a mask, wondering how the moon could have seen fit to burden my little *behrserk* with such a mate. I'd heard stories about him from many members of this pack. Well, perhaps it was more accurate to say I'd forced stories from the lips of former pack members, before I killed them to add their entrails to my bouquets for Flor.

Only two of them had shared tales of this dark-haired male standing up for his true mate. An older male had mumbled something about Luke as a child taking a beating meant for my little mate when she was barely old enough to walk. He'd died before I could glean any details, and no one else seemed to remember that moment.

A younger shifter had shared that a few years ago, not long after the rest of the worthless males had begun to hunt my mate-to-be, Luke had stepped in again, protesting her treatment. Supposedly, he'd been starved for weeks, locked up for months, and beaten on the Alpha's orders. I might have softened toward the useless Heir, except for one thing. After that, he'd allowed the Hunt to go on, leaving Flor to evade forty males for years on her own.

Though had she truly done that? I suspected the mate bond, even if he hadn't felt it, would have driven Luke to do something to protect her. Small things, perhaps. Unnoticeable by the other Enforcers.

*Enforcers.* I stifled a growl. In my first centuries, I'd culled hundreds of shifters like these. Their removal was no loss to the world, and the paltry few I'd slaughtered at Southern would never be missed.

I'd devoted myself to killing every single one of her former pack who had chased her down. Every hand that had touched my little mate needed to be cut off, every head removed from unworthy shoulders, after they'd confessed their part in her torture.

My rage had grown with each story, along with my frustration that I could not find two of the wolves who needed killing most. I paced around the room as I thought, my senses alert for any noise from the hallway or outside. I had to be cautious. If I was stronger, I could cloak myself in shadows and erase any trace of my presence. As it was, I had to sneak. I glared at the unconscious shifter who was the root of my current weakness.

He was the reason I had to remain here. I had to protect him, not only for my little mate, but for myself now. I rubbed absently at my chest, feeling the painful pull there. It was an unusual, unwelcome sensation. My well of power had been full, or nearly so, for centuries. Even when I'd needed to use a more significant portion of my magic over the years, I'd had more than enough time for it to replenish, and I'd never felt... emptied. Weak.

But I'd expended so much, saving Luke. No, saving the Southern Heir wasn't all that had weakened me. I didn't like to admit it, but the distance from my true mate was sapping me at a dizzying rate. It didn't help that I'd sent a burst of power, one I didn't have to spare, to answer her need at the Mountain pack. Answering the desperate call of her mate, Brand. I needed her beside me, soon. I needed her claim on my body, and mine on hers.

Her dying mate, Luke, needed her as well. If moving him wouldn't have meant his death, I would have taken him away long before now. Carried him to her, or dragged him at least. A wave of vertigo flooded me.

She would have to return here, even if I wanted her to stay far away. I closed my eyes and reached for her along the narrow ribbon of magic I'd planted in her soul the first time I touched her, and reinforced at Northern, in the forest. *I need you, little one. Come to me.*

I felt her startle, felt her fumbling inside her own spirit as she reached for me, listening.

*He needs you. I need you. Come to me.*

There was no answer, but I had faith she would come. I had made Southern as safe as I could, though at least two of her enemies still lived.

At least I knew Trevor Blackside and Calvin Callaway were nowhere near Southern. At first, I'd suspected the old Alpha was hiding among the rogues outside the pack's borders, but there had been no sign or scent of him there.

The white-haired woman, Lily Rain, was the leader of that group, and she kept them all well-hidden.

They were a pitiful group of half-feral, starving outcasts, though I had a feeling that Sergeant had been feeding them recently, taking care of them along with Lily. I'd watched him running with some of them in the woods, saw them bring down a deer. The two scrawny males who'd hunted with him hadn't known what to do with the beast once it was downed. Sergeant had shared the kill, then shifted and carried the rest back to the pack.

I turned the word over in my mind. *Pack*. Yes, the rogues were a pack, though I hadn't seen it on my first visit to Southern. They hunted together, so far as they were able, and denned together. Even though they were led by the crazed female, they had an Alpha in their midst now as well, his presence steadying the group. If I trusted Sergeant even the smallest bit, I would approach him, enlist his aid in watching for Callaway to return.

Pity that I trusted no one, other than my little mate.

Another wave of fatigue swept through me as I crossed to the window, sliding it up soundlessly and dropping to the ground below. When Flor arrived, I would need to be rested enough to protect her, not only from the rogue pack on the border, but the newly appointed "leader" of Southern, Torran.

Something was wrong with that one. He spent his days torturing various small groups of ranked Southern shifters who had balked at his commands, though he called it training. Most of the ones he'd damaged were those I'd planned to add to my bouquets anyway. He hadn't actually killed any of them, so I could still add them to my collection. But even if none of the Southern pack were worth a moment of my concern, his brand of leadership made my wolf rage.

Though my mother had not been a shifter, she had been the one to instruct me in what the moon had intended. Before pack laws were ever written down, they were sung and chanted at firesides for centuries, and she'd spent enough time in my father's St. Petersburg pack to have heard them all. She'd whispered them to me at bedtime, when I was very young, before my father understood my power and took steps to contain me.

Packs were formed to protect the weak, to give children a safe place to grow, and the elders a place to share their knowledge. Alphas were meant to lead by example, to sacrifice their own safety and comfort for the ones in their care. No one had informed Torran of that, I assumed. And none of the shifters at Southern seemed to expect anything other than his abuse.

The ranked shifters moved about the compound with wary expressions. The unranked, metal tags still glinting on their ears, worked in fearful silence, with heads lowered. The single females had all been sent to live in one dormitory, six and seven to a room. I had a suspicion that Torran visited the dorms during the daytime, when I was hidden in the forest, sleeping. He wasn't there now, but as I passed it in the darkness, running silently, the stench of despair that wafted from the building burned my nose, and the sound of muffled sobbing was louder than the hum of cicadas.

This pack had been close to ruin before, but thanks to Torran, it was beyond saving. The world would be better without him in it, and even though I knew I didn't have energy to spare, I began pondering how best to bring about his end.

He would be my final courting gift to Flor, I decided, as I vanished into the darkness of the woods. I would kill him, skin him, thread every one of the unrankeds' ear tags on a silver chain, and hang him from the tallest tree by the Pack House, like a... I searched for the word in my memory as I ran. Many of the humans in the South had them by their doorways, to frighten away evil spirits, I assumed.

*Ah, yes.* A wind chime. A perfect courting gift.

# 16

## LEAVING MOUNTAIN
### FLOR

"He's a natural," Glen murmured at my side as he watched Brand move from shifter to shifter, accepting their vows of loyalty. I hummed in agreement, but my gaze was fixed on Samuel.

He sat on a folding chair that was far too small for his frame, sipping a cup of hot tea that had so much whiskey mixed into it, I could smell it from a dozen feet away. His face was frozen in an expression that was equal parts pride, amazement, and awe, his dark eyes shining. I swallowed to keep the tears that had gathered in my own from falling.

Tears of gratitude. Samuel was wounded, but healing. He was no longer the Alpha of the Mountain pack, but he was still *something*. I could sense the residual power that emanated from him in gentle, almost comforting ripples.

When I'd asked Samuel if that was what normally happened when an Alpha handed over their power in front of the Council, he'd said no. "Shouldn't be here," he'd muttered, his shock making him sound like the nearly-silent giant he'd been when I met him.

"What he did shouldn't be possible," Glen murmured in

my ear as a mated pair bowed together in front of Brand, and he laid his hands on their shoulders. "No shifter has ever been strong enough to do that."

"He wasn't strong enough," I corrected. "You were. You and me and him together." *And Grigor,* I thought to myself. I would have sworn I'd felt him, sensed him at the end, reaching out.

Glen ducked his head, pressing a kiss to my shoulder. A few shifters around us began whispering, and a couple even moved away. One of them hissed, "*Shame.*"

Instantly, Brand was there, facing them. "No," he announced, and everyone went quiet, responding to the Alpha power that rolled off him in invisible waves. "Flor is your Alpha Mate. You will treat her with the respect you promised to me."

A tall male, one I'd met at Southern in the Enforcer Games, pointed out, "She wears the mark of another shifter, Alpha. Glen's mark. How can she be your mate, and his as well?"

His tone was not disrespectful, and that may have been why Brand only snarled. "You dare?"

I wasn't sure why he was shocked. The looks I got weren't all that different from the ones I'd faced at Northern. At least no one had yelled whore or witch this time. Of course, the night was still young.

Glen leaned down and murmured, "They've seen *my* mate mark? Have you been running around in a bikini, Dream Girl?" I elbowed him hard in the gut, glad for the distraction, though his mention of the hidden claiming bite made my inner thigh pulse slightly.

Brand held up his hands, and every shifter who'd arrived for the challenge sank down, listening. Then he nodded to me, though I stayed right where I was, holding Glen's hand. I didn't need to be in the center of the pack.

"But you *are* the center, Flor," Brand said, obviously reading my thoughts again. I glared at him and thought very hard about the maggot-filled squirrel I'd once found outside my dorm room door back at Southern. He snorted a laugh, before he addressed the gathered pack. "The moon has made it clear to us that our packs have run down a path that leads only to death," he said quietly, though his voice carried as if he was using a microphone. "Fewer wolves find their true mates every year. Almost no children have been born at the other main packs in the past decades. Even our own is dwindling, though our adherence to many of the old ways has kept us strong."

My heart was swelling with pride, when I heard something. A whisper, a humming.

*I need you, little one. Come to me.*

Who was that? I concentrated while Brand talked about what needed to change at Mountain. The insularity that had led to the current mess. The isolationism that had allowed corruption to infect every pack.

The voice interrupted again, pleading. *He needs you.* I had a vision of Luke, in a bed, alone. Unconscious. *I need you.* Dark eyes, gleaming with red fire, flashed. *Come to me.*

"But you and her... and *him.* Those aren't the old ways," someone in the crowd shouted at Brand.

"No, they aren't," he agreed. "And my eyes are not my old eyes." Those bright twin moons flashed. "The world we live in is not what it once was. For some reason, my love has been given more than one true mate." The crowd burst into chatter, until he sent out another wave of dominance to silence them. "I am in her heart, in her very thoughts, and I tell you, there has never been a shifter born who was as brave and strong as this small female. If you do not accept her as my mate because her heart was made to hold more than one bond… then I will leave this pack, and you may find a new Alpha."

A few shifters looked to Samuel, who shook his head. "I no longer have the force of an Alpha in me. My son did what no other shifter has ever done, a feat that always takes the power of death, or the power of the entire Council, a gathering of strong Alphas filled with the connection to all of their pack's wolves, to effect. The moon has blessed him in many ways, the greatest of which is Her choice for his mate, who is more than worthy. If he leaves, we are all rogues. Packless and lost."

He stood and walked to his son, then kneeled on the ground in front of him. "Before the moon, I vow to serve the true Alpha of the Mountain pack, Brand Becker." Then he bowed his head to me. "And I vow to protect his mate, Florida Wills, from anyone who would dare to question her place at his side."

All the grumbling stopped. I wiped my face, pretending to be annoyed at my tears. "I think I'm allergic to something up here. Pine trees, probably," I grumbled when Glen handed me a handkerchief from somewhere.

Brand went on. "Mountain, I must warn you. The Council will not accept me, or my mate, or even the moon's judgment that was made today. They have grown used to holding the power of the pack, of *our* pack, on their own leash." A growl rose from the crowd, and Brand roared back. "I will *not* accept the collar of a corrupt Council leader, who has already imprisoned the Alpha and Alpha Mate of the Northern pack. Who has placed their deranged Head Enforcer, Torran, as a figurehead at Southern. Change is here, whether we are comfortable with it or not. War is coming, and we must be prepared to protect our home, and to shine the moon's light on all the packs."

The crowd burst into howls, shouts, and cheers, and as one, they rushed toward their Alpha.

Glen pulled me closer to Samuel, who shook his head at the raucous, fiercely joyful scene. "He'll be the best Alpha we ever had. I'm so damned grateful I'll be here to witness it." His dark eyes speared me. "Brand needs to stay in the Den for the next few weeks at least, gathering our forces, preparing for the battles that will come."

"Patrick is already doing the same at Northern," Glen murmured. "How soon can Mountain be ready?"

"Normally? Months," Samuel replied grimly.

"What... What do you mean, months?" We didn't have time to wait. Luke needed me. Grigor needed me.

Samuel shook his head like he was clearing away cobwebs, and answered slowly. "Every pack member must travel to the Den and pledge their loyalty. The ritual must be completed before they go to war."

"Shifters need a leader to fight effectively in a pack this large," Glen explained. "Once the ritual is complete, Brand will draw strength from the pack, and the pack from each other. We may not even need Patrick's army. Mountain will be unbeatable." He sighed. "Even if they hurry, though, this pack is enormous. It will take weeks."

Samuel grunted. "Good. That means we have time to read." I blinked at him, until he explained, "I'm taking you back to the library." He set his cup down and stood, but I didn't take the hand he held out. I couldn't.

"I can't stay."

Samuel frowned.

"I can't stay here. Luke is dying." I pressed a hand to my heart. "I can feel it inside me. He's being kept alive by machines, but his spirit's connected to mine. He's draining all five of us."

"All five?" I raised an eyebrow, and he sighed heavily. "Brand can't go with you, Flor. He needs to accept the pledges, and then gather weapons for the fight." He scowled. "If they figure out Luke is your mate as well—if they even *suspect* that you're connected to the Heirs—they'll kill him to get to Brand. Or Finnick, or Glen."

Glen cursed. "We have to get Luke away from them, from Torran."

It wasn't the first time I'd heard his name. He sounded like a real rat bastard, but I'd dealt with plenty of those before. "I know every hiding place and rabbit path in that pisshole pack. If anyone can get in and out without being spotted, it's me. I think..." I didn't want to say Grigor's name and set Samuel off again. "I think I'll have help when I'm there. Someone on the inside. Just get me close, and I'll be back with an extra Heir before you know it."

Samuel nodded slowly. "You can't fly. You don't have identification, and the Eastern pack will have eyes on the airports around here. Eyes on the roads. They're waiting to catch Glen leaving the borders. They know I won't have killed him." He scratched his beard in thought. "Can you drive?"

"Nope. But I'm a fast learner."

Glen's hand tightened in mine. "I'll take her. We'll drive to Southern. Not to the gates, but to the back of the packlands' hunting grounds. Flor knows the way in."

I gripped his hand back. Just what I'd never wanted: to go back to Southern. But I didn't have a choice. Grigor was there, with Luke. I had to get them free before Brand declared war.

"Let's get those books, Samuel. I'll need some light reading on the way."

BRAND and I made love that night, over and over, until the sun rose, like we might never see each other again. Glen slept in his own room, though I could feel his presence in the bond.

When I asked, Brand admitted he could, too. "It's not as odd as I had feared," he said, as he toyed with one of my nipples. "When you claimed Finn, I didn't feel much change."

I shrugged, brushing back my hair, which fell past my shoulders now. Being mated to powerful males came with some side benefits, it seemed. My hair and nails grew super fast and strong, and I healed from small wounds almost instantly.

If only the pain from Finnick's infidelity would heal as fast. He hadn't done anything else, not since that first hour or two of what felt like acid in my veins. But I could still feel the ache, and wondered if it might happen again.

"Maybe Finnick doesn't feel the bond at all," I mused.

"I think he does. How could he not be longing for you? You're perfection."

I rolled my eyes, even though my insides were flipping around at his matter-of-fact tone. "You know, Cityboy and I only bit each other. We didn't butter the biscuit." Brand groaned. "What, you prefer baking the potato? Planting the pars—"

He placed a hand over my mouth, his fingers covering

half my face. "Please don't use Grandma Ida's expressions when we're naked together." His eyes, almost silver in the dim light of the bedroom, gleamed with humor... and heartache.

How could I get along without my Bearman? It was silly to feel so desolate at the thought. I'd been more or less alone for years, with only Del to help me when he could. But I'd grown dependent on Brand in a few short weeks. It wasn't that I needed him to protect me. I mean, I wasn't nearly as strong as him, but I was a hundred times meaner and sneakier, and even without my wolf, I could rain hell on anyone who tried to fuck with me.

But I would miss him.

"I'm in your thoughts, my love," he murmured. "If you need me, I'll know it, and I'll come for you. Taking on this pack, being Alpha here, was only so that you and Glen would be safe. If I have to give it up, I will."

I kissed him soundly, then scooted out of bed, hunting for my clothes. It was time to go. "No, Alpha Becker, you're needed here. Glen and I can sneak out, and if they catch us—"

He grabbed me up in his arms and kissed me again, his beard soft on my face. "If they catch you, if they *dare* to hurt you, I will bring down the Mountain on their heads."

"I don't know about you, but I'm swooning," Glen sighed from the doorway. He leaned against the open door-frame with one hand resting at the top, and the other tousling his golden hair, a pose I'd seen on a romance novel cover more than once. "Bring down the Mountain? I never knew you had such a romantic side, brother. I'm not certain I can measure up."

Brand grinned suddenly. "You never could, Glenda."

Glen leaped across the room to tackle him. The two of

them tumbled off the bed and around the room, wrestling and mock-snarling, until they knocked into the lamp and I punched Glen in the kidney.

"Ah, shit!" he groaned, falling to the floor, in real pain.

Of course he was in real pain. I was his true mate, and I'd just punched a vital organ. I winced. "Sorry, Glen, I forgot."

He whined from his spot on the rug. "Forgot I was your mate? I see how it is. Brand gets your sweet side, and I get your—" He shut up when I lay next to him, reaching under his shirt to rub my hands over the spot I'd punched.

"Feel better?" I asked after a minute.

A sweet smile on his lips now, he stroked the side of my face, and I moved so that I could brush his curls back from his. He took advantage of the position, pulling me close for a long, lingering kiss. By the time he broke it off, my toes were curling and my core clenching like it was ready for more.

"Good morning, mate. I would ask if you slept well, but I know you didn't. You can sleep in the truck."

"Thanks." I reached around to rub his lower back again. "All better now?"

"Mostly. It would feel even better if you rubbed a little lower, and around to the front..."

A flannel shirt landed on his face, and I was sailing through the air the next second as Brand picked me up and handed me my clothing, "Dean's got everything ready. It's time to go."

Dean came up to us once we were dressed, shaking hands with Glen, giving a little bow to me, and handing over a set of keys to his truck. It was weird seeing him next to Glen. The two were wearing the same outfit, from the identical work boots to the Denver Broncos baseball caps that obscured their features from above.

I'd been confused about some parts of the plan, until Samuel had admitted that the Eastern pack was modern, which meant drones and maybe even satellites. "For all we know, they'll have eyes on the front door of the Den." That made sense, even if the idea of shifters using technology like humans made my wolf curl her lip. He went on. "Dean will be seen walking in. Then it'll look like Dean is the one leaving, with Ida."

"Ida?"

"You."

My disguise was minimal, but effective, and it made me laugh when Dean handed me the pieces to pull on in the middle of the upstairs hall.

In less than a minute, I had one of Ida's broad-brimmed straw sunhats covering my red hair, and a long-sleeved cotton dress over my own clothes. Apparently, Dean took Ida into a nearby town every week on this day to get baking supplies. We would leave the truck in the town and switch to another, older truck that Samuel had unearthed from somewhere on the packlands, and donated to the cause.

Dean bowed to Brand, murmuring, "Alpha." Brand nodded back. I was glad Brand would have him as his Head Enforcer, or whatever they called it at Mountain.

*Wait.* Samuel wasn't Alpha, so I wasn't sure what Dean's position was now. Had he lost his job?

"Brand? Who is your Head Enforcer going to be? Is it still Dean?"

"Mountain only ever used those titles in war, and when the Council insisted we have one for full Council votes. I've decided not to have one at all."

Glen gave him a surprised look as we walked to the side door of the Den together. "We *are* at war, brother."

Brand growled. "When we go to war, I may name officers. But I think those positions will be temporary."

From our matching scowls, I knew we were all remembering the clusterfuck at Northern, when Glen's parents had adopted wartime measures and kept them going, creating a permanent lower-class tier of vulnerable shifters who had no hope of rising to the rank their wolves deserved.

Still, the logistics of it confused me. Who would hold down the fort if Brand needed to leave the Den? "Won't you need other shifters to help lead, when you're not around or—"

His grin stopped my words. "Flor, if everything works out, I'll have plenty of help leading the pack. You, Glen, Finn, and Luke."

I hummed, thinking, *And Grigor,* then winced as his smile turned into a frown.

"Do not bring that one back to the Mountain packlands. I know he claimed to be a suitor; I know he's fascinated with you. But he's a mass murderer, a conscienceless monster. Some of those books in your bag will tell you more about what he's done. Read them. He's not safe for you to be around. And I sure as hell don't want him near our pack."

My wolf bristled. Safe for me to be around? He was acting like I was some weak-ass bitch who needed a mate to protect her. Him calling it our pack was all that kept me from giving him a quick kidney jab as a goodbye present.

"Our pack," Glen chimed in, opening the door. "I like that. I'll pick my own title. Not Head Enforcer. Maybe... Chief Provider of Flor's Orgasms? Senior Wolf in Charge of

Flor's Bliss? He Whose Name is Screamed Loudest by the Shared Queen—*ow!* Damnit, Brand! Now my shirt's wrecked."

I had to muffle my laughter as Brand pulled back his hand, the claws already retracting. Glen's shirt sleeve was torn, and he was bleeding the tiniest bit, but when I pressed a kiss to his forearm, the cuts healed up instantly.

Brand pulled Glen close and murmured something in his ear, as they hugged in that way males did, where I wasn't sure if it was an affectionate touch or if they were trying to break ribs. Our embrace was far more intimate, and painful in a way I had never encountered.

"I'll miss you," I croaked, when he pulled away, my face still tingling from his beard rubbing my skin as he kissed me.

"I'll be right here," he replied, tapping my head, and then my heart. "I'll never be more than a thought away." I nodded brusquely, then followed Glen out the door, fighting to keep my tears from flowing until I was outside of the pack's borders.

# 17

## PARTING GIFTS
### FLOR

"You ready, Dream Girl?"

Glen's simple question was filled with compassion. He could probably hear my wolf already howling for Brand as we left him behind.

"Try to keep up, Glenda," I retorted, pushing my way out the side door. We both ignored the rasp in my voice.

The sunlight was bright as I stepped out into it, but the sunhat hid my face. No one walked us to the truck; they didn't want anyone to see them aiding and abetting Glen's "escape from the pack jail cell," which was the cover story if the Council came down on Samuel or Brand before they managed to complete the Alpha handover.

Of course, Ida had kissed and hugged me plenty of times, and packed us all sorts of food for our journey. Verona had stuck a stack of required shifter reading in my bag, but she'd shared more than that the day before. After Samuel had brought me back to the library and handed me over to her, she'd given me priceless information. And after she'd shooed him back out, she'd given me something else. Weapons.

Her words rang in my memory as Glen started the truck and drove us down the gravel road toward the nearest town.

"I'm breaking a number of Council laws right now, Flor," Verona whispered, as she locked the library door behind us. "But I need to share a few things with you before you leave tomorrow."

"What do you mean?" Did she have more contraband books for me?

"I gave you a book. Now I need to give you an explanation that no one else older than you, and no one who ever attended a Conclave, would be able to share: the reason why even speaking of the Western pack was forbidden."

My jaw dropped. I'd assumed, from our conversations, that she couldn't speak openly about them either. Wasn't she under the same command as the rest? She was plenty older than me. "How can you..."

Her smile was sly. "I wasn't at the great gathering after the war, when all the remaining shifters agreed to never speak of the Western pack again. So I wasn't personally bound under the Council's command. I never attended a Conclave after that, either, when that particular command was reinforced by all the Alphas. I knew better." She sighed. "Samuel figured it out, of course. He commanded me not to speak of Western. But his Alpha command for me is no longer in effect." Her lips twitched. "I love a loophole."

I loved the sneaky way she thought, and told her so.

"Thank you. As the Centralis librarian, I have a sacred duty to share knowledge to help our pack."

"Centralis?"

She walked me back to the locked cabinet and pulled out an assortment of things, laying them out on the table. "That was our pack's name, years ago. My mate warned me that the back-lash against magic would be severe, after the fighting ended. We were... broken, by the way the remnants of the Western pack had allied with the Russians and betrayed us, as well as the weapons they used to attack us."

On the table in front of us, she had placed a small, plain-handled silver knife, a book, and something in a narrow leather case. I wrinkled my nose at the stench wafting up from the knife. "They used silver?" For some reason, my wolf paced restlessly at the thought.

"Yes, but more importantly, they used magic. They were the only pack in North America that had magic wielders in their ranks. They'd been punished for this after the Betrayal—that's what many called the disastrous Southern Conclave four decades ago. At the end of the war, the victorious packs decided defeat wasn't enough. They chose to eradicate them."

We both sat in silence for a few heartbeats, thinking of that. An entire pack, killed. That would have been just before I was born. Not all that long ago. Had Samuel been a part of that deci-sion? Had Margarette, or Bradley?

I didn't ask. I wasn't sure I wanted to know.

Verona went on. "The Council Head at that time was Bradley Hillier's father. He commanded the packs to round up and execute every single Western shifter that they could find, even the prisoners of war. Any who were left were named rogues, and the Council ordered them to be killed on sight."

Even if it made me sick, that made sense. But I didn't under-stand why there'd been a command that no one could speak of them. I asked Verona, and she snarled.

"Fear makes people stupid. And stupid people do stupid things, like burn books. As if you can burn ideas with fire. Destroying these books would only mean that the next time magic wielders come against us, we will be defenseless."

The way she spat the words magic wielders made me think of Grigor. Was he one of the ones we'd fought against? He was

*Russian, and he definitely used magic. Was he the enemy? My enemy?*

*Verona was still talking, so I shook the worry away.*

*"You know that pure silver blades are not legal for anyone other than Alphas and their mates to wield. There really aren't many in existence; the metal is too soft to be practical. But if a metalsmith is clever, and wraps silver around the steel..." She pulled on gloves before showing me, picking up the small, plain dagger that I assumed had been made the way she described, then slid it into the spine of a book on Alpha ascension rituals.*

*I peered at the book. You couldn't even see the knife inside, and the scent of silver was completely suppressed by the binding and the flap of leather she pulled over the top. "Nice."*

*"Lethal," she corrected. "Use the knife if you have to, but read the book as soon as you can. Remember that knowledge is one of the strongest weapons you can possess."*

*Del had told me that. I nodded as she picked up the leather case and pulled out another small item, which looked like a metal dowel, or a fancy pen. On one side, it had a button like a pen, and it was silver colored, but it didn't have that awful odor that made my stomach turn. "This one is more dangerous than the knife. It's pure steel on the outside. But when you push this..." She pressed the tiny button to one side and then up, and a narrow silver blade, almost as thin as a needle, popped out.*

*"Ugh," I said, fanning my face. It now smelled incredibly potent.*

*My wolf began pacing faster, panting, wanting to run far away from the odd blade, but I knew I might need this. I needed every weapon I could get my hands on, if I was going back into Southern.*

*I reached to take it from her, but she pulled it away quickly. "Not so fast. This blade is exceptionally dangerous. The silver is pure and brittle, made that way on purpose. If you stab someone* with it, the metal will fragment inside their body. There's no shifter alive who could survive this."

She carefully tucked the blade back into the cylindrical holder, then the leather sleeve. I waited until she'd slid it into my bag to give her an enormous hug. "This is the most thoughtful gift I've ever been given. One of the only ones, to be honest. Though Margarette did give me clothes, and Sergeant gave me a sword."

Verona perked up at the title. "Sergeant? What was his name?"

I swallowed hard. "I never caught his last name. Or his first. Is Sergeant a first name? Or a title?" I described him to her, and she pursed her lips.

"He must be the same shifter who came through our pack-lands. The one whose journal I gave you."

My heart raced. I'd felt like Sergeant was related to me, the first time I'd met him. He'd given me his mother's sword as well. What if... I tamped down the hope that he was related to me. I wasn't even sure he was one of the good guys; he'd been in on the oppression of the unranked at Northern, and he'd defected to go who-knows-where after the Russians had bombed the Lodge.

Verona walked me to the door of the library, unlocking it, her expression concerned. "You said you hadn't received many gifts. What about Brand's courting gifts?"

I opened the door to find Brand there, holding a forest-green velvet bag. "He hasn't given me any courting gifts yet," I said as he leaned down to kiss me.

"A failing I am about to rectify, my wildflower."

He had outdone himself. Now, as Glen drove us away from the Alpha's Den, I held one of the carvings Brand had given to me. There had been seven in the small bag, minia-ture representations of his parents and grandparents. They were treasures, and had to have taken weeks to carve each one. "The next time I see you, I'll have one of you, Glen, Luke, and Finn. Our pack."

I'd left the bag with him, afraid the carvings might get damaged or lost. The only one I was taking with me was the one he'd done of himself. It was no larger than my thumb, but it was a perfect likeness in dark walnut of my Bearman, down to the hairs of his beard, his broad shoulders and chest, and the way his second toe was longer than the first.

Silent, I stared out the window for the first hour, until we reached the town. Glen stayed quiet as well, lost in his own thoughts. Worry and fear thrummed in our bond, but there was nothing either of us could do to stop that. We left the truck in a parking lot, took our backpacks and roamed through a bustling farmer's market, then followed Dean's directions to the next truck.

"This piece of shit?" Glen groaned. It was a Ford F-150, at least forty years old, with what looked to be three colors of paint and significant hail damage. I laughed as we got in and the engine roared and sputtered, a cloud of dark smoke pouring out of the tailpipe. "The whole damned pack will hear us coming."

"Nah. This is perfect camouflage for Southern," I told him as we pulled out onto the main highway, heading east. "Remember, Southern is the piss tank of all the packs. The burst septic line of shifterdom. The festering abscess on the hemorrhoid of—" He gunned the engine with a laugh to drown me out, turning on the radio to a country singer wailing about an ex-girlfriend, a broken-down truck, and a questionable number of beers that made all of the pain fade. I laughed and sang along, even though I was going home to hell.

Because I wasn't going home alone, or unranked, or unarmed.

THE TRIP to the ass-end of Alabama should have taken twenty hours, more or less, but the gas-guzzler Samuel had found for us made that impossible. We had to stop for fuel for the first time in New Mexico, and about five hours after that, at a wide place in the road outside Abilene, Texas. I was glad for the stop; my bladder was bursting, and my head spinning from all the pages I'd read so far.

Glen followed me to the ladies' room in the back of the gas station, where I took care of business and washed my face with water that smelled like gasoline fumes and lead pipes. We didn't bother going inside for food. We had provisions from Ida, and the fewer people who could identify us in case someone came looking, the better.

Another hour down the road, I shut my book with a sigh, closing my eyes. "What have you found out, Dream Girl?" Glen asked softly. "You feel..." He pressed a hand against his heart, and finished, "Conflicted."

I slipped the book that I'd just finished into my pack and pulled out the one I'd been itching to begin—the journal. "Conflict is right. I've been readin' that history about the war. I guess I knew it was bad—Del told me some stories—but I hadn't ever seen it written down. So many shifters died. Like, half of all the remaining packs, and the whole Western one."

"That pack wasn't really whole by then," he said softly, his eyes on the road. "The war ended a little over twenty years ago, but it began before that. Forty years back, at the disastrous Conclave at Southern."

I nodded. I'd read about that, but I still had questions.

"It said there was a fight, and an Alpha died. The Southern Alpha before Callaway's uncle took over?"

Glen nodded. "Yes, Morton Callaway's father. I think his name was Hollis."

"Hollis got into an argument with the Western pack Alpha. The book didn't name him."

"I don't remember his name, or maybe I never knew it," Glen said. "We don't speak of... them."

"Yeah, I guess if I'd been at a Conclave, I wouldn't be able to either. Do you think it'll wear off? The command, I mean?" Glen raised an eyebrow. "Well, now that you're, um, in between packs. If you aren't under the Council's command, and you don't agree to it again..."

"I guess I'll find out. I guess I'll find out a lot of things," he said, his tone grim.

I knew what he meant. Rogues had a reputation of going feral. Without an Alpha to lead them, they lost themselves to their wolf natures, or at least that's what I'd been taught. That was why so many of them sort of hung around their old packlands, or the borders of other pack's territories, trying to slip back in.

Their wolves wanted to belong, to have a family to protect them, and to protect.

It made me feel sort of bad for the rogues, though the ones in Canada hadn't seemed feral at all. Murderous and violent, sure. But they'd had a leader, that Russian guy. He had been enough of an Alpha substitute that he'd kept them sane, more or less.

When I asked Glen, he seemed disturbed, but then nodded. "Maybe so. Or maybe they had an Alpha somewhere else. They didn't act like rogues."

"More like mercenaries or terrorists," I mused, opening

the latch on the journal. It almost flew open, like it wanted me to read it. Like it was as impatient as I was.

I thought about Verona, how she'd admitted she couldn't open it. I had a weird feeling my blood on the latch had been what had done the trick. She'd said this book was forbidden. Was it magic?

A chill ran through me as a few puzzle pieces clicked into place. Things I really should have put together a long time ago, only they'd seemed so impossible. The journal warmed on my lap, like it knew I was feeling cold.

*Ah, skunkshit.* Magic for sure. I tucked my hands under my armpits, half-wishing I'd left the dang thing back at Mountain.

"Do you have any more questions?" Glen asked, our bond shifting slightly, ripples of reassurance and love moving through me.

I had more questions than answers now. "I still don't get exactly what happened at that old Conclave. They'd already been worrying about infertility, right? The birth rates had dropped, and they planned to discuss it at the meetings they always hold at the end. But then the Southern Alpha got involved in some fight at the start of the Games, and died. So instead of working out why there weren't enough babies, they ended up disciplining the Western pack. I can't figure out for what, exactly." The book had been long on blaming the Western pack for everything, but there had to have been something that started it. Or someone.

"They used magic to attack a young Southern girl who was at the Games, and then, during the fight that broke out, one of them killed the Southern Alpha, Hollis."

I thought for a moment. "Maybe it was an accident, though? A fight that got too rowdy?"

"No. That was when witchcraft was outlawed entirely. From what I pieced together from my lessons, and what I remember overhearing when I was little, magic was used to kill at the Conclave, not just claws and teeth. I assumed that meant witches were at the Conclave. After that, witches weren't allowed to cross any pack's border." For some reason, Verona's cackling about loopholes echoed in my mind.

I frowned. I'd missed a lot of lessons after dropping out of school; maybe there were more books that went into greater detail about what had started the fight at those Games. They covered the ending well enough. "The history book said the pack name, the Western pack, was removed from the North American rosters like it never existed, and they were sent back to the West Coast without their Alpha. How could they survive without an Alpha?"

Glen shrugged. "It may be why their pack crumbled so fast."

I thought for a moment about what I'd read. "There was a lot of infighting, Western wolves fighting for dominance. Within ten years, almost all the former members of the pack were either dead, injured or weakened, or had left the pack and become rogues. A core of them stayed, and made an alliance with Russian shifters to take over the continent. Russians like that Ivan guy, the general."

I rubbed a hand over the spot where he'd scratched me with his silver-tipped claws. Somehow, Grigor had healed those cuts up until they didn't show at all.

Glen hummed. "The Russian wolves were always rumored to have witches or wizards in their packs. There were stories about the old Alphas stealing young witches to use to breed magic-wielding wolves, though of course that's impossible."

"Is it?" I asked, thinking of Grigor. His mother had been a witch.

Glen shot me a weird look. "You know humans and shifters aren't compatible that way. Right?"

"Sure." I knew shifters and humans couldn't breed. They'd taught us in school that there hadn't been a single pup ever born that came from a human and a shifter. I'd wondered if it was true, but I'd overheard some of the ranked males in my old pack saying it was a good thing, or the closest city outside our borders would have had a hundred tiny Callaway babies running around. But... were witches not human?

Before I could ask, Glen went on. "If it were possible to have shifter babies by breeding with humans, or outside our own kind, there would be a hell of a lot more shifters in the world. Of course, it's taboo."

Of course it was. I forced my thoughts away from my biological father, and back to the conversation. "Still, it seems like overkill, to hypnotize all the remaining shifters in the whole country after the war not to be able to even talk about magic. Or the pack they wiped out." I wiped my eyes, feeling an odd connection to shifters I'd never met. "It was a far smaller pack by that time, from what I read. Almost all women and children when the war ended."

"Maybe they don't want us to talk about it because they're ashamed." Glen's pain seeped through the bond, and I laid a hand on his leg. He took it and held on as he spoke. "I am, though I never really thought of it that way."

We rode in silence for a few more miles before I added, "If no one talks about it, someday none of the packs will even know what happened. What if shifters invade again, ones who have magic, or have witch allies? We won't know how to protect ourselves."

"That's why for the last twenty years, the Council has had groups of Enforcers who do nothing but hunt witches, or rumors of magic. It's one of the reasons the Council still exists, because of that possibility. Magic and shifters don't mix." He shot me a look, and I knew he was thinking about Grigor.

But I was thinking about another shifter, Sergeant J. Rain. I only had another hour or two to read before it got too dark, so there was no time to waste. I opened the journal and began to read from the beginning. It began very formally, but quickly became personal, and I could almost hear a rough, gravelly voice reading the pages in my mind.

*I am Sergeant Julian Rain, son of Alpha Mother Dahlia Rain, and the late Alpha Ithil Mar, who fell to a silver blade and treachery at the fifty-second Conclave held at the Meridion packlands, leaving me as the last remaining male member of the Moonblessed Warrior division. Mad with grief, my mother attacked both enemies and allies at that Conclave, and was struck down as well, leaving no leader ready to hold the collected power and magic of the Occidens pack.*

*This journal contains the notes of all I learned from my father and the last Alpha Mothers of the West, of the nature of both wolfcraft and witchcraft. It is my hope that in breaking tradition and committing this knowledge to the page, it will not be lost forever upon my own death. I will also attempt to lay out my own theories of how the imbalance in the two great magics given to Her children by the Moon Goddess may have created a rift that draws energy away, not only from the remaining packs as a whole, but also those things that every individual shifter holds most dear: our true mate bonds, and our pups.*

*I have guarded this book with magic and blood, so that only one of my family, though we are all but gone, will be able to open its cover and read what I have written.*

*It is my hope that if she is alive, my niece Lily, the daughter of my twin sister Camellia Rain and the last child born to Occidens, may find it. That she may take up her natural role as Alpha Mother, though the survivors of our pack have lost all honor and may not welcome their rightful leader.*

*Lily, if you're reading this, I hope you remember me. I wish I had spent more time with you before you were forced to flee our green home, the magic-filled, ancient forests that nurtured us all.*

*I pray the coven was the safe place we were promised. The war that I fear approaches may mean that there is no such place left for our line. Anger and resentment has festered in the hearts of those who remain, and their desperation has borne evil fruit.*

*In the years following the Conclave Betrayal, after the dissolution and diaspora of the Occidens pack, our pack was shunned entirely. Any Occidens wolf discovered more than one hundred miles from the Blue Mountains was put to death as a rogue. Trade was shut off, and our young were not allowed contact with other shifters, thus ensuring they would not find their true mates. Mating between one of ours and any other pack was outlawed. Any shifter who broke that law, even if they were answering the call of a true mate bond, would be cast out, rejected and reviled by the Council and its allies.*

The world went dark as my mind spun, understanding blooming like a razor-edged flower. My last name was Wills, or so I'd believed. I'd thought my mother's was, too. Lily Rain Wills. But it was just Lily Rain.

Who the hell was she? And who was I?

# 18

## HIDDEN
### GRIGOR

*Flor. Flor. Flor.* Her name and her essence pounded in my heart, like a drumbeat, pushing the blood through my veins. I could feel her coming closer, and that was all that kept me from despair.

That, and the burning desire to kill the shifter, Torran, who had gotten tired of only torturing the Southern shifters and had started cutting into Luke's helpless body during the day when I wasn't in his room.

I wasn't sure what had changed, but the Council Enforcers had taken the medical equipment out of his room five days before, leaving him without food or water. Only my power had kept the air circulating in and out of his lungs, the blood moving through his veins. I'd been forced to bind myself even more tightly to him, going so far as to graft a portion of my magic onto his faded soul. It was similar to what I'd done to my little mate, though I'd only left a thread of power there, linking us. The strands that bridged the gap between my own dark soul and Luke's were braided tightly, and irrevocably.

I'd been shocked at what I'd found when I'd completed

that task. His wolf spirit still fought for life, and I felt a growing respect for him. He wasn't as useless as I'd thought, and if he survived, I knew he would do anything he could to protect Flor.

He needed to survive, for her. There was an odd connection between him and my little *behrserk* that I didn't quite understand. A blood bond, it felt like, more than just an unrealized mating claim.

I'd sent a call to her the first evening when the machines had been removed. The next morning, I'd felt a lessening of the painful stretch in our own destined bond. I hadn't doubted her for a moment. Even without a mating mark, I'd known she would come to me.

Luke's abused body shivered on the bed. I was still in a significant amount of pain, but I tried to ignore it as I placed my hands on his wounds and pushed more of my magic inside him. He should have been dead. Without the permanent connection I'd placed there, he would be.

But his apparent unwillingness to die had roused curiosity. Torran had come to the pack with silver-laced blades, it seemed, or found some when he arrived.

From the evidence I found when I entered Luke's room tonight, Torran had been slicing into the younger shifter's unconscious body in some sort of macabre experiment, making deep cuts in places not easily seen: his armpits, the crease at his groin, behind his ears, even under his thick dark hair. Those would all scar, if he survived. I was concerned about what he might do if I healed Luke too much, but a few of the wounds might have been fatal if I hadn't made the attempt.

I had a suspicion Torran knew that. What had he hoped to achieve? I'd assumed they'd been leaving Luke alive for some reason. Had his usefulness to the Eastern pack expired?

I may have miscalculated when I'd killed so many of the stronger shifters in this pack. If Luke died in this bed, and the old Southern Alpha was found and executed per the Council's orders, then Torran would be the obvious replacement as Alpha here. Perhaps the only replacement.

I couldn't regret my actions. So many of the males here had been Flor's abusers. Their continued breathing had felt like an affront to my soul... and their entrails had made such lovely formations.

I panted shallow breaths, suppressing a groan as Luke's wolf siphoned energy from me through our spiritual connection. I hadn't been this weak since I was a child. My ability to keep him alive, while simultaneously preventing Flor from feeling the pain of the neglected mate bond between us, and concealing myself, was sapping my strength.

For the first time, I wondered if I might die. If Torran came upon me in this state, with silver in his hands... I shook the thought away. My mother had warned me not to dwell on possibilities. *"Guard your thoughts, little Grisha. Those like us have a way of bringing dreams to life, for good or ill."*

I let my mind move to my own dream come true. Thought of her blazing hair, her sharp amber eyes, her rare smiles. The way she had smiled in her sleep as I sang to her in those nights when she dwelled at the Northern pack. I needed her.

*Faster,* I sent down the fraying bond between me and my mate. *As fast as you can.* I staggered away from the bed, heading for the window, but froze when I heard footsteps in the hall outside.

"Stay out here, Enforcer. I'll just be a moment."

That bastard Torran. I didn't have time or energy to cloak myself in shadows, or slip out of the window undetected. I might have enough power to kill him, but not silently, or quickly enough. My hands were trembling with fatigue.

As the door began to open, I slid under the bed, cursing myself for landing in this position. I formed a bubble of silence around myself, though I was too late to fully cover the faint hint of magical scent, which smelled to me like burning ozone, before the male had closed the door behind him. I held still as he inhaled audibly, then exhaled, moving around the room to inspect the closet and the window, sniffing everywhere he stopped.

I allowed my claws to extend when he approached the bed, and dug deep into my waning well of power for enough energy to cloak myself. When he kneeled down, his eyes glinting as he stared directly at me, I wasn't certain I'd succeeded. But he rose again, standing at the bedside.

I heard the sounds of a phone ring, then a woman's voice. "What?"

"Alpha, were you here at Southern t—" he began.

The distant voice interrupted him. "I've told you not to call me that. Or to call me at all."

The shifter chuckled. "My apologies, Mistress. I thought I caught your scent here."

"Wishful thinking on your part. I should punish you for calling."

The room filled with the thick musk of Torran's lust, and he began to graphically describe the ways in which he wanted to be punished by the woman, all of them involving pain and blood. From the sounds, he'd pulled out his cock and begun to stroke it.

I felt my cheeks burn, not at their banter, but at the situation. I was Grigor Dimitrivich, the most powerful and feared shifter alive, reduced to hiding under a bed, eavesdropping on a worthless, twisted male and his dominant lover. How had I fallen this far?

*"Love makes you weak,"* my father had warned me centuries ago, as I lay broken and bleeding in his dungeon. His hands had still been wet with the blood of my mate, Anya. *"Love is the true enemy."*

He had been so wrong. I'd never been stronger than after he took my love from me, took the only creature in the world who might have stopped me from killing not only him, but every single member of his pack. I'd burned them all alive, warming my cold hands over their ashes.

Though now I wondered if loving my little sharp-thorned flower had weakened me, knew that perhaps it had. But I was weary of living alone, in the shadows. And her brilliance, her indomitable spirit, made me long to warm myself in her glow from now on.

The male came quickly, his seed spattering the floor near my face. He groaned into the phone, "Mistress, when can I come to you? When can I see you again?"

"When the Heir dies, Torran."

"I can make that happen—"

"You cannot kill him. I told you he must appear to die of natural causes. Why hasn't he already?"

"I don't know. He's breathing on his own. There's no explanation, unless... perhaps he is mated."

The woman's voice grew louder. "He had no mate mark. You told me."

Torran swore. "I swear he didn't. You examined him yourself."

"I ordered you to check again."

151

"I did. I've gone over every inch of his body, as you asked. I've done it all; I turned off the machines days ago. He's had no water, no food. His organs should be shutting down. Even a strong Alpha would be dead by now. He's been healing, Mistress. I'm not sure how."

"He must have a mate. It's the only way." She went quiet. "You said you thought you smelled *me*?"

"Not exactly, but something like your scent," he murmured, heading for the door.

"I'll check on it. Make sure no one goes in or out of that room, Torran. We need that shifter to finish dying so you can be named the Heir. We need you to be Alpha." The lock turned, and footsteps moved away.

It was safe to leave, but I was still too weak to rise. Perhaps I would stay here until my little blade arrived. If Torran returned to make his hidden cuts again, to hasten Luke's death, I would need to be close to heal him. Close to protect the only one I had allowed to touch my magic, besides *her*... I drifted into a troubled sleep under the weakest of my Flor's mates.

Though I wondered if that might no longer be true. My power had been drained until I felt like a starved wolf, lost on the tundra. I fell into the dream, the memory of when I was exactly that, and all I had to fill my belly was snow.

*Faster, Flor.*

# 19

## GHOST STORIES
### FLOR

"Faster. We have to go faster!" I woke up shouting.

Glen's eyes glowed faintly blue in the dark cab of the truck. For some reason, we'd stopped, and I knew we would be too late to save... who? For some reason, the word *everyone* echoed in my mind.

Glen's voice was intense, but quiet. "Flor, what's wrong? Are you awake?"

"Where are we?" I sat up and glanced around. The sky outside the slightly cracked windshield was beginning to blush pink along one edge, and trees surrounded us. It was morning, which meant we were there, or almost. But when I craned my neck to look around, I didn't recognize this part of the forest, or the gravel path we were on. It wasn't wide enough to qualify as a road, and the kudzu was so thick here, the whole landscape was covered with a thick blanket of camouflage. "How long have we been here?"

Glen reached into the back seat for our packs. "I just pulled over. You slept through Louisiana and Mississippi. We're halfway across Alabama now, on the back road that you said leads to the hunting grounds. It's time to ditch the truck and go on foot."

"Got it," I whispered, unbuckling my seat belt. On the seat next to my leg, the journal lay, the latch on the front closed again. "Did you read—"

Glen shook his head. "I shut it when you fell asleep. What did you find out?"

"So much," I said, my mouth dry. "I'll tell you on the way. We have to hurry."

"Is it Luke?"

I nodded. "Not just him. It's... I think Grigor is dying, too."

"Good riddance," Glen muttered, opening his door, then racing around to open mine. "One less magic-wielding serial killer in the world." When I flinched, I felt Glen's remorse in the bond, but it was mixed with a good dose of stubborn caution.

I got out and placed a hand on his chest. If he hated magic that much, I had some bad news for him. "Glen, I need to tell you what I read."

"We're still thirty miles from the border of the hunting grounds." He pressed a kiss to the top of my head, then handed me my pack. "We can talk while we walk."

"While we run," I corrected. "Or we won't be there in time."

FOR THE FIRST FEW MILES, I panted out the story, glad Glen's shifter hearing was keen enough that I didn't need to shout. I could feel him taking it all in, the bond between us humming with wonder and a little fear, when he realized who I was. Who I was related to, and what that meant.

"Your mother," Glen whispered, the words as soft as the leaves underfoot. "That has to be why your father hid her from the Council."

That, plus he was a rat bastard. I nodded as I ran. "He'd have been thrown out of his own pack. He'd have lost his Alpha spot, right?"

"He might have, even if he set her aside." He thought for a while. "That must be why he hired the Florida witch." I stumbled at the last two words, and he slowed up to wait for me.

"I know these trees. We're getting close. We need to run quiet from now on." We weren't all that close, but my mind was buzzing, and I needed time to think.

If anyone found out I was the child of a Western shifter, I'd be cast out as a rogue, and all my mates would be as well. I let that bother me for a moment, then shook it off like rain. Del had always reminded me to focus on the fight I was in, not on one that might never happen. I needed to get Luke out of Southern—possibly Grigor, too, if he was as weak as his voice in my dreams had sounded—and then worry about witchy mate bonds.

Anyway, Glen was already a rogue, and I supposed I was technically already in the stink for being mated to more than one Heir. So even if I hadn't been from shifterkind's eradicated pack, I was already a good two-thirds of the way up shit creek with no paddles in sight.

*Magic.* I was magic, at least partly.

I rubbed at my chest, at the scar hidden under my shirt. The journal had all sorts of confusing explanations about mystical markings, and the kinds of scars that magic made. I remembered Sergeant's scars, all the whorls and patterns that covered him from neck to toe. I'd thought they were tattoos, possibly made with silver, but maybe they weren't, or at least not just that. Some of the designs had been doodled in the margins of the journal. From the notes, it seemed like he'd been focusing on marks for hiding something, or finding something. If I ever saw him again, and he didn't turn out to be some asshole traitor or dishonorable possumdick, I'd ask what his were.

I wanted him to be a good guy, more than I should. He was the only blood relative I had in the world, other than Callaway. Well, if he was even still alive.

I reached behind me and touched the sword that was strapped tightly to my back. Sergeant had given me that sword, the one that had belonged to his mother—my great-grandmother—before my first fight. It was perfectly sized for me, and as beautiful as it was sharp.

He'd known who I was, or suspected. There was no other explanation.

I ran without a sound, letting myself focus on the bonds. Glen's was a bright, solid cord right now. Brand felt muted, but every bit as strong, and there was something that hummed like tiny sparkles along our connection. I had a feeling it was the Mountain pack bonds that were connecting tighter to him as the shifters there took their oaths, making him more powerful.

Glen ran noiselessly behind me for over an hour, and I was impressed at his skills. We heard others in the woods twice, and avoided them successfully—hiding behind a boulder as a group of four unfamiliar males in wolf form loped past a few hundred feet away, and climbing two tall pines as fast as we could when a couple of boys wandered straight toward us not twenty minutes later.

I recognized these two, and for a moment, I was thrown

back to the night a few months before, when I'd hidden from the Hunt by the shifter dorms. They were named Bo and Leroy, and were greasy-haired, low-ranked members of Southern. But what were they doing out here on their own?

When they stopped to catch their breath at the base of the tree Glen was in, I listened to find out, the breeze carrying their pungent scents and raspy words clearly.

"Bo, I can't run no more," Leroy complained, his voice cracking. "Can't keep on. We gotta... go back."

"There's no back to go to," Bo hissed, pushing his hair away from his pimpled forehead. His eyes flicked to the branches above him, and I wondered if he'd spotted Glen. But he looked back at his friend without reacting. "We can't stay at the compound, Leroy, you know that. Even if that fucker Torran don't give a shit about us, the Flower Arranger's still in there somewhere. There's only us left from the Hunt. We're the only ones still ali—" He stuffed a grimy fist in his mouth and bit down to stave off tears.

I mouthed the words, *Flower Arranger*, wondering what he was talking about.

"Maybe he ain't comin' for us," Leroy whimpered. "We only hunted her that one time, and we didn't even *wanna* catch her. Maybe he knows that, somehow. Maybe he's gone back down to Hell, done with his killin'."

"Might'a beens won't help us now. We oughta just let him catch us; we're all starvin' to death."

I squinted down through the pine needles. Bo wasn't exaggerating. He didn't have a shirt on, and his sharp bones stuck out at hard angles. His wrists and ankles were bruised for some reason, and he had belt or whip marks littering the exposed parts of his body.

"Don't be a pussy, Bo. Anyhow, we're just as likely to be caught by the Ghost Lady, if we don't find a place to hole up." Leroy slumped down to sit on the dry pine needles and dirt at the base of the trunk. "She wanders the hunting grounds every night, lookin' for her lost mate. If you hear her howlin', you're dead before sunup. Two of the Council's assholes died just like that. They heard that odd howl, then turned up dead the next mornin'."

Bo leaned over, close to hyperventilating, and put his hands on his skinned knees. "I can't... I don't wanna die. I don't want my guts to be flower petals."

I glanced across the pine branches at Glen. I could just make out his face, and could tell he was fighting not to laugh. Did he know what these boys were talking about?

At that moment, the breeze shifted direction, and I grimaced.

Leroy sniffed. "I smell somethin', Bo." He sniffed again, standing up. "Cinnamon."

*Crap.* Was it me? I'd rubbed my arms and legs on some vines and bushes near where we'd left the truck, but I'd been sweating a little as I ran in the heat. I froze as Leroy stood, sniffing the air.

There wasn't a single sound, not a leaf rustling, or a branch cracking. Just a voice I hadn't heard in four years, calling out, "Is that my baby? I smelled... I smelled my baby." And then a long, ghostly howl.

When I saw her, it felt like someone had punched me right in the gut. I couldn't breathe. I couldn't even think clearly. At the bottom of the tree stood a ghost. One that looked up and directly at me, her head tilted to one side, her long hair a tangled mess, and her clothing an odd assortment of patched-together hides.

I knew every angle of her face, every line. The hair was different, silver-gray instead of dark curls, but the scars that Callaway had put all over her were the same, criss-crossed silvered marks where her skin had never healed from the endless torture. And the madness in those eyes was exactly like I'd seen the last day I'd seen her, when she'd saved me from Trevor Blackside and warned me to run.

Trevor the toadfucker, who'd taunted me for years with stories of her death. She'd been thrown to the rogues, begging and pleading, he'd said. They'd ripped into her... He'd described it in detail, over and over, just to see me flinch.

He hadn't been lying, or... Maybe he hadn't thought he was. She'd been attacked, been dragged off into the woods, but somehow, she'd survived.

*Magic,* a little voice reminded me. It was in our blood.

I could feel turbulence in my mate bonds, but I pushed it all aside, focusing on the bedraggled form that floated across the forest floor. *Mama?* I mouthed the word, but no sound came out. Not that anyone could have heard me.

At the base of the pine, Bo was hyperventilating, managing to squeak out, "G-G-Ghost Lady," before his eyes rolled back in his head and he fell to the ground.

His friend, to his credit, didn't run away. Leroy grabbed hold of one of Bo's limp arms and started dragging him off, begging, "P-please just let us leave. We ain't babies; we won't taste good, I swear it. We're stringy and smelly, and—"

She cackled, the sound straight out of an old cartoon, then started mumbling something that sounded like "stupid little fucks" before she whistled three notes—the "hey sweetie" call of a black-capped chickadee.

A barred owl answered back, and not five seconds later, an entire group of young male shifters poured into the area under the trees. They wore a combination of deer hides and sweatpants, no shoes at all, and every one of them had a beard as ragged as Mama's hair.

Where the hell had they come from?

Leroy froze, staring at the group of rogues like he expected them to fall on him and Bo and chop them into stew meat. Instead, one of the males reached into a pocket, pulling out a handful of what looked like jerky. I thought he was going to hand it to Leroy, but he stuck it in his own mouth, gnawing at it, until a voice snapped out from a few yards away, "Duane, drop it."

"Yes, Alpha," the young guy barked out, letting the jerky fall to the ground. Leroy's eyes followed it all the way down, and I thought he might have darted over to pick it up, but I had my eyes on the familiar man who had joined my mother and wrapped an arm around her shoulders.

Sergeant lifted his head, his eyes meeting my own wide ones. "Why don't you come on down, Flor? Your mother would like to see you." I glanced at Glen, who was shaking his head when Sergeant let out a dark chuckle. "You, too, Alpha Heir."

Glen dropped down before I could, and jogged over to the base of my tree. My legs were weak as a baby lamb's when I finally stood, facing the group. Glen was wary, his hand on the hilt of his dagger.

The sword Sergeant had given me was strapped to my back and my steak knife sat at my waist, but they might as well have been left in the truck. I was so shocked at the scene in front of me, I couldn't think.

"Mama?"

She looked up, sniffing, but there was no recognition in her dark eyes. "You're not my baby." She pulled away from Sergeant, moving around the area, dropping to sniff at the ground every so often, then moving on.

Two of the males I didn't know followed behind her, and I took a breath to ask what was going on, but Sergeant shook his head. "They've doubled the patrols on this side of the hunting grounds over the past few days. We'll talk in the cavern."

"The what now?" I sputtered, but the group was already moving on.

Glen stood firm. "How can we trust you? You deserted your post. You were a part of the corruption at my pa—at Northern."

Sergeant's jaw ticked, but he dipped his chin once. "I did desert my post. But I was bound to a vow I made long before the promise I gave your father, Alpha Heir."

"I'm not the Heir anymore," Glen murmured. "I'm a rogue."

Sergeant's eyes shone. "Then we have that in common. I'm the Alpha of a whole pack of rogues, and I promise you'll be safe when you're with us. If you choose to come with us." His gaze fell on me. "I vow to the moon that I will not harm you, or see you come to harm while you're in my company." His words rang with truth.

I could feel Glen's hesitance, but I squeezed his arm. "Let's go with him. We need to know what's up before we head into the compound. Plus, he's right. You're both rogues. What's he gonna do, turn you in?"

Sergeant swallowed, almost nervously. "We have something in common, too, Flor."

"I know, Uncle," I said calmly, loving the way his jaw dropped. "Or should I say, great-uncle?" Reaching into my pack, I pulled out the journal. "I've read your book."

Clearly shocked, he took it and turned it over in his hands for a moment, then handed it back. "I'm glad. I'm sure you have questions."

"You've got no idea." I felt more than one pair of curious eyes on me as Glen and I followed him around a clump of limestone boulders, and through a close-set grove of elms and hackberry bushes. No one spoke, though, and I heard more of the chickadee calls, along with some ravens, owls, and a red-tailed hawk, though that one could have been a real bird.

We walked in silence for fifteen minutes at least, Leroy and a now-conscious Bo both staring at me like I was going to snap and chop off their heads if they so much as blinked. We were in a part of the forest I hadn't spent much time in when my mother, who'd been at the front of the group, suddenly vanished.

"What the..." Glen breathed.

Sergeant shot him a quelling look, motioning for us to follow. Between a wide pine and a boulder, there was a gap that led to a sharply angled tunnel, leading down into the ground. A sinkhole?

From where we'd stood, you couldn't even see it, and something about it made it hard to look at. Hard to approach, even, like it didn't want to be noticed.

Someone cleared his throat softly, and I startled. "Flor?" Glen murmured. "What is it?"

"Magic, I think," I replied in a whisper. Moving forward, I nodded at the male who stood by with a screen of leaves and branches, obviously planning to obscure the entrance after we'd gone inside.

I was the only one who didn't have to duck my head to walk inside the long, narrow tunnel. There was no light to see where we were going, only the sounds of feet scraping on rock, and breathing. The walls grew cooler as we descended, and I even felt my ears pop at some point, but it wasn't until we'd been walking slowly for at least five minutes, that I realized I could see.

The shifters who'd come in with us whisked Bo and Leroy off to one side, going in the direction of what smelled like smoked meat. I ignored them for now, taking in my surroundings.

I'd never imagined this was here. Del had never found it, as far as I knew. No one in Southern knew anything about this place.

The cavern we'd reached was at least two hundred feet across, and a hundred feet deep, the ceiling covered with glittering stalactites that sparkled and shone in the reflected light of a small campfire. There were about thirty shifters here, none of them in wolf form, but the scent of wolf urine and scat was strong, especially to my left, where a long tunnel disappeared into darkness. A latrine, possibly.

Del had taught me to assess every new place I found myself in for ways to escape, weapons to use. Other than the way we'd come in, I had no idea how to get out of here. The ceiling of the cave was at least fifty feet overhead, and the tunnels my eyes made out could lead anywhere, or nowhere.

But weapons weren't going to be a problem. The walls were lined with them: swords, daggers, pikes, spears, and knives. Some of the weapons were homemade, mop handles with crude steel blades duct taped on, or screwed in. Some of them were antiques, it looked like.

I blinked at a stack of swords, then sniffed. "Those are actual silver blades," I muttered. "Real ones."

"Holy shit," Glen whispered. "What *is* this?"

Sergeant walked toward the fire, offering us seats on the wide flat stones around it. "This is your mother's pack, Flor," he said, pouring water from a wine bottle and handing me and Glen each a cup. The rest of the males in the cavern moved closer, surrounding us. Glen's warm leg against my own cold one was all that kept me from wanting to bolt. "Welcome home."

"Home?" I choked, setting down the cup.

Sergeant shrugged and waved at the room. "You're the Heir. This will be your inheritance."

# 20
## BROKEN AND WHOLE
### FLOR

Sergeant's gaze on me was as heavy as the sandbags Del had once forced me to carry as I ran through the hunting grounds during training. The words my great-uncle said were every bit as weighted, too, with expectation. What did he want from me, though?

I sat stunned for a moment, then finally found my tongue. "I'm not Callaway's Heir. That's Luke." When he frowned, I went on, my voice tight. "I'm not back to stay. I'm here to get my... to get Luke out of Southern. They're doing something to him. Killing him."

"And you know this how?" Sergeant asked quietly.

"Ah, I... have a—"

"Mate collection," Glen said. I shot him a glare. He winked back. "What? It's true."

Sergeant stood, the gathered males moving aside with whispers of "Alpha" as he went to my mother's side, took her arm, and escorted her to the fire to sit with us. He was incredibly gentle with her, but when he tried to sit her beside me, she hissed.

"He's not here," she muttered. "Who took him? Somebody took him, hid him. *En tenebris, en tenebris.*"

I didn't know who she was talking about, or even what she was saying. When Glen lifted an eyebrow, I shrugged it off, surprised when I didn't feel the familiar embarrassment. She'd been this way since I was little, and my pack had made fun of both her and me for years. But I thought I'd lost her. I'd take her alive any day, even if everyone around us made fun.

But to my surprise, the males in the cavern clustered around Mama the instant she sat down, and began offering her small things. Bits of jerky, shiny buttons, even a small, polished squirrel skull. She accepted them all like some sort of queen, pressing kisses to their greasy heads. No one mentioned the way she would have what looked like a small seizure and start mumbling. When she coughed, two of them even argued over who would give her water.

None of them acted like I'd been taught rogues did. They looked feral, but they weren't. They were kinder to her than our own pack had ever been.

Once I got Luke out of there, I was just gonna light a match and throw it behind me, and let that whole place burn. It was all they deserved.

"What did you mean, Flor is the Southern Heir?" Glen asked Sergeant, who watched my mother holding court, with a mixture of pride and despair on his normally expressionless face.

"I didn't say Southern. I meant the Heir to *this* pack, her mother's pack."

I didn't even know where to start. For one thing, I wasn't a male, and a dick and balls were requirements to be an Alpha Heir of any pack, as far as I knew. But the bigger issue was what he meant by my mother's pack.

Before I opened my mouth to ask, I took in the bearded faces and eyes that glimmered in the firelight. I thought I might have seen a few of them before, years ago. Two of them were males who'd been beaten for loving each other. Del had mentioned that they'd even claimed one another, and when I peered through the gloom, I saw mate marks on their exposed shoulders.

I thought they'd been killed, since those sorts of relationships were against pack law, or so Callaway had said. Had they been thrown out of Southern, and stayed close, like Mama?

How could this group be any sort of pack, let alone my mama's?

"What do you mean by that? These are rogues, right?" My eyes moved to the stacks of weapons. "Or are they some kind of army?"

Sergeant muttered something that sounded like, "I wish." Then he sighed, shaking his head. "These boys haven't had training. Most of them haven't had more than a few solid meals over the last few years. An army? Maybe someday."

"We're going to need armies, and soon." Glen's eyes darkened as he told Sergeant what had happened to his parents, and how his brother was preparing for war against Eastern, if necessary.

I told him about Brand becoming Alpha, though when I spoke, Mama got agitated, like my voice hurt her, so I left out a lot of the details.

Sergeant sighed heavily. "Well, we have weapons if we need them. But not enough strong hands to hold them." That was an understatement.

"Where did they come from?" I asked.

"As far as I can tell, they're leftovers from the last big

Southern Conclave, forty years ago. There was a great battle, and that was the beginning of the end for what you call the Western pack. Afterward, I imagine some witch or wolf hid the silver blades that were left on the field in this cavern, then sealed it." One corner of his mouth twitched. "A few of the weapons are newer, though. Someone fought valiantly with a mop handle at the Conclave earlier this summer, and the boys have been asking me to show them how to fight with those. They've brought more than one mop-sized branch down here."

I felt eyes on me and heard slight whispers, but there was no threat in their curious stares. One of them crossed the cave floor to hand me a piece of jerky. I nodded my thanks, and shared it with Glen. "Who'd have thought rogues would be so... welcoming?"

The flickering firelight made Sergeant's tattoos seem to come to life as he thought for a moment. "They were more typical rogues, until your mother found them. Fought for her place to lead them. Do you know what it means to be pack, Flor?"

"The pack protects each other," I whispered, echoing what I'd been taught when I was a child.

"That's right. These shifters are family. Even if none of the other packs on the continent recognize them."

"And the Alpha protects the pack," I went on, finishing the law.

Sergeant hummed. "Yes. Even if they're illegitimate, even if they're insane. Even if they are all but eradicated. The bond between the shifter and the Alpha is what makes a pack whole. This pack is whole."

"She's not an Alpha," Glen began, but I cut him off.

"No, she's an Alpha Mother, isn't she? Like her mother was before her."

Sergeant nodded at me. "Exactly. It was enough to keep them going, keep them alive. Though it wasn't until I showed up that these males' wolves started to waken. They can't all shift yet and keep control, so I've commanded them not to try unless their lives are in danger."

"You have the power of an Alpha over them," Glen breathed.

"They gave me their bonds willingly; their wolves recognized their need. An Alpha Mother is a great blessing, but every pack needs an Alpha to be whole, to balance the magics. I am honored to take that role at my niece's side."

I stared at my mother, who was cooing and playing with the trinkets the males had brought her, and fought a sudden wave of tears. Her odd white hair and scars made her look old, but the madness in her eyes told a darker story. "The pack's whole now. But she's not, is she?"

"No. To be whole, she would need her true mate. And that's the one thing she'll never have."

I wanted to say that she was better off without him, but now that I had mates of my own, I understood there was no getting rid of them. They became a part of you, a spiritual limb that couldn't be amputated. But you could bleed out if they were dying, and they could take you with them.

I felt the pull on my own inner strength from what must have been Luke, but felt more significant. Luke and... Grigor? It made my head hurt to focus on them, and I shook the thought away.

"He's still alive, then," I said, knowing it had to be true. If he had died, Mama would have died, too. "Callaway, I mean."

Sergeant winced, but Mama had already swiveled her head toward me. Her nostrils flared. "He's here? No, he's not. But I know you. You better stay away from him, you little witch. I won't share my mate with you. I won't share him with—" She launched herself at me, but the males at her sides grabbed her arms, gently but firmly, and kept her from crashing through the fire to reach me.

Before I knew what had happened, Glen was in front of me, his fingers sprouting wicked claws and sharp canines poking out over his lip. The males responded to that like he'd threatened to kill them all. More than one began to growl, a terrifying chorus, and an odd scent—musky and harsh, like tar, old blood, and smoke—wafted through the cavern.

My steak knife was in my hand as I crouched on the balls of my feet, ready to fight to the death. I'd smelled that scent before somewhere. It was sour and pungent, with a hint of dark smoke. This time, it was coming from the shifters nearby who were on the verge of losing control, but I'd had to breathe it in at Southern, more times than I wanted to admit.

It was the odor that clung to my father.

"Be ready to run, Flor. They're going feral," Glen whispered. I nodded wordlessly, but Sergeant stood, his back to Glen.

"At ease, shifters," Sergeant barked, and a powerful wave of dominance rolled over us all. The males responded first, falling to their knees, the odor dissipating almost as quickly as it had appeared. Mama giggled like she'd been tickled, turning her attention back to the trinkets on the cave floor.

Glen and I stood firm, the thrum of strength that came from Brand making it as easy as balancing on one foot.

Sergeant's bushy eyebrows rose, but an oddly satisfied gleam shone in his eyes as he took us in. "I think you two have some more stories I'd really like to hear. You have my apologies for my pack's reaction. They're very protective of their Alpha Mother."

My heart ached as I watched Mama settle, the males around her distracting her with silly games and antics. I'd known that coming back to Southern would tear the scabs off old wounds.

I just hadn't realized how badly it would hurt.

# 21

## SWEET
### GLEN

For the first time since I'd met her, my little mate seemed to be out of her depth. She'd dealt with everything life had thrown at her—fighting her way out of her abusive pack, leaving it and going to another, then repeating the process and finding her way at every turn—with a confidence that I'd assumed was unshakable.

She seemed composed on the outside, but standing a few short feet away from a mother who didn't recognize her and a great-uncle who was a stranger, even if we both thought we'd known him, I could sense the wall of panic that was rising inside her.

Threatening to pull her under.

"Dream Girl," I murmured in her ear. "We need to go, soon. Luke needs you."

"Yes." She gasped the word, like I'd thrown her a life preserver, and quickly squared her shoulders. "Stories later. We have to go. Sergeant, what can you tell us about the state of things inside the fence?"

The cavern went silent, except for a few smacking

sounds from the two young boys from the forest, who were gnawing at pieces of dried rabbit with gusto.

"In the compound?" Sergeant asked at last. "We can help with the hunting grounds, but that's all. We don't go inside."

"Can't." Flor's mother raised her voice, surprising us all. "They've patched the fence."

Flor swallowed hard, but didn't look at her mom. I spoke for her. "Oh? Where did they patch it?"

"Where Del used to get through, to hunt. They found the hole and closed it." She sounded lucid for the first time since I'd met her, and her voice was much like Flor's. Her eyes met mine across the fire, and my wolf moved restlessly inside. Her dominance was incredible, more oppressive and wilder than Flor's, but every bit as powerful.

But mine was a match for it, and more. Flor had given me that. I felt my wolf gently, inexorably, push Lily's sharp-edged wall of power down.

She gasped. "Alpha?" When I shook my head, she blinked. "No, you're not my Alpha."

"No, ma'am," I said softly as she crumpled to the cave floor, two of the males catching her before she hurt herself. I didn't think I'd done anything to her to cause her weakness, and no one growled at me, so I assumed this sort of spell happened a lot.

Sergeant let out a dissatisfied grunt. "They've got triple guards on the main gate to the hunting grounds, and the patrols are out in force. And once you're in, there's no telling where Luke's at, or what shape he's in."

"Oh, he's fucked ten ways to Sunday," one of the new boys volunteered, with a mouth full of masticated meat. I was pretty sure his name was Leroy. "A few days back, they done took him off the machines, and there's all sorts of bets about when he's gonna kick it."

*Shit.* My blood went cold. We really had no time left.

"Um, ah, we got out, Sergeant, sir," his friend stammered. "We know a place someone little can get in."

Flor snorted. "Why should we listen to you? Last time I was here, you little rat's asses were hunting me."

They both dropped their heads. Leroy muttered, "You got no reason ta, I reckon. We're sorry-ass sons of bitches, that's a fact."

The other one, Bo, choked out, "But we're sorry, too. Sorry we helped them Enforcers hunt ya. We were just hungry. They was gonna give us food, and my ma died two years back. My little sister's starvin' just like us. Nobody's got enough to eat anymore." When Flor's expression shifted to concern, he went on. "When you go in there, can you... can you maybe get her out, too? I mean, not just her. All the little girls, if you can find a way. That Torran's doin' bad shit to them in the dorms. He took my neighbor's kid in, and she's only eleven. Even if we go feral out here, this is better than what's goin' on inside."

"Fuck," Flor muttered. I nodded in agreement. I had a feeling our rescue mission had just been upgraded. "How do we get in?"

Bo squinted. "Well, you're gonna have to be small. And wade through guts."

"What?"

Leroy scowled at the jerky in his hand for some reason, then set it down, looking back up at Flor. "There's only one place no one goes near, not even the guards. And one itty-bitty hole in the fence line. You'll probably fit, but the big guy's gonna have to shift."

At that moment, Flor staggered, and I caught her arm. I felt an echo of pain in our bond, and swore. "What is it?"

"The chickenshit," she panted. "Finnick's..."

"Is he—" I began, but she shook her head.

"I don't think so. Maybe. Feels... different. He's being hurt? I think."

"Maybe we should wait."

She huffed. "Nah. It'll give me something else to focus on. Bo, Leroy? You two show me the way in, and I'll do what I can for your sister."

HALF AN HOUR LATER, we stood a few yards away from the edge of a long, razor-wire-topped metal fence. Bo whispered, "See the hole? We cut it just big enough for us." He wasn't wrong about me needing to shift to get through; I was shocked anything bigger than a rabbit could squirm through it.

"I see the hole, but what the fuck is *that?*" Flor replied, staring past the fence at a stack of something pink. It looked like entrails from here, arranged somehow, but there was no scent, no flies, no carrion birds circling overhead.

"The Flower Arranger's been makin' those piles ever since the end of the Conclave," Leroy squeaked. "It's, ah... the guts of all the males who hunted ya, Miss Flor."

"The guts?" Flor breathed, moving closer to the mound. "Whose?"

Bo looked like he might throw up, but he answered bravely. "Well, we're pretty sure this 'un is one of the Enforcers, a guy named Lyndal." He shot a look at Flor.

"Nobody knows who's doin' it. Ain't been caught, has he? But everybody knows he's doin' this for you."

"Why do you think that?" Flor speared the kid with a cold look.

He shrugged. "Well, he writes your name on the... You'll see. There's at least twenty other piles like this, all inside the fence. Some of them are more than one. One of 'em is nothin' but skulls, all cleaned and shiny and stacked up like a... a weddin' cake or something.'" He swallowed hard, like he might be sick. Flor was eyeing the mound of entrails, but not with a look of disgust. She seemed fascinated.

"How can you tell who that is?" I whispered, stripping my clothes off and stuffing them in the pack that Flor would carry through the hole in the wire.

Bo wiped his hand down the front of his t-shirt. "Lyndal had a scar on his thumb, from messing around with a silver blade when he was s'posed to be doin' inventory inside the armory."

I didn't understand what he meant until I shifted into my wolf form and followed Flor through the hole. I left more than a little fur on the sharp wires, but the scratches healed within seconds. I was so much stronger than I'd ever been, but I had a feeling I would need it in the next few hours.

Bo and Leroy moved quietly back to Sergeant's side, and the older man nodded to us. I nodded in return, but Flor was already nudging the mound of guts with one sneakered toe. I padded over to her side, touching my nose to her leg and breathing in her cinnamon and jasmine scent.

There was still no odor of blood, and though the scene was violent, it also held some macabre beauty. I'd heard something about this at Northern, back when reports had still been coming in from the shifters who were loyal to my father, before Torran had tightened his control. Brand had confirmed the rumors.

But seeing it was something else.

Someone or something had taken a shifter apart here, and created a strange tableau out of the remains. Bouquets, was what they'd called them, and that was exactly what they were. The pink entrails made the petals, with femurs, tibia, and fibulas as odd stems, helping to give the bouquet a three-dimensional shape. Although the lack of scent or decay was a pretty clear indicator that magic was involved as well.

"Why haven't they cleaned them up?" Flor wondered aloud. I couldn't answer and tell her about the magical shields we'd heard speculation about, but seeing it made it clear that was exactly what was going on.

I felt slightly ill as I noticed the care that had gone into the placement of the teeth, ears, and other parts as details on the petals. When I looked at the bottom of the bouquet, I recognized four letters spelled out with fingers and thumbs —one of them scarred, just as the boy had promised.

"He spelled my name," Flor whispered. "That's so sweet."

I whined and nuzzled her leg, but when she didn't respond, I grabbed the pack in my teeth and carried it with me across the open ground to the dark cover of some trees, hoping she would follow.

The boys had made sure we knew that only Torran's Enforcers were allowed to shift, so I needed to change back into my clothing before we headed any further. According to Bo, there were work squads of two to three shifters, whose job it was to check the fences. That's how he and his friend had escaped. From a distance, we might be able to pass as workers on our way home after a long shift.

Flor had left all her own things back in the cavern, except for her steak knife, of course, which was in the bag I dropped on the ground. The sword had to be left behind, since it had been too bulky for the small pack. I could tell my mate had hated to leave her things, but we weren't going to be inside the pack's fence for long, and it would be hard to disguise, even from a distance. She had tucked the small, lethal "pen" that Brand's grandmother had given her into her back pocket, though she'd seemed oddly conflicted about taking it with her. When she'd described how it worked, I'd been relieved and repulsed in equal measures. It was always good to have an extra weapon, though.

I'd brought my clothing and some packages of dry crackers and jerky, just in case it took longer than a day. But if we could hide out in the sewers that Flor knew about until dark, and sneak into the Lodge where the boys said Luke was being held, we hoped to get back out before daylight.

If Flor could hold it together, that was. She let out a string of nearly-silent curses from where she stood by the preserved entrails, and staggered, her hand plastered to the mate mark that was hidden under her shoulder-length red hair. I could feel the pain of whatever Finn was doing—or what was being done to him—leaking through the bond, and an increased sense of urgency filled me. She would need to be at her best to make it across the compound without being seen.

Of course, I'd no sooner thought that than someone did see her.

"Hey, you! What are you doing out here? On your knees!"

# 22

## CAUGHT

### GLEN

I snarled, my wolf ready to run back to our little mate's defense, just as Flor sent a sharp wave down the bond that was almost a word. *No.*

She was still standing, in the same easy stance she adopted when she was ready to fight. I thought she might dart back through the hole in the fence, distract the guards, and get away. That would be fine. *She* would be fine. I could rescue Luke on my own, and stay the fuck away from the insane wizard who was courting her. I'd probably move faster alone, and knowing she was safe in the woods she knew like the back of her hand would help me focus on the mission.

Instead, her fingers flew to the tag on her ear as she dropped to her knees, her head bowed instantly and her neck tilted to one side so that her hair didn't cover the tag. "Apologies, Enforcer."

The man was on his own, but another Enforcer stood a few hundred yards away, watching. My blood went cold. The boys had told us that no one was supposed to be on their own, that unranked shifters in particular weren't even allowed out of the dorm without a guard, or a ranked partner.

The Enforcer who'd barked the command moved closer, leaning down to pull Flor's ear by the tag. The scent of her blood carried on the breeze to me, and my wolf crouched, ready to spring. "What are you doing alone out here?"

"I w-wasn't alone, sir. I had a partner, a ranked one, but he ran off. He had important work to do." She was being careful not to lie, but she was also making sure I knew what she wanted me to do. Go on with our mission.

"As if any Southern dog knows what a day's work looks like. Probably trying to sneak out the main gate. We've killed seven in the past three days alone, little bitch."

"Please don't kill me, sir. I promise I'm not plannin' to head to the gate. I promise I wasn't even thinking that. Please let me go—" Her accent got thicker the more she begged, until the male shook her harder.

*Fuck!* The damned tag was going to rip clean out if he did that again. It took everything I had not to react when she cried out. The man let her go, and she flopped to the ground, pretending weakness. He pulled his leg back to kick her, when something—no, *someone*—darted along the fence line. The other Enforcer who was watching from farther away saw it, too, and raised the alarm, running toward the gate that led to the hunting grounds. Other voices joined in, and howls.

Young-sounding ones. It had to be Bo or Leroy, distracting the guards.

"I think we found the asshole who left you alone. He a friend of yours? Because he's about to be a dead one."

Flor just whimpered, covering her head. "Please let me go back to my room. I swear I won't do nothin' but go. I won't stop; I'll run right there." Her voice rang with truth.

But the man hesitated, squinting down at her face. "You think I trust you to go back on your own? Start running, girl."

"Yessir." Flor jogged ahead of him without even glancing in my direction, holding a hand over her neck. I used my nose to shove the pack into a ditch, then slunk behind them in the shadows. I moved silently under the clouded sky, keeping her faint scent in my nose as they moved into the section of the packlands where the dorms sat, dark and grim. My attention was on my mate, but I couldn't help but notice the changes all around.

When I'd first arrived here for the Conclave, I'd thought Southern was shabby. But now, even if the paths and yards were clear—almost eerily quiet, as if everyone was hiding in their homes—there was a palpable sense of foreboding that lingered. A few curtains twitched in the houses we passed when the Enforcer was greeted by others. I fell behind as we neared the dorm where Flor had lived before.

My wolf growled low, not wanting our little mate to enter that building. It was well-guarded, with two alert Enforcers at each door, who were checking in some women, marking them off on a paper roster. *Shit.* If they kept track of the individual shifters, they'd know Flor didn't belong. This was the most dangerous moment.

"Hey, Stan, I got one of your girls here. Her escort ran off into the woods, left her by one of the piles."

The red-haired guard moved closer, eyeing Flor. "Which floor are you on?"

One of the women waiting by the door spoke up. "Lor, there you are. Better hurry, Holly's gonna whip you bloody for bein' late. Both of us, if we ain't careful." Before I could wonder at the name she'd called my mate, the blonde had looped an arm through Flor's. The stranger twirled her pale hair around one finger in the worst pretense of flirting I'd ever seen, batting her lashes at the door guard. "Let us in quick, and I'll see if I can slip back down later and make it up to ya."

The red-haired male licked his lips and reached out to grab her, but the other guard growled. "Let 'em go, Stan."

"Thanks, Iris," Flor muttered, glancing over her shoulder at me. I took one step toward her. She lifted her hand and scratched her nose with her middle finger. Then she did it again.

I froze. Was she... telling me to fuck off?

The finger changed to a thumb, pointing in the direction of the Pack House. Then, sending a burst of emotions down our bond that was equal parts impatience, encouragement, and trepidation, she entered the dorm.

I almost smiled. The little minx was confident enough for both of us. I hoped she was right to feel that way. I waited three minutes before I slipped back into the deepest shadows I could find, and went in search of Luke.

Finding him was easier than I'd thought. The Pack House wasn't a mansion by any stretch, just a sprawling ranch-style house with one story, if you didn't count the holding cells in the basement. I was slinking along the outside of the building, listening for guards and taking in the slightly foul scents of Southern when I smelled Luke.

Well, I smelled Luke, blood, and something else: a crisp ozone scent I'd noticed in the woods at Northern when we were hunting the rogues, and then again when I'd recovered from the attack delivered by General Ivan.

Magic.

I stopped and sniffed at the windowsill. The window was slightly open, and when I went up on two paws, I could see a man—or a corpse—in bed, covered only with a sheet, and about the same shade.

*Hang on, Luke*, I thought, and began to shift. I'd need hands to open the window. My change was swift and nearly painless, and as silent as it could be, the sounds of the bones breaking and reforming as quiet as dry leaves blowing on pavement.

As I straightened and reached for the window, I felt distant twinges in the bond with Flor, and focused. She wasn't scared, but in a little pain, and a lot angry. Most likely Finnick was still pulling some shit I would eventually beat his ass for, if Brand didn't get there first.

I went still, listening for others, then opened the window and vaulted through. My feet made a soft thudding noise, right before the floorboard I'd landed on creaked.

*Oh shit.*

Footsteps sounded in the hallway, approaching fast. I ran to the door and stood behind it, cursing myself for a fool. But a voice called out down the hall, "Shaun, tell Torran we have a report of a shifter outside the fence line. We found tracks, a decent trail for once."

The footsteps retreated. After a long moment, I approached the bed and stared down at the man who had been a friend, if not a close one. Of course, now I knew why he hadn't been closer, why he alone of all of us hadn't been able to bond with the other Heirs and foster at all the packs. It hadn't just been Callaway keeping his Heir close.

Back then, I'd thought Luke was weak, before I'd learned the truth. Somehow, Luke had known Flor was his mate since he was ten. He'd been separated from her again and again, sometimes for days or weeks, somctimes by thousands of miles. He'd been forbidden to shift for years at a time, to weaken him. And still, he was alive. Fighting to be at her side.

I wasn't certain I'd have been able to survive such a long separation from my mate, especially before we'd exchanged mating bites. I wasn't at all sure how Luke had managed to, even before whatever Brand had done—whatever had turned his eyes white—to funnel strength all the way to Southern.

I laid a hand on his forehead, shocked at how cold he felt, like he was already dead. "She's here, Luke. She's here, and I'm going to take you to her."

"Not alone," a raspy voice replied, just as a whip made of fire wrapped itself around my ankles and dragged me to my knees, and then the floor.

I was frozen, unable to move a single muscle, even to blink, though all I wanted to do was close my eyes when I saw what had me.

It was a demon with glowing red eyes, wrapped in darkness, lying in wait under the bed. As I stared, helpless, it inched closer, placing one clawed hand on my face. "Ssssso young," it hissed as its talons sank into my hair. "Ssstrong."

*Fuck.*

# 23

## HOME SWEET HOME
### FLOR

"Walk fast, keep your head down, and don't make eye contact with any of the males," the blonde shifter at my side whispered as we hurried past the door guards, her voice almost too quiet to hear.

I knew this woman, or I had, when she was a girl. Her name was Iris, and she'd been the closest thing I'd had to a friend back when we were both eight years old.

One day, she'd found me crying behind a shed outside the schoolroom at lunchtime. I'd been starving hungry, as usual. That wouldn't have been enough to bring me to tears, of course, but the teacher had given homemade cookies in honor of the Alpha's birthday to everyone in the class that morning. Everyone except me.

Iris had snuck over to me, a rolled-up brown bag in one hand, and whispered, "Flor? You want some of my sandwich? I'm not hungry."

It had been a lie, of course; the unranked kids like us were always hungry. She'd shared her sandwich, though, and I'd hoped she would be a friend. But she'd been pulled out of class later that day and hadn't come back for a month. When she did, she didn't talk to me, or even look at me.

Bad memories. That was all this place held for me now.

We passed another guard who leered at us, and I added him to the mental list I'd been making all the way here. When it came time to leave, I'd need to know how many to kill.

As we climbed the stairs, I checked in on my bonds. Glen was sending confident, on-a-mission vibes my way, which was exactly what I'd hoped he'd do. I sent some back, or tried to. If he could find Luke and get him out of the Pack House, I could handle the rest. I'd lived in this pisshole long enough to know every single potential weapon, bolt-hole, and exit, so I had no fear of being trapped here again.

I was closer to Luke and Grigor now, so the amorphous ache that had grown so constant I'd almost forgotten about it didn't really hurt, and Brand was pouring strength down the solid bond between us.

Finnick had finally stopped sending pain down our connection for the moment, thank the moon. If he'd been fucking around again—or whatever had made me feel like our bond had turned to acid and my brain to jelly—I was going to rip him a brand-new asshole at the very first opportunity. My mind kept returning to that moment back at the lake again and again, trying to make sense of it.

Maybe we weren't real mates yet; maybe our bond wasn't fully formed. But no matter how hard I tried, I couldn't come up with a problem he'd need to *fuck* his way out of.

Though my wolf snarled when I even thought of him fucking someone else. And I had a feeling she was snarling at *me*. Maybe I had it all wrong.

*Ah, well.* No need to stew about Finnick. I had problems enough of my own.

Iris's soft voice reminded me of that. "I'm taking you to my room. Your old one was trashed after you left. Holly was so pissed." I'd bet she was.

"Why are you helping me?" I breathed the question.

"Because I can," she said. I almost laughed. She hadn't helped me—no one had—when I was a child being beaten and starved. No one had even spoken to me, not after that day outside the school. But I'd let myself be pissed about that later.

She knocked a short pattern on one of the doors, waited for the count of five, then opened it, half-pushing me inside. The room was dark, but my vision was so much better now, my wolf stronger.

I blinked, taking it all in. It was a standard dorm room, maybe a little nicer than the one I'd lived in for years, but not much. There was a single window, but it had been nailed shut. The two twin beds in the room were pushed against the walls, and the chest of drawers was missing. The bathroom was missing the door, and I could see figures crouched in there, staring out like frightened mice.

"Who is it?" one of them whispered.

"It's me, Iris." The girl nodded toward the bathroom, and I followed her inside, breathing through my mouth. The stench of fear, urine, blood, and vomit was almost overwhelming.

There were five girls in the room, two older ones wiping down a small, dark-haired younger girl in the shower, pink water dripping from her hairline, and one cradling another one on top of the closed toilet. In one corner of the room was a mop pail, with a mop and dirty rags stuffed inside, and some cleaner ones rolled up on the edge of the sink.

No, they were bandages. One of the girls on the toilet hopped down at a soft noise from the shower, handing a rolled-up bandage to one of the older shifters.

"Jeez, it's Flor," the girl croaked. "Look, it's her."

Every eye turned to me, staring so hard, I began to fidget. I knew their names, even if they had never spoken to me. "Hey, Tami. Hey, Deb. What's up with... uh, is that..." The youngest girl, the one getting bandaged, dropped her gaze. In fact, all of them did.

"Delia," Courtney said gently. "She's just arrived tonight."

"Arrived?" I almost couldn't get the word out.

Courtney moved to the side, and I could see what had happened to the little girl. Her hands had been either cut or whipped enough times to make them a mass of bloody flesh. I saw bone through some of the gashes on the tops of her fingers, and at one wrist. She wasn't crying, though, her expression almost resigned. Immature shifters, especially weak and starved ones, had the same ability to heal as a normal human, but the severity of the wounds she had made me wonder if she might lose her hands before she was old enough to shift.

"What did they *do* to you?" I breathed.

Courtney answered for her. "Silver-edged knife. Council fucker. She was caught taking scraps from the cans behind the dining hall when she was supposed to be inside." I swallowed bile. Those wounds wouldn't heal until she'd shifted. She couldn't have been more than eleven. She'd be maimed for years, and carry the scars in her psyche for her entire life.

I leaned close so only Courtney would hear my question. "They cut her up for eating outta the trash?"

She nodded. Delia whimpered as Tami wrapped the gauze, but she looked up at me. "I was just so hungry."

I was pissed. "Those cocksucking, motherfucking sons of bitch *fuckheads!* You point me out who did it, and I'll pull his spleen out through his throat. I'll take my knife and peel that toadfucker's skin like I used to skin squirrels, one nice long piece so it's useful to make something to wear when it's cold."

Delia stopped whimpering. Courtney stifled what might have been a laugh. "She can do it, too," Iris said behind me. "One winter, my ma was... sick." Her eyes met mine, and I remembered. Her mother had been mated to one of the low-level Enforcers. He'd cheated on her ma often enough that it had made her take to her bed from the pain, though she hadn't gone crazy like mine. "Flor snuck over to our place and left a lap blanket she and old Del had stitched together outta rabbit and squirrel fur. It was the softest thing I ever felt. It was the nicest gift Ma had ever got. I always wanted to thank you for that."

I swallowed hard, holding back a sarcastic retort. I didn't need thanks; I'd have settled for a scrap of kindness the size of a mouse's pelt. Instead, I said, "Well, if you let me know who did this to ya, Delia, I'll skin him and make gloves for all of us."

Delia's eyes welled with tears, but her lips trembled into what wanted to be a smile. "You'd do that?"

"Nothing would make me happier," I promised.

The other girls helped her stand and half-carried her out of the bathroom. No one spoke over a whisper, and from somewhere else in the building, I heard crying and male shouts and laughter. The other girls sat on one of the thin mattresses, and Iris gestured for me to join her, Courtney, and Delia on the one closest to the bathroom.

"Where have you been, Flor?" she asked. "After the... After you killed Van Blackside. Where did you go?"

"Northern," I said quietly. "And then Mountain."

Iris craned her head slightly, peering at my neck. "You have a mate?"

Deb let out a soft squeal. "Please say it's the Alpha Heir from Mountain, please say it's him!"

I almost laughed. "Yeah. He's mine. But I have a..." I almost repeated Glen's joke about having a mate collection, but stopped when Delia let out a sob. "Hey, what do you need, sweetie?"

"I need my brother back," she said through her tears. "He went out the fence to get some meat for us. It's just him and me now. Our pa's been killed. Ma, too. Bo p-promised he was gonna find us some food."

"Bo. Your brother's Bo?"

"Was Bo," Deb said, standing. She padded into the bathroom and brought out the mop, using it to sop up some of the blood spatters that were drying on the cracked linoleum. "Torran's wolves tear any of us to shreds if we so much as walk in the direction of the back gate."

"Bo's dead?" Delia gasped.

I shot Deb a look. "No, he's not. He's fine, and he and his friend Leroy are the ones who got me into the compound." The room exploded into whispered questions. I held up a hand. "They're living in the woods with an Alpha I met up at Northern. His name is Sergeant." I decided not to mention my mama, her being the Ghost Lady and all. "They're fine. There's a bunch of other shifters—"

"You mean the rogues?" Iris asked, shocked. "They don't have an Alpha. They're feral!"

I shrugged. "They're not really. The Alpha—he's not the Alpha from Northern; this one is from the Western pack."

There was another volley of whispered questions, which ceased abruptly at the sound of hard-heeled footsteps approaching in the hall outside. All the girls scrambled to the floor and kneeled in a line. Deb dropped the mop on the floor with a clatter just as the doorknob turned.

*What?* I mouthed at Iris, dropping to my own knees beside Deb.

*Inspection,* she mouthed back.

I wanted to ask who was doing the inspection, but I didn't have to. I knew the sound of the voice that came from the hall outside, shouting a room number and a command to open up.

Holly Grier.

*Ah, snakeshit.* She would drag me out of here and get me stuck in the holding cell—if I was lucky—faster than I could spit.

Before I knew what was going on, a piece of cloth that smelled like piss and mop water had landed on my face. *What in the chicken-fried fuck, Courtney?* I mouthed.

"Wrap!" she hissed back, motioning to my face.

I understood at once. Grabbing the roll of cloth, I unrolled it quickly around my face, covering it like a burn victim. Just as I'd tucked the end behind one ear, Holly opened the door.

"God, this room smells like shit." She stepped inside, a metal rod the size of a rolling pin in her hand, and the room went utterly silent. She grunted as she moved closer, taking in Delia's hands. "Stealing, I see. Well, I bet it's the last time you'll try that." She tapped the end of her metal stick on the little girl's wrist.

Holly looked healthier than she had before I left, her hair shiny and her arms fleshier, like she'd been eating

191

better than ever. Next to the starved children in this room, her obvious health was obscene.

Delia chewed at her lip furiously, clearly trying not to cry. My muscles had tensed, my wolf inside waking up more fully than she ever had before, ready to tear out our enemy's throat. I flexed my fingers, trying to keep claws from forming, though my nail beds itched as they began to lengthen. Damnit, this was the worst time for my wolf to come out to play.

Holly stopped walking in front of me. "Who the hell is this? Uncover your face."

"She's new, she and Delia both. They just got the bandages on; they shouldn't take them off," Iris volunteered.

Holly pivoted on one heel and shoved the baton into the center of Iris's torso. "Did I give you permission to speak? What did I tell you would happen the next time you gave me any lip?" She waited, her breath loud in the dead silent room. "Well, tell me what I said."

Iris struggled to inhale, but managed to speak. "You said... you'd break... my jaw."

"That's right. You had fair warning. So put your hand down and your chin up, you little bitch. We'll see how much lip you give with no teeth." She pulled the baton back, raising it high over her shoulder.

*Aw, hell no.* I didn't even have to think. Del had taught me well, and though I was too far to grab Holly's arm and stop her from striking, I was right next to one of my favorite weapons of all time. A mop.

I'd snatched it up before the baton had started to descend, and swung it with all the rage I felt at this bitch hurting little girls and women, and thriving while this whole pack was suffering. Dying.

Luke was gasping for breath across the compound, and here I was, having to deal with her shit again. She needed to die. But I'd start with teaching her a lesson.

The mop handle wasn't strong enough to break the baton, but it was plenty strong to break her arm. I shifted to a low crouch and brought it up fast and hard, relishing the sickening sound of her humerus snapping.

She sucked in a breath to scream as she dropped the baton. Iris caught the metal stick before it could hit the ground and make a noise. I kicked Holly's knees out from under her and had her in a chokehold on the tile in two seconds.

She screeched once. "*Flor?*" Her face was equal parts rage, fear, and shock as I rolled her onto her stomach and threaded my arms through hers, one knee pressing into her back, the other on the floor. I yanked the bandages off my head, quickly stuffing them into her mouth before she could make a second sound, or call out to the guards.

In this position, my face was close to hers, and I whispered, "Don't even try to get away. I'll break your other arm, and then your jaw. Hell, I'll work my way down your whole body, break every fucking bone like I'm snapping green beans. I've got plenty of time and *years* of bad memories."

"Let me break some," Iris said quietly. "And the others. Tami and Deb." Something in her tone had me twisting my face away to see hers. The other girls were frozen, staring at Holly like she was a rattlesnake that might still bite them, even though I was smashing her face to the floor.

I was about to give suggestions on where to start breaking when, suddenly, the bond between me and Glen lit up with fear, like he'd been taken by surprise. *Shit.* He might need me. I didn't have time for Holly.

"She's yours, then. As far as I'm concerned, y'all can spend the rest of the night playing with this old bitch. I've gotta go."

"We can't keep her alive," Iris breathed in my ear. "We have to kill her."

"We?"

Iris's eyes were haunted. "Tami and Deb at least."

They both gasped. Deb let out a sob.

"What did she do?" I asked. When no one spoke, I shook Holly's arms, grinding the broken one under my now-clawed hand. "What did you do, you walking piece of dogshit?"

Of course, she couldn't answer with her mouth full of dirty cloth, but her eyes flashed with something like panic.

Courtney finally sucked in a breath. "She sold us. She's taken food and presents for... for all of us. Even the younger girls."

"Who?" I was shaking with rage now. "*How old?*" I let my grip on her other arm tighten until blood spilled out from beneath my claws, and heard the smaller bones in her other arm break. "Give me that baton, Iris. I'll make sure she can't go running for help anytime soon."

"You said you had somewhere to be," Iris said, smacking the baton on Holly's skull neatly and knocking her out, like she was conking a catfish on the head. "We'll take care of this one."

Within seconds, Deb and Tami had tied Holly's arms behind her back, and dragged her into the bathroom with Courtney's help. Iris sat next to Delia on the bed, who stared in fascination through the open bathroom doorway as the two girls went to work.

With a heavy sigh, Iris picked her up and turned her away from the grisly scene. "Thanks again," she said to me as she rocked Delia on her lap like she was much younger than her age.

Unable to stay still, I was already up and at the window, cursing when I saw it wasn't just nailed, but welded shut. I'd hoped to get out and escape by way of the treetops. My wires and cord should still be there, probably in decent enough shape to get me down from the dorm roof. Getting out through the hallways would be a lot harder.

For a moment, I listened to the sweet, muffled sounds of Holly being tortured by three girls who were discovering one of the least appreciated, yet most effective forms of therapy available. Getting bloody, thorough revenge.

Then I turned back to Iris. What had she just said? "Thanks... again?"

"Of course again. You think the girls in this pack like me don't know how much we owe you?"

"What?"

"The food. The squirrels and rabbits in the lean years when you were still a kid yourself. The rice and grain from the kitchen after you started working for Del. Ma and I would've starved more than once without the extra you brought us."

*Oh yeah.* I remembered dropping two rabbits off on her porch one December, when I'd heard her mother coughing from three streets away. Shifters rarely got sick, but that year, too many weak ones had died of starvation and the cold.

"So thank you *again*, Flor."

I swallowed a lump in my throat, my heart aching. "I wish you'd thanked me then," I said quietly. "I wish anyone had."

"We weren't allowed. You knew that, right?" She sounded shocked.

I was, too. I shook my head. No one had talked to me; no one had ever befriended me since...

I blinked as she pulled the neckline of her shirt lower. "You probably don't remember, but when we were eight, I shared a sandwich with you at lunchtime. The teacher caught me and turned me in to Blackside. He used a hot silver poker to give me a necklace." She angled her neck so I could see a row of irregularly spaced, permanent welts—about the size of a cigarette end—placed along her collarbone and disappearing behind her long, dark hair. "Our whole class was warned that if anyone so much as smiled your way, they'd get far worse."

I wanted to throw up. Of course Blackside had done that. "I guess... I can't blame you for not helping me after that."

The last thing I expected was for her to laugh. "Not helping?" She patted Delia's hair and smiled down at the girl, who was now sleeping somehow. Then she glanced back at me, her dark eyes gleaming with a fierce, stark fire. "We helped you for four years, Florida Wills."

"What—what do you mean?"

"You know what they say. The pack protects, right? Well, the males in our pack did a shitty job of that. But the females? We did everything we could, even if you never knew it. We cut the hole in the fence back at least five times after someone on patrol mended it, making sure it looked like some animal was digging it out. They eventually gave up fixing it. We made loud noises when you were running along the dorm rooftop so Holly wouldn't hear you. We brushed dirt over your footprints, and swept bleach over the spots where you holed up that had your scent. The ones we could find, anyway. You were really good at hiding. Maybe just not as good as you thought."

My jaw was hanging open, but she kept on. "We made sure you had cinnamon to cover your scent, even when the kitchen was running low. Some of us even grew the ghost peppers Del dried for your secret weapon in our backyards. You think you stayed safe all on your own? Every unranked female in our pack helped keep those bastards from catching you. And we'll do it again now, if it means you get clear of here."

She met my gaze and held it for longer than any other shifter besides my mates had been able to, since Brand claimed me. "We'll get you free tonight, but you have to promise me one thing. Don't come back. Don't ever let them catch you. You're our hope, do you understand? Hope is the only thing we have left, and we can't lose it now."

# 24
## THE WORST PLAN IN THE HISTORY OF PLANS
### FLOR

Her words pounded into my mind like sledgehammers, changing not only my plans for the near future, but my memories of the years I'd lived here before. So many small things I'd noticed and dismissed while I was being hunted began to make sense. The bleachy smells had been them. The windows left unlocked. Who even knew what else.

*The pack protects.* I'd thought it was a lie for so long. But what if I'd only been seeing the worst parts of my pack? If they'd been helping me all along, how could I leave them to suffer here now? Even with Holly taken care of, they were caged in this building.

I was their hope. That word taunted me like a pissed-off mockingbird dive-bombing my focus.

I closed my eyes and sent my attention to the bond with Glen. *Huh.* He wasn't scared anymore. He felt wary, excited... fascinated, even. But not afraid. That meant I had time. It wasn't even midnight yet. I could get clear.

At that exact moment, Delia let out a tiny, snuffled sob

as she slept. The sound was like a silver dart in my chest. Not just me. I had to get the women in this building out, too.

My throat tried to tighten, but I forced out a question. "How many?" Iris raised an eyebrow. "How many girls, how many unranked women are in this building? How many need to get out?"

"Get out—" Her jaw snapped shut. With tears shining in her eyes, she rasped, "Twenty-four, besides us."

I had no idea how I could get twenty-nine girls out. But I'd have to. From the sounds of the muttered, "Oops," and the sudden absence of Holly's muffled shrieks, we had a dead body. The guards would notice her absence in the morning.

"Can they be trusted? Can they all run? Or climb?"

"Flor, if it means getting out of Southern, they could fly."

I walked to the window and thought. I *had* to get Luke out. That was my primary goal. But I couldn't leave these girls here to die, either.

*Fuck.* What should I do? I stared outside for a moment. Brand would let them live inside Mountain's borders. But that was too far from here. There was only one place, one group, close enough to hide them. Sergeant's rogue pack.

"How much time do we have?"

Iris answered quickly. "Five hours. The bell rings at four-thirty."

Five hours to get twenty-nine women out of this dorm, across miles of guarded packland, outside the fence, and underground. It would take a miracle.

I glanced up at the sky outside. The clouds were obscuring the moon, keeping everything dark. I could see some lights on in one of the houses, and in the Pack House.

I closed my eyes, trying to think of a plan that didn't end in death for me, Glen, Luke, or these brave women.

The answer came in a flash. *Grigor.* He was here, somewhere. He'd been weak; I'd felt it. Maybe even dying. But now, I didn't feel the weakness, that diminishing of my power. My wolf was strong, like she was ready to emerge. Except for the place where Finnick was connected to me, the bonds—even the ones I hadn't completed with Luke and Grigor—felt steady for the first time.

I set my hands on the metal of the window frame, closed my eyes, and focused on that place inside me where I'd felt him, heard him. He'd sent words to me. Could I send them back?

*Grigor, help. Help me.*

Of course there was no answer. How could there be? I wasn't some powerful witch wolf. Or was I?

I was connected to Brand, who was moonblessed and could hear my thoughts, or at least he could when I was back at Mountain. And I was connected to Glen.

*Glen!* I focused on the bond there, pressing against it.

It felt... odd. It had felt strong before, but not like this. Now it had a strange texture, like it was a braided rope of spirit. I repeated Glen's name in my mind, and felt a surge of affection that was undeniably him. But the staticky whisper of a voice that replied wasn't my Northern mate.

*Yes, my queen?* An odd shiver ran down my spine at hearing his voice in my head, almost like an invisible hand was stroking me.

*I have to save the girls here.* I tried to think of all the things that had happened. How I needed Grigor's help to find Luke and Glen, and get them out to join me and the others, and what I needed to do next.

Grigor's reply was a wave of confusion. I let out a shuddering breath, focusing on Delia. Blood was leaking from the edges of her bandages, and her sleepy whimpers tugged at my heart. I had to get her out of here.

His voice was faint, and I felt a strain on the bond, but heard, *Peace, little queen. We will come. No. Not here.*

*Where?* I got a sudden mental image of pink flowers. The bouquet he'd made for me. I felt my cheeks heat up, and hoped the thought I sent back was gratitude.

*Perfect for me. For us.*

My blush deepened, and the sensation of a hand stroking my spine returned, stronger, lighting up all my nerves. My wolf whined, and I opened my eyes when a cracking sound at the window got my attention.

I'd broken the weld. I had no idea how. It almost looked melted, allowing the window to slide open noiselessly.

"Whoa," Iris whispered. "I guess we're going out the window after all."

"I guess so." I filled her in on the worst plan in the history of plans. So much could go wrong. But I had to hope it wouldn't.

Iris and Courtney volunteered to sneak into the other rooms and bring the other girls to this one, since the window was unlocked. "How do we get down?" Deb asked. She and Tami had wrapped Holly's body in a sheet and left her in the shower.

"We go up," I said. "I left rope and leather up there. As long as the wires have held up for the past few months, we can slide down. I know every single way out of this pisstrap of a pack. I'll get us out."

I hoped I wasn't lying.

It only took an hour to get every one of the females in the dorm onto the roof. So many of the faces I'd expected to see were missing. When I asked Iris where they were, she just shook her head. I used a sheet to tie Delia to her back, and they were the last ones to go out the window.

The others had already filled everyone in on our plan, though a few of the women shook their heads. One of the older women whispered, "It won't work. They've got guards patrolling every street, all night long."

I took a moment to ask where the patrols were, and how often they passed. "Do they have cameras?"

"Yeah, but only a few that still work. We've taken out the ones we can with rocks." She described where the remaining ones were, and I rethought the escape route. *Shit.* Going around those would take a lot longer.

"All right. There's no time. We'll just do our best."

"With no weapons? Torran's guards are all armed. Some have silver-edged blades."

I shrugged, thinking about the pure silver blade in my pocket that Verona had given me. That was a weapon I'd only use as a very last resort. "I killed Van Blackside with a steak knife. Use anything you can find. A branch can be a staff. A sharp rock can take out an eye."

"We're not trained to fight like you," a younger girl said with tears in her voice. "We'll just die."

I caught her eye. "Then die fighting. Don't lie down for it, do you hear me? If you have to die, let your death have meaning."

Her jaw dropped, and I turned away before I could say

anything else. This girl was probably right. They might all die. But the captivity and servitude that waited for them inside the dormitory was worse than death.

"Let's go."

It took another hour to get them all down from the rooftop and hidden in bushes and culverts nearby, rolling in mud on the way to obscure their scents. They hadn't been lying about the guards; they came past at very regular intervals. What had my heart racing were the patrols that came at unexpected times. Whoever this Torran fucker was, he was smart.

Iris was a natural leader, and the other women, even the older ones, followed her without question. When I asked her to move to the front so I could guard the rear, she shook her head. "We can't lose you." She set Delia on the ground, who wrapped her arms around my waist, careful not to touch me with her hands.

I pressed a kiss to Delia's head, then whispered to Iris, "You won't. Just stick with the plan if anything happens."

"The shitty plan."

We exchanged grins. It really was shitty. If the alarm was raised, I would raise hell, too, luring the Enforcers away from the girls while Iris led them out the hole in the fence behind the remains of Lyndal, and to the forest. She knew how to do a decent barred owl call, as it turned out, and since that would get Sergeant's attention, I figured he and Mama and their wild boys could take care of the rest. Sergeant would never let these girls be hurt, if he could help it.

"I'm a fast runner, and if I can get to the drainage pipes, I can hide. Just get these girls out. You remember where I told you to go in the forest?"

"You sure they'll let us in?"

"Just tell Sergeant I sent you." I'd described both him and Mama to her, and she'd been relieved to hear that the Ghost Lady was on our side.

The wind that picked up as we began our way across the compound in small groups, crouched low, rustled enough leaves that the sounds of our feet moving blended in. We made it without anyone seeing us all the way to the edge of the housing rows, with Iris at the lead carrying Delia, and me at the back. We were still far too close to the Pack House when our luck ran out.

I froze, hearing a growl. The shifter who noticed me was in his wolf form, and that was the only warning I had before he was running straight for me.

*Shit.* I started to run, away from the girls and in the direction of some trees I knew I could climb. But in a few steps, he was no more than ten yards away, too close to outrun. If he howled for help, the others would be caught. Even if he didn't call for help, this was one of the biggest wolves I'd seen, other than Brand's. I didn't know if I could beat him.

I had to try anyway. And I had to kill him quickly. Silently.

I grabbed the pen from my pocket, popped the cap off, and crouched down just as he leaped for me. When his dark gray body was a split second from landing on me, I extended my hand, the silver blade plunging into his throat.

He fell on top of me, his claws scratching my arms, his teeth snapping too close to my face as I held him up and away the best I could with my elbow.

I didn't see the silver blade shatter, but I saw the realization in the wolf's eyes as he felt it. The air around us filled with the scent of blood and silver.

This close, I could see that this wolf was young. For all I knew, he was my age, or younger. The silver burned through his throat, as he tried frantically to cough it up. It smelled wrong. It *felt* wrong as he staggered and fell into my arms, his eyes begging me for something. To help him.

When I'd killed the first time, I'd been in some sort of altered state. Rage had filled me, and my mind had shut off. Van Blackside had needed to die more than any shifter born, and I hadn't felt a second of guilt.

When I'd killed Clara, I'd known I was right to do it. She'd deserved it, too. But the way this wolf curled up in my arms, falling on top of me, made me ashamed.

Hot tears stung my eyes as I heard someone call out in the night, an unfamiliar male. "Tanner? Little brother? Brother!"

"Brother?" I repeated in a whisper. His form changed slowly on top of me, fur shifting to flesh, jaws shrinking, until all that was left was a skinny, naked young man. So young, he couldn't even be twenty. His face was etched with terror and confusion as he fought to speak. The stench of silver wafted from his wounds like invisible, lethal smoke.

*What have I done?* This wasn't how shifters were meant to fight, or kill. We'd been given claws and teeth, strength and cunning. We used knives and swords, if we were in human form.

We'd never been meant to use poisons and silver.

The moon came out from behind a cloud for a split second. Then the boy's eyes went cloudy, and he fell limp. Sliding out from under him, I ran for the closest storm drain like the devil was right behind me.

# 25

## A BARGAIN WITH THE DEVIL
### GLEN

The devil itself had me in its grip, but I wasn't going down without a fight. Its claws were still tangled in my hair, its breath warm on my face, as I dug deep into my well of power and called on my wolf to answer. I couldn't move, but fur prickled on the backs of my hands, and my claws and teeth lengthened. If I could somehow manage to open my jaws, I would—

"Peace, little brother," the beast with the glowing eyes rasped, then let go of me.

I scrambled away on the floor, trying to stay quiet. I had to get Luke out of here, away from this. The creature pulled himself out from under the bed and lay panting, propped up against the wall.

Only it wasn't a creature. It was a man. One I knew.

"*Joaquin?*"

"Grigor," he corrected with a soft groan.

I shook my head as he pulled himself up to sitting. He looked awful, his normally bronzed skin almost gray, his face drawn. "What the fuck were you doing under Luke's bed?"

"I was... keeping him alive." He rasped out a few short sentences that were so ridiculous, they had to be true. Crazy, cruel shit. Torran cutting into Luke, the machines being taken away. "He's only alive now... because I breathe for him. My power is moving the blood through his veins, pumping his heart."

"How?" I stood, skirting Joaquin until I stood next to the bed again.

"Magic, little brother. I am Grigor Dimitri—"

"No." I cut him off. "I don't want to hear that name. I'm not going to stay in a room with the fucking boogeyman of all wolf shifters." His eyes flew to mine, and I immediately dropped my gaze. *Damnit.* I forced myself to look back up, though I had to stare at his nose. "You are Joaquin Villalobos, from the Borderlands. Got it?"

He nodded and tried to stand, but pitched over. I caught him before he could hurt himself, helping him up onto the bed beside Luke. Joaquin was shorter than Luke, his skin dark against the white sheet, and he looked almost innocent as he lay there, panting. But when he opened his eyes, and the red flames there danced...

"Close your eyes," I snapped.

He sighed heavily. "You're here for me."

"For Luke," I corrected.

"Of course. But Flor came for me, when I called, yes?" I just sneered, not willing to answer. "I won't be able to leave this room and go to our mate with my eyes closed." He hesitated. "Or not in my current state, in any case."

"Cryptic fucker," I muttered, checking on Luke again. He was no closer to waking up than he had been, though his skin felt slightly warmer. When I remarked on it, Joaquin looked resigned.

"I had to... connect our souls, in order to save him."

"You *what?*"

He snarled, the fire in his eyes flashing like red and blue lightning. "He was dying. No, he was *dead*. His wolf was all that was left, and I wasn't certain I could even save that part of him. But our queen will need all of her mates to be whole. So I made the choice. I bound myself to him. I brought him back."

"His wolf?"

"I think... I think he will be whole. I'm not certain. He hasn't awoken since. I've poured everything I have into him, to try and heal both of his natures."

"Why would you do that?" I was beyond shocked. I'd known that Flor felt an unrealized mate bond to this guy, though I'd tried not to think about it, hoping that if she had to let one mate go, it would be this one.

But he'd tied himself to Luke, to save his life. *Why?*

His mouth turned up at the corners, and I saw the answer in his flickering eyes. "Is there anything you wouldn't do to keep her from harm, from pain? I would burn down the world."

I blinked at him for a moment, understanding. Wishing I didn't. "Again. I heard you already did it once. Heard you killed more shifters than all the wars since time began."

"How could I have done that?" he asked calmly, trying to sit up, but failing. "I'm only Joaquin, an unimportant shifter from the Borderlands." Against my better judgment, and ignoring the way my wolf cowered inside me, I leaned over to help him up.

This time when I touched him, it felt like grabbing a live wire. Energy began to pour out of me. "Let go," he ground out, his jaw tight. "Let go *now!*"

The command in his voice was so much more powerful

than any Alpha dominance I'd ever felt that my body obeyed before my mind could process the words.

"What was that?" I stared at my hands. They didn't look burned. The weakness I'd felt vanished as suddenly as it had appeared.

"Apologies, young brother. I didn't mean to pull your strength away. I'm weaker now than I've ever been, and it was instinct."

I ignored him, because Luke's eyes were opening slightly. His lips formed my name before he fell back into unconsciousness.

"He woke up!" My voice was far too loud for the situation we were in, and Joaquin glared at me. With a wince, I whispered, "He spoke, or tried to."

"You are young, but very powerful. Your new bond with our little mate is a seductive source of energy for my wolf, and for Luke's. It is best you do not touch me again."

I thought for a moment. "You're saying if I touch you, you could accidentally suck me dry?"

He lifted one dark eyebrow. "Crudely put, but yes. It is possible."

"What about Luke? What if I touch him? Could he pull —" Joaquin was already shaking his head. "I meant, could *you* pull energy from me through him, enough to wake him up, so he can walk out of here? I don't think I can carry him to the fence without being caught." I didn't mention that Joaquin looked almost half-dead himself. There really wasn't a safe way to tell an immortal, evil, uber-powerful creature that he looked like shit.

"It might work," he admitted at last. "I had to create a significant bond... I could facilitate the transfer, though it might mean another bond..." He let out a long exhale that might have been a laugh. "I have done many things over the course of my long life. I find this... not knowing... exhilarating."

I was almost certain "exhilarating" was another way of saying "terrifying." I focused on a different part of his rambling. "Another bond?"

He nodded slowly. "You may become connected to Luke in the same way that I am. And..."

"Connected to you as well."

"Yes."

*Fuck.* My breath was shaky as I let it out. I couldn't do this without knowing. "Will it hurt Flor?"

"No. I would never allow it. I would use the last of my power to keep that from happening, even if it meant my own death."

"And Luke's."

He nodded.

I understood. But did he? "I'm a rogue now, but I still follow the moon's laws. I can't be bonded to a wolf who has no honor. Who'd kill indiscriminately. Who'd make flowers out of intestines, for fuck's sake."

He regarded me for a long moment, then asked, "Did she like them?" I didn't want to answer, but finally, I nodded once. "What did she say?"

"She said... Damnit, she said it was sweet."

That eyebrow arched again. "You are already bound to a *behrserk*, little brother. What will you do when she kills again? Will you cast her aside? Will you make her feel that she is not worthy of your bond, because she was forged in a hotter fire, made for greater feats than you can imagine?"

I was already shaking my head. "She's not like that. She's not a cold-blooded killer."

"We are all *like that*, as you say," he murmured. "Given the right spark, we are all one breath away from embracing the worst of our natures. I'll understand if you would not risk a bond with me. If Luke dies, if I die as well, she will survive. I will ensure it. The magical bond I made with her is tenuous, and I could make its cleaving painless." His gaze bored into me, and I shivered under its weight. "But I believe she would not thank you for taking that choice from her. I also believe you have too much courage not to try."

Outside, the wind picked up, whistling around the corners of the Pack House, a sense of urgency in the sound. "One condition," I managed to say, though my tongue was dry in my mouth, and my throat clogged with fear. Joaquin nodded. "You can't call me little brother. I'm at least six inches taller than you."

His quiet laughter spilled through the room, somehow painting the walls with shadows. "We have a bargain."

"A bargain with the devil. What could go wrong?" I muttered before I closed my eyes, and laid my hand on Luke's chest, right over his heart. It was time to wake him.

# 26

## RESCUE
### GRIGOR

It had been many years since I'd admired another shifter's courage, other than my own little queen's. But this young pup was dealing admirably with his fear. A justifiable one, given my past and my reputation. A fear of magic, as he had been taught, and the more universal fear of the unknown.

But as I felt his spirit connect with Luke's, through the bond I had with that one, I found even more to admire in the way he opened himself up fully—in spite of his fears— to whatever the bond required.

For her. Like me, he would risk all for her safety. Her happiness.

His spirit glowed a bright yellow like distilled sunshine, and flooded into the dark, cavernous place where Luke's life force had been almost totally extinguished. The small, flick- ering flame that I'd wrapped my own shadowed energies around leaped for the light of Glen's power.

Leaped, and held on, drawing too quickly. Glen let out a garbled moan of pain, and I used my shadowy power to throttle the connection between them—between us—down to a steady, smaller stream.

The void that had to be filled was so deep, though, that I was unable to keep the connections stable. Luke's wolf, the part of him I'd tried hardest to save, roared to life, and demanded that I give more to drag his human side back as well.

If I had been at my full strength, I could have ignored him. But his wolf was unbelievably powerful. How?

I fell onto the bed, my body draped over both of the others, as Luke's spirit wolf dug its claws into me and dragged me into the dream his human side was having.

Perhaps not a dream. A vision? It felt utterly real.

"Mine," I whispered, echoing the young boy in the vision that drew me in and clamped jaws as strong as the moon around my spirit.

*"Mine." I threw myself over the tiny, wailing child, her warmth my only comfort as the world exploded in pain. Lines of fire raced across my back, the skin peeling and blistering as I huddled over the girl who had been under the belt only seconds before.*

*The pack protects, they'd taught me. I wasn't the pack. Not an Alpha, or an Enforcer, or even old enough to shift. I was a child myself, only ten, but the little girl was no more than two.*

*"Blackside, stop! That's the Heir!" voices around me shouted. The entire pack was here, watching. Just as they'd watched the Head Enforcer punish the little girl for tripping and falling over her own tiny feet, and against his legs.*

*She hadn't hurt him, but he had taken his belt to punish her. Perhaps to kill her.*

*No matter how the crowd muttered and shouted, Blackside didn't stop. He redoubled his efforts, as if he were determined to* beat the girl through me, cut me in half with the leather strap if necessary, to get to her.

My blood ran in rivulets down and over her skin, the hot, metallic scent of it mingling with her own cinnamon-laced blood and saltwater tears. Inside my mind, a howling began, as if a beast was running from somewhere far away to save me.

It would be too late. Instead, a tendril of something soft, unready, like the first leaf of spring unfurling, stretched from the tiny one beneath me and wrapped a delicate spiral around me.

Mine, it echoed. Mine.

The scene changed.

"Luke, there you are," the husky voice muttered. I rolled over to see her, naked, perched on the edge of my bed. Her hair was long, her limbs strong, glowing with health. Her breasts were still small, but the nipples peeked through the curtain of red hair that tumbled around her shoulders. "I've been looking everywhere for you, mate."

I smiled back at her. I loved this dream. "I've been right here, waiting for you."

She rolled her eyes and slid over the sheet to me, lining her small form up with mine as best she could, her warm fingers skating over my sensitive skin. I placed my hand on the five-armed scar over her breast.

Her fingers trailed across my chest, teasing the sparse hairs there, then dipping to press against my cock. "I've missed you," she said softly. "Close your eyes, and I'll show you how much." Her warm body slid lower on mine, her knees bracketing mine, her hair falling all around my stomach and thighs as she leaned down and took me into her mouth.

Slowly, patiently, she worked her clever tongue up and down, around and even below, teasing every inch of my flesh until I had to hold the sheets in my fist to keep from pulling her back up and on top of me, burying myself in her wet heat. Filling *her until she was overcome with pleasure, her body tightening around mine.*

*"Love me," she murmured, as she did exactly what I'd dreamed, burying my length inside her. "Love me, Luke."*

*Hot tears ran down my face to the sheet below as our eyes met, as I lifted my hips to meet her. "I have never done anything else, little fighter."*

*Suddenly, she cried out. Not in pleasure, but pain. "Luke! Where are you? What have I done?" Terror filled her gaze, as she held up her hands. Blood dripped from them, though she wasn't hurt. "What did I do?"*

*She vanished, my body cold in an instant. I felt her pain, through some new connection. Felt others there, with me, in her place.*

*In the place inside my soul, where only she belonged. They had taken her.*

*Had they touched her? Her pain echoed along the ropes that connected to me, inside me. My wolf roared to be let loose, and even though I knew Callaway would kill me for it, I couldn't let her be taken...*

*Where is she? Where is my mate?!*

I pulled myself away from the memory mere seconds before the others woke, and was deeply grateful. It gave me time to slap my hand over Luke's mouth just as he drew a deep, shuddering breath, ready to roar out the questions his wolf had uttered in the dream.

His eyes blazed with blue fire, like the sky itself was boiling inside him. "Stay quiet," I warned him. "We're still in the Pack House. Her enemies are all around." I lowered my hand, noting Glen sitting up on Luke's other side, and prepared to quiet him as well, if necessary.

Luke's whisper was as close to a wolf's growl as I'd ever heard a human sound. I pulled on a thread of my power to wrap silence around us, ignoring Glen's disgruntled complaint as it took energy from him as well. Luke repeated his silent question, his voice raspy with disuse. "Where is my mate?" His wolf was challenging mine, meeting my gaze. And to my surprise, holding it.

"She is close. She came to rescue you."

"We both did," Glen added.

Luke's head swung around, and the tension in his body, along with the threat of imminent attack that had been present, dropped away. "Glen?" He sniffed, taking in his friend's changed scent. "You... You're her mate?"

"We all are," Glen whispered, almost cheerfully. "At least, I am, and Brand. Finn and she are... complicated, but claimed. You and Joaquin here are the only two who can't technically call her your mate yet—oh, okay, let's not get carried away." Luke and I had both turned to him, snarling, at the same instant.

"His name isn't Joaquin," Luke hissed, as I stood next to the bed, slightly dizzy from the magic I had performed with the new bindings. "It's Grigor Dimitrivich. And if you think I'll let you within a hundred feet of my mate, you are sorely mistaken."

I stopped for a moment, wondering how Flor would feel about one more bouquet. A large one, made of Luke's entrails. I forced myself to remember the dream, or vision. He had saved my little queen, and I had—foolishly, perhaps —tied him to me. I suppose I had to let him live.

"I will not pretend that I am worthy of her. But you allowed her to suffer for years. You allowed the ones who hurt her, who terrorized her, to live. I do not need your permission to continue to court the one whose soul is bound to all of us. And if you try to keep me from her, may the moon have mercy on you. Because I will not."

"Good talk," Glen interrupted. "Luke, we don't have time to measure dicks or dominance. Flor's somewhere alone in the compound. She's trying to get the women and girls out." We both glared at him.

"What?" I muttered just as Luke demanded, "You left her *alone?*"

Glen let out an exasperated breath and headed for the window. "We ran into a guard. She still had her ear tag, so he thought—"

"Why? Why would she keep it? Didn't she earn her rank at Northern?" Luke rose slowly to his feet. "Shit, how long was I out?" His legs were shaky, and I slung an arm around his waist to keep him from falling.

Glen opened his mouth to answer just as a cry went up somewhere in the Pack House. "There's an intruder! An Enforcer has been killed!"

"Oh, fuck," he sighed.

We moved quickly, Glen in front. I helped Luke stay on his feet while Glen opened the window once more. "I know a place we can hide, not far—" Luke began in a whisper.

"The storm drain," I finished, plucking the image out of his thoughts. "Where our mate hid before her fight."

He curled his lip. "Yes."

Glen helped him out the window, and I followed, using the magic I had to keep our passage quiet, and encourage the Enforcers who might see us to look in another direction. It was a simple piece of magic, in normal circumstances. But I had never attempted it with three, and with my power so drained.

I kept the spell unspooling around us as we staggered from one shadow to the next. Enforcers ran mere yards away, and even if some in their wolf forms sniffed at the air, they ran to the fence. To the forest.

I found myself smiling, though blood trickled from my nose as I depleted my strength once again to cover us as Glen worked at the bolts on one side of the circular metal drain cover.

I could smell her. My little queen wasn't in the forest. She was here, with us, now.

And her heart was breaking.

# 27

## CONFESSIONS IN THE DARK
### FLOR

If I hadn't immediately known who was coming into my hiding place as I felt them approach, I would have been terrified. But I knew them all.

Glen and Luke... and Grigor. Glen's bond was bright and strong, but the odd connection I felt with Luke still buzzed with a draining sensation. And Grigor. His power was dimmed, somehow.

I watched the cover of the storm drain move away with no noise at all, the silence so absolute I recognized it as magical. Then the faint light from outside was obscured by three bodies, dropping one after the other into the tunnel. But I wasn't afraid. I was grateful.

"Dream Girl?" Glen whispered. "Are you—"

I scrambled across the damp tunnel floor on my hands and knees, my arms tangling with Glen's as he caught me. He held me as I cried, murmuring soft words of comfort. I would have stayed there for hours, except a voice filled with a rage so palpable and dark it felt thick in the air distracted me.

"Who has hurt you, little queen? Tell me."

"Grigor," I said softly, reaching a hand toward him. I gasped when he took it, that strange surge of wind rushing through me, his eyes sparking fire in the darkness. Touching him, I could sense so much. A connection between him and... "Luke."

"Flor." I couldn't see his face, but his voice was a rasp of pain. "Are you hurt? I smell blood."

"Not mine," I replied softly. "I'm not hurt." My body wasn't, anyway. My heart, though, ached like a piece of it had been carved away. I kept seeing that young wolf's eyes as he realized what I'd done. The scent of silver was still in my nose. "I... I killed a wolf on my way here. With silver."

"The pen from Brand's grandmother?" Glen asked, one hand in my hair, pushing it behind my ear.

"Yeah."

"Did he hurt you?"

"Not really. He barely scratched me, tried to do more, but—"

"Then you did him a kindness," Grigor said, his other hand wrapping around mine. "I can hear the pain in your voice, but I promise, the death you gave him was far more merciful than what would have happened if he had succeeded in truly harming you." The tunnel floor trembled around us as he kneeled in front of me in the darkness, his breath warm and rich as he murmured in my ear. "Though I wish you never had to lift a hand to protect yourself, I am proud to have such a fierce and deadly mate."

"Mate?" I was glad it was dark, since my cheeks were flaming. "Pretty good at counting chickens, ain't ya?" His laughter was like melted chocolate. It soothed some of the raw places inside me, softened the pain. "What are you doing here, Grigor?"

"That's not his name," Glen said for some reason,

settling onto the floor next to me. His naked skin was warm, and I ran a quick hand over him. With both males touching me, the invisible wind rushed even harder through me, through us. It was odd, but I could feel something between me and Grigor, and Glen. "His name is Joaquin," Glen finished.

*Huh?*

"Pup, you have no reason to fear me." Grigor's tone was half exasperated and half amused.

"Said the boogeyman in the dark," Glen grumbled, but I could tell he was trying to distract me.

I was plenty distracted, but it was by the sound of Luke's body hitting the ground. *Oh shit. Luke.*

"I've got you, brother," Glen murmured, shuffling away from my side.

"Is he okay?"

"He's weak." Grigor moved away to do something. "Ah, good," he muttered, before returning. I heard something slosh, and then, "Drink slowly." I remembered the last time I had hidden here. Grigor had slipped me energy bars and water, and sang songs in Spanish outside to keep me company. I had left some water and an energy bar down here, and when I heard the telltale sound of a wrapper, I knew Grigor had found the remains of that meal.

"What happened?"

"He's been comatose. Starved. When he didn't die, that fellow Torran tried to kill him. He was very nearly successful."

"And you saved me," Luke rasped. "You... tied us together, didn't you, Grigor?"

"I did," Grigor said. "I am as bound as you are, brother."

"I know. I can feel you inside me."

It was definitely not the time to laugh. But after a

moment of holding it in, Glen and I both let out a long, breathy gasp. Glen's chuckle bounced around us, like we were sitting inside a bubble. I supposed we were, with Grigor using magic to keep us all safe.

It took me more than a minute to collect myself, and when I finally had my laughter under control, I apologized.

"Your laughter, little queen, is the most beautiful music I can imagine," Grigor replied. "May I hold you while I explain what has transpired? Touching you gives me more power to conceal us."

Glen muttered, "Slick move, grandpa," when Grigor shifted position to pull me onto his lap and wrap his arms around me. He had on pants of some kind. Leather, maybe. I tried not to be disappointed.

But his arms were bare, and his hands. I shivered, but not from the temperature. The feeling of his skin on mine was incredibly distracting, and I had to force myself to pay attention as he sketched out all that had happened.

Grigor had followed Sergeant to Southern, thinking he might be an enemy, then discovered the rogue encampment in the woods. "Of course, they're not rogues now. Sergeant has the power of your family line, as do you." Luke made a shocked sound.

"You know about my family? That we came from the Western pack?"

He hummed a yes.

"I'm not sure how Mama ended up here, though."

"Once the eradication began during the war, I would imagine that all of the shifters who could leave, did. Especially those of the ruling bloodline, like your Sergeant and your mother," he murmured, his hands gentle in my hair. "That pack's destruction was a great loss to the world. I'd heard of Occidens—what you call the Western pack—

when they formed two hundred... No, *three* hundred years ago. They were the only shifters who welcomed witches inside their borders. Well, the only *wolf* shifters."

"What the fairy tale fuck—" Glen began, but Grigor tsked.

"A sad story for another time. When I arrived, this shifter Torran had taken over, searching for a killer."

Glen scoffed. "Searching for whoever was slaughtering all the males of the pack."

"They earned their deaths," Grigor replied calmly. "My only regret is that I was unable to locate the younger Blackside. And Callaway himself, of course." Grigor sounded more than pissed about that, and I patted his arm. Shocks of power, like static electricity, ran from his skin to my fingers. "He was also torturing Luke at the request of a female I cannot identify. Someone he spoke to on the phone."

"Someone from Eastern. Finn's mother?" Glen breathed.

"I do not know. Now, we need to get water and food for young Luke, and find a way out of the compound before the sun rises." He went silent, as if he were listening for something. "I am much revived, thank you, my queen. I will go outside and gather provisions." He pressed a kiss to my hairline that felt more intimate than it should have, and rose. "You could share your energy with Luke, if you feel compassionate. It may give him enough strength to stand on his own."

*Share my what now?*

Before I could ask, in a rush, he was gone. All at once, the noises from outside filtered in, though they were still muffled. Shouting, the sounds of running feet and the metallic clank of weapons.

"That is one spooky fucker," Glen whispered after a moment. "Let's leave while he's gone."

I almost laughed again, but when Luke said, "Can't. Little shit's still inside me," I lost it. Luckily, I slapped a hand over my mouth and kept the sound from traveling. Or at least, I hoped I had.

Glen cleared his throat. "I'll, ah, go check out the tunnel back here. You two catch up."

Luke and I let out matching sighs. "So, sharing energy, huh?" I moved toward him, wishing I could see his face, but kind of glad he couldn't see mine.

"I'm not sure what he meant by that," Luke murmured as I crouched next to him, and found his arm with my hand. His muscles had atrophied in the months I'd been away, and his arm trembled as I touched him. I slid an arm around his narrow waist, until we were sitting on the hard ground side by side. "You don't... I can sit on my own."

"I know you can. And I know what he meant." I thought I did, anyway. I wasn't sure how to do it, but I could almost feel some of my strength moving into Luke now. It felt like spitting on desert sand, though. It wasn't nearly enough. "I should probably tell you everything that's been going on while you napped. Mind if I rest my head?"

"Please." He was naked, but I ignored that as best I could, letting my forehead fall against his shoulder as I got ready to tell a long-ass story.

I started at the beginning, with the car ride to Northern, and Vanessa's welcome. When I got to the part where Brand saved me from dying, I swallowed. "Pretty sure that's what Grigor meant. About the, ah, compassion or whatever. If we mated—"

Luke let out a soft curse. "No, Flor. I won't do that. I won't allow you to do that."

For a second, I was offended. "Why not?"

I felt his hand in my hair, stroking it behind one ear. He felt the metal tag and hesitated. My wolf took that moment to rise up just enough to whine.

Luke chuckled almost silently, and kept stroking. "Not because I don't want you. Or want a bond with you."

"You do want to be with me, like, ah... even though I've got a, a—"

"A plethora of mates," Glen muttered loud enough to hear, still moving away. Luke cleared his throat.

I shot the finger in Glen's direction. "More than my fair share, though if Glen pisses me off anymore, there might be one less by morning."

Luke's voice was raw when he answered me. "Yes, Florida Wills, I want to be your mate. I've always wanted it. I've loved you from the time I was a child myself."

"I don't get that," I admitted. "I heard that before. Brand said it, but wouldn't tell me the story. What did you mean? That you knew I was your mate."

"When I was ten..." He told his own story then, of Van Blackside beating me. How Callaway had been late for the pack run, and Van took out his anger on me, then Luke. How Callaway had forced Luke to shift before he bled out.

"I don't remember any of that," I whispered. "That's when you shifted for the first time?"

"Yes. I shifted, and my wolf knew you. I think something happened, when I was trying to protect you that night. Our blood mingled? I'm not sure. But I knew who you would be to me, someday. My wolf was obsessed with protecting you."

I stiffened. "Not all that obsessed. Where was that protection during the Hunt?"

"Callaway commanded me not to shift for years," he

murmured. "To weaken my wolf. It was only one of hundreds of commands he laid on me, in secret. I wasn't allowed to shift. I wasn't allowed to speak to you, unless I was acting as an Enforcer. I wasn't allowed to step in if you were being punished..."

"Oh." This was a familiar story.

"My wolf was more dominant than his from the beginning, but he bound it with commands. Not just about you, but all sorts of things. But my wolf resisted the ones that kept us away from you the most. He... gnawed at them over the years, if that makes sense. And when those started to unravel, the Alpha forbade me to shift or run with the pack. I was cut off."

"He knew we were mates?"

"He may have known all along. But I'm almost certain Van figured it out when you were fifteen. He caught me watching you walking home from school. When he said something about letting Trevor have you when you were older, I shifted without meaning to and attacked him. Even under all the commands. Even though Van was far more powerful than me at that point."

His next words were quiet, but each one was as heavy as a boulder. "That was when he told my fa... told Callaway that you needed to be the prey in the Hunt. That you needed to be mated to someone, *anyone* else. To make certain I could never challenge him."

# 28

## SECOND KISS
### FLOR

We sat in silence for a moment, while I tried to process everything he'd said. Callaway had tortured Luke, and me, to keep us apart. The whole Hunt had been to force me into mating with anyone besides him. Luke had saved my life when I was a baby. Had loved me since he was a little boy. He'd waited for me, tried to protect me.

It was just like Iris had said, how I hadn't been alone for all those years during the Hunt. I'd had protection I never knew about. A broken pack, silently guarding me as best they could. A broken mate, bound by commands not to step in and protect me.

Now, Luke shifted restlessly at my side, until finally I let out a sigh. "That rat bastard Callaway. What an absolute toadfucking piece of dogshit. I wish you'd killed him in the ring."

Luke hummed. "I should have. If I had, none of this would be happening."

I wasn't sure I believed that. The whole mess with the Council and Finnick's parents taking control had been brewing for a hell of a lot longer than this summer. "So he didn't want his adopted Heir mating his daughter." I snorted. "It is pretty damned Southern, when you think of it, *brother.*" Somewhere down in the tunnel, Glen sniggered.

Luke groaned. "Please don't ever call me that again."

"I promise." I bumped against his side, trying not to think about how good he felt. "So, rain's wet, toast lands butter side down, and Callaway was an asshole. No shockers yet."

"*Is* an asshole. I'm almost certain he's alive somewhere."

"He's still the Alpha?"

"Yes. I can sense his connection, but it feels like a spiderweb. There's no discomfort when I talk to you now. I think whatever Grigor did unraveled most of his hold... What are you doing?"

I had twisted around, remembering what I'd done to Luke with my steak knife. "Checking on that damned stab wound I gave you. Grigor wasn't lying; I can make it better by touching it. I did it when I stabbed Glen—" I reached for his abdomen, or at least I thought that's where I was aiming. He was hunched over, though, and instead of pressing my hand to his stomach, my fingers landed a little too far south, on his dick.

His hard dick. It was smooth, and warm. I must have been possessed by some sort of demon for a second, because instead of letting go, I wrapped my hand around it and gave it a quick squeeze. Like a nice-ta-meetcha hand-shake on his private parts.

"Flor?" His voice was strained. "That's not where you hurt me."

I let go quickly, even more glad the tunnel was pitch black. "Ah, sorry. I won't—I mean, I didn't mean to..." I was just about to crawl down the same tunnel Glen had gone into, curl up and find some nice place to die of embarrassment, when Luke's hand circled my arm.

"I didn't mean I wanted you to let go."

My mind stopped working for a few seconds, a white noise replacing all my thoughts. "But you said—"

"I meant I didn't want to mate with you under duress. I'm not going to exchange mating bites in a filthy tunnel, for one thing. And definitely not because you feel sorry for me."

"I mean, it's medicinal," I half-joked. "If it makes you stronger..."

"The thought of you being willing to give me another chance, after all the times I failed you, gives me as much strength as I'll need." He pulled me closer, until I was sitting on his lap, that very firm erection pressing against one of my thighs. "Anyway, I think the skin-to-skin contact was doing the job. Why don't we just..."

"Make out?" I smiled into the darkness.

"Yeah. Make out," he agreed, then drew me close, his lips finding mine instinctively.

The only other time he'd kissed me had been my last day at Southern. Our first kiss had felt like a prayer. This one felt like a sin.

It was all heat and need, passion and desire in the darkness. His lips owned mine, his tongue plundering my mouth. I writhed, my core tightening quickly as the scorched caramel scent of him, the feel of him, erased every other thought from my mind.

My chest ached; my body burned. My wolf howled softly, almost purring. "Luke," I gasped into his mouth. It felt like we were vibrating together, two strings plucked almost at the same time, a silent harmony being played.

"My heart," he breathed back, kissing me even more passionately. "My Flor."

His body may have gotten weaker, but his grip on my waist was firm and strong. The short beard that had grown on his face rasped against my neck as he lavished kisses down each side, one hand gliding from my waist to circle my throat gently.

My own hands were on his shoulders, then his back, the skin there warm but slightly rough, as if he had mud or something stuck to him in patches. I moved them to his nape, tugging slightly at the hair that had grown longer over the months. It was surprisingly soft and thick, and I inhaled deeply, dragging his warm, sweet scent inside my lungs.

"I dreamed of this," he murmured, before his head dropped lower. He pushed the thin t-shirt I was wearing up, and lifted me slightly to draw one of my tight peaks into his mouth. "The taste of you. The feel of you."

He moved to my other breast, one hand holding me around my waist, the other dropping to my thigh. His fingers slid up my leg, under my shorts, moving them aside. Or trying to. He couldn't quite get his hand turned the right way to—

"Fuck it," I swore aloud. I pushed him away momentarily, then wriggled free of my clothing, tossing it all to one side. As soon as I was naked, Luke's hands were on me again, drawing me back onto his lap.

"Perfect. You're *perfect,* Flor." He kissed me again, his hands on my arms, until I opened my thighs and guided his fingers back to the bare skin of my stomach, glad for the darkness. Not because I was ashamed, but because I wasn't.

I was overcome. This was everything I'd dreamed about in my darkest days, the fantasy that had given me just enough distraction to keep from falling into despair. This kiss. This moment.

Luke settled one hand between my legs, tracing uncertain lines around the tops of my thighs, finally reaching my opening, sliding through the wetness. Staying there.

"Um," I murmured, not sure how to tell him what I needed. "A little—"

"Oh, right," he whispered, his fingers inching closer to the right spot until I cried out.

"Yes! That's it..."

"Good," he murmured. "Tell me what you like. Show me how to please you."

Something in his voice made me understand that he had never done this before. My heart pounded as I slid a hand down to cover his, my fingers alongside his, and I showed him how to trace circles, widening the pattern, keeping the pressure even, until I had to bury my face in his arm to muffle the shout of pleasure that wanted to fly from my throat.

He kept moving his hand, more gently, as I spiraled back down, until I panted out a request for him to stop. He pressed kisses to my hair while I recovered, the humming between us still resonating in my head.

"That was good?" he asked.

"So good." I shifted to one side, his erection still rock hard on my thigh. "But you—"

"Can wait," he said. "Otherwise, I'm not sure I'll be able to keep my wolf from claiming you."

"Um, well, I could..." I slid off his lap and took his length in my hand, leaning over to lap at the sticky tip.

"Flor!"

I stifled a giggle. I'd shocked him.

I shocked him a bit more when I took the end of him in

my mouth, sucking, and snaked one hand under his balls to cup him.

"I won't... last long," he whispered.

*Not if I do it right,* I thought, but didn't stop what I was doing. I wanted to feel him come apart under my hands and lips, on my tongue. It only took a minute before he was groaning softly, my mouth filling with his warm salt.

"That was... magnificent," he managed to say.

"First time in a storm drain?" I teased, wiping my lips on the front of my now-filthy shirt.

"First time ever," he admitted. "When your wolf meets their mate at ten years old, there's really no settling for less."

"I think my wolf wants to meet yours." I set one hand on my chest, over my scar. "I haven't shifted again, not since I was here. But now, it feels like she's close. Like I'm almost ready to—"

Suddenly, Luke's hand landed over my mouth. "Listen."

The distant noises from outside had diminished, but the voices of two males approaching were clear, panting along with running footsteps. "...heard Torran called them already. He said to make up the rooms."

"Shit. When will they be here?"

"No telling. I'll wake up some of the females. You let the others know that..."

They were too far away to hear, but it was clear. We had to get out of here, *now.* Luke handed me my clothing, and I dressed quickly.

A moment later, a shadow fell across the tunnel opening. I knew without asking that it was Grigor. His eyes sparked red in the darkness as he lifted the round cover away, that unnatural stillness a blanket around us as we stepped out into the night. "The fence is heavily guarded."

His whisper sounded strained, like he was in pain. "We must go. I'll try to conceal us. There is a place we can hide until..." He staggered, and Glen caught him.

The scent of blood and silver in the air had the hairs on the back of my neck standing up. There was no time to ask what was wrong, not a second to spare, as he poured all of his power into creating a cloak to conceal us as we crept down an alley, across a secluded stretch of packland, and to the back door of a house.

Glen tried the handle. It was locked, and he let out a soft curse. I didn't hesitate. I leaned down, felt under a rock, and dug out a mud-encrusted metal key.

Then I opened the door, tears coursing down my face when I stepped inside and took a deep breath.

The house still smelled like Del.

# 29
## WORTH ANY SACRIFICE
### FINNICK

A soft, feminine hand rested on my back as I retched into the toilet. I'd been violently ill on and off for days, ever since Stella's visit to my room.

I'd felt my mate at the other end of our bond. Felt Flor's shock, pain, and then her rage. I might have been able to live with that, but her anger had changed. Turned to something that might have been acceptance.

Or pity.

I sat up, my eyes closed. It was hard to focus. As soon as Stella had left the room, I'd shifted, and my wolf had tried to claw his muzzle to ribbons, to get rid of the taste of betrayal. It had taken all my strength to wrest control back from him, and hours to heal from the self-inflicted damage.

The next night, while I slept, he forced another shift, and I woke with a muzzle covered with blood from chewing at the locked door. My wolf had gone feral, and I was using every ounce of my training to keep from shifting, and fleeing to go to her side.

A cool cloth was pressed to my forehead. "Finny, what's wrong?" Tana asked quietly.

I glanced at the door, and she rose to close it. I'd made certain to disable the cameras in my bathroom, but she turned the sink and shower on as well before she spoke again. The servants came in and out daily, and I didn't trust any of them not to leave a bug in a stack of towels, though I checked every time they left.

"You're sick. Shifters don't get sick. Finny, what's *happened* to you?"

I sighed, turned so I was sitting with legs crossed on the black tile—though not moving too far from the toilet, just in case—and stuck out my tongue.

"Finnick McDonnell, what are you doing?" Her outraged laughter was the only reason I'd had to smile in a week, and I took it.

"Showing you what happened."

She moved closer as I stuck out my tongue again, her jaw dropping as she saw. "You're... You're mat—" I pressed a hand over her mouth before she could say the word aloud.

I rose on shaky legs to turn the heater on for more noise, then returned and sank back down. "Yes, I am. To the most infuriating, wonderful, strong, powerful female I've ever met."

Tana's eyes welled up as she threw herself at me, embracing me. "Oh, I'm so glad. So glad! But... where is she? Who is she? Mother... Oh, no. *No.*"

"Oh yes," I said, as her thoughts flashed over her face, her expressions showing she understood. "She can never come here."

"Never," Tana agreed. "And you... you can't leave. But Finny, you *have* to."

I sighed as she leaned against me, her presence calming my wolf slightly. "I'm going to. We'll both go."

Her whisper was shaky. "We'll be rogues?"

"No. Father said the Mountain pack has a new Alpha. My friend, Brand. He hasn't joined the Council, and..." I barely breathed the next words. "I'm not sure he will. They follow the old ways. And he's... My mate is his mate as well."

She breathed a word I hadn't realized she knew.

"Tana!"

She ignored me. "That's not possible. She can't be your true mate, then."

"She is, though. Mine, and his, and Glen's. And do you remember Luke?" I knew she would. Luke had visited our pack years before, as a foster. He'd brought Tana a box of crayons and a coloring book of teddy bears. She'd been recovering from a punishment from Mother, for eating cakes away from the dining table. She'd been ashamed of the marks on her face and arms, but the two of them had spent hours together while she healed. Then Luke had gotten ill.

No one had understood what was wrong with him, though one of the doctors had suggested an unknown poison might be to blame. Luke, however, had hinted to me that he knew what was going on, and that suffering a dozen doctors' questions and prodding was better than what would happen if he shared.

"She's worth any sacrifice," he'd whispered, just before he'd left. "And so is your sister. Don't forget that. Good luck, Finn."

As I gazed into my sister's wide green eyes, so much like mine, I wondered if there was a limit to how much I would have to sacrifice to keep the ones I loved safe.

Love.

"I love Flor," I whispered, shocked at the thought.

"Finn?" Tana's eyes filled with fear, but not because I'd

accidentally admitted my love. "Flor? The one Mother's been ranting about, the wild girl from Southern? Father said she was dirty and foul-smelling, and she cut a male's head off with a steak knife." My hand went back to her mouth until she calmed.

"Be nice. That stinky Southern killer is your sister-in-law now. I actually think you'll get along like a house on fire."

I didn't know her eyes could get wider, but they did. "Really?"

"No. I think if the two of you were left to your own devices, you'd burn down at least one house. Maybe a whole pack." I tugged at her hair, and she made a grumpy face before she got up to brush it at my sink.

"I'd burn this one," Tana muttered. "Then we could leave."

I opened my mouth to tell her about the plan I'd made. I'd exchanged encrypted emails with an Italian Enforcer just the day before, hinting that I had information on the death of the missing Heir. I'd made sure the pack knew that I would provide far more than information if Tana were taken to safety, ideally to Brand.

Before I got the chance to tell her, I heard a knock at my bedroom door. It was one of the maids. "Your father has requested your presence in the lower levels."

I nodded and shut the door, grabbing a clean shirt from my closet and rinsing out my mouth. Tana had turned off the sinks and shower, so I breathed my instructions in her ear. "Stay here, Tana. I have no idea where Niall is, and he'll take any opportunity to get you alone." She nodded, her chin trembling.

Niall had been absent—I assumed busy in the lower levels—all week, while I had been "indisposed." But I'd glimpsed him in the hall outside our private wing the evening before. If I was working in the lower levels, he'd take the chance to get his hands on my sister. I didn't think he'd enter my room, but I couldn't be certain.

"Don't leave my bathroom. Don't make a sound. Lock the door after I go, and if you have to, you know what to do."

Her eyes flicked to the sink. I'd taped a short blade, no bigger than a pocketknife, to the back of the fixture, inside a sturdy holder. It wasn't silver, but the blade was coated with an extremely strong powdered sedative that worked on shifters, at least for a while.

"Good luck," she whispered. I knew I'd need it.

Father met me at the entrance to the lower levels, impatience in every line of his face. He handed me a set of the white coveralls that indicated what kind of work we would be doing.

Bloody work.

I slipped them on without speaking. The color white had been Mother's idea. She said it was more effective for our prisoners to see their blood on the fabric, and resulted in quicker and more comprehensive information. Unfortunately, in my experience, she was right.

"We think you were poisoned," Father said. "We questioned the ones who would gain the most, but they were... not forthcoming."

"Niall? He's not that much of an idiot."

"We both know he is." Father's thin lips curled into a smirk as he opened a white bag, checking on the contents. The stench of silver swirled through the air, but there was also... peanut butter? I focused on what he'd just revealed.

"You have no intention of letting him mate with Tana, do you?" I blinked, my mind putting together hints and clues. "That was a threat to keep me in line. You're going to send her away. Italy, or... No. Russia."

If I cared about pleasing my father, I would have been happy at the look he gave me. "Nicely done. I've already brokered the deal with the Alpha of Novosibirsk. She leaves on her birthday."

I had to force myself not to react. I'd heard stories about that particular Russian Alpha. His father had died in the war twenty-two years ago, and he'd been making noises about getting revenge ever since. He was at least forty, and had a reputation for brutalizing young shifters, males and females alike.

"The Russians who attacked Northern this month. That was one of your plans?"

"Hardly. We'd been in contact with that rabble, of course. Keeping an eye on them. But that Ivan fellow was a wild card. No, we've been playing a deeper game. All I need is to ensure that I am lawfully elected as the permanent Head of the Council. Then every piece will fall into place." His eyes closed for a split second. "The Long Hunt will be over."

The way my father whispered those words revealed more emotion than I'd almost ever heard him express. Longing and wistfulness, like a dream just out of reach. A dream of power.

To be elected the Head of Council, he would have to obtain a majority of votes from the other members of the Council. Even if he could make a case that he had authority over Southern while Luke was in a coma, that was only two Alpha votes. Somehow, he'd have to convince the Hilliers.

*Oh, fuck.*

The silver tools in his bag. The white clothing.

"How?" If he expected me to assist in "questioning" the

Hilliers, I would need to find some argument to stop him. "How are you planning to get the votes? You know torturing the Hilliers will only result in a bloody war. They'll never give you the position."

If Northern's shifters felt their Alpha's life end, the response would be fierce and immediate. Northern would come in force for revenge, though we outnumbered them. They wouldn't be alone. The Mountain pack was slow to anger, but this would do it.

"As if torture would work on either of those stubborn fools," Father spat out, pressing his hand to the keypad. "Bradley and Margarette are confined, yes. They are being investigated. But we're not animals. We don't torture our peers." My shoulders relaxed slightly, until he continued. "We merely kill them when the moment is right."

I was glad he had his back to me as we entered the locked hallway. It gave me time to mask my reaction. "Why the delay?"

"Brand has taken his father's seat, and his power. We felt Mountain's bonds to the Council break. But somehow, Samuel is still alive. Not that the Council has been informed officially. But we have satellite images of him sitting outside after the fight."

"What?" That was impossible. But when I thought about it... I'd felt an odd disturbance in my bond with Flor, only a few hours before Father had informed me of Brand's ascension. If I hadn't already been in my room, recovering from the fictitious "poisoning," I would have collapsed from the maelstrom of sensations. It wasn't possible to take the Alpha power of another shifter without also taking his life, not without the help of the Council, backed by all their respective packs.

We'd all learned the hard way that if a former Alpha

was left alive without transferring the power, the new Alpha ruled in name only unless the Council stepped in—or unless the old Alpha could be found and killed. My thoughts went to Luke, wondering how he was managing to hold on. Wondering where in the hell Calvin Callaway was.

"Samuel's alive? How did they pull that off?" I muttered.

"We'll ask the new Alpha, if he answers the summons to Council."

"Council? You've called a meeting."

"We've invited Brand to come here within the week to discuss Alpha Hillier's competence to rule, and ordered him to bring the rogue Northern Heir, Glen, as well as the Southern trash mate as well. Can you imagine her as Alpha Mate at that pack? At *any* pack. It's an offense to all decency."

As if he knew anything about decency.

I hummed, my mind already calculating a way to use this information. "Brand is a new Alpha, though. They did this in the old ways, not at a Council meeting. He won't have made connections to all his wolves. He'll need to stay at Mountain for months to receive their pledges of loyalty." If he came to Eastern before that, he wouldn't be strong enough to stand against my parents. At least, not against Mother's dominance.

"True. But I made certain he understood that if he wants a chance to vote on my election as permanent Head of the Council, or be a part of the decision on what befalls the Hilliers, he'll come immediately."

Ahead of us, a door opened, and I heard someone sobbing inside the cell. "Who?"

"A Southern shifter," Father said, his tone guarded. "We

have two of them. Your mother's pet project. She asked for your help with one of them. But let's make a quick detour."

I didn't ask for more information, since he already had a hand on the keypad to one of the larger cells, only one door down from where I'd been tortured after my return. When we entered, though, I gasped.

Margarette and Bradley were bound with silver chains at their wrists and ankles, lying side-by-side on what looked like a towel, laid on the floor, obscuring the place where the metal drain sat in the center of the room. This wasn't a prison cell; like the one I'd occupied, this was one of the wet work rooms.

There was no bed here, nor furniture of any kind. In fact, other than the towel, there was only an empty water bottle and, in one corner of the space, a metal bucket with a lid and a bare roll of toilet paper.

They struggled to sit upright as Father approached, Bradley putting himself between him and Margarette. She began cursing my father out, while Bradley sat silently watching us. His eyes met mine, and I saw disappointment in them. I swallowed, knowing my father was watching me.

Bradley cleared his throat. "Finnick."

"Bradley," I drawled. "How the mighty have fallen."

Margarette went quiet, her head swiveling to me. "Finn, tell me you're not a part of this. You know Bradley's not incompetent. You were *there*."

"I was. I was at your pack when you allowed rogues to plant a bomb practically inside the Lodge. When your own family abducted a guest and sold her to a Russian-backed rogue. After all of that, you executed your own Enforcers for who knows what reason. If the only thing my father is holding you for is gross incompetence, count your blessings. If I were in charge, Alpha heads would roll."

I wasn't lying, but only I knew which Alphas' heads would be on the floor. Margarette's jaw clenched, and Bradley closed his eyes, pain etching his features.

Father's smile widened, and he patted me on the shoulder. "Well said, son. Now, let's give our guests their dinner and leave them to ponder their gross failures in leadership." Reaching into the bag, he pulled out a bottle of water and a package of peanut butter crackers, tossing them to the floor.

I forced myself not to give the Hilliers any indication that I was on their side. No hope. I knew there were cameras in the room, and that my father would watch the footage carefully later. But when I left the room and heard Margarette's muffled sob, I let myself imagine my father's head rolling free, painting the white hallway a bright red.

We turned a corner, and he opened another door with his fingerprint. "Enough amusing ourselves. This is today's job." This room smelled of bleach, blood, and traces of urine and shit. The male pinned to the opposing wall with thick, silver-lined manacles didn't even look up when we entered, though I could hear his breathing begin to saw in and out as we drew closer. "This is Trevor Blackside, who was found driving his defeated Alpha away from the Southern pack to Florida, of all places."

"On their way to a theme park, perhaps?" I mocked as the male's dark head slowly lifted until he was looking at me.

"That's what we need to find out, before we finish up with him. So far, he's been... resistant." Father set the white bag down and opened the door again to let himself out, and I understood. Trevor Blackside would not be leaving this cell, at least not in one piece. "Take as long as you need, son. I'll be—"

Mother's voice from the hallway interrupted. "Aidan. I have to make a quick trip back to Southern. There's been a development. We think she's returned—" The door closed on the rest of her words as Father slipped through.

I stifled a curse, desperate to know what was being said, but the soundproofing on these rooms was the best laundered money could buy. I opened the case and removed a long silver scalpel, ignoring the stench. "Well, well, Trevor Blackside. I almost want to pinch myself. It's like my birthday came early."

"I didn't do nothin'," he rasped. "I didn't do anything but what my Alpha told me to. I was followin' orders. Please don't... don't hurt me."

"You did so much more. And I'm afraid I'm following orders as well." I crossed the cell and leaned toward him, pulling his head close enough that I could whisper directly into his ear. "Though I want you to know when I kill you, I'm not doing it because my father wants me to. I'm doing it because—what was it? Four years ago now?—you chose the wrong wolf to hunt."

# 30

## THEY KILLED ME FIRST
### FLOR

The best part about living at Southern—maybe the only good part—was it taught you how to take a shovelful of shit to the face and keep on going.

But a knife to the heart was still tough to handle, when so much else was going to hell. My heart ached to be standing in the small house Del had lived in for my entire life. So I focused on the shit.

"Glen, help Grigor inside. Luke? There should be cloth and bandages in the bathroom. Maybe some bottled water, too." I kept my voice as quiet as possible, as Glen grabbed Grigor and did as I asked, locking the door behind them both and carrying the injured male to the threadbare sofa.

"Where did he keep the water?" Luke asked.

"There was a jug under the sink." I followed him into the bathroom, hoping the gallon jug of water Del had kept for emergencies would still be there. It was, and I kneeled down to check the cabinet, searching for anything else useful. Luke grabbed clean rags from the shelf and turned toward me, our bodies taking up too much space in the tiny room. Especially his body, all six foot two naked inches of him, though most of him was covered with dirt and mud from the storm drain.

*Most* of him. His dick was practically at my eye level. When he tried to cover it with the bundle of rags, I realized I was staring. I slammed my eyes shut.

"Isn't the water still hooked up?" he asked.

"If the pipes make noise, the neighbors will know someone's here." I kept my eyes down, filled my arms with supplies, and Luke followed me back to the sofa. "Sorry we don't have fresh water," I apologized to Grigor. "Del's pipes practically yodel. We can't risk it."

Grigor groaned. "Give me... a minute. I'll use magic... to contain..." He stopped talking when Glen moved away, and I let out a curse.

His abdomen was a mess. He still had the black trousers on, but they had small holes clear though, and bloodstains gleamed a darker black on the material. The skin of his torso was even bloodier.

There wasn't one silver blade in him, but a bunch of... "Buckshot?" I wondered aloud. "The bastards used silver shot?" I felt an odd stirring of rage inside. "They brought *guns* here?"

Luke had grabbed Del's ratty old bathrobe from a peg on the wall and was pulling it on. "Callaway had a shotgun in the armory. We didn't ever use it, and I didn't know he had silver shot. But it was probably already here."

Glen muttered, "Fucking Southern," as he examined the wounds.

The smell of the silver was even stronger now. I sighed and ran into the tiny kitchen area, fishing out some leather gloves from a drawer, and grabbing a pair of tweezers from the bathroom. By the time I got back in, Luke was pouring water over the bloody entrance wounds, and I nudged him out of the way.

"You look like a whole-ass scout troop got their BB gun merit badge on your stomach," I grumbled as I started picking out the silver. A bowl appeared on the sofa next to Grigor, and I nodded a thanks, dropping the silver pellet in it. "What happened?"

"I wanted to make certain... the women got out. There was one who had fallen, carrying an injured girl. They had your... scent on them."

"Iris and Delia? Are they all right?" I took a deep breath, steadying my hands for the next piece, and the next. He was bleeding too much for my comfort, and I couldn't stop. There were dozens and dozens of silver pellets in him. If I left even one in...

"They both escaped. I was not quite so fortunate. I'm afraid I have... very little strength." He groaned. "At least I destroyed... the gun that did this."

Small favors, but it made me feel slightly less enraged. "Food," I said firmly. "How long has it been since you've eaten?"

Grigor closed his eyes. "Luke needs it more than I, my queen."

I glanced at Luke. He was drinking a glass of water at the small table, while Glen rummaged in the cabinets. He'd found a pair of sweatpants somewhere, maybe some of Del's. I'd need to find clothes for all of us, and more towels, and...

Glen's voice interrupted my thoughts, bringing my attention back to the job at hand. "We can't cook, but I found some crackers and a jar of mustang grape jelly, whatever that is."

I almost smiled, but kept working on Grigor, wiping the

blood away and using the tweezers without hesitating. "Wild grapes. Really good. Big seeds, though. Del and I perfected that recipe. I reckon that's the... the last jar." Drops splashed on the bloody skin beneath my face, but I kept going. "There oughta be some canned beans somewhere in there. Spoons in the drawer left of the sink."

Glen found enough food for a sparse meal. He served Luke, then carried a bowl to me. "Not yet, thanks," I murmured. "I need to finish with the silver." I knew I couldn't eat with that stench in my nose.

"Your hands are shaking, Dream Girl. You have to be thirsty, and hungry. Let me take over."

Grigor's eyes snapped open. They were wild with pain and power, bright red fires burning in the pupils. "My wolf... is very near the surface, little br..." For some reason, he stopped, and when he spoke again, his voice sounded odd. Different. "You are my brother. Yes. You may help me."

Glen moved closer, keeping his head bowed and slightly tilted to one side in submission. "Thank you, brother. Flor? Please eat."

For some reason, watching me eat the cold beans and jellied crackers seemed to soothe Grigor. No, Grigor's beast. That's who was watching me, unblinking, out of those fire-black eyes, as if he were deciding whether to claim me or kill me.

My gaze kept returning to his, then sliding away, my own wolf intrigued and wary. She liked seeing his wolf rise. Honestly, I did, too. I knew I shouldn't find it attractive, that show of magic and slipping of his control. He was a killer and a criminal. A monster.

I shivered. I guess I had a thing for monsters.

I perched on the edge of the sofa next to him, giving him a sip of water and feeling very much like I was hand feeding a dragon, or a gator. "I read about you in some books back at Mountain. They said you killed thousands. Tens of thousands." He snarled slightly, and Glen went still. I just took another drink from the cup. "So, did you? Kill a whole lot of people?"

His voice was still odd when he answered. "Winter kills every year, little queen. Ice and snow and frost take countless lives. The ocean drowns ships and submerges entire cities. It is the way of things."

Was he comparing himself to natural disasters? "Well, I'm not about to consider a whole season of the year or the Pacific Ocean as a suitor. So answer my question, *Joaquin*." I arched an eyebrow and met his gaze, even if the fire there was way over the edge of creepy.

This time, it sounded like the man I knew was speaking. "I did, little queen. I killed many. At first, I killed for my father, at his command. Later, I killed my father, and his pack, and everyone who ever raised a hand to help him, or pledged allegiance to him." He paused. "But they killed me first." Grigor's words hung in the air for a long moment, ominous and confusing.

"What does that mean?" Glen muttered, saving me the trouble. "They killed you first? Did they shoot you with silver back then, too?"

"No." My throat was tight, but I spoke clearly as his meaning dawned on me. "He's talking about his mate, Anya. They killed *her*. You loved her, didn't you?"

Grigor was still staring at me, but a flicker of unease dimmed the flames. "I will tell you my story, little queen. But you have no reason to fear. My heart is yours."

"Was she your true mate?"

"She was... my soulmate. But—"

Gutted, I closed my eyes and turned away. I'd wondered

about the woman who'd been mentioned in the books. The spark that had ignited Grigor's most famous killing spree had been her death, and his own father had been the one to kill her. But hearing that Grigor had loved someone else was a pain I hadn't been prepared for.

I looked over at Glen, who was still picking the shot out of Grigor's stomach. "Glen, you finish up. I'm going to put Luke to bed." Luke had fallen asleep at the table. I got up, made sure Del's bed had a pillow and sheets, and helped Luke shuffle into the small bedroom. He was asleep again before his head hit the pillow, and I got clothing out of Del's drawers for all of us.

I let myself cry for a moment then, holding one of his old t-shirts up to my face, and smelling him. I missed him so much. He'd been my one safe place in this pack. My rock.

Pulling off my own filthy shirt, I replaced it with that one, then left a set of clothes for Luke on top of the dresser, before carrying more out to the main room. Glen had finished, taken the bowl of silver away somewhere, and was now holding a cup of water to Grigor's mouth. I took another damp cloth, wet it, and kneeled next to the sofa, ready to wipe the remaining blood away.

"Please don't," Grigor rasped. "Never kneel to me."

"I don't want you getting blood all over Del's shirt, so shut it, old man."

"Old man?" He blinked at me as I pushed his hands away and wiped him down. His skin was healed, only the faintest traces of the silver shot still evident. They would be gone in minutes.

Glen winked at me. "I'll let you get on your knees for me, Dream Girl." I reached over and punched him in the groin. Not hard. Just enough to remind him not to be a degenerate.

I ignored Glen while he pretended to be injured, and held a shirt out to Grigor. "How old are you, then? And how did you live this long? I want to know everything."

"Why?" Grigor's question was subdued. "It will not make you love me. I've done... shameful things."

"Who hasn't?" I shrugged, thinking of how many times I'd eaten out of the trash, or stolen bits of food from the ranked shifters. I'd broken dozens of rules over the years. I'd sawed off a man's head and... "I did a shameful thing tonight."

Both men waited, and I took a breath, still on my knees. It felt right, for a confession like this. "I killed a shifter with silver. I didn't have to. I could have knocked him out. I probably could have run, and gotten away. He wasn't as fast as me; none of these wolves are. But I panicked, and I... I had a weapon, and I used it. But he was just a kid. Not much older than Bo and Leroy. Doing what he was told, what his Alpha ordered."

I lifted my eyes to Grigor. "The silver I did it with, it splintered in his throat so he couldn't howl for help, or bark, or breathe. It was a terrible death. An avoidable one." Probably. I wasn't certain he would've given up without me doing some real damage. Most males saw a scrawny female shifter and thought they could take me, then got pissed when they started to lose to one.

Suddenly, Glen was on his knees beside me. "That wasn't shameful. That was *necessary*. Joaquin, you said the girls all got out safely? Well, that was because you gave them that chance, Flor. You saved them, and if the cost of that was one shifter's life..."

"I killed ten thousand." Grigor admitted. "I killed my father first, then burned his palace, then hunted down every one of his pack—villainous and innocent alike—and erased them from the earth. And I did not mourn their loss. I did not feel regret."

Glen's hand closed around mine, and I could tell he was one more confession away from grabbing me and forcing me out of this house, away from the serial killer.

I wasn't completely against that idea. But then, I remembered something. "Brand's father said you left your own mate there. In the palace. Did you... burn her along with the rest?" If he said yes, it wouldn't matter how many of my tormentors' hands he made into arrangements, I was not going to add him to my mate group.

Brand could help me figure out a way to cut those ties to Luke and Glen.

"I would never have hurt Anya. She was the other half of my magic. My..." He said a word that had far too many consonants and swallowed vowels—and sounded like he was coughing up a hairball—then smiled softly at my expression. "The word is in an old language, but it means witch mate. She was incredibly powerful, far more so than I. When we bonded..."

His hand moved to his upper arm, and I noticed something there. A very faint scar in the shape of a small x, two lines crossing. It looked a little like my scar, only made of two lines instead of five that originated from a central point. "You know that the power a shifter gains from a true mate is what creates the most powerful Alphas. My father was the Alpha of Alphas, ruling over an entire continent. He did not share power."

"He had a true mate?" Glen asked. "Your mother?"

Grigor shook his head. "No. My mother was not his true mate. My father's true mate was like your own mother, Lily. Mated to a monster, and driven mad. My mother, she was gentle. From an immensely powerful line of dark witches, but she had chosen to live differently. She taught me all she could." He closed his eyes. "I haven't spoken of her for centuries."

I decided to ask about the whole "centuries" part later. My wolf was sniffing around the painful heart of this story. His witch mate.

"My father hadn't known my mother was a witch when I was conceived. It was forbidden in that country to mingle the lines."

Glen muttered, "I thought it was impossible, not just forbidden."

"Humans cannot procreate with shifters, brother. But witches and shifters share the moon's magic. It's entirely possible, but rare. When it happens—especially when two overly powerful beings come together—the result can be a creature so terrible, it cannot be allowed to survive." He winked at me.

I scowled back. "Anya. Tell me."

His amusement vanished. "Yes. I did leave her, I suppose. My father knew what I was, but believed my mother had been a weak witch, since she mostly used her magic for small things. When he discovered I had mated with my Anya, one of the most powerful witches on that side of the world, he sent his warriors to bring her down. They brought her to the center of his judgment hall, where he bound her in chains and slaughtered her. Tore her into pieces so small, no healing magic has ever existed that could revive her. I made a pyre for her out of his palace, and his pack."

"You didn't leave her." I would need to tell Samuel, and make sure the pack history books were corrected.

"We had a child. Anya had taken him to her coven. I hid him in another village, making certain no one would be able to find him. I left no one alive who knew he existed."

Glen sucked in a breath.

"You killed them, too?" I asked. "Her coven?"

"They were the ones who gave Anya over to my father. They kept our child, but let my witch mate die, because she had rejected their ways."

"What happened to him? Your son?"

He closed his eyes. "I failed him in every way but one. I gave him to a family that loved him, and allowed him to live without anyone knowing who his true father was."

"Is he... Is he still alive?" If Grigor was who-knows-how-old, I had to assume his kids might be just as long-lived.

"No. He died too young. But his human wife survived, and their children, and theirs, and so on. I made certain all of my line have never lacked for wealth. But the true gift I've given them all is anonymity. No one knows they are mine. Not even they do."

"Maybe you should give that gift to Flor," Glen muttered.

"If I could have done so, I would have," Grigor admitted, but something in my face must have alarmed him, because he grasped me tightly. "For *your* sake, my queen. Your safety. You should refuse me, though I must warn you that I cannot let you go, no matter what you decide. Whether I worship you in the light or from the shadows. Whether I am allowed to stand at your side, or fight without any recognition. I cannot regret what I have done. I would do far more for you; my wolf would demand it."

"Your wolf?"

"You are his mate, Flor. His true mate. When they killed

Anya, only he kept my witch side alive. Only by allowing me to kill everyone who needed killing."

The hairs on the back of my neck stood up. "Needed killing? You know you sound really crazy, right?"

He made a noncommittal sound. "I do not pretend to be sane. My wolf has waited in madness for you, has kept us alive for this moment. Anyone who would hurt you— human, wolf, or witch—he would snuff their lives out."

He went silent, since I'd climbed up on the sofa, onto his lap, and was kissing his mouth. I held his face in my hands, tasting him. It felt a little like kissing a winter storm, or the ocean. Like I was flirting with death just by being this close to him.

But it wasn't my death I was flirting with. It was that of anyone who tried to hurt me or mine. This future mate would do anything to protect me. To protect the ones connected to me.

And his "anything" was something any shifter should fear, even a whole corrupt Council full of them.

"Grigor Dimitrivich?" I announced, ignoring Glen's muttered, "Call him Joaquin," as he slipped into the bedroom and closed the door softly. "You may be crazy, but you're my kind of crazy, aren't you? I guess I ought to give you a chance. I've gotta let you know, I don't think Brand's gonna be so easy to convince."

A smile slid across his face, as his hands lifted to hold my cheeks as well, both of us gazing into each other's eyes, the house shaking slightly as he pulled my face to his for another kiss. "I'll work some magic, little queen."

# 31

## DIRTY MOVES
### FLOR

Grigor's kisses were like dark chocolate. Smooth and addictive with a slightly cold edge, the invisible wind that I'd always felt when he touched me somehow moving through my veins.

"Sure you're not a vampire?" I muttered as he moved his hands through my hair. It had grown far faster than it normally did since I'd cut it in this house months before, and fell past my shoulders now. He lifted it with one hand and used the backs of his fingers to trace the outline of my ear, ending up at the top, at my tag.

"Why do you still wear this, my queen?" There was no judgment in his tone, only curiosity.

"It's a good thing I kept it. Otherwise, I wouldn't have been able to get into the dorms." His eyes narrowed, a predator waiting. "Okay, it's dumb, but... I'm kind of attached to it. It reminds me of Del."

He frowned, then smiled gently. "Del? Your true father. The one you loved. He left a mark on your soul."

"Yeah." I swallowed the lump in my throat. "When I first got this tag, I was little. I cried, and begged Del to take it out. Of course, he wouldn't. They would've killed us both if we'd broken that rule. I told him I didn't want the other kids to see it and know what it meant. That I was weak."

"You were never weak, little mate."

"That's what Del said, too." Here, in his home, it was almost like I could hear his voice again, saying the words he'd whispered in the kitchen when I'd come running to him after a group of the older boys at school had taunted me for being unranked trash. "He told me, 'They want us to be weak, girlie. They want us to believe they can define us. But you know what I see when I look at your tag? A full moon, shining silver. Power that can never be contained.' When I look in the mirror, I see the way he saw us. Valuable, powerful. Children of the moon, like any of the others, whether we held rank or not."

"I would have liked your Del very much."

I snorted. "He'd have kicked your ass from here to the ocean, one leg or not. He was more protective than any dad I knew."

"That is exactly what I would have liked most about him. I might have allowed him to get a few good hits in."

I pretended to be offended. "Allowed? Someday I'll show you what he taught me."

Grigor's jaw dropped. "You would... fight me."

I closed his mouth with two fingers on his chin, then squeezed his face. "Spar, sure. Might even win. I fight dirty."

His eyes sparked with delight as he wrapped his arms around me, flipping us so I was lying on the sofa with him over me, growling low. "I will hold you to that. I want to see you use everything at your disposal. Especially the dirty moves."

He was only a few inches taller than me, so our bodies

lined up, more or less. Before I could get used to the feeling, his pelvis tilted forward, one of his legs in between mine, and I felt a surge of what had to be magical heat move from his body to mine.

Now it was my turn for a jaw drop. "Grigor. Did you just..." I was going to say, "Make a dirty joke," but he traced a finger over the seam in my shorts, and my mouth dried up.

"Let me, my queen?"

I blushed so hard I felt a little dizzy, but nodded. I thought he would undo my shorts, but he just settled his hand over my private parts, cupping them. Then he smiled, and I felt another wave of magic, with little vibrations starting up down there.

"No earthquakes," I squeaked.

He nodded, a dark smile curving his lips. "No screaming."

I wasn't sure I could keep that promise, but I bit my lip and nodded.

Luke had given me an orgasm in the storm drain not two hours before, but my body acted like it hadn't been touched in years, the waves of Grigor's magic lighting every nerve on fire in seconds.

When Brand touched me, he'd always been focused on my pleasure. Luke had been uncertain and sweet. Grigor wasn't either of those things. He knew, whether from magic or experience, exactly what to touch, where to press and how hard, to make me reach my peak.

His laugh was wicked as I fell over the edge, expecting him to stop. He shook his head, the dark hair that fell around his face making him look mischievous rather than evil.

"No screaming, little mate," he reminded me, as he sent

a larger wave of magic to my core. It felt almost like he was inside me, like something thick and hot and... getting wider!

"Grigor!" I gasped, the word muffled as he covered my mouth with one hand.

"How much can you take, little one? How much pleasure can you stand?"

Another climax tumbled over me, and I glared up at him when it was waning. "I can take whatever you dish out, old man."

"Holy shit," Glen said from the doorway. "This would be even hotter if she was naked, Joaquin."

"True," Grigor murmured, moving away from me. "Well then, brother. Come and help."

Glen's ocean-blue eyes flew to my face, an unspoken question in them. I rolled my own eyes, pretended like I wasn't blushing so hard my cheeks might stay this way permanently, and nodded him over.

Glen took Grigor's place and had my shorts off and on the floor in seconds. He pulled my thighs apart, looking like he was trying to memorize my pussy for a final exam. Grigor just watched from behind, standing with his arms crossed, the muscles on his arms and chest taut.

"What?" I snapped, as he circled behind the sofa. He lifted my arms and pulled my shirt off, distracting me from Glen's inspection.

"You're just so incredibly beautiful," Glen explained, then leaned forward and pressed a kiss to my inner thigh.

"And dirty," I protested, twisting. "I haven't had a bath in—"

"Sponge bath," Glen announced, grabbing a clean rag and pouring some water on it. He gave my parts a cursory wipe down, followed by a more thorough cleaning with his tongue.

"Glen!" I giggled at the way his stubble tickled my thighs. I would have said something else, but Grigor had leaned over the back of the sofa, and his lips were on mine, upside down. I closed my eyes, luxuriating in the feeling of mouths and tongues, and pleasure building again, the waves of vibrations traveling from where Grigor was kissing me, to my nipples, then lower, circling my core on the inside the same way Glen's tongue did on the surface.

How many times was Grigor planning to make me orgasm?

A voice answered in my mind. *You said you could take whatever I dish out. Are you giving up?*

*Not even close.*

Grigor's carefree laughter felt like watching a beautiful sunrise after a storm. After I came again, Glen's tongue teasing me to a long, lazy climax, I asked, "Grigor? Do you want to..."

Glen backed away, but Grigor shook his head once. "I cannot. I told you that when we come together, the earth will move. I am afraid I would not be able to hold back my reaction. It is best for our first joining to take place in a less perilous situation."

*Oh yeah.* We were literally surrounded by enemies. Probably not the best time to trigger an earthquake with the epicenter in Del's shack.

I sighed in disappointment, but Grigor surprised me. "However, your young mate might have a suggestion."

He hadn't even finished the thought before Glen had pulled me forward, lifting me up. He sat on the sofa and settled me on his lap facing him, his cock curving up between our bare stomachs. "I thought you'd never ask."

260

"What am I gonna do with you, Glenda?" I teased, kissing him before I slid up and notched the tip of his cock at my opening. "It's a good thing I love fucking you so much."

"So good," Glen groaned as I lowered myself down over him, the stretch of his cock making me ache in all the best ways. I rose up and down a few times before Glen took over, gripping my hips and driving me down on him, filling me more on every thrust.

"So... good," I managed to say.

"Not good enough if you can still talk," he snarled.

Grigor circled the sofa so that he was at my back once more. He made a soft sound, drawing Glen's attention. I'm not sure what passed between them, but in seconds, Glen was turning me so that my back was to his chest, then positioned us so he was inside me again, seated to the base. I was so full, I ached. I needed more.

Grigor moved to kneel in front of me, as low as he could, then leaned forward. "What a vision. May I taste you?"

I nodded, shocked, as he dropped his face and took my clit into his mouth, sucking gently, his tongue moving. His face was only inches away from where Glen was buried inside me, and his tongue was practically vibrating.

I shivered at the intensity of the sensations. Glen groaned again. "Don't move, Flor, I'm begging you. It's going to make me... I don't want to come until you—"

The idea of Grigor tormenting Glen by simply licking me had my core tightening, my back arching, and my walls clamping around Glen's cock.

"*Fuuuuck*," he gasped as he flooded me with his warmth. Grigor gave me one last swipe with this tongue, then leaned back.

"That was... amazing," I moaned once I could finally talk.

"Was?" Grigor's brow creased, but the mischievous look had returned. "You cannot think we are done?"

Beneath me, Glen whimpered.

I bit my lip. "Bring it on, old man."

"HE'S EVIL, Flor. He's evil, and he's killed us both." Glen groaned. He lay beneath me on the sofa—a sofa that would need to be burned after tonight—with one hand over his face, and the other arm around my waist.

I grinned stupidly. Of course I did. I'd been fucked stupid for over an hour. It was probably four a.m., we were stuck in this house for another day, and I hadn't slept a wink. If a curious pack member came knocking, if any Enforcers came to investigate the place, I was dead. I was too exhausted to stand. Fighting was out of the question.

But if I had to die, at least I'd die with a smile on my face and a pleasant ache in my lady parts.

"This evil man needs to go," Grigor chirped from across the room. Well, as much as a serial killer wearing all black would chirp. He had on his own trousers, but had put on a black t-shirt of Del's that fit him perfectly. He looked refreshed as fuck.

"You sucked all my energy out, didn't you?" I accused softly, since Glen had now fallen asleep and was snoring lightly.

He shook his head. "Being near you makes me feel centuries younger."

Centuries. He kept using that word, a little too casually, if you asked me. I wanted to get some answers—how had he ended up living this long, when the oldest shifter ever had only made it to a hundred and twenty? What had he done all that time?

Did he still miss his dead mate?

Had he had a lot of lovers in all those centuries?

But I felt like I could sleep for a week, and if he answered wrong, I'd have to get up, find a knife, and stab him, or something.

"You rest, little queen. I'm going to weave a small spell around this place."

"A spell?" I mustered the strength to sit up. Glen let out a snort, then rolled over, still asleep. "What kind of spell?"

"It's one my mother taught me. A look-away. Very simple, though it would usually require a full coven to weave a solid one around an entire structure." I almost called him on his bragging, but then realized he was probably only stating a fact.

"I wish we could shower," I mused aloud.

Grigor ran a hand over his chin in thought. "I could include a silencing spell. It should muffle the sounds of the pipes. And of your young mate's unfortunate snoring. Wait a half hour before you use the water."

I nodded. "Aren't you tired? Won't all that magic take a lot of energy?"

"A fair amount." He winked. "I find myself much rejuvenated, though. Sleep. I will remain outside, watching. No one will enter while I stand guard."

He slipped out the door, and I wandered into the bathroom, finding a toothbrush and using the bottled water to brush my teeth. Once I'd done as much as I could to get clean without running water, I lay next to Luke on the bed and crashed.

I dreamed of Finnick and Brand. Not sex dreams, though. Clearly, I was too exhausted for that to seem fun. But in the first dream, Finnick was in a cell somewhere, with...

*"Trevor Blackside." Finnick spat out the name like it was poison. His hands were slick with blood, and he held a scalpel in the bloodiest one. "You disappoint me. I thought you Southerners were tough. Chased a girl in the Hunt for years, night after night, didn't you? Tormented all the unranked shifters at your hellhole of a pack, and I assumed you'd be this big, bad Enforcer. But look at you. Begging, covered with piss and blood. If you'd been born into Eastern, you'd have been culled years ago."*

*A shape—it was almost unrecognizable as a man—quivered on the wall opposite Finnick. "Please... no more."*

*I hadn't recognized Trevor, but I knew that voice. It had taunted me about my mother's death, and threatened me in graphic detail for years about what he wanted to do to me after he caught me in the Hunt.*

*I wanted him to die slowly, and as painfully as possible.*

*But as Finnick stepped closer to him, I saw something in his eyes that disturbed me more than any of the wounds on Trevor's body. The brilliant green of them had dulled to a flat gray, and I had a feeling that his soul was changing. Like whatever it was that made him Finnick was fading. He was as filled with shame and self-loathing as I'd been when I'd killed the young wolf.*

*Killed with silver.*

*I heard Brand's voice in my mind. "Finn seems hard and cold, but he is the gentlest of us all. The most broken. Help him, little flower."*

*I thought my reply. "This isn't a dream."*

*"It is not," Brand's voice said before he drifted away. "It is the nightmare his parents created. Only you can help him wake up."*

*I didn't know how to help Finnick, but I knew I didn't want him to torture Trevor any longer. Not if it was hurting him.*

*But even if this wasn't a dream, even if it was some kind of vision, I couldn't do anything, change anything. I let out a frustrated scream.*

*Finnick's head shot up, and his eyes darted around the blood-spattered room. His lips formed my name. "Flor?"*

*Could he hear me? I felt the vision fading, like I was being pulled away. Suddenly, I knew what he needed to do.*

*"Drop the blade," I whispered to myself. "Claws and teeth."*

My eyes opened before I could see if he'd heard me. "Flor, you were crying out in your sleep." Luke's voice had me sitting up in the bed. Del's bed.

I had on one of Del's t-shirts, and a pair of boxers. Luke was holding a cup in his hand. "Coffee?" I scrambled out of the bed and took the warm mug. "How?"

I blew on the liquid and sipped carefully, taking in Luke's appearance. He was standing straight, and even though his arms seemed a little less muscular than before, and his beard a lot scruffier, his eyes were bright.

"You look rested," I said after a moment. "How long did we sleep?"

"Most of the day," he replied, holding out a hand. I took it, loving the feel of his skin under mine. He had on the shirt and pants I'd laid out for him. "Glen's made us a late lunch."

"He cooked? I could eat a gator. I guess Grigor got the look-away spell going?"

"He did. He's watching the house, but so far no one has come anywhere close. The compound is teeming with activity, though it's hard to hear. The spell, I guess."

"It's weird to have someone who can do magic around, isn't it?" I asked as he pulled out a chair for me at the table. Glen grinned at us both, carrying over a plate with an odd collection of food on it: pieces of cold Spam, some crackers, a small pile of canned mandarin oranges, and a vanilla pudding cup.

"I wouldn't call my meal prep skills magical, but you're welcome," he said, dropping a kiss on my head. "Your Del's food-hiding skills were pretty spectacular, though. He had cans in just about every place no one would ever think to look."

I grabbed my fork, nodding. "Yeah, he was the one who taught me about camouflage, and hiding in plain sight. As long as nobody could smell something interesting, he always said they probably wouldn't look too hard."

"You smell pretty interesting, mate. You might consider a shower when you're done eating—*ow!*" I'd pinched his butt as he passed me, and he whirled around with a pained grimace. "I was only teasing. You smell fantastic."

The scent of his lie had us all crinkling our noses. That and... "Is the silver still in the house?"

Glen answered. "Joaquin took it out. He said it made the spell harder, so he took it off and buried it somewhere just before dawn." He yawned. "Wake me when it's dark, Luke."

Luke nodded, grabbing some food for himself. I sipped the coffee, then dug into the food. When I thought about this being Del's provisions, it made my throat tighten up, but I was getting used to being in his space.

"Why does Glen call Grigor *Joaquin*?"

Luke smiled down at his plate. "I think it's easier for

Glen to have a magic-wielding wolf named Joaquin around than to grapple with the reality that he's bonded to Grigor Dimitrivich."

"Bonded," I repeated, fascinated. "You said he was inside you. And I can feel... I felt it, when you were being pulled away. He did something to save you. Are y'all really..."

He swallowed, nodding.

"How did that happen?"

Luke stared down at the table for a long moment, then answered like he was tiptoeing around a sleeping porcupine. "I didn't do well after you left. The pain was worse than I'd expected. It was only a week before I wasn't able to stand for more than a few moments. I had some things with your scent on them, and they helped. I snuck back into your old dorm room, and... Well, my wolf went a little crazy there. Brand had warned me not to shift, and it took a full day to get control and shift back. By the time I was back in skin, Torran was there, and had me confined to my room for observation."

He ate a few bites, then set down his fork. "I thought I would die. I wanted to. Not because I didn't want to live, but because it felt like I was losing my mind. I think... someone was there, Flor. It felt like my mind was being flayed, like someone was reading all my memories, asking me questions, and all I could do was try to keep them out. Keep you safe."

"Questions about what?"

He swallowed hard. "About you."

I had to remind myself to breathe. Me? Why would anyone want to know about me? Unless someone knew who I was. What I was.

Luke let out a breath. "So I let go. I gave up."

"But your wolf didn't, did he?"

"He tried. But Grigor wouldn't let him go. He grabbed him—by the tail? It felt like that. By the tail hairs of my wolf's spirit, and hauled us back from..." His eyes closed for a moment. "That's when he braided our souls together. It's not a mate bond, but it's something like that. Every bit as permanent. I'm stronger now, even if I have a ways to go to be worthy."

"Worthy?"

"Of his gift. Of you. Of Glen's sacrifice."

I blinked. "Glen?"

"Grigor was all that was keeping me alive. But Torran kept coming into the room, cutting me with silver, trying to get me to die faster, and by the time Glen arrived, both of us were on the verge of dying. Glen gave Grigor permission to tie us all together. He gave us the strength to hold on for you. If Torran had come back..." He went quiet, and I realized I was growling.

"Sorry." I had no idea what this Torran looked like, but if anyone pointed me in his direction, everyone was going to find out what he looked like without skin.

Luke's lips twitched. "Don't be. You have a cute growl."

"Cute?" I stood, pretending to be offended. "I'm fierce and fearsome."

"You're five feet tall and wearing an undershirt," he replied. "But Glen was right. You do smell a bit fearsome."

He ducked away from me as I lunged. "Go play with Glen then." Sticking my nose up in the air, I stomped to the bathroom. "Couple of princesses with sensitive noses." I tried to act offended, but it was hard when I could smell myself.

I took the world's longest shower, crying just a little as Del's soap brought back memories of the painful past. And to my surprise, I ended up smiling as I thought of the two worthy males who were waiting outside the door for me, and the future we might have. I just needed all my males together, and safe.

And my damned steak knife back.

# 32

## SCARS AND SECOND CHANCES
### FLOR

"I'm worried about Grigor," I admitted later that afternoon. We could still hear the sounds of a hunt outside, and I'd been trying not to let myself think that it was my mysterious suitor who was at the front of what sounded like a pack of wild wolves. More than once, a wolf had come close to the house, one even snuffling at the front door before it gave up and wandered away.

We'd decided not to use the stove, of course, since the smell of food would definitely be noticeable in a pack that was this starved, magic spell or not. Del's house wasn't in the nicer parts of the compound, and nobody out here had ever had much food.

The Pack House was in the center of the fenced compound, more or less, with dorms and barracks on two sides, and houses and double-wide trailers in sloppily concentric half-circles for a mile or so. Del's house was just about close enough to the fence line to make getting us all out possible, but not before it got dark, and not without Grigor's magic.

That's what had me worried. Even though he'd said he

was feeling better before he left, Luke and Glen both seemed a little fatigued, and I wasn't certain why. Was Grigor still weaker than usual? It could have been the magic he was using now that was draining all three of them somewhat.

Luke and Glen had spent the first hour after Grigor left hunting for even more cans, but hadn't found anything else. So we wouldn't have long before hunger would drive us out. At least we had water, and knives to sharpen. So when the sun went down, we would make a run for it.

I had Del's whetstone and the last few paring knives from the kitchen, and was spending my time at the kitchen table, making them sharper than they'd been brand new.

Luke and Glen were playing cards on the sofa—with a towel covering the desecrated fabric, thank goodness—and conversing in quiet voices. I could hear every word they said, of course, and I was learning more than I'd counted on, about Luke, mostly.

"I didn't expect to see you again," Luke murmured. "I still can't believe you came for me."

"Of course we did. You're her mate. Or you will be, once you two figure your shit out."

"When did you two...? Was it a life-saving thing?"

Glen laughed. "You heard about Brand, huh? Poor bastard, it about killed him to have his claim be a medical emergency. Then Finn, in the family parlor at Northern, right before he had to go back to Eastern—"

"No way. She's really bonded to Finnick as well? How the hell did he pull that off?"

"*She* did it, man. Or her wolf did. Bradley had Alpha-commanded him to tell him everything about what had happened with the Russians who abducted her—"

"What the fuck are you talking about?"

I'd finished two knives by the time Glen got to the end of that story.

"Holy shit," Luke muttered. "I thought she'd be safe once she got away from here."

"Yeah, not so much. Trouble seems to follow our girl wherever she goes. Anyway, she bit Finn on—get this—his tongue."

"That's... probably good, given where he's stuck right now." There was a moment of silence before Luke went on. "Okay, so I can see where she claimed you. And Brand? He's wearing her mark, too?"

"Yeah, that's the... Oh right. I forgot about your pack's, ah, tradition. I can't imagine claiming my mate, and not having her return it, you know? It would feel like nothing would be complete. I'd wear ten of her bites if I could."

Outside, a shadow crossed the sun, and the only sound was cards flipping for a long moment. Then Luke murmured, "We all knew it was wrong. The shifters who were older than Callaway always claimed one another. I think that's one of the reasons that he started up the 'tradition' of males not allowing females to return the mating claims. It made what he did seem less..."

"Evil? Twisted?"

"Profane," Luke supplied. "He twisted everything the moon intended. And when anyone spoke out, he punished them. Killed them more often than not, or had Van Blackside do it for him. It's why our pack was so small, and so weak. He made us weak."

"You could make Southern strong," Glen said gently. "If you stay here—"

"Like you stayed with your pack?" A soft laugh filled the room. "If she'll have me, I'd leave everything and not look back once. I'll do exactly what you did—become a rogue, abjure my pack, and follow her anywhere. I'd follow her into Hell, Glen. Just like you would."

"You might have to do something harder, Luke. You might have to stay here, and take the Alpha position."

"I don't want it. What the hell would I stay for?" It was exactly what I'd said to Glen when I'd left here months ago.

"To fuck up their plans. Finn's parents were trying to kill you, or get you to die. They're planning something big. Samuel told me he suspects they've been setting this up for years. Setting all the pieces in place, funding the Russians who took Flor, maybe. Giving information and even weapons to Callaway and Blackside—the ones Joaquin found during the battle. Samuel said there have been far too many coincidences for it not to be a plan."

Luke muttered the word that was on my own lips. "Fuck."

"Exactly."

I set down the knife, trying to remember what calm felt like. The only place I'd ever felt that was Brand's lake. I closed my eyes and pictured it.

It was working until Glen said, "Speaking of fucking, when are you gonna give up the old V card?" I heard the sound of someone punching someone else, and when Glen wheezed, I grinned.

"This... This isn't the time," Luke sputtered. "There are enemies all around, and—"

"Come on, Luke, we're not in a sewer now. You know there's never going to be a good time. Go do the bitey mambo with our girl, and level up. It'll make you stronger. Her, too. I bet it helps her wolf come out."

I stood and put the paring knives and whetstone away, considering Glen's words as I sat back down at the table. He might be right; I wasn't certain why my wolf hadn't emerged, not even during the full moons since I was forced to shift for the first time, but she felt close.

I didn't really need a reason or an excuse to bond with Luke. I'd known he was my mate—or one of them—for a while now. And I'd been in love with him since I was a girl. It was just hard to get past the knowledge that he'd lived all those years knowing I was his mate, but not stopping the abuse the pack's Enforcers and the Alpha had heaped on me.

If anyone tried to hurt one of my mates, I would stop at nothing to make sure they couldn't make a second attempt. He said he'd protected me, but it was hard to see when, or how exactly. Even if he'd been forbidden to shift, or to stop the beatings I took... I sighed and sat back down, wondering if I could forgive him. I knew I'd need to before we went any further.

"Has she seen you without your shirt?" Glen asked. I thought he was teasing Luke about being shy, until he added, "Has she seen the scars?"

"Of course not." Luke whispered the answer, as my mind spun, trying to remember if I'd ever seen him with his shirt off. I'd seen his abs, for sure. I'd stabbed him in them. I'd seen him shirtless from a distance over the years, but I'd never had the chance to get an up-close look.

Come to think of it, Luke had almost always kept his shirt on. And he hadn't been allowed to shift for so long, meaning he'd never really run around without clothes at all. More than once, I'd wondered what he looked like under his clothes, and been disappointed that I never even got a glimpse of his human form right after a shift.

I'd felt his skin the night before, in the storm drain. And there had been some places on his shoulders that had felt bumpy. I'd just assumed he had mud or something stuck to him, making his skin feel uneven. Could they have been scars?

Glen was whispering, now, too. "You should let her. I don't think she really knows what you went through. That Callaway whipped you with silver, and why."

"Does it matter?"

Glen's voice was pitched loud enough for me to hear it, and I could feel in the bond that he wanted me to pay attention. He knew I was listening. "That he was going to whip her with it if you didn't stop trying to protect her? Yeah, it fucking *does.*"

Luke's answer was so quiet, I almost couldn't hear it. "I don't want her to pity me. If she claims me, I want it to be because she thinks I deserve her love. Not that I do."

"Not that any of us do, brother," Glen said. I heard cards being put down, and a second later, Glen was standing behind me. He tilted me and the whole chair back, balancing it on the back two legs, and kissed me upside down, his stubble tickling my nose until I batted him away.

"Do it right, you goofball," I grumbled, and he grinned, plucking me out of the chair entirely and setting me down on the table. I still only had on the t-shirt and a pair of boxers, and the laminate top was cold on my butt. "What are you doing?"

When Glen sat down on the chair where I'd just been, and wrapped his hands around my thighs like he was about to dig into his favorite meal, I had my answer. "I'm doing *you*. Right. Like you asked." He set his face over the seam of the boxers and growled, sending vibrations to my core.

"Oh yuck, not on the table," I groaned, trying to wriggle away and failing.

Glen wiggled his eyebrows and leered from between my

legs. "We're leaving tonight. Why not go out with a bang? One last perfect meal?"

I almost laughed. Glen's bright spirit in our bond was like sunshine in the darkness. Once we left here, we'd be in the cavern with Sergeant and the others, and I sure as heck wasn't going to be doing anything with my mother and great-uncle listening in. I half-wanted to let Glen have his kinky way with me right there. But over his shaggy blond head, I could see Luke, standing beside the sofa, his arms folded, and his eyes filled with longing.

"I think you're right," I said, leaning over and pressing a gentle kiss to Glen's mouth, then his cheek. I whispered in his ear, hoping he understood, "But you'll have to wait your turn."

The surge of joy in the bond made it clear Glen not only understood, but that this was exactly what he wanted. A split second later, a distant echo of that happiness trickled through the bond with Brand. And then, as if a wire were sparking, then dying down, Finnick's connection with me flared to life before it was choked off again.

Glen kissed me more deeply before he let me go. "As you wish."

# 33

## A PERFECT MOMENT

### LUKE

I'd always thought Flor was the most graceful shifter I'd ever known. But her strength and self-assurance practically radiated from her now as she approached me. She stopped a few inches away, her amber eyes almost glowing. I would have believed the almost-cool expression she wore, if her cheeks hadn't flushed before she spoke.

"Luke," she began, then swallowed.

"Flor." I tried to say her name with all the love I felt, but my voice trembled. "Little fighter."

She lifted a hand to my face, then let it drop down to my heart, where she pressed it slightly, her smile widening. "Your heart is racing." I nodded dumbly. "So is mine." Taking my hand, she placed it on her own chest. Through the thin t-shirt, her nipple beaded up under my palm, and I felt my cock go stiffer than it ever had. "Come on."

We moved together to the small bedroom, and I smiled when Flor shucked off the boxers, then lifted her arms and waited. I grabbed the edges of the oversized shirt and pulled it off, then dropped to my knees. "You're exquisite," I rasped. "All my dreams, come true."

I kissed her stomach, my hands spanning her narrow waist, then tasted her warm skin, drawing letters with my tongue. Spelling out passages from the love letters I'd written years ago. She wove her fingers in my hair and moaned softly when I reached the final words, right over her red curls. I pressed my face into her, breathing in the heated cinnamon and jasmine scent of her, surprised when she pushed me away.

"Your turn, Luke," she insisted.

I knew what she meant, and I stood again, dropping the borrowed shirt and trousers to the floor. I leaned over, slowly, and picked up both pieces of clothing, then carried them to the dresser, knowing what she saw. "I always thought I would wait until dark, in my dreams. So you didn't see... me."

"So many." She breathed the words.

There were a lot, crisscrossing my back. The ones higher up weren't as noticeable. The worst marks were at the base of my spine and over my buttocks, where Callaway had whipped me with silver. The scars burned under Flor's gaze.

I took my time folding the shirt, giving her a chance to leave. When I heard her move across the room, and the door click shut, I let out a shuddering breath, my eyes closed. I didn't blame her. My scars weren't a beautiful star like hers, or marks of valor, like other shifters sometimes wore. They were proof of my weakness. I hadn't ever wanted her to see them. And I suppose she hadn't wanted to, either. I bit my lip so hard I tasted blood, knowing I needed to keep the pain inside.

"No." Flor's voice was quiet behind me, and I startled as I felt her hand move over the rough skin on my back. "Whatever you were thinking, you're wrong."

My breath caught. "You didn't leave."

"I already left you once, Luke. I about got myself killed getting back to you. From now on, let's stay together." Her hands moved around me to my front, locking together as if she was planning never to let go. That was exactly what I wanted, too.

Her lips pressed against all the scars she could reach on my back, and then she pulled me over to the bed, climbing to stand on the mattress before she turned me around, and finished kissing the ones on my shoulders. She laughed when she got to the topmost one, at my nape. "Sometimes I hate being so short."

"Good thing you have plenty of mates to help reach things on top shelves, then."

She growled, hooked a leg around me, and in less than two seconds, had me flat on my back on the mattress, while she sat on top of my chest. Her move had been so fluid that I couldn't quite figure out what she'd done to get me there.

"How—" I managed, before she slid down and pressed the tip of my swollen cock to her entrance. Somehow, she was already drenched. When she descended a little, I made a guttural noise. "Flor... let me... first..."

She put two fingers in her mouth and swirled them around, then placed them exactly where she wanted them, drawing what felt like figure eights over her clit. "Shush, hot stuff. I'm making a whole stack of fantasies come true."

"What?"

Her eyes twinkled as she moved her hips, taking just the first two inches of me inside her as she touched herself. "I dreamed about this when I lived in the dorms. I'd lie in my cot late at night, wondering what it would feel like to have you underneath me, inside me. Looking up at me."

It was the most erotic, honest, emotionally charged

moment of my life. I tried to let her see how intense and perfect she felt, wanted to tell her so, but I was afraid I might come too soon and spoil the moment, so I stared up at her and hoped she could see it.

Her eyes gleamed gold, and I knew I was seeing her wolf. My own battered, hungry wolf rose to greet her. Howled in ecstasy at being so close to our mate.

"Mate," I murmured. "My mate."

Deep in her gaze, twin moons shone as she replied, "Yes."

As she moved, it felt like we were waking from a dream that had begun a long, long time ago. Like the spirals of bliss that caught us were carrying us into some bright, new morning.

There was a roaring in my ears as she began to climax and rode me faster, leaning over me, her face by my ear.

Her breath in my hair.

Her teeth in my neck.

"Mine," she growled, claiming me.

I twisted to one side, and my teeth found her shoulder, sinking deep, as I snarled out my own release. *"Mine."*

Our souls became one, twisting and binding. Her wolf fought to surface, and my own nudged her, showing her the way. Our hearts began to beat at the same rate, and I felt her. Her passion, her strength. The love she'd hidden from me, and even herself, for years when she was young. Her forgiveness.

It was a perfect moment, until it wasn't.

Grigor's voice roared through our joined consciousness. The joy turned to panic, and the pleasure became pain. *Get her out. Now. GET HER OUT!*

# 34

## A TERRIBLE ERROR
### GRIGOR

Harsh sunlight shone all around the culvert where I'd been forced to squat for hours now, holding the look-away spell over the hovel where my little queen's true father had lived. It was more difficult for me to do any work of magic without shadows and moonlight to draw from, though I hadn't admitted that to my future mate. She'd been concerned enough, hearing my confessions earlier, and after she had given me the chance to touch her, taste her, I'd felt like I could do anything.

I should have known this task would be far more difficult than I had anticipated. Not only was my magic still diminished from the days spent lying under Luke's sickbed, funneling my power directly into him to keep him alive, my physical body was exhausted.

I hadn't slept since Luke's machines had been unplugged. I needed rest, though I couldn't afford to slip into unconsciousness now.

I also needed food, though there was almost none to be

had here. I'd left what little had been found in the house for the others, hoping to snare an unsuspecting squirrel or rabbit while I guarded from outside, but the whole compound was buzzing with shifters searching for the missing females. Not even a songbird flew overhead, with this many agitated predators making so much noise, though a black vulture circled lazily above.

I exhaled slowly, my stomach burning, my hands shaking with fatigue. Only the memory of my queen's face when she was transformed with bliss would—

"Torran, I found this at the base of a pine close to the fence line." An Enforcer jogged down the closest street, and I saw the Eastern Alpha stand-in approaching from the direction of the back gate that led to the hunting grounds. I marveled again at what effective camouflage he had.

Torran was the most nondescript powerful shifter I'd seen in a long time. He had short brown hair, with flat, dark eyes, and was not quite six feet tall, short for an Enforcer. Most curiously, he didn't hold himself like a powerful being. His shoulders were hunched slightly, his head swinging from side to side as if he were looking for something, and his hands held no weapons, though I knew he had at least one silver blade on his person at all times. When the wind blew the right direction, you could smell it on him, though it was faint.

Today, he wore his usual black clothing, though his hairline was damp with perspiration. The Enforcer who ran up to him stopped in the center of the dusty road. "It smells odd, sir. Like—"

Torran already had the backpack in his hand, unzipped. "Like cinnamon," he said softly, rifling through the contents before pulling out a steak knife.

Her steak knife.

I bristled as he lifted it to his nose and sniffed delicately, as if he were tasting a wine. "And jasmine. What a lovely... bouquet." Before I could do something foolish, he dropped it in the pack and handed it back to the Enforcer. "Thank you for bringing this to my attention. Where is your second?"

"My younger brother. He was... the one killed last night." The Enforcer's jaw worked as he swallowed convulsively.

Torran didn't blink. "Ah, yes. We'll need to reassign someone to you. Reinforcements are coming from Eastern. Keep this for me. I'm on my way to the Pack House. Bring this there when you're done checking the houses on this row."

"Yes, sir," the young man said with a salute. He slung the backpack over his shoulder and jogged to the door of the next house, knocking three times. When no one answered, he kicked the door in, shouting, "Inspection!"

It had been too long since I'd given my little queen a courting gift, I decided. And she'd admitted a strange attachment to her ear tag, so I didn't think the wind chime I'd planned to make of Torran's corpse and the unranked shifters' tags would be as well-received as I'd hoped.

But she loved that knife. It was the first weapon she'd ever used to kill a man, and I knew how special those could be. I would get it back for her.

I waited for Torran to move out of sight, then spun a thread of magic around myself and slid along the ditch, before following the Enforcer inside. I was prepared to kill him to take the backpack, but he'd dropped it just inside the door of the empty house. Grabbing it, I slid back out in seconds, before he knew I'd been there. I took a moment to carry the backpack to the back door of Del's house, ready to open the door and take the knife inside.

But when I got close enough, even though I'd shut down the connections as much as I could, in order to keep my focus and not draw energy from my new brothers... I couldn't help but feel the shivering sensation of Luke and my queen kissing.

For a moment, a deep need to rend the one who would touch her into pieces threatened to consume me. I dropped the backpack at the door, feeling the beast who shared my body roaring to be let free.

She was mine. *Mine!* I'd waited for so long, and it wasn't right that I be the last one to join with her. This one, in particular, was the least worthy of her mates, the one who had failed her day after day...

No. *No.* I knew better now.

Slowly, I backed away from the door as the sound of a lustful groan reached my ears. This had to happen. If they mated, when they did, it would be one step closer to her being stronger, her wolf emerging, and our group becoming what it was meant to be.

I could wait. But not this close, I knew. I reached into myself and pulled far more magic away from my center than was safe, wrapping it around the small house to dampen the sounds for those inside, and out. Sealing the doors and windows shut to intruders.

It would have to do. I slid back next door, quickly broke the neck of the Enforcer who was coming out, and dragged him back inside.

A moment later, I stepped out wearing his uniform and jogged toward the Pack House. Reinforcements, Torran had said. I'd need a closer look at any new additions to the Southern packlands.

The Pack House was a frenzy of activity, and I was able to enter by the side door closest to Luke's sickroom, carrying a basket of laundry. I kept my head down, but my senses alert.

There was something strange in the air, like a storm racing in. I heard others I passed whispering about "her," their voices filled with awe.

Or terror.

It had to be the one Torran had spoken to on the phone. His mistress. I turned the corner just as the front door of the Pack House opened, and a tall woman with reddish-gray hair stepped inside. Torran was beside her, practically trembling with lust. She ignored him, and set her hand on the doorframe.

"Someone is inside," she said. The cold power that filled those simple words had me stepping backward, slowly, trying not to draw attention to my movements.

But every other shifter in the entire house had gone still. Frozen by her power. I had made a terrible error, allowing myself to be this close to one like her, while I was so weak.

I had to get out, *now*. Had to get my little queen out, and her other mates. Had to—

Too late. The woman pressed her hand into the door-frame, the wood giving under the pressure of her hand, and spoke three more words—in a blood-soaked, ancient language that told me exactly what she was.

A shield of power fell over the Pack House, trapping everyone inside.

Her voice was soft, almost gentle, as she spoke again. "An unexpected visitor. How fortuitous." Then she turned, the gleam in her eyes razor-tipped and cruel, and I knew not only what she was, but who.

I used more power than I should to send a plea down the braided bond to Luke and Glen, begging them to listen, but she was always my priority. Even now.

*Get her out. Now. GET HER OUT!*

# 35

## BAD ODDS

### FLOR

In one breath, Luke's soul was humming, that silent music that had always started up when he touched me, but inside my innermost being.

In the next, the waves of passion turned to fear. "Grigor," I gasped.

Luke was frozen above me, a smear of my blood still on his lower lip. "Someone's hurting him," he snarled, throwing himself off me and grabbing his clothing from the dresser. "At least I think so. He's shut down the link between us."

Glen opened the door, his face nearly white. "Not to me," he said, gritting his teeth. Blood trickled from his nose. "I can't—" He fell into my arms, and I staggered under his weight until Luke was there, rolling him onto the bed.

My Northern mate was shivering, almost like he was having a seizure. "Can I give him some of my strength?" I wondered aloud. I knew it was possible.

Luke and Glen both snapped, "No!" at the same moment.

Glen's eyes were bloodshot, but he stopped shaking

long enough to glare at me. "I've got this. Just need a minute. You get dressed. Find... weapons."

"Hold on, brother. Hold on," Luke muttered as he finished dressing. I wasn't sure who he was talking to, Glen or Grigor.

I grabbed clean clothing from the drawer, knotting one of Del's shirts at my waist, and pulling up two pairs of his boxers, tight-fitting ones this time. Luke was ahead of me in the kitchen, grabbing the knives. There were only three, not much bigger than paring knives, but at least they were all sharp.

Luke made me take one, keeping the other two for him and Glen. I tried to think, to plan. Three small knives weren't enough to go charging into danger with. He had better weapons. "Maybe you should shift, and fight as a wolf?"

"There's no time," Luke admitted. "I'm slow. Not much practice."

"Got it." I thought about taking the broom from the closet, but it would be too noticeable, and would slow me down if I needed to run.

Glen appeared in the doorway again, holding onto both sides of the doorframe, like he couldn't stay upright without help. He'd wiped the blood away, though, and looked less pale.

"Is Grigor doing better?"

"I don't know. He found some way to cut me off."

Luke growled, "So that's a no. For a mass murderer, he sure likes to play the martyr."

Silently, I agreed. "Glen, can you shift? We're short on blades."

He was shaking his head before I finished speaking. "I'm not sure I can spare the energy." He grunted like he'd been punched in the gut, and we all swiveled in the direction of the Pack House. "Feel that?"

"Yeah," I replied once I could breathe again. Grigor was taking some hits, and even though it seemed like Glen was getting the worst of it, we could all feel him in the weird-ass bonds he'd made with the guys. "Silver lining, at least now we know where he is."

"What's the plan?" Glen asked, staring hazily in our direction.

I looked at Luke, who was also staring. At me.

"Wait, y'all are the hotshot Alpha Heirs. Why're you looking at me?"

Glen scoffed. "You're the one who kept safe for years in this compound. You're the one who saved us all the last time we were this fucked."

"We weren't *this* fucked. We had Enforcers then," I argued. "Or you did. The Mountain troops—"

I felt my first mate then, in our bond. Brand was already waiting there, a bright pulse of power. Reassurance. "Glen, let Brand in." When he blinked in confusion, I waved at his chest, and mine. "I think he's sending some Mountain mojo our way."

I wished he could come in person. I missed him, and I had a bad feeling about how this day was going to end. The three of us against the Council Enforcers and the remains of the Southern pack? Those were shitty odds. Of course, I'd never had any other kind.

My mind started spinning. Planning. In a few seconds, I had a rough plan for finding Grigor and getting us all out. It was gonna be ugly, even if it worked.

It would have to do.

"How—" Glen had been propped up against a wall, but

he let out a low whistle, standing on his own. "Brand. He just... How'd he do that?"

"I mean, magic is the short answer," I half-joked, motioning for them both to follow me to the back door. None of us had shoes on. That was good. If the guys needed to shift, they could. I'd lived most of my life without shoes, and could run, climb, and fight better without them anyway.

"Here's what we do. We can't stick too close together; we'll be too noticeable. It's not full daylight, but not dark enough to use shadows to hide. I'll go first, and head for the back door of the kitchens. No, the dumpsters off to the side. The smell will cover ours. If Grigor's been caught some-how"—I hesitated, as we all wondered who could have got the best of the boogeyman—"then I'll need to cause a distraction, while you two get him free."

"Why you?" Luke's eyes blazed.

"Because I run the fastest, and I know where to hide." He nodded curtly, opening the door. "I just wish I had a better knife—" I looked down to see the backpack Glen had ditched the night before. "My knife!" I grabbed it out of the backpack and sniffed the blade. It smelled of ozone and darkness.

Grigor. Now *this* was a solid courting gift. After I rescued him, I'd have to figure out a way to thank him properly.

I passed Glen the paring knife Luke had given me. "Okay, I'll go first, then you, then Luke. We'll circle around a bit and approach the Pack House from the west. The sun'll be in the eyes of anyone looking that way, and we'll be downwind. Stay quiet."

I went up on my tiptoes to Glen, who leaned over, giving me a quick, soft kiss. Then Luke did the same. I scowled at them both. I hadn't even wanted mates, mostly because I hadn't wanted to be hurt. But now I realized I should've been more afraid of this. That they might be injured, and I would care so damned much.

"Don't get hurt. You're all my mates now."

All except Grigor.

WE GOT LUCKY, staying clear of the Council forces. A few of the Southern males were running in small groups, and I would have sworn some of them saw us. One even pointed to Luke, but then they ran off.

I wasn't sure if that was good or bad. I guessed we'd find out.

When we got close to the eastern edge of the training ring—the only exposed area we'd need to cross to get to the dumpsters—I slowed down. It felt too easy.

There was a lot of yelling and the sounds of engines at the front of the Pack House, though, like something had their attention. Maybe my luck had changed.

I waited a minute as Luke and Glen caught up, stopping behind separate trees only a few dozen feet away. *Me first,* Luke mouthed in my direction. I shook my head. This was the most dangerous part of this run, and even if he was much stronger than he'd been, he was still recovering.

Not waiting for him to silently argue, I darted out into the open, hoping to skirt the edge of the dusty, flat space, and duck behind the edge of the main building. But a wolf appeared out of nowhere, running on my left about thirty yards away, and I was forced to change my course.

*Shit.* Another wolf joined him, and then another. From the way they were coming together, as a hunting pack, they'd been following me for a while. I ran faster, but was forced to zigzag, and then, when four more wolves stepped out from behind the dumpster, I turned and ran to the center of the ring.

A man stood there, waiting. Where the fuck had he come from? My mouth went dry as I felt his gaze rake me— an odd, clinical look, like he wanted to take me apart, piece by piece, tendon by tendon, and see what made me tick. He wore all black, and was medium build with brown hair. In one hand, he held a small silver blade. I could smell it from here.

"You," he called, lifting a hand. The wolves formed a circle around me, ten of them altogether.

At first, anyway. Before I could take a breath to answer, ten more shifters, dressed in black—Enforcers, judging by their size and demeanor—had formed a circle behind them. My brain buzzed with panic, but I gripped my steak knife firmly in my hand, and tried to do what Del had taught me.

I scanned the area. There were no trees to climb. No storm drains or sewers to escape into. Nowhere to hide. I couldn't run. I definitely couldn't fight this many shifters.

*Time to talk shit.* I grinned cockily. "Yeah, me, asshole. You know how hard it's been trying to get you alone... Torran?"

It was a lucky guess, though Del would have smacked me upside the head for even thinking that. He didn't believe in luck. *"Observation, preparation, and premeditation, girlie. Don't ever think that luck will save you. Only training will."*

He hadn't been wrong. I wasn't certain I'd trained hard enough for this showdown. I was surrounded, and the way the other wolves and shifters kept glancing at the man, then at me, waiting for his signal, made it pretty obvious who was the head honcho. It had to be Torran.

The only thing that confused me was, if this guy was the big baddie, where was Grigor? There wasn't anyone else at Southern with more power than Torran, or so I'd been told repeatedly. Even if he looked like a slightly undernourished, shorter-than-usual plain shifter, I could sense a swirl of dominance around him that was a thousand times scarier when paired with the absolutely batshit crazy gleam in his eyes as he looked me over.

I couldn't sense or hear Grigor in my head, even when I called out now. Had the Council Enforcers all ganged up on him somehow, or taken him by surprise with some sort of silver trap?

The small silver knife flashed as Torran began cleaning under his nails with it. It had to hurt like fire, but he didn't flinch, just tilted his head and made a weird little humming sound. "So you're the one we've heard so much about. Why would you be trying to find me, Florida?"

I had very fucking little to say that would impress this guy. I was closed in by dozens of enemy shifters. It was time to play my only card. "I mean, I kinda wanted to meet the fucker who's been killing off my shifters. If you don't get a grip, psycho, there won't be anyone left for me to lead."

The training ring was silent. "Your shifters? Lead? What could you mean by that? I am the interim Alpha, little girl. You are... well, not no one. But no one significant."

"Sticks and stones, crazypants." I shrugged. "I meant this pack is mine. I'm the most dominant shifter, and you're about to find that out. I challenge you, Torran of Eastern, for leadership of Southern." I raised my steak knife. "Fight me."

I'd only half expected him to agree to fight me. I knew

what I looked like: skinny, armed with a steak knife, and looking like five foot nothing of Southern trash. But I hadn't expected him to put his knife into a small case, drop it in his pocket, and walk away without a single word.

Well, to me at least. I heard him give an order before he passed through the first ring of wolves. "Don't kill her. I want to play, and our Alpha Mate would like to meet her. Bring her to the cell."

The wolves circled closer, and I knew I was in for a world of hurt. Good thing I'd learned how to take a beating and get back up every time. But I needed some advantage. A weapon these wolves wouldn't be ready for.

I dropped to the ground, grabbing a handful of dust, and using my other arm to cover my eyes as I burst into crocodile tears. "Please... don't hurt me. Please. I didn't mean to..." I had to dance around telling an actual lie, since they'd smell that. But I managed to make it sound like I was planning to come quietly. In fact, by the time I'd blubbered a bit more, half of the wolves had turned their backs. Only the main one, a big gray wolf that reminded me of Glen's, came within striking distance.

So he was the first to die.

I shocked myself with the speed I moved. I jumped up from my crouched position just as the wolf was rising over me, and flung my handful of dust into his eyes. It wasn't as effective as powdered cinnamon and ghost peppers, but it did the trick long enough. He wobbled mid-air, and I leaped upward, grabbing his neck. Pulling him down and to the side, I drew the steak knife in a long, bloody arc through his fur, and across his neck.

Blood sprayed me, but I was already gone, moving to the next wolf, who was staring at his fallen companion in shock. That only lasted a heartbeat.

Then the battle really began. In seconds, I was caught in the middle of a ball of raging wolves, my steak knife no match for the sheer number of claws and teeth that tore at my skin. Pain bloomed all over, but it wasn't nearly as bad as when I'd been whipped as a girl. My wolf simmered under the surface, longing to sink her teeth into these beasts. But she was still trapped inside.

The attacks became more vicious, the teeth biting deeper, tearing jagged swaths of my skin. But somehow, I was healing almost as fast as they bit into me.

I heard shouts, and knew Luke and Glen were fighting the shifters in human form, trying to get to me. I stabbed and spun, doing impossible somersaults over the heads of the wolves, never losing my balance, landing perfectly in position to stab and weave. My knife sliced through fur, muscle, and tendons, leaving wolves unable to stand and fight. All I had to do was think of a move, and it happened. I was a good fighter, sure, but this was... something else.

Was it Brand, or Grigor, feeding me power? Or was this what had happened when I fought Van Blackside, all those months ago, and I was just aware of myself now? I didn't have time to figure it out, and I didn't care. It was working.

But the wolves kept coming. There had to be more than thirty of them already, and I could hear the guys fighting just as hard. For a second, the leading wolves fell back, a few whimpering, stumbling over the dead bodies I'd left behind, and the healing ones, who were still out for this fight anyway.

There was no way I could take them all on. Even with my new speed and my healing, I couldn't fight this many.

I glanced over the wall of fur to see Glen and Luke, back-to-back. Glen was in a half-shifted form, like I'd seen Brand once, back at Northern. He stood on two half-transformed wolf legs, his clothing almost gone. His arms were furred, and his clawed hands soaked with blood. His hair was a mane of fur, standing out like a gold and gray halo around a face that was bloody and bore a long snout. Luke was still human, and held both paring knives, spinning them faster than my eyes could track.

Not that I should have let myself be distracted. The wolves around me were regrouping, working as a pack. Two of them moved in front of me, harassing me with concerted, consistent attacks. The rest massed behind me, and I knew they were about to fall on me like a tidal wave of pain.

Was this it? Was this where I died?

I kept fighting, trying to work my way closer to Luke and Glen, whirling with the steak knife, wishing I had brought the broom handle now. It was far more effective for this kind of fight.

One of the wolves leaped for me, and I rolled underneath him and had my exit from the circle. I raced to fight with the guys, taking one human-shaped shifter off guard as I vaulted over him, doing a somersault before I landed next to Luke.

That somersault was a mistake. Sure, it had caught most of the enemy by surprise. But the enemy had surprises, too. Suddenly, they all fell back, leaving the three of us standing next to one another, panting, the shifters massing on the side opposite the Pack House. Were they leaving us a way to retreat?

Absolute panic flew through our bonds as Glen suddenly whispered, "Fuck. Get down!"

Then there was a loud shout, a word that made no sense. "Fire!"

In that instant, I felt a blaze of fire move through my gut, entering from the front and exiting at my spine. My legs went numb almost instantly. Pain sheared from the place, and I looked down, confused. My shirt was already too blood-soaked to see what had happened.

"Not her!" someone yelled.

And then another voice. "Fire!"

Luke screamed and began to shudder next to me, like he was having a seizure. Glen was doing the same thing, but he managed to fling himself toward me, crushing me to the earth underneath him. At the last second, I managed to angle my steak knife so it wouldn't go through his stomach.

I couldn't breathe. I couldn't move. And as Glen continued to shudder on top of me, I knew what was happening, though I could hardly believe it.

Del had taught me about all sorts of weapons, but there was one I'd never touched. I'd never even seen one, except on television or in pictures. It was considered the least honorable weapon a shifter could use, and even if he owned one, not even Callaway had broken that taboo and used it.

But these shifters had done the unthinkable. They'd brought guns into the compound. Into the fight.

Into my pack.

# 36

## HALF A PACK
### BRAND

"Look at your pack," Dad murmured at my side, as the line of shifters who had formed that morning dispersed without a word.

Well, not from me. They'd had a word from Grandma, an important one: dinner. The scent of her brisket and cornbread, along with the appearance of a dozen of the pack's best cooks bringing out the food, and what looked like an endless number of homemade pies, had everyone ready to stop for the day. Or the hour, at least. They would form the line again after we'd eaten, and continue until midnight.

They were as anxious and excited as I was to have the pack whole once more, though I knew hundreds more were still traveling here. It would take a long while.

"It's only half the pack," I replied, rubbing my chest. "Three thousand and forty-seven down, three thousand and twelve to go?" I glanced at him for confirmation.

I'd had an official phone call from the Council days ago, congratulating me on my ascension. Aidan McDonnell had been extremely curious as to how my father was still alive, a fact he shouldn't have known. I'd known his pack was watching us, but hearing him refer to having eyes inside my borders—even if they were merely electronic ones—made my wolf howl for his blood.

He'd insisted on my immediate presence at the Mansion in the next few days to accept my pledge to join the Council, then to attend a Council vote on his installation as permanent Head, knowing it wouldn't be possible. He'd insinuated that perhaps I would do as my father had, and adopt a hands-off approach to Council matters. I'd made sure he knew that would not be the case, but left his invitation hanging. I had to consolidate power before I confronted him.

Dad shrugged and settled back in the wide Adirondack-style chair, made of logs and cushioned with Grandma's quilts. "Wouldn't know. Sounds right, unless someone's died, or been born. It's odd not to feel the connections."

I grunted in agreement. "It's even more odd to suddenly have them, like moths fluttering in the back of my thoughts." It was distracting, but that feeling had been all that kept me from throwing myself in a truck and driving to Alabama to be with Flor. That and the knowledge that it was only once I'd finished this process that I would have the full power of the Mountain pack behind me. And the right to take them to war.

"Moths, huh?" Dad grunted a thank you to the young shifter who'd handed him a plate piled high with food, as well as a cloth napkin wrapped around some cutlery. Another young shifter ran over with a large ceramic mug of cold water. Dad nodded his thanks, then turned back to me. "They felt like caterpillars inside my brain, not moths. Don't worry. Once they've all pledged, that'll go away."

I scowled at the image of brain caterpillars. My brain

was already so full of extra input, from the currents of energy that flowed between me and Flor, and the lesser ties to Finn, Glen, and now Luke.

The young male bringing my food had stumbled twice on his way to me, and now stared red-faced at my feet as he offered now half-filled plate, promising to bring me more. I took the plate and dismissed him with a gentle nod. But instead of eating, I pondered the sensations and thoughts that had tumbled through my mind over the past two days.

After the first few hours on the road, Flor had slept, and I'd had a short respite from her thoughts. That hadn't worried me, since I could still sense that she was safe. Glen would keep her that way, I knew. But when she woke up and her thoughts—which had been so clear to me while she was inside my pack's borders—grew fuzzy and faint as they kept going, my wolf began to pace. It had only been two days, but something in my soul was urging me to drop everything and run to her side.

Except dropping everything might hurt all of us more in the long run. I needed an army. I needed the full power of the Mountain pack tied to my own soul, so I could protect her and all of the honorable shifters who were vulnerable to the Council's machinations. So I stayed.

But something was now telling me that I needed to leave, *fast*.

The moon chose that moment to rise over the horizon, a deep red hue tinging it. Like blood. A howl began, from within my soul. I stood abruptly. "I have to go."

"Son?"

I didn't answer. I couldn't. It was all I could do not to shift. "She's in danger. They all are." I whirled on my heel and grabbed Dad's arms when I almost fell over.

I wasn't certain what Dad saw in my face, but his own

was glowing from the light that must be shining from my eyes. "A plane," he said. "You'll have to fly."

"You have a plane?"

"No, you do," he told me, shouting as we ran to the house. "Dean! Get your plane ready. Now!"

It took an hour to get everything we needed packed. The plane only seated four, and we'd have to stop every eight hundred miles or so to refuel.

"I don't like you going on your own," Dad muttered as I packed a quick bag with weapons. Grandma already had a hamper of food ready and in the plane, and Grandmother had come in a moment before and hugged me goodbye, an unusually affectionate gesture.

"Your mother would be proud," she'd said, with tears standing in her eyes. "She was the strength that made your father the Alpha he was, and is. Go and take care of that magical mate of yours. Save her, so she can save the rest of our packs."

"Magical?"

I'd hugged her back, and she'd whispered in my ear, "Magical, moonblessed. There are many words for what she is. What you are. Go quickly."

I would. The pressure to leave was growing intense, and my wolf clawed at me to run. Dad handed me a short sword. "I could go with you."

"No. I need you here. The pack will be arriving, and they need to know what's going on, why I'm not here to meet them. Put together a group of our best fighters. Brief them, get supplies and transport. I want them on their way to Southern by morning," I said as we went through the front door. We jogged side by side to the long stretch Dean had chosen for a landing strip. A few shifters were still hurriedly mowing the tall grasses there, and chasing out a few startled rabbits.

Above us in the sky, something glinted in the late afternoon sun. It was too small to be a plane.

A drone. "Eastern is watching," Dad muttered.

"From a distance, like the sneaks and cowards they are. Let them watch. We'll give them a closer view of our wolves soon enough." And with that, I was running to the plane, where Dean was waiting.

The flight was silent, and almost peaceful, though after our first refueling stop, that changed. A rough voice shouted in my head: *GET HER OUT!*

I fought to control my shift, Dean sweating next to me as he took off from the rural airstrip. "Is she okay?" he asked.

I couldn't answer. I had no idea.

Thirty minutes later, I felt a surge of need that had me shifting, my clothes tearing. "Shit!" Dean shouted as the plane rocked. "Sorry, Alpha." He kept his head tilted away, his neck exposed. I was in my half-shifted form, and the cockpit echoed with my growls.

I closed my eyes, fighting for control. She was hurt. Not only that, she was *being* hurt, again and again. Worse, Luke and Glen were being injured too fast for their shifter healing to matter. The oily power that I'd sensed connected to my flower was... absent.

Had Grigor turned against her? Against all of them? The need to kill him filled me like a flood coming down a canyon. I pushed power down the bond to Flor, more than I ever had, even when I'd reached through her to Luke in the river. It wasn't enough.

No. I would not allow this. I took a deep breath, then let it out, and instead of pushing, I pulled. I gathered the bonds of all the shifters who'd tied themselves to me, who'd given their vows.

"Alpha, I have to fly," Dean wheezed. I flicked a glance at him. His face was pinched, and his hands shaking on the controls. I focused, and stopped pulling at the strand that connected us, putting it to one side.

Then I turned my attention back to the other three thousand and forty-six souls who had promised to serve me, and I held them to their vows.

# 37

## MY HELL
### FLOR

They'd brought guns into my pack.

*My pack?*

Yes. It was mine. I didn't have time to pick apart why that thought sent a wave of acceptance through me—as if my wolf was curling around the idea of pack, of home, here of all places. I'd hated my life here. It had been hell. But it had been *my* hell. Filled with other shifters who'd been suffering right alongside me. And then, after I left, these fuckers had come in like they owned the place.

Glen went still on top of me. When I pushed at him, his limp body tumbled away, but I couldn't muster the energy to sit up. Not that I would have been able to fight. My back was healing, but I still couldn't stand.

Whatever had happened to my spine had been bad, but I could almost smell Brand's pine and wild berries over the acrid bite of what had to be gunpowder. His power still flowed into me like a cold mountain stream. The hell I saw when I was able to focus my eyes, though, made my heart stutter.

Luke stood in front of Glen and me, his back to the ones

who had been firing at us. He'd been wounded so badly that I didn't understand how he was still standing. Then I realized the guns had stopped. The fighting, all of it, had ended.

Or had it?

I heard a voice, a female one. "What have you done, Torran? Shooting the Alpha Heir of Southern?"

"I had no idea he was here, Mistress. I only knew about the girl, and the rogue."

"Hm, yes." I half-closed my eyes as the woman came nearer. She kicked my steak knife out of my hand with her shoe. A high heel, with links of silvery chain that criss-crossed her ankle and vanished under black wool trousers.

I had a ridiculous thought that Vanessa would have killed for those shoes.

I couldn't get away. I couldn't protect myself. Best I could do was play possum.

So I held still, trying not to react when she picked up the steak knife and stabbed it through my stomach. It hurt like fuck, though.

I held my breath as she leaned close, humming. Sniffing. She smelled like magic. I knew all I smelled like was blood... though I was afraid she'd nicked an intestine, from the added odor.

"This one won't make it. I'm vexed, Torran. The Heir told me she had magic. You knew I was hoping... Well, in any case. Take the Heir, clean him up, and put him in my vehicle. Alive. Not injured any further, do you understand? I need him."

Her accent was weird, I decided, trying to focus on anything other than the pain I was in. Like the time I'd watched *Pride and Prejudice* with Glen at Northern, and we'd tried talking in those voices the next day. I'd still sounded Southern underneath. She sounded that way, too.

Luke's eyes were still on me. I could tell he didn't want to go, but he didn't have the strength to fight. None of us did. In seconds, he was hustled away by two burly shifters, struggling weakly before he collapsed into their hold. In no time at all, he was out of my line of sight.

"And the Russian?" Torran's tone was uncertain.

"He's been contained. I'll take him to the lower levels myself when I get home." I felt her prodding at Glen with her foot as well. "Won't this be sad news to give to the Hilliers when I do. Maybe I won't tell them yet."

"You can't stay—"

She cut him off, already walking away. "After I go, make sure these two are dead, won't you? You know what to do."

Torran snapped out an order for someone to bring gasoline. "At least have a meal with me. I've missed you."

"I can't look at you right now. You've failed me too many times. Losing half the females? Allowing the rogues to run unchecked in the woods? Honestly, I thought I could trust you to do this one task on your own."

"Mistress..."

"And leave a few Southerners alive to clean up this mess, unless you're planning to do it yourself." Her voice was faint when she added, "Though I suppose we could just burn it all down and rebuild. I've hated this place since I was a girl."

Torran called out, "Wait for me," but I wasn't certain who he was talking to.

The voices were gone then, and the only sounds were from the shifters who'd been fighting me. I could sense that Glen was alive, but only just. I kept my eyes closed, letting

Brand keep healing me, and concentrated on pushing some of that healing power on to Glen.

I smelled the gasoline before I felt it, and wished I could close my nose to the pungent fumes. I sucked in slow, shallow breaths, waiting for my moment. I was hoping at least some of the Council Enforcers would leave, but none of them seemed inclined to do that.

A few made crude jokes about which packs made the best barbecue. Two of them called out that they were going to get some sticks and marshmallows. One of the men kicked Glen closer to me before they dumped more gasoline on the ground.

I wanted to laugh. These fuckers had no idea what they were doing. Once, a couple of stupid boys had decided to build a bonfire, and they'd used a half gallon of gasoline to wet the wood. They'd stepped back plenty far, but when they'd lit the match, the fumes all around them had caught as well. The younger of the boys had died from the burns, and the older had been forced to shift to heal, though his hair never came in right afterward.

I felt wood landing next to me. I was healed now, more or less, though no one had noticed. I opened my eyes a crack and saw Glen facing me. His eyes were still closed, his chest not rising noticeably enough to see him breathing, but I knew he was still alive.

Alive, but not for long.

The number of shifters around us diminished, and the ones left sounded restless. The scent of the fumes had to be bothering them, too. I heard engines in the distance, and the main gates of the compound ratcheting open, then shut.

Finally, the Enforcers nearby started moving around,

though they didn't seem to be doing much. "Looking busy," is what Del would've called it. One threw a few more pieces of wood down by me. A heavy bit landed across my outstretched hand, and I peeked at it.

It wasn't a mop or a broom. It was even better. An actual bo staff, one of the practice ones our Enforcers had always trained with, but broken to about two-thirds the normal length. This was a real weapon.

I shifted, trying to feel if my spine was healed enough to stand. It was, though the spot felt fragile. One good hit there, and I'd be down again. But I would die fighting.

"We're ready to burn the corpses, sir," a voice called out.

"Have you decapitated the rogue Heir?" Torran replied, his voice growing louder as he returned. "You know the traditional punishment for betrayers. Let's not get sloppy just because we're away from home. Mattias, hand me that machete."

Glen was still out for the count. I didn't have long, and if I didn't time this right... Out of the corner of my eye, I saw the machete rise. In an instant, I had the broken staff in my hand and my feet under me, ready to throw myself at Torran.

But the blood around me made me slip. I fell back on my side, just as the machete came down with a hard thunk.

My mind began to buzz. Someone was screaming. Time stood still. When it started again, the world ran in slow motion as I found my feet.

Torran stood on the other side of Glen's body, his head lazily turning toward me, though everything else was still nearly frozen. I couldn't look down at Glen. If I did, if I saw what had happened, I might fall again. The buzz in my brain had done something to cut off the warmth where the bonds between me and my mates had been before.

Now everything was cold. Cold, dark, and razor-sharp. Something strange and malevolent—a beast?—slid into my thoughts. Into my core, where my spirit lived. Was it my wolf? Was it... Grigor? It felt powerful, magical. Evil. I didn't know if it was. I didn't care.

It pressed against my skin, filling me with power, pulling it into us until I felt bloated with it, then shoving it out into the world, into the air itself, holding everything still. The wind. The light. All of it. Particles of dust hung around me, like fireflies pinned to the air itself.

Somehow, my clawed hands already held the broken bo staff. It moved almost on its own, toward my enemy. Torran's smile curled the sharp edges of his lips as he tumbled out of the way of my first strike.

"You," he said, the word strangely elongated. Other shifters around us drew closer, circling me. "You're alive." My enemy snarled, showing blunt teeth. He raised his voice. "Kill her."

Others leaped at me, four or five at a time, all in human form. The beast was pleased. It was so much easier to tear through skin than fur. It wanted—I wanted, *we* wanted—his skin, though.

His head.

The staff battered the others out of my way, and I sliced with claws at the few who managed to dart inside the circle. I slipped away again, allowing the beast to kill as it wanted. They deserved it. Deserved to die for what they had done to... to...

The beast wrenched my mind away from the pain.

Time skipped.

We stood in a pile of bodies, our true enemy out of reach. Enraged, we leaped over them, landing softly, like a dry leaf, like a spark. He bared his weak, small teeth, like he wanted to growl. All that came out was a whimper.

We breathed in the sound, tasting his fear, and batted three more shifters out of the way as he scrambled back. Did he think he could escape us? We would never allow it. We crouched to chase him, confident he would not elude us.

He barked a command, one word. "Now!"

Then, to one side, a hint of sulfur. A small flare of light. Fire. A distraction.

I fought for control of my mind. Fought to stay, rather than flee. Why? There was nothing here for... The beast clawed at my concentration as the enemy drew farther away.

"Flor." The whisper of a name came at the very moment that the match was held up, to be thrown into the air.

Glen. He was alive. He was alive and... *close to the fire.*
*The fire!*

I wrenched control back from the beast, whose whole focus was on the enemy, and leaped back to my mate's side. It took all my newfound strength and speed to drag him away as fast as I could, pulling him over dead bodies and away from where we had fallen.

Time skipped again, once more, and I was a hundred feet from the pile of bodies and wood when the fire caught.

The match had landed exactly where we had been, and the conflagration roared as high as the Pack House roof, then higher, forty feet into the sky. Small explosions went off, and a chunk of something came flying in my direction. I tried to run, but all the unnatural strength that had filled me before was gone, emptied out. I felt as weak as I'd ever been, before I'd shifted.

I flung myself over Glen at the last second, and felt the projectile hit me in the back, right at the spot that had been broken before. It didn't make a sound as it broke, but I did. I screamed. Well, cursed. "Ratfucking, possum-jawed, toad-licking piece of snakeshit! That fucking *hurts!*"

Screaming was probably not my smartest idea, even if the cussing helped numb the pain a little, as usual. I heard some of the Council fucks running my way, the ones of them who hadn't caught fire or been exploded, or whatever.

I flipped myself over, locking eyes with the last person I wanted to see. "Why the hell couldn't you have caught fire?" I muttered, though I noticed he was scorched on one side of his head. He marched toward me, his silver knife in one hand, his teeth bared. My death was in his eyes.

There was no beast to call on now. Brand's energy had dried up. My bonds to the others were thin, like wisps of cotton wool pulled too far, too thin. *Damnit.* I wished I had my steak knife. Or any weapon.

I'd always feared dying at Southern with no weapon in my hand. With no friends at my side, no...

"Need a hand?" The voice came from directly behind me, just as a woman hurtled over me and Glen to land in front of us.

The voice was Iris, and she wasn't alone. Suddenly, a whole slew of the wild boys, the Southern rogues, were there, surrounding me, and some of the girls, too.

But the woman who'd jumped over me wasn't any of them. "Mama," I breathed. She didn't look my way.

The appearance of my mother, dressed in animal skins with her wild white curls flying, and screaming like a banshee, stopped Torran in his tracks. It stopped all of the Council Enforcers, at least for a moment.

But not the Southern rogues. In fact, it was obvious they'd planned Mama to be the diversion for my rescue. She was screaming gibberish, the crazy talk that Trevor Black-side had teased me about for so long. But somehow, it sounded like words. Maybe it was. Maybe it was a spell, or something.

I didn't have time to wonder.

Iris had my arm over her shoulders, and two other girls had Glen in a hammock hold, carrying him toward the back of the compound, and the hunting grounds. My eyes widened as I saw a half dozen of the rogues, armed with long sticks and swords—though none of them had the antique silver ones, from what I could tell at a glance—wading into the middle of the Council Enforcers.

There were more fighters on our side than theirs, but the rogue males were so much weaker than the skilled Enforcers they faced. The boys fought bravely, but were still half-starved, and while I could see that Sergeant had trained them for a couple of weeks, it wasn't nearly enough. The Council Enforcers started shifting to wolf form and attacking, and the boys didn't—or couldn't—respond in kind.

Torran reached my mother and leaped at her with his silver knife. Suddenly, her wild curls disappeared from my view. The boys cried out as one, as if they'd been struck. The ones closest to me staggered. One was immediately pounced on by two shifted wolves, who savaged his exposed stomach. Another three wolves attacked the boy closest to Glen, tearing out his throat.

"Lily!" Sergeant's cry came from my right, and I saw him running toward where Mama had fallen, his Alpha roar affecting every shifter who heard it. He did have a silver sword, or at least it shone like one, and I heard the clang of metal as he ran to intercept Torran's next blow.

There was too much to see, too much to follow, but Iris slid a sword into my hand as she stumbled, carrying me away from the worst of the battle, into the small grove of pines that marked the boundary between the main compound and the first ring of houses. A dozen of the women who'd fled the dorms with me the night before ran past us, armed with more of the weapons from the cave, and yelling some word.

*Tenebris, maybe?*

I couldn't make it out. The shouts became screams of pain and anger as the women met up with the Enforcers who'd been chasing behind us.

Iris set me down at the base of the tree for a moment, panting. She was skin and bones, like the rest of the women had been, and I could tell she didn't have magical reserves of strength like I did. Or like I'd had.

"We can't leave them," I managed to say as she picked me up again, a look of sheer determination on her thin face. "We can't leave them to die."

"Sergeant gave orders," she grunted, moving through the trees, the two shifters carrying Glen right behind us. It was dark under the cover of the pines, and I realized night was falling. The light from the bonfire back by the Pack House was all the light we had here. "Gotta get you out. You and the pretty boy. They got Luke, I guess?"

"Yeah. That Council bitch took him to Eastern. But I'm going to get him back."

"How?"

Before I could answer, she'd stumbled to a halt. Both the girls carrying Glen cursed under their breath.

I cursed right out loud. "What the fuck?"

There was a wall of shifters standing between us and the first row of houses, all of them armed with various things. Knives and sticks, mostly, though I spotted a couple of baseball bats. These shifters weren't dressed in fancy uniforms, though. They wore cut-off jeans shorts and tank tops, ragged tennis shoes and shirts that had been washed until the colors were mostly faded.

These were the Southern shifters. The ranked ones, though none of them were the males who'd hunted me. Probably because Grigor had exterminated them.

I swallowed hard as Iris gripped me tighter. I could tell she was looking for a way out. There wasn't one, though. But I didn't think these shifters were here to kill me, or they didn't want to, at least.

One of them, an older male, stepped forward. He had one of the baseball bats in one hand, held low, and I swallowed hard. I'd been hit with a bat before, and I knew exactly how much damage they could do. This guy was meatier than most of the others around him, and held my gaze for a few seconds longer than usual.

"Our Alpha's been taken?"

I blinked. "Callaway?"

He turned his head and spat to one side. "Luke. Our Alpha. Or he's gonna be. Those assholes had him locked up in the Pack House."

"Yeah," I said, my heart pounding. "The Council was trying to kill him, or get him to die. Almost did. He got free of the Pack House, but they took him to Eastern not a half hour ago." I closed my eyes. I could feel him moving farther away, and I put a hand to my neck. "They're moving fast."

"That his claim?"

My eyes snapped open, and I sneered. "Yeah. What of it?"

He almost grinned. "Makes you our Alpha Mate-to-be. Second in command, accordin' to pack law." All the shifters in the line moved restlessly. This wouldn't sit well with a lot of them. But this guy was their leader, or was acting like it for now. "Heard that Torran asshole say they's gonna burn the whole compound down. Maybe we oughta ask for your orders about that, Alpha Mate." The whole group went silent.

I didn't wait. "As the Southern Alpha Mate, I command you to go beat the tar outta all those fuckers who came to burn us out. Kill every last one of them. Use whatever weapons you can hold, teeth or claws. Don't kill the rogues, the Ghost Lady, or the tattooed Alpha named Sergeant. They're on our side." His eyes went wide, but he nodded. "Be careful. The Council brought guns into our packlands."

He sucked his teeth. "Silver shot?"

It didn't stink of silver. It was lead, or steel, or whatever humans used in bullets. I thought about mentioning the silver buckshot that we'd dug out of Grigor. But that seemed counterproductive, and Grigor had said he'd wrecked that gun. "Nah. But the shit still hurts."

"It does indeed. Thank you, ma'am. Let's whup some East Coast ass, boys." At that, they all slid off into the trees, as fast as bare feet and treadless shoes would carry them. Only a few were shifted, probably because Callaway was still alive somewhere, and had forbidden shifts without his permission for most of the pack.

It was a ballsy move this guy was making, to declare Luke was the Alpha. But maybe the ranked shifters had been sick of Callaway, too. Or maybe they'd realized anyone was better than Torran.

I wouldn't ever forgive them for the shit they'd pulled on all the unranked shifters here. For the abuse they'd heaped on us, and the way they'd all looked aside as long as it wasn't them getting treated like crap. But who knew? Del had always said a common enemy could make friends out of anybody.

We'd find out.

# 38

## ANSWERS

### FINNICK

*rop the blade. Claws and teeth.*

The words that had spun through my mind the day before still echoed now, as I stood before the doorway to the lower levels once more. This time, Father had returned my access so I could go in alone, keying my fingerprint in on his way to a final meeting in the city with the heads of Imregin.

"I don't know why your mother thought you'd gone soft," he'd said the day before, as I'd come up from killing Trevor Blackside. "I've never seen anything more brutal than what you did in that cell. It made me proud." Of course he'd watched on the cameras.

I couldn't care less what he thought of me, though I was glad to have my access restored to the lower levels, and to the main tech room for the entire Mansion that was at the end of one of the locked halls. Since Mother had not returned my access to the Mansion's computer systems, I had to use the computers down here to contact the pack who'd promised to help rescue Tana. I might even have a moment to speak with the Hilliers. I'd pocketed a few supplies, though I wasn't certain I'd be able to deliver them without being noticed.

*Proud of me.* I'd wished for so many years for him to say those words, and he never had. And of course he didn't understand what had happened down there. Why I'd dropped the scalpel and used my hands to finish the job.

*Claws and teeth.*

My parents believed that silver was a more civilized way to deliver pain and death, and it left a lasting memory for the scarred souls left alive. I'd gone into that room ready to skin the one who'd hurt my mate with silver, the weapon of choice in Eastern's torture rooms. But Flor's voice had changed my plan, somehow making the murder I'd delivered cleaner than any of the ones that I'd committed before.

I lifted my fingers to the keypad and waited for the soft click. My first stop was the tech hub of Eastern. Two of my father's favorite Enforcers guarded the room from the inside, but I knew neither of them had any idea what I was doing when I sat in front of the desk and logged in. They were, in human terms, goons. Muscle that knew their place, but never aimed any higher.

The only one who would have known I was up to something was my mother's favorite, Torran. And perhaps Niall, though he was still recovering from the wolfsbane-laced coffee I'd had delivered to him that morning. He'd been shadowing Tana as often as possible, even following her to school until I asked Father casually if Niall didn't have enough to do, that he could haunt our pack's school when the rest of us were working. He had not been pleased to hear of Niall's dereliction of duty. He'd probably laugh if he knew I'd poisoned him. Maybe even be proud of me.

With Mother away, Father was the only one who might come down and discover what I was doing. I typed quickly, writing up reports for Mother about some new tax laws that we could use to our advantage for long enough that the two guards stopped paying attention. Then I began recording a video loop of the empty hallway outside where the Hilliers were being kept. I'd need that for later.

While the recording ran, I opened a new window and spent the next few minutes making certain everything was lined up for Tana's rescue, and leaving precise GPS coordinates for where the body of their Heir was buried behind the Mansion. It would be up to them to exhume him, but I'd given them enough details to satisfy them.

Tana's extraction had to come first, of course, before I could even try to rescue the Hilliers and escape. She would be taken from school the next day, and the Italians had assured me she'd be kept safe. I hadn't told her anything about it, except a general warning to be ready for anything at any time, but I'd given her rescuers the private code words we'd used for years, between the two of us. I hoped it would be enough.

After a few more moments, I saved the video loop, then cleared up as much evidence of my online activity as possible—though I knew a skilled hacker would be able to see I'd done something unusual—and spent the last few minutes rebalancing the pack's investment portfolios.

I was almost certain my financial acumen was the only thing my parents valued me for. At least their paranoia about security meant I had access to this room, and that meant I could visit the Hilliers without being discovered. I grabbed a bottle of water from the minifridge in the corner, opened it, and pretended to drink.

The guards grunted at me as I left, not bothering to notice that I turned in the direction of the cells rather than the exit. In a dozen steps, I stood in front of the Hilliers' cell. This could go so wrong, but I had to try.

Everything I did down here, including my entrance to the cell, would be recorded in the electronic logs. I hoped I could make them understand what I was going to say, and get what I'd brought in to them.

The door opened with a soft click. Margarette and Bradley looked even worse than they had before. The silver chains were obviously taking a toll. Margarette's hair was limp and hung around her eyes, and she shook incessantly.

Bradley wasn't any better. He held her, stroking her arm gently, though even that small effort was costing him. The water bottle I'd seen before was empty, and there was no smell of food at all, only blood, silver, and urine from the pail in the corner.

"What a lovely sight. The devotion of true mates," I gritted out with a sneer. My eyes pricked with tears, and I circled the pair, moving between them and the metal bucket. They'd used the rough toilet paper to make a flimsy barrier between their skin and the chains, along with strips of their ragged clothing, but blood still seeped through. Stopping with my back to the camera, I waited for them to look at me.

"You bastard," Bradley muttered.

*I wish*, I mouthed. Bradley's eyes widened for a moment. His hand tightened on Margarette's arm, and she looked up at me as well.

Then I said clearly, letting the truth of my words sink in, "I had no idea you two would end up here. No idea you would put yourselves in the position to be brought so low." I let a tear fall as I went on, knowing the camera wouldn't capture it. Not ashamed for these two to see my pain. My grief. Margarette stifled a gasp. Bradley's eyes warmed.

Knowing they would scent the lie, while the recordings would not, I went on. "But I'm glad I finally get to see you getting what you deserved. It was becoming impossible to pretend that I enjoyed being at your pack. That you or your shifters would have anything to teach me about being ready for leadership. My parents are ten times the leaders you could ever be." As the familiar, acrid scent of deception hit their noses, I pulled a thin package of what looked like chewing gum out of my pocket. I pretended to put a piece of gum in my mouth, then balled up the package and tossed it on the floor by Bradley's foot.

It wasn't trash, of course. I'd placed small strips of a special tape inside an empty pack of gum, an invention Father's spies had come up with to help conceal silver blades.

The tape was lined with a thin coating of lead, but was flexible enough to bend. If they put it on under the cloth and toilet tissue, they shouldn't feel the silver. I'd worn it more than once, when I'd gone on hunting trips to do jobs as the pack's torturer. A layer stuck to the skin, and another on top of a hidden blade, and not even the keenest shifter's nose could tell where the faint scent of silver was coming from.

It wasn't much to give the Hilliers, but Tana came first. I tapped my wrist subtly, then lifted an eyebrow at the wrapper.

Bradley's gaze flicked to it, and his lips parted. For a second, I thought he might thank me, but he went still. "I'm ashamed I let you past my pack's borders, Finnick. You're never welcome there again." The stink of lies almost covered up the silver, and I swallowed hard.

Margarette cleared her throat and spoke, her voice raw. "We obviously didn't teach you about honor, or what it means to be a decent Heir. I may have treated you like a son, fostered you with my own, but I never loved you, Finnick McDonnell. I never truly thought of you as my own."

I almost sneezed from the pungent odor. I did smile a little, and saw an answering gleam in Margarette's eyes. *Be ready. Two days,* I mouthed, before I muttered a few more insults, tossing the bottle of water at her as I left. I'd done what I could for them, and given them the hope and answers they needed.

Now I needed to get a few for myself.

I was only a few steps outside the room when I heard a voice inside my head. *GET HER OUT!*

I staggered, catching myself with one hand on the wall. *What in the hell?* I shook off the sense of doom that threatened to drag me under, and stalked down the hall to the room next to the one where Trevor Blackside had spent his final moments.

The window in the door of this one had been blacked out, and there hadn't been a camera feed, at least not one that showed up on the monitors. I was almost certain it was occupied, though. The day before, I'd seen a maid coming down to the lower levels with food, then going back up, looking like she'd been attacked.

I had a feeling I knew who Mother had hidden in here, and when I pressed my fingers to the keypad and opened the door, I discovered I was right. "Hello, Callaway."

The old Southern Alpha cursed when I entered. "Dammit, I was hopin' you were that sweet little female they sent me yesterday. Day before yesterday? Fuck, the days are runnin' together. What day is it?"

"Thursday." I blinked as the door slammed shut behind

me, shocked at the room. They'd given the Hilliers a bucket and silver chains. Callaway had a queen-sized mattress, a sofa, and a table with two chairs, where he sat now, holding a tablet that was emitting the unmistakable sounds of sex. There was a long table against one wall covered with snack foods of every description and cans of beer and soda.

He'd been watching porn when I came in. But now he stood, tucking his dick back into his dark blue sweatpants and crossing his arms over his burly chest. In the months since he'd vanished, he'd grown even less impressive than he had been before. He smelled sour, worse than ever.

And when his eyes rose to my face, there was a sly, feral glint in them, though he didn't meet my gaze for more than a second. Perhaps he wasn't able to.

"So this is where you disappeared to," I remarked, trying to put it all together. There were no cameras in here, from what I could tell. It was as close to a comfortable hotel room as one of our cells could appear to be.

"Where I got disappeared to, ya mean," he grumbled, wandering over to the food table and grabbing a purple bag. "Want some a these Takis?" I forced myself to shake my head politely as he popped the bag open, and began eating and talking at the same time. "Yeah, your bitch of a mother had her Enforcers on my ass before Trevor could get me out of Alabama. Threw me in here, keeps coming down and making all sortsa pretty promises about putting me back in power, but I'm startin' to think she's full of shit."

A few orange pieces of chewed chip fell onto his belly. He picked the biggest piece up and ate it, then went on. "I been through your mama and your dad. Is it Junior's turn to grill me, see if I know anything else I ain't told them?"

"How did you know?" I pulled up to the table and forced myself not to react as his peculiar, foul odor washed over me when he did the same. "If I can get more from you than they did, maybe I can talk them into letting you move up to the main house. There's really no reason for you to be down here, is there? The Mansion is safe enough, and you deserve so much more than this."

"You want secrets? If you can get me outta here and the kind of set-up I deserve, I'll give ya secrets I ain't told nobody yet."

I grinned conspiratorially at him and described the elaborate meals we had upstairs. "Steak, lobster, everything you could desire. And all of it presented beautifully by lovely young females."

Halfway through my description of the maids who served in the dining room—and who I would never, *ever* let this piece of breathing excrement get near—he was cursing and rubbing his dick through his pants. "All right, all right. Let's get this done. Long as you get me out of here. Swear it."

I told the absolute truth. "Once you tell me what I need to know, I will make sure you get everything a man like you deserves."

That was all it took. Before I could take another breath, Calvin Callaway, deposed Alpha and absolutely delusional idiot, started spilling his darkest secrets.

And they were dark indeed.

"You know about the Southern Conclave, the one forty years back? We used to call it the Betrayal, before everybody stopped talkin' about it, and about the pack that started all that shit." I nodded, knowing he meant the Western pack. He got up and grabbed a beer, and popped it. "Well, they was 'sposed to be killed, right? We cut 'em off, the rest of the packs did. Forbade 'em to come back to Conclaves, forbade our shifters to go out there looking for mates, and vice versa. My uncle was the Alpha after that mess, and he told me all about it. It should have worked. It mostly did. But some of them sneaky fuckers came across the whole country, lookin' for trouble."

He went quiet, and I said, "Looking for mates?"

He swallowed, and the scent of menthol and sour laundry got stronger. Suddenly, I remembered where I'd smelled this before. Years ago, a rogue wolf had been caught skulking around behind the Mansion. Nobody had any idea how he'd gotten that close, but Father had captured him, and taken the rogue into the lower levels to do experiments.

It had smelled like this. Sour, putrid. Did my parents know Calvin Callaway was going feral? I focused on his story again, looking for more signs of madness.

"...was out with my pack huntin' some rogues northwest of the compound, with my uncle. We heard somethin' coming across the woods, a whole lot of wolves, and the rest of the Enforcers went after them. They were rogues, for sure, but they'd been chasin' a girl. Well, a witch."

I must have reacted, because he smirked at me. "You heard me. A witch, from the dead pack. Look at ya. You look as shocked as I felt when I found it out. Not that you should be, with that mama of yours, and her witchy fuckin' ways."

I narrowed my eyes. "Witchy ways?"

"You can't think a low-class wolf like her got to where she is without some sorta dark magic, can ya?"

I almost choked. It had only been six years since I'd learned where my mother had come from before she mated with my father at an Eastern Conclave. Father had been drunk, and forgotten himself. How had this man known? "Low class?"

"Hard to forget, your mama, even if she don't look much

like she did back then. She was sweet, skinny, a dime a dozen on the outside. But that power—she had it even when she was a girl. It just oozes off her, doesn't it?"

"It does," I agreed, and wondered, not for the first time, when she'd learned to control it. Now, her power only showed when she wanted it to, though she stayed within our pack's borders as much as possible for an Alpha Mate. "So you know she's from Georgia. The St. Mary's River Pack that was eradicated by rogues."

He laughed for a long minute. "That's what you heard? Boy, that may've been her pack before 'rogues'"—he made quotation marks in the air—"killed them off. But the river has two sides, and your mama's packlands spanned both." He rubbed at his ragged beard. "Fuckin' Florida. Not a damn good thing ever came outta that state."

I felt something in the bond then, a sharp feeling that had to be fear. Intense fear, coming from Flor.

I ignored it for now. "Enough about my mother. What happened to the girl you found? The witch?"

Callaway grunted. "Speak of the devil and she may appear, eh? Well, that's the truth." He rubbed his chin. "I should'a known what Lily was when she popped up outta nowhere. One second, the forest was empty, and the next, she was running at me. Bitch threw herself at me. Lit up the bond with her dark magic, and before I knew what was happening, we were ruttin' right there in the woods." For a split second, the stench of him abated slightly. His blood-shot eyes softened, as he was caught in the memory. But then, the moment was gone.

"I nutted and bit her neck, but when she tried to bite me back, I smelled something. My uncle had warned me about the stink of magic, how it was like lightning and fire. He'd smelled it at the Betrayal. So I pushed off her, and looked down in her eyes. They weren't regular. They were red and blue, fires blazing inside. She was a fuckin' witch."

"Is that why you hired Verbena Flock, from the coven, to sever your bond?"

He looked confused for a moment. "Verbena Flock?"

"The witch."

He grunted. "Never could remember her name." That was the truth, but the next words he said were a lie. "Sure. I needed to cut the bond."

Sniffing the air, I stood. "Try again. You can't lie your way out of here."

His face went red, and he seemed to swell up, fur prickling over his skin in an odd wave, then subsiding. "Fine, ya little shit. I took Lily back to the compound and stuck her in my room. My uncle came draggin' ass in an hour later, giving me shit for running off, bitching about how the rogues had killed his top Enforcers, and I could have made the difference. He tried to knock me around, but he couldn't even look me in the eye." He let out a short laugh. "For the first time in my life, he dropped his gaze. So I challenged him, right then and there. He died, and the Alpha power came to me." He went silent.

"But you knew you couldn't have a wolf from that pack as your mate," I finished for him. "She was your true mate, and very powerful. So when you claimed her, her power came to you. That was why you were strong enough to defeat your uncle." I fought to hide my disgust. "You claimed her, but instead of owning up to it, you hired a witch to sever your bond." He twitched, and I knew I was almost right. "To sever the bond and kill her."

Calvin hung his head. "There was no way they'd let me keep my spot with her at my side. I had to do it. It was the only way."

I didn't remark on the scent of deception this time. Something terrible was happening in my bond, and I couldn't afford to show any weakness in front of this male.

"But it didn't work," he said, his tone bitter. "When it came time, Lily was already knocked up. The witch didn't have the juice to sever the bond and kill both of 'em, not without taking me out along with them. She got all worked up, made me promise all sorts of shit if she tried to just sever the bond anyway."

I had exceptional control of my wolf, but hearing his mate spoken of this way was testing the limits. He longed to rip this male's throat out for what he'd done. "What did you promise?"

"She made me swear it on the moon. Did some scary blood magic shit, too." He rubbed at the palm of his hand. "First off, I had to make a vow I wouldn't kill the pup when it came. And I'd name it after her."

"The pup?"

"Some sort of magic thing. And I did, didn't I?" He started to laugh like he'd just told a joke. "Even though that bitch died doing the spell, I did what I promised. Never did kill the pup. And named her—well, I never could remember that gal's name. But I got close enough, I guess."

"Florida?"

"Florida Witch," he finished, then collapsed in laughter that held more than a hint of madness.

I stood silently and glided to the door, pressing the keypad to let myself out. By the time Callaway heard me, it was too late. I was outside, and all I could hear was the muffled thumping of him throwing himself against the wall.

A wall I was clinging to as agony wracked my body.

She had been injured. Attacked by an entire pack, it felt like, from the searing phantom pain all over my body.

The pain abated for a few seconds. Then, a thousand miles away in Alabama, all hell broke loose.

But I felt every lick of the flames in the sterile, quiet hallway where I lay.

# 39

## TENEBRIS
### FLOR

Iris exhaled heavily as we watched the last Southern shifter vanish into the trees. "Well, time for us to scoot on back to the cave."

The other two shifters with Glen had already headed off, and I saw two young males—Bo and Leroy, from the way they moved—greet them and help them carry him down the middle of the street.

"Don't worry about the Heir," Iris murmured, watching him go. "He was breathing, and he's young and strong. There ain't anyone in the hunting grounds but us now, anyway. They'll get him to safety, and get him cleaned up."

"Good." I needed to know at least one of my mates was safe. Iris tried to lift me again, but let out a pained sound that had me stopping her. "Don't. I can walk." When she set me back down gingerly and stepped away, I was pleased to find that was true. I was still in pain, but not dying.

What worried me more were the hidden wounds I suspected were there, though I couldn't feel much in my bonds. The dead spot where Grigor's little tendril of a connection had been now felt like what I imagined an amputated finger would. Luke's bond was weak and staticky, like somebody had poured a bunch of metaphysical cement all around it.

Glen felt weak, but was getting stronger. He was pulling power through me, somehow, even while he was unconscious. I was glad; I had a feeling if he knew what he was doing, he'd stop. He needed whatever Brand could give him.

My heart lurched. Finnick... Finnick felt distant but quiet, like he was asleep.

The bond with Brand, though, was slowly roaring back to life, like a souped-up car on a gravel backroad. I could almost feel the vibrations of his energy beginning to fill me again. He was coming closer every minute, and fast. My spine was still not good, but I could walk again. Knowing he was on the way gave me the strength to say what I had to.

"I need to go back."

But Iris wasn't having it. "Bullshit, Flor. You're running on fumes. And smell like them, too. All it would take is one match and you and I'll both go up like a whole packet of firecrackers."

I had to get her to understand. "I won't fight. But I can't run away when my pack is fighting for their lives." My pack and my family. If Sergeant and Mama died, and I hadn't tried to help... It all felt wrong.

Iris was silent for a long moment. "Your pack. You mean *this* pack? Southern?"

I almost laughed. "Yeah. It's a shithole, but it's my shithole."

"Damn, I wish I didn't know exactly what you mean." She let go of me, watching me sway for a moment, before we started back through the trees, side by side. "You always did get back up," she whispered. "Every time they knocked you down. Every time anyone came for you. You got back up and got stronger."

I glanced at her. "Didn't know anyone noticed."

She laughed silently. "The girls did. We watched and wanted to learn. If there had been another Del, one who could help the rest of us, train all of us unranked girls, things might have been different."

"Another Del?" I whispered as we got to the edge of the trees. We both stopped, in awe. Shifters fought in both forms, and with every weapon they could. Aluminum baseball bats swung and caught the firelight in the darkness, along with swords and knives.

Like an answer to my question, Sergeant stood in the front of the battle, fighting the Council Enforcers with a deadly grace and efficiency that was beautiful. Like watching a hawk dive, or a deer leap over a stream, he knew precisely where he needed to be to protect the younger shifters around him, and to hurt his enemy the most effectively.

"Tenebris!" he shouted, as the line of Council Enforcers broke. One or two of them were still firing guns, but it seemed like almost all of the ammunition had been used up, as most of them had reverted to the swords or long knives that every Enforcer wore.

"Tenebris!" the rest of our side shouted, though some of the fighters yelled, "For Southern!"

I heard a howl that came from a human throat, high-pitched and strange, and saw my mama running through the battle—almost skipping, like she was playing, though she was bleeding all down her front. She had a knife in one hand and was stabbing randomly, laughing like a child. She sounded absolutely insane. Every once in a while, she uttered a word that... did something. The earth would rumble, and dust would fly into the air.

It had to be magic.

I scanned the battle, looking for Torran. But he was nowhere to be found. In fact, there were only twenty or so Enforcers left now, fighting against Sergeant, Mama, and at least a hundred rogues and Southerners.

"Where did they go?" I wondered aloud. Iris pointed in the direction of the front gate, where we could see taillights appear and vanish as they crested the only slight hill on the drive out of Southern.

The last of the Council Enforcers tried to follow, and the rogues broke off fighting at Sergeant's command, but the girls weren't having any of it.

"I want to kill that fucker right there," Iris said. "I need to." Her gaze was locked on a shifter who was fighting in human form. Normally, that would make them an easier opponent, but this guy was closer to seven feet than six. He had a shaved head and a sword in both hands, and was holding off five of our fighters.

I took in the way Iris stood, practically vibrating with rage. "Yeah, I can see that. You'll need a weapon." I jogged a few steps forward and picked up a discarded sword. "You know how to use one of these?"

"No. I've never used any weapons."

*Ah, right.* The damn Alpha command was still affecting her. "You shifted yet?"

"Yeah. Sergeant helped me find my wolf last night." She blinked, and a tiny, evil smile crept over her face.

"I bet she'll know what to do."

"Hell yeah." In less than a minute, she'd stripped out of her clothes, dropped to all fours, and shifted into an underfed golden wolf. Her fur gleamed in the dying firelight.

"Go fuck his shit up, Iris," I encouraged. "You've got this." She gave a quick bark and ran at the guy.

He never stood a chance. Between Iris and her equally revenge-thirsty friends, Sergeant and his wild boys, and the ranked and unranked leftover males from Southern, the combined packs of Southern and Tenebris had it covered.

THE HOUR after the battle was messy and satisfying. Three of the girls had died, but the ranked Southerners were treating their bodies like war heroes. One of the rogues was close to death, but Mama went over and laid her hand on his cheek, whispering in his ear, and holding his shoulder. He died, but he had a smile on his face when he did.

I didn't understand it. When I tried to approach Mama, she got a peculiar, heartbroken look on her face, and started mumbling again. Somebody had wrapped a bandage around her middle, but I could see blood already seeping through. She needed to stay calm, so I steered clear.

Sergeant was the center of all the work after the fighting was done. He directed the rogues to move through the bodies and finish off any of the ones who were dying slowly, the girls to collect all the fallen weapons, and the ranked Southerners to stack the Enforcers' bodies and burn them.

The unranked girls got upset when they couldn't pick up the swords and guns, though. Sergeant cussed a blue streak when he realized Callaway's orders were still hurting them. "Tenebris! You five"—he pointed to some of his shifters—"pair up with those girls. They'll find the weapons, you stack 'em. Look for any ammunition, too."

"Yes, Alpha!" they chorused. The ranked shifters seemed unsettled when they heard the word Alpha, but no one asked about it. Everyone was too tired.

Sergeant approached me once the pyre was burning. It smelled awful, but no one left the area. We had to see this through to the end. "Where's Glen?" he asked, holding out a knife by the blade to me.

Not just a knife. My steak knife. I took it with a nod of thanks, and thought about Glen. "He's in the cave. I think he's sleeping. It *feels* like he's sleeping, but restlessly. Like he's having a dream." A good one, actually. I kept getting flashes of his wolf running with mine, or at least I thought it was. It was small and an almost-reddish black color, running with his large gray one.

"Just like your grandmother," Sergeant mused as we both stared at the fire. "She always knew what her mate was up to. It's the way of bonds, for our kind."

"For... *blended* shifters?" I wasn't certain I should speak about it out loud, even if we were surrounded by our own side. I knew how fast shifters could turn on you. It had happened at Northern quick enough.

"Exactly. The wolf bond is more solid, from what I've been told. But the *other side* gives a more flexible connection."

"The kind of connection that would let you talk to your mates through the bond, even from a long way off?"

"Maybe don't tell anyone about that, hm? That's not something that happens in wolf bonds. Ever."

"Ah. Got it."

Iris came over with cups of water, and we all drank.

"Glen's not awake yet, but the ones guarding the cave sent word that he's healing faster than they've ever seen."

I thanked her, and we handed back our cups. Another Southern shifter turned on a hose, and we took two-minute turns underneath it in the dark. I almost cried when someone scrounged up a bar of soap and let me get some of the gasoline smell off. My clothes were soaking wet when I finished, but I felt a thousand times better.

Sergeant found me again when I was done. "What's next for you, little warrior?"

It was so much like Luke's nickname for me, tears stung my eyes. "They took Luke," I said once I could talk. "Finnick's parents. They have him, as well as Finnick and the Hilliers. And Grigor."

"Grigor?" Sergeant faced me, his eyes narrowed. "The Russian? Grigor fucking Dimitrivich? They did us a favor with that, Flor."

"Tell it to my wolf," I muttered. The crazy thing was clawing at me, wanting nothing more than to run after him and Luke, to save our mates from the woman who'd taken him.

Sergeant's silence was worse than one of Del's lectures. But I wasn't going to back down. Grigor was mine, as much as the others. Or he would be.

"She had magic," I said softly. "All along. She had magic."

"Your mama?" Sergeant sighed as we watched Mama dance at the edges of the flames, her wild boys dancing along with her, all of them howling as loud as they could. "She did. She does, a little. It's been coming back to her. But it's like trying to fill a cracked pitcher with water. She can't use it reliably."

He scanned the area, barking out a few orders to his

rogues to get food for everyone. Some of the ranked shifters walked across, shaking hands with the boys, and showed them the back door of the dining hall. It was the older guy with the baseball bat who busted the lock off the door, but all of them carried food out, as well as some tables, and started setting up a feast. Well, as much of a feast as Southern could provide.

One of the rogues ran over with a hot dog and handed it to Sergeant. "Alpha, first one's for you," he said, his head lowered. Sergeant patted it and sent him off.

"Cute," I teased. "You got a real little pack here. Tenebris?"

"Means darkness," Sergeant grumbled, and tore the hot dog down the middle, handing me half. "I'm not sure about the name, but they'll be a good pack. We can't stay in the cave."

"No, you can't. Why not bring them..." I stopped, knowing it wasn't my place to make the suggestion that had come to mind.

"Alpha Mate! Can I bring you a plate?" one of the Southerners called out.

I blushed when I realized he was talking to me. "Ah, sure. Anything you got."

I could feel Sergeant's stare on my shoulder, where Luke's claiming mark showed just a little. "Coulda sworn that was on the other side before, Florida."

"Yeah, I've got a collection," I grumbled. "Luke." I pointed to the new one. "Finnick." I tilted my head. I pulled down my ragged shirt so my shoulder showed. "Brand."

"Where's Glen's?" Sergeant asked.

My face flamed. "Nowhere you'll ever see." He laughed, and every shifter around looked at him, most of them in disbelief.

Yeah, Sergeant laughing was pretty unbelievable.

Finally, he settled down, and Iris wandered over, two hot dogs in her hand and one in her mouth, and I remembered what I'd been thinking.

Luke wasn't here. The boys and Mama and Sergeant didn't need to stay out in the woods. And with all the girls who'd run there, they probably couldn't. There wouldn't be enough food or water, for one thing. Maybe it *was* my place to offer what help I could.

"Hey, Iris. Would you and the girls be happier in the compound, now that the assholes are gone? Or dead, whatever."

"Not all the assholes are either one of those things," she said, cutting her eyes to some of the ranked Southern shifters, who were talking quietly on the other side of the fire. "I for one don't want to come back to the life we had here."

"What if it was different? What if there was an Alpha who'd protect you, teach you to fight?" I glanced at Sergeant, who nodded slightly. I thought about the way they'd treated Mama in the cave. The way they'd treated Bo and Leroy. "What if there was a whole pack of guys who had honor?"

She swallowed her mouthful. "Wouldn't know what that looks like, to be honest. Those males... Not all of them know what it looks like either." Her gaze moved to the dorms. "Even if it was safe, we couldn't go back in there. We'd rather burn it down."

I could tell she wasn't going to go for it. "Sergeant, what if you bring your pack inside the fence?" I suggested. "Let the Tenebris pack and the unranked set up in the Pack House. Let your boys be given the job of protecting the pack. The females."

"They could do that," Sergeant said slowly, as he considered it. "It might be what gives them the last bit of control they need. The pack is meant to protect. They need something more than just Lily to take care of. It's a good idea, Florida."

Iris wrinkled her nose. "All of us in there together?"

I shrugged. "It's connected to the dining hall. It's got lots of bathrooms and guest rooms. Nice carpet, and I don't know... The rogues—the *Tenebris* boys are used to sleeping together."

"Denning," Sergeant told me. "That's what it's called. In some smaller packs, they still den. All in one room, or one house."

Iris hummed. "We could den together, I suppose. The females, I mean. If we could use weapons ourselves, we'd be even safer." She was practically batting her eyelashes at Sergeant, clearly hoping for some sword lessons.

I snorted and held up my steak knife. "I never had any problem keeping myself safe with this. And there's a shit ton more of 'em in the Pack House. A couple dozen, at least."

Iris nodded grimly. "Let me go ask the girls."

When she left, I pressed a hand against my heart. It was aching. "So, Tenebris. Sounds badass. It's a good name. And they have a truly great Alpha."

Sergeant stayed quiet, as we watched the females gather together. He put a hand on my shoulder. "Your pack will, too. Don't stop fighting. Your pack needs you."

"Southern isn't mine. Not really." *Not exactly.* "It's my past."

"I didn't mean Southern."

# 40

## ONE DARK THREAD
### FLOR

Sergeant's pack and the unranked females moved into the Pack House that night. I spent it in the cave with Glen, curled up in front of the small fire on a rug made of deerskins. Someone had washed him off and put clean clothes on him, before I arrived. He still smelled a little like gasoline, but I didn't care.

We were safe, it was quiet, and when he woke up just before dawn, we were able to hold each other and cry without anyone seeing.

Well, anyone besides Bo and Leroy. Bo had greeted me at the cave the night before by falling at my feet and thanking me so profusely for saving Delia that I was embarrassed. I had to threaten to kick him to get him to stop trying to kiss my feet.

He'd said I could kick him to the moon if I wanted to, but he was never gonna stop looking for ways to show his gratitude. "I'll even make you some more piles of guts, Miss Florida," he'd vowed, his eyes wide. "I'd do anythin' for you." Leroy had finally pulled Bo away, and I'd ordered them to guard the cave from the outside, so I could sleep.

I had nightmares for all four hours I lay next to Glen, visions of Brand dropping from the sky, and Luke being pinned to a table and cut apart by witches. Finnick making love to dozens of women, one after the other, each one more beautiful than the last. And Grigor, dead and crumbling into silvery ash.

I woke to soft fingers in my hair, and blinked my eyes open to see a pair of ocean-blue ones smiling down at me. "Hey, Dream Girl," Glen rasped. "We're alive."

I scrambled to sit, and poured some water from the pitcher the boys had filled. "Just barely," I muttered, handing him the cup.

"How?" He beckoned me to him. As soon as I was close enough, he pulled my face to his and kissed me sweetly, gently, as if I were the most precious treasure in the world.

After a moment, he sat up as well, running a hand over his torso. The bullet holes were all healed, but the flesh was pink where each one had gone in, and where he'd taken wounds from blades and claws.

"How, princess?"

"Sergeant says it's a witch thing," I whispered, not sure what Bo and Leroy might think. "That the way those kinds of bonds work is different. Wolves have solid connections, but the other ones..."

"The moonblessed side," he supplied.

"Sure." I shrugged. "That's how Brand was able to send all that healing through the bonds. Normal shifters can't do that, right?" I checked in on my bonds. Grigor was still absent, Finnick felt the same, and Luke was... *Huh.* Luke felt contorted, like the bond was twisting around. It didn't hurt, but it was peculiar. But Brand—

I gasped as I felt him close. Really close.

Glen didn't notice that my attention had drifted.

"...never heard of it anyway. Mates can share a little. Alphas and their mates, of course, share and increase power. But not healing, not from thousands of miles aw—"

The voice that interrupted him was deep and rich, and filled with emotion. "I'm not thousands of miles away."

Brand stood at the entrance to the cave, dressed in nothing but a pair of ruined, torn trousers. In one hand, he held Leroy off the ground by the collar of his shirt. Under his other arm, he had tucked Bo tightly against his side. Both of the boys looked like they'd been knocked out.

"Bearman!" I shouted and ran across the cave floor. "Put those idiots down and kiss me."

Instantly, he dropped the boys, who I didn't think were hurt, mostly just stunned. They'd obviously been playing possum, too, since they both scrambled to their feet instantly.

Leroy whispered, "Ghost eyes," gaping at Brand for no more than a second before he and Bo started backing out of the cave.

Those odd, white eyes met mine as I jumped up into his arms. "I missed you," I mumbled before I couldn't speak any more. His kisses were wild, desperate, hungry. They felt savage, almost, and when I explored his mouth with my tongue, his teeth were definitely sharper than human.

Since he was supporting my entire weight, I held onto his face, then ran my hands lower as the kiss lengthened. His beard was oddly furry, and so were his shoulders and arms. Even his chest was furrier than normal. What was up?

I pulled back to catch my breath. "Did you just shift or something?"

He made a sound that was half despair and half delight as he wrapped his arms even more tightly around me—

definitely furry arms—and buried his face in my neck, inhaling deeply. "I did," he growled, his voice breaking. "I needed you... Flor! You were hurt." He held me away now, off the ground, inspecting me for injuries.

"It was my back." I wriggled to be put down. "I got shot, and then there was a huge battle, and my back was broken again, and if you hadn't been sending all that mojo—*uh-oh*."

I guess telling him all of that wasn't exactly smart. Brand started growling and dropped to all fours, his nose elongating into a snout.

"Ah, they're all dead, if that helps?" I finished, ignoring Glen's soft laughter behind me.

"Never again," Brand said, or at least that's what I thought he said. By the end of the last word, he'd transformed completely into the familiar, dark chocolate-brown shape of his wolf.

Though I was almost certain he hadn't been this big the last time I'd seen him.

"Holy cow," I breathed, as Brand circled me, scent-marking me with his fur everywhere he could. Which was pretty much from my chin down, since he was almost as tall as me.

"No, holy wolf." Glen eased up next to me, Brand's wolf growling slightly as Glen embraced me from behind. "Brother, I'm glad you're here. Thank you for healing her, and all of us." He led me by the hand back to the furs, where the three of us sank down, wrapped around each other.

"I need to tell you what happened. Can you shift back?" I whispered.

Brand whined slightly.

*Can you understand me?* I thought. I took the lick he gave

my chin as a yes, and told him—and Glen—everything that had happened in the night.

By the end of the story, Glen looked almost as enraged as Brand's wolf. "If they weren't all dead, I'd go now and kill them."

"They're not. I think Torran got away. And Finnick's parents have Luke," I reminded them. "They have Finnick, and Luke... and Grigor. We have to rescue them."

Brand's growl reappeared, and his face was suddenly in front of mine, his pearly eyes glowing. "Don't you start," I said, bopping him on the nose. He looked at his own nose cross-eyed, like he couldn't believe I'd done that. "Grigor isn't all bad."

"He's ninety-nine and a half percent bad, Flor," Glen said, before he got up and began rummaging around in the crates for food. He came back with jerky, handing some to me and Brand, then taking a piece for himself. Neither one of them would eat until I'd taken a bite. I rolled my eyes and started chewing. Brand ate his piece in one big bite, and I would've put money on him imagining it was Grigor's face or something.

"Okay, he's not a good guy. But he's not pure evil. He's had a hard life."

"A hard, immortal life, killing thousands upon thousands of shifters—"

"He gave that up," I argued. "And we all make mistakes." They both stared at me like I'd lost my very last marble. "Whatever. The point is, we need to get the guys out of there." I wiped my eyes, annoyed at the tears. This wasn't the time to cry. This was the time to kick ass. "They're gonna torture them, maybe even kill them. We have to go now. He was just healing, not even back to full strength, and then was shot—"

Before I could finish, Brand had transformed and pulled me into his human arms. "We'll rescue him, I promise. But we need to plan. Finn isn't in danger. I don't think they have any idea he's mated to you. He wouldn't have told them, and his mate mark is on his tongue, remember?"

I nodded.

He hummed. "I don't think they'll hurt Luke either. Or at least, they won't kill him. They've called an emergency Council meeting in three days to vote on Aidan's position as Head, as well as sentencing for Margarette and Bradley, for killing their own Enforcers without cause."

Glen and I both cursed a blue streak at that. Glen started to pace as he thought aloud. "They won't kill Luke as long as they think they can force him to vote their way. Since Northern is implicated in the sentencing, they'll be recused from the vote. All they need is one of the other main packs—Southern, since they must know you won't vote their way, Brand—to ally with them, and they'll have the majority."

"Don't underestimate Aidan McDonnell," Brand growled. "He's called me to Eastern as well, no later than the day before the emergency meeting, to submit to the Council's leadership, as my father did. As all of the other recognized Alphas have." He sighed heavily. "They know you're my mate. They suspect you're also Glen's. If they know that you're tied to Luke, or Finn, I might be forced to..."

"No," I gasped.

His jaw hardened. "If I must pledge to the Council in order to keep you alive, or keep them alive, I might."

"You won't. You *can't*," I said softly. "You're going to follow the old ways."

Brand's eyes flared, then dimmed. "That is my plan."

345

I didn't like the way he'd said that, like there was some question as to what he would do. I turned his face toward me and mock-glared at him. "Brand Becker, one of the things I love most about you is how much you are like your pack's name. Your integrity, your character, is as solid as a mountain. Following the old ways, following the moon, is the only way we'll get all this shit sorted out. It's how you were able to take on being Alpha without killing your dad, and how Glen and Luke and I are still alive. You channeled all that energy to me, and through me, right? You were able to do that because of this."

I moved higher on his lap and kissed his eyelids softly, then stared into them. "We're going to get Luke and Finnick free," I whispered, silently tacking on Grigor's name, though I knew Brand could hear my thoughts. I ignored his silent snarl. "I mean it. If I have to chop every Eastern head off myself, I'm getting them back. Then we're going to the fucking lake. All of us."

"The fucking lake?" Glen murmured in my ear. "Are we renaming it? Wait. That's your safe word, isn't it?"

"It is." Brand's lips twitched. "Little flower, are you saying lake?"

"No, I'm pretty sure she said fucking. What a great idea." I laughed as Glen picked me up from behind and spun me around. "Fucking first, then saving all our brother mates, then the lake?"

"I like your priorities," Brand agreed, before he stole me back, laid me down on the deerskins, and showed me—one kiss, one touch, and one whispered word at a time—just where his priorities lay.

My world was still a trash fire. My other mates were in danger. But for the next few hours, these two stood between the uncertain future and me, blocking out every worry about tomorrow. Replacing the fear with desire, and stoking the flames of our passion until they roared brighter than the darkness that threatened us all.

And somewhere in those hours, I felt four connections blaze to life, the energy of our joining supplying them with strength... and one dark thread snap.

# EPILOGUE
## INTERROGATION ~ LUKE

I woke inside a vehicle of some kind, in a back seat that was soft and smelled of expensive leather. A car, a large one.

I stunk of battle. Gunpowder and lead, blood and smoke. My skin felt as if someone had sanded it, every nerve blazing with remembered pain. Time had passed. I wasn't sure how much. I was exhausted, but also... drugged? Maybe. It felt like I'd been kept unconscious.

My wolf was still asleep. I let him rest, as I forced myself to think. Think, and remember.

We'd gone to rescue Grigor. Flor had been caught. Glen and I had moved between her and... There was a hole in my thoughts, a place in my mind itself with scorched edges, as if something had burned it out.

Burned. *Fire*. Someone had shouted *fire*. There had been guns.

That was all. I couldn't remember anything that had happened after I was shot.

I had been shot, hadn't I? Silently, I ran a hand over my abdomen. There was no wound, but there was definitely a hole in my clothing. I lifted my hand to my throat. Flor's mark was there. I could feel her, as well, alive.

I thought about the braided rope of spirit that had pulled me out of my coma two days ago. It was still present. Glen's energy was, anyway, but the other strand felt odd. Numb, almost.

Where were they?

Where was I? It was dark outside, the windows tinted, and some sort of opaque partition kept any illumination from the car's headlights from reaching me.

I blinked, lifting a hand to rub my eyes. An interior light clicked on at once, and I startled as I realized I was not alone, though I hadn't scented anyone else. A woman sat across from me, her legs angled to one side, her head tilted slightly. She wore a black pantsuit, high heels, and a curious expression.

"Alpha Mate McDonnell?"

I'd never spoken to Finnick's mother when I was fostered for those few short days at his pack. But I'd seen her, and even if I hadn't, I would have recognized her face. She was an older, harder, female version of Finnick. The same cold strength resided in her, though hers made my wolf's hackles rise.

But her reply had the hairs on the back of my neck rising as well, and fear filling my belly. It was the voice of my nightmares.

"I'm so glad you're awake, Luke. I have so much to ask you." Her eyes flashed with red fire as she lifted her hand to point at the mating claim Flor had left on my neck. "Starting with that. Who gave you that mark?"

I held my jaw shut, intent on saying nothing. But when her eyes flashed with fire again, I knew this was a battle I would not win.

"Her name is Florida Wills," I said through gritted teeth, then opened them and bit my tongue hard enough to bleed, trying to stop the words from coming out.

Another flicker of red fire.

"Her name is Florida Wills," I repeated, blood running down my chin. "And she is... my true mate."

A smile as cold as the heart of winter curled her lips. "Excellent. Tell me everything."

And I did.

# Acknowledgments

Thank you so much to you, readers, for giving me a reason to keep dreaming up these characters and their stories! My Ream and Vella supporters in particular have kept me going, day after day, with their insightful comments, questions, and encouragement. This book is for you, and especially my muses/cheerleaders Tami and Iris.

My Bearman Betas are the kind of readers authors dream of. Thank you for the patience, honesty, and for laughing along with me. Clothes? Who needs them? Certainly not Kristin, Deb, Bek, Courtney, Lorna, and Maria. Thanks as well to Yve Vale, Sarah Reynolds, Raewyn Ash, and everyone else who waded through the typos to help me polish this one.

# ALSO BY MERRI BRIGHT

### *The Forgotten Angel Series (RH Paranormal)*

Lost Feather

Fallen Feather

Rising Feather

Glittering Feather

### *The Lost Lines Series (RH Omegaverse Fantasy)*

*Vali's Stories:*

The Omega's Mischief: A Short Story Prequel

The King's Omega: The Lost Lines Series Book 1

The Queen's Nest: A Lost Lines Series Novella

*Haven's Story:*

The Guards' Haven

*Cilla's Story:*

The Duchess's Designs

*Roya's Story:*

The Assassin's Promise

*Wren's Story:*

*Part One* The Leviathan's Debt

*Part Two* The Wyvern's Redemption

*Ratter's Stories:*

The Spy's Solstice

The Goddess's Spy

### *The Billionaire's Betasitter Series (MF Omegaverse)*

# ABOUT THE AUTHOR

Merri Bright spends her days dreaming up naughty angels, misunderstood demons, sexy shifters, growly Alpha males, and frequently refuses to limit her heroines to just one love interest.

Please join Merri's Mischief Makers on Facebook where you'll discover random giveaways, sneak peeks of new novels, book recommendations, and silly/sexy/funny stuff. You can also email her at merri@merribright.com, or follow/subscribe to reamstories.com/merribright for stories in progress.